Fiver
and
the Psychology of Rabbits

Frank J. Page

D1298207

ISBN: 1493794868
ISBN 13: 9781493794867
Library of Congress Control Number: 2013921252
CreateSpace Independent Publishing Platform
North Charleston, South Carolina

This book is dedicated to my dog Fiver and my brother Vaun Paul Page, two major sources of inspiration in my life. Also, my thanks to many kind friends and family who generously helped in the editing and gave me encouragement.

#

Chapter One

#

When the song ended, Mitchell was headed up the canyon. With the white beams of its headlights reaching out in front of it, the big, wedge-shaped sports car looked like an alien craft shooting along the ground. After taking an exit from the freeway, he was on a two-lane road that wound upward into the mountains west of Denver. With one hand on the wheel and the other on the gearshift, he was passing through small farms and ranches clustered peacefully around the mouth of the canyon. At the side of the road, white fence posts flashed by in the darkness, while behind them, the fields and pastures sat in quiet repose. Caught in the glare of the headlights, the fluorescent eyes of small animals shined back at him. Surprised and ruffled by his intrusion, they seemed to stare indignantly.

As he left the farms and ranches behind him, the road began to climb and wind around the narrow part of the canyon. Keeping his eyes on the road, he reached toward the radio, and after some fumbling with the small, square touch controls, managed to turn it off. As the road got steeper, he shifted down, and straining to a higher, shriller pitch, the engine moaned as he increased the revs. Accelerating as he went through the gears, he glanced at the tach, and as he gained speed, the trees and dark shapes at the side of the road fell behind him.

Up ahead, the switchbacks marked the steepest part of the canyon. As he entered them, he slammed the shift lever into second, and with the rear wheels breaking away and spewing out rocks and loose gravel, he powered through the first corner. Shooting forward, he pumped the wheel in the other direction, and keeping the revs up, he slid, and in a controlled drift, rounded the next bend. With the rear end popping and swaying from side to side, he accelerated hard. All around him, he could feel the power from the engine. Swirling and rolling through the drive train, like a huge ocean wave, it thrust him forward.

Accelerating and just coming out of third gear, directly in front of him, he saw it. "Move!" his mind yelled, but the big brown rabbit froze and glaring back at him, his eyes widened. Mitchell grimaced as he snapped the wheel to the left and hit the brakes. But it was too late. Then there was a thud, and sliding sideways down the highway the big sports car came to a stop in a cloud of dust on the other side of the road. "Dammit!" he shouted as he hit the steering wheel with his fist. "Damn!" Flinging the door open, he jumped out of the car, but after taking a few guarded steps, he stopped and probed the blackness of the canyon. Freezing in mid-stride, he saw the rabbit a few feet away, lying on his back. With his legs pawing desperately at the air he was still trying vainly to escape. In halting steps, Mitchell moved closer through the darkness. As he watched, the rabbit's long back legs stretched out for two spasmodic kicks, and with blood trickling down from his mouth, he stared up curiously at Mitchell.

Standing over the rabbit, Mitchell felt trapped, trapped in a dark tunnel, and looking down at the rabbit, he had an urge to turn and flee. But held fast by his shock and pity, he couldn't move. "Don't die," he mumbled. "Don't die." Then, with one last flick of his ear, the rabbit was still, and the circles of his big gray eyes hypnotically drew Mitchell in. "Why did you do this to me?" the rabbit seemed to say. "Why did you do this? You and your big machine." Then, as if he could see through the rabbit's eyes, Mitchell saw his world of meadows and fields. The rabbit was crouched next to a winding blue stream that glistened. Behind him, the sun was yellow, then white, and it seemed to move. But, in a blink, things got darker, and the vision of the rabbit faded away. Coming toward him from far down the canyon, Mitchell saw two small headlights wandering back and forth.

Taking his eyes from the approaching headlights, Mitchell looked back to the rabbit, and falling to his knees, he scooped up the animal's limp body. As he carried him to the side of the road, he could feel his tiny ribs beneath his fur. "I'm sorry," he whispered as he put him down in some tall grass next to an aspen tree. "I didn't realize. I.., really didn't." When he stood up, the leaves of the aspen trees rustled overhead, while beyond them a dark navy sky was filled with yellow and orange stars. Beneath them, silhouetted against the canyon walls, Mitchell stood fixed as he gazed down at the now silent rabbit. Then he sighed, and turning, he headed back toward the car.

Still idling at the side of the road, with its big red door swung open, the car seemed to be waiting for him. As he moved toward it, he could smell the acrid exhaust. Cutting through the cool canyon air, the scent was like pepper on sweet corn. But with each step, his stomach tightened, and the red car, like a whore, suddenly seemed vicious and cold. Getting closer, he eyed it like someone measuring his opponent. Then his despair gave way to rage, and with his fists clenched, his foot flew out, and yielding to the kick, the car door slammed shut. About to pound it with his fist, he paused abruptly, and dropping his head, he collapsed against the car. "What am I doing?" he moaned. "What the hell am I doing?" Then, lost in a swirl of grief and doubt, he felt something warm flash across his back, and turning away from the car, he looked down the dark canyon. On the canyon walls, meandering circles of light signaled an approaching car. Straightening up and trying to gather his composure, he looked one more time to where the rabbit lay in the tall grass. Opening the car door, he fell into the bucket seat and wearily pulled it shut. As the car passed, it slowed down, and the couple inside leaned forward and studied him, but lost in his thoughts and the red glow of gauges on the dash, he was indifferent to their scrutiny. "Aw, hell," he said sadly, and glancing up at the rearview mirror, he watched the red taillights of the passing car recede in the darkness. Then after releasing the hand brake, he pushed the shifter into first, and with gravel crackling beneath the car, headed slowly down the canyon. Following his own narrow path of light, his remorse turned to shame, and by and by he felt as if the canyon and all its minions were watching him leave.

#

Chapter Two

#

Mitchell slept fitfully that night. As he tossed from side to side, he kept seeing the rabbit at the edge of the road. Looking up at him, the rabbit's hypnotic eyes, like a kaleidoscope, kept pulling him closer and closer. Then, over and over again, he would hear the thud and the sound of the car skidding on the highway.

Unable to sleep, he was up early the next morning, and he was sitting at the piano in his pajamas when the phone rang. The piano was a small baby grand with sheet music strewn about on the top of it. Ignoring the phone, he kept playing, and with a pencil between his teeth, he stared hard at the music in front of him. With the phone still ringing, he took the pencil, and scratching out a B^b7 chord symbol, he replaced it with a B^b9. "That's better," he thought. "Yeah, much better." Then, looking over at the ringing phone, he laid the pencil down. As he rose up, he brushed his long brown hair from his forehead and stepped over to the desk. When he picked up the phone, his blue eyes narrowed.

"Hello."

"Aha! You don't sound sick to me."

"Oh, hi, Susan."

"Well, what is it? The flu or a hangover?"

"Uh...well, really, it's...well, I'm just not in the mood for work today."

"Boy, some people have it good. You're not in the mood, so you just don't come to work."

"Yeah, something like that, I guess."

"You know, if you had a real job, you couldn't get away with stuff like this."

"I do some of my work here, but if I had a real job, I might like going to work!"

"Well, how about the party tonight? Are you in the mood for that?"

"What party?"

"The party for Howard's retirement."

"Oh, I forgot about that. But I don't think he'll miss me. He'll be so drunk he won't know where he's at."

"That's not the point, Mitchell. You know Preston wants to talk to you tonight."

Mitchell rolled his head back. "I know," he said wearily. "He wants to put me in the trading room with the big boys."

"Well, isn't that wonderful?"

"I don't know...I don't know if I want to spend the rest of my life talking through my teeth on the phone."

"Do you know how many people would die to get that offer?"

"Yeah, I know."

"Well, are you going to hear him out?"

"Yeah, I guess. How 'bout I pick you up at six thirty?"

"But Mitchell, you know the party starts at six."

"Um...huh? Yeah, I know, but let's not drag it out, huh? If I have to talk to Preston all night, I'll be brain damaged. Let's just go at six thirty and get it over with. Then maybe we'll catch a show or something. I really don't wanna hang around and talk shop all night. I just don't want to do that right now."

"All right. How about a late dinner? Dinner at a nice place, not that diner you hang out at."

"What's wrong with Eddy's?"

"Well, for one thing, the food, which is usually terrible."

Mitchell looked down at the floor. "Yeah, I guess the food isn't great. I just feel comfortable there, and I like the jukebox."

"Jukebox?"

"Yeah, I like the jukebox, good old tunes, some old blues on that thing."

Susan chuckled. "Don't you think a jukebox is a bit outdated? I mean, it's kind of quaint, but really."

"I suppose it is, but it still lets you choose. I mean it's better than being force-fed all that canned music you get everywhere else, a bunch of vacant bubble-gummers in hot pants. Hell, a jukebox is the last vestige of democracy."

After a long pause, Susan replied. "Mitchell, can't we go to a nice place? The people in that place!"

Rolling his head back again, Mitchell closed his eyes. "All right," he said. We'll...we'll go to a...a better place. Just as long as I don't get stuck with Preston all night at the party."

"Good," said Susan cheerfully. "And try and get in a better frame of mind, will you? You sound like you're getting into one of your moods again. I really think you've been spending too much time alone. You know, you're thirty-four years old. We're in the eighties now, and the sixties are long gone. It's time to get it together."

Mitchell laughed and half coughed. "I'd do that if I knew what the hell it meant," he said, his voice trailing off.

"I know what it means," Susan said confidently. "Trust me. And baby, why don't you get a haircut today? And no Levi's and no blue work shirts, please. You're looking just a little raggedy lately. Still handsome, but a little out of it."

"What?" Mitchell was about to protest, but Susan cut him off.

"Boy, it's good you have me around to give you some direction, isn't it? See ya tonight."

After a moment, the phone started to buzz, and Mitchell hung up. "Right," he said softly. Then, still barefoot and in his pajamas, he trudged back to the piano. Sitting down at the keyboard, he was about to play something when the image of the rabbit stole back into his mind. Lying on his back on the road, the rabbit pawed at the air ever so slowly. Struck by the sight of him, Mitchell sat mesmerized on the bench. Then, slowly, the black and white keys of the piano came back into sight, and with a sigh, he shook his head and began to play a slow, rolling blues riff.

#

Chapter Three

#

After they left the restaurant, Mitchell accelerated hard as he whipped the shiny sports car around the entrance ramp onto the freeway. When he shifted into third gear, he saw a stream of bright red taillights ahead of him in the darkness. Holding onto the armrest, Susan waited until the car was heading straight down the freeway before she pulled down the visor. Then, looking into the mirror on the back of it, she straightened her shoulder-length blond hair, and with long, delicate fingers, she adjusted the white silk bow around her neck. Still looking into the mirror, she said, "Thank you for dinner. That was very nice, and I thought the food was quite good, didn't you?"

Mitchell nodded. "Yeah, it wasn't bad," he said, and reaching down to turn on the radio, he pushed the little square button that scanned for a channel. Picking up a bit of music and a blurb of news and then some more music, the radio kept scanning. As he tried to make it stop, he groped at the other buttons on the front of it. "You know, this thing has given me fits from day one. All this digital stuff! I'd just like to have a knob I could turn! You know, when I was a kid, I had a crystal radio set. If it broke, I could fix it. If it needed a part, I could just go downtown and buy one. I actually understood how it worked, but not these things. If this breaks, you're at the mercy of some giant cartel."

Indifferent to Mitchell's complaints, the radio continued to scan, and in contrast to the chaotic music and verbiage that was flowing from the speakers, Susan's voice was cool and confident. "Are we a little frustrated with the car?" she said as she pushed the visor back up. Still fumbling at the switches, Mitchell finally managed to turn the radio off. "I guess I am a little," he said.

Susan looked askance at him. "But I thought you liked this car. You're always talking about how you like the way it handles and how quick it is. Maybe you're getting older."

Keeping his eyes on the road, Mitchell scoffed. "Naw, it's not that. It's just...uh...I don't know. It's somethin' else."

"I see," said Susan. "I see." And for a while they didn't talk. As he drove, Mitchell pondered the rich blanket of stars overhead, and how on the horizon they seemed to merge with the multitude of lights that made up the city. "How did it go with Preston?" Susan said finally. "I saw you talking to him, and he didn't look too pleased." With his mind still fixed on the stars, Mitchell barely heard Susan. Then she reiterated. "Mitchell, you're not listening again. Tell me, how did it go with Preston tonight?"

Wanting to say something about how the stars and the taillights gave him the impression of flying through the galaxy, Mitchell looked over at her, but seeing the determination on her face, he succumbed to her question. "Oh, I suppose it didn't go too well. I mean we got into a discussion of sorts."

Susan shot him a questioning look. "A discussion? You mean an argument. What did you argue about?"

Throwing his hands up from the wheel, Mitchell signaled his own frustration. "We didn't argue that much," he retorted. "We were just talking about the Fenninger deal, and I told him I didn't like it. I told him I thought we were taking advantage of the old man."

"You told Preston that?"

Mitchell shrugged. "Yeah. Why not? He asked me."

Nonplussed, Susan shook her head. "So, what did he say?"

Glancing over at her, Mitchell changed lanes. "Aw, you know Press. He told me it's just business, that if we didn't do it, someone else would. He's deep, isn't he."

Looking down at her lap, Susan continued to shake her head. Then, picking some lint from her suit, she looked out the passenger window. "How could you do that?" she moaned bitterly. "My God, you don't lecture your boss!"

As the traffic up ahead began to back up at an exit ramp, Mitchell shifted down, and the car whined as it slowed. "I don't know," he said. "But where the hell are you when you can't give an honest opinion to somebody you work with all day?"

Now in heavy, slow-moving traffic, Mitchell revved the engine and shifted down again. "Hey, it's no good," he declared. "The market's corrupt, and so is Preston, and you know I'm just as bad. We don't produce anything, make anything, all we do is make bogus profits, manipulate, and skim. That's really what we do."

Without responding, Susan turned away, and staring out the passenger window, she watched as a copper-colored Mercedes sedan passed them in the right lane. The Mercedes was almost out of sight when she finally spoke. "Mitchell, I really think you should go see Dr. Matheson. Don't you think he could help?"

Mitchell cocked his head to one side. "Your shrink, Mr. Rent-a-friend? Nope, I'm not goin' there," he said with irritation.

Susan's face tightened. "You know, Mitchell, I think you have a real problem," she said somewhat scornfully. "You seem depressed or something, particularly in the last few days. I think he could help you."

Up ahead, the traffic started to thin out, and Mitchell accelerated as he replied, "No, hey, he's just a company man, like most of 'em. I saw a shrink once in college. When I told him how I felt about the world, he gave me all this stuff about not feeling guilty, and 'that's the way of the world stuff, accept it.'" He actually told me that I was at the top of the food chain and I should appreciate it. Then he handed me a bottle full of pills to calm me down. That's what most of 'em do. They sedate us so we can't see what we're doing or what's happening to us. Then we stay in our cages and do what we're told and we don't bitch. Christ, I can do that with a bottle of bourbon. That's what Howard's done for thirty years. Just because I don't wanna spend the rest of my life in a box with a phone jammed in my ear doesn't mean I'm crazy."

Pausing, Mitchell waited for Susan to say something, but when she didn't respond, he went on, and as he spoke his frustration grew. "You know, the office is nothing but a cage to me. In fact, all those buildings downtown look like cages to me. Just cages stacked one on top of the other. You've got to be crazy to adjust to that! Matheson's the one who ought to check his hand. He's gonna spend his life in a cement box, and he doesn't even mind. He thinks it's normal! Christ, talk about the blind leading the blind, and then to make fifty bucks an hour for it. How's that?"

In obvious frustration, Susan reached into her purse for a cigarette. "So you won't talk to him."

"Listen," said Mitchell with both hands on the wheel. "I don't like what we do. We exploit people, and then we have people like Matheson coach us on how to cope with it. It's not a psychological problem; it's a moral problem. It's a matter of character, plain and simple. Right's right and wrong's wrong. My old man always said that, and he was right. Your shrink friend is just a corporate cheerleader. He's an ad man posing as a priest, and I'm not gonna spill my guts to him or anybody else!"

Susan took the lighter from her cigarette slowly. As she exhaled, she glanced scornfully at Mitchell. "You know, you're impossible sometimes," she said. "And you only get away with it because you've made lots of money for the company. The 'golden boy.' You ought to think about what you'd be without it, without the company. You've got to get over all this guilt or whatever it is. I think Matheson could help with that."

"I have thought about that," said Mitchell. "Guilt, I mean." Then, slowing down, he caught the exit ramp and brought the car to a stop at an intersection. "You buy the stuff about too much guilt, don't you," he said as he pulled away from the intersection. "Myself, I don't think people feel enough guilt. Around here everybody's a nice guy. I mean, as long as you don't kill somebody, you're OK. If you cut a deal and put people out of work, deflate their stock portfolio and leave them penniless, that's OK too. Around here self-respect grows on trees. Doesn't that bother you? I mean, how can the world be so messed up and everybody be so God-damned good?"

Agitated, Susan rubbed out her cigarette in the ashtray. Then, turning back to Mitchell, she lashed out, "We're not crooks! And who the hell are you to say that Dr. Matheson doesn't know what he's talking about? I swear, sometimes you sound like a crazy sixties radical or something! The sixties are over, Mitchell! You get it? That's the way it is! C'mon, it's time to grow up! It's a tough world out there, and we are on top of the food chain, and I want to stay there, and so do you. Get real!"

When he pulled into Susan's driveway, Mitchell turned off the car, and looking at the dashboard, he spoke. "Look, I didn't mean to run on about Matheson. I..."

Leaning over, Susan kissed him on the cheek like she usually did when they had a tiff. "It's OK," she said with a sigh. "I know what you're like sometimes. But, you know I think we'd better talk, sometime soon. Seriously."

Mitchell sighed as he looked out through the windshield. Then, nodding his head, he said, "Oh, I get it. That means I'm not coming in, huh."

"Not tonight," replied Susan softly. "The mood is wrong, don't you think?" Then, seeing his disappointment, she changed the subject. "What are you doing tomorrow?"

"Uh...I'm going to the pound again."

"Still looking for a dog? How many times have you been out to that place? It's such a depressing place. I really don't know how you can stand it. And what are you going to do with a dog, anyway? You're a stubborn one, Mitchell Black."

"Well, I just think..."

"I know, you're going to fetch one from death row, and you think it's better that way." Shaking her head, Susan opened the car door. "I'll talk to you tomorrow," she said as she got out.

Sitting back in his seat, Mitchell watched her walk up the sidewalk to her door. "Ah, hell," he muttered. Then he started the car and abruptly backed out of the driveway. As he drove away, he was frustrated, and yet somehow, in some way, he felt slightly relieved.

#

Chapter Four

#

Late the next morning, Mitchell left the house and headed across town toward the pound. It was a bright sunny day, and he drove with his arm resting out the open window. With his head cocked back a little, he felt the warm summer air as it wafted about his face. At the stop sign at the end of his street, he looked over at a new construction site where an old home was being torn down in preparation for some new condominiums. At the side of the partially demolished house, a bulldozer began to ram and claw at an old apple tree. Seeming to cling to the earth, the tree at first withstood the lunging machine, almost defiantly. Then, with a snap, it fell slowly back, and its naked grasping roots surged up from the ground. The sight of it made Mitchell wince, and suddenly, without warning, the vision of the rabbit intruded into his mind. Again he saw the rabbit gazing up and pawing in the darkness. Behind him, with hot smoke pouring out from its exhaust, the big, wedge-shaped sports car was idling in the background. Then, hearing a horn, Mitchell flinched, and he started off from the stop sign with a jerk, and then sped away.

Out on the freeway, he reached down and opened up his tape box. Thumbing past Vivaldi, Chet Baker, Bob Dylan, and Elvis Sings the Blues, he grabbed a homemade tape that had "Joe Cocker," scribbled on the cover and snapped it into the tape player. The music started with a highly syncopated piano riff, and once the band was in full swing, Joe Cocker howled, "feelin'-all-right, ah huh" in his husky voice. As Mitchell accelerated, he smiled and indulged in the sensuous mix of rhythm, speed, and power that surrounded him, all of it inhaled at once.

He had been on the freeway for about half an hour when up ahead he saw the pound, and not taking his eyes off it, he turned off the stereo. When he shifted down and the engine whined, the car felt like a jet coming in for a smooth landing on the runway. As he got off the exit ramp, he could see the tall chain link fence surrounding the lot. The main building was canary yellow, and two large, red-and-blue rainbow-like stripes had been painted on the side. "Hell," he said to himself, "this place looks like a playground. I wonder if Dachau was painted in the same cheery colors."

As he closed the car door, he read the sign above the front entrance. In big, blue letters it said, "WE LOVE ANIMALS." Beneath it, in smaller print, it said, "We afford these animals humane treatment using the latest scientific and medical methods. Stray animals suffer from hunger and disease. We are here to ease their suffering." Mitchell scoffed. "I bet if you asked the animals, they'd rather take their chances on the streets," he thought. "That's bull," he muttered to himself. "They don't pick them up to help them. They pick them up to keep the damn streets clean. They kill them because they're a nuisance," he thought. "What lies they tell, all these good people."

Inside, Mitchell walked up to the counter and studied the receptionist. She was talking on the phone, and she was muttering something about what a drag her date on Saturday had been.

"And after that, he had the nerve to come on to me. Can you believe it? Linda, hold on, I've got someone here." Acknowledging him, the receptionist dropped the phone to her shoulder. "What can I do for you today?"

"I'd like to look at the dogs again, if I can."

"Well, they're right through the door. You know the way."

"Thanks."

When he turned away, Mitchell took a deep breath, and after walking a few steps, he pulled open the big aluminum door that led into the area where they kept the dogs. As the door slammed shut with a loud clank, the dogs began to bark, and in seconds there was a terrible howling racket. In the midst of the crying and yelping, Mitchell's heart sank as it always did when he went in there. Trying not to think about just how terrible this place really was, he immediately began his search for the right dog.

As he walked toward the rows of large cages that housed the dogs, he passed the smaller cages where they kept the stray and abandoned cats and smaller animals. In one of the cages there was a litter of kittens. Peering in, Mitchell saw that most of them hadn't yet opened their eyes. "Yeah, keep your eyes closed," he thought. In the cages next to them, other cats just stared out blankly, as if they had already retreated into some protective form of insanity. In one of the bottom cages a huge gray rabbit lay sleeping, and for a moment Mitchell couldn't help but stare at it. Fighting off images of the rabbit he had hit on the highway, he turned away suddenly. In his haste, he tripped over a hose that was lying on the floor. As he fell forward, he grabbed onto one of the large dog cages. In the cage, a big German shepherd lunged at him, snarling and growling. After jumping back, Mitchell stood fixed on the dog's bared fangs.

Leaving the snarling shepherd behind him, Mitchell walked slowly between two rows of cages. The air was foul with the smell of urine and feces, and the barking and crying of the dogs was now almost deafening. At the far end of the first row of cages, one of the attendants, a young man in rubber boots, was hosing down the dogs and stalls. For a moment, Mitchell watched as one of the dogs being doused crouched helplessly in the corner of his cage. In the cage next to him, a gray-and-white Husky growled and snapped. Amidst this pandemonium, Mitchell looked from one cage to the next. Inside the cages, many of the dogs would light up and start to jump up and down as he approached. Others sat attentive and wide-eyed, like fearful children trying to control and compose themselves.

In a cage by herself, a little black-and-white mongrel was crying and running in circles. As Mitchell approached, she bounced up to the side of the cage, and standing on her hind legs, she forced her nose through the chain link. Her eyes were big and round, and as if she had been crying, there were wet marks below them. Crying and pawing at the fencing, she seemed to plead with Mitchell. Looking down at her, Mitchell stopped, but then forcing himself to avert his eyes, he walked on.

A few cages away, a high-stepping Irish setter nervously padded to the front of her cage, and seeing Mitchell, she pushed her side up against the wire mesh. Knelling down beside her, Mitchell reached through the fencing and rubbed her back. At the touch of his hand, the setter whined. "It's all right," said Mitchell. "You'll make it out of here. You're pretty, and I can see you've got expensive tags."

In the next cage there was a cocker spaniel with three little puppies nestled up to her. With her puppies sleeping contentedly, she looked guardedly at Mitchell. There was a terrible hopelessness in her eyes, and it filled Mitchell with remorse and anger. "What kind of person would abandon a mother and her puppies," he thought.

As he pushed on, Mitchell continued to peer into all the cages on both sides of the aisle. In one of the cages there were two black Labradors. An Afghan across from them looked skinny, even for an Afghan. Lying down with her head on the cement, she didn't move when Mitchell approached. When he tried to coax her over, she just stared straight ahead. "She's given up," thought Mitchell. "Too genteel a breed to survive in this place."

At the end of the aisle, Mitchell came to a cage where a few days earlier he had seen a jaunty little English pointer. A smart little guy with bright eyes and a frisky disposition, he had made a strong impression on Mitchell. A man in rubber boots was washing out the cage. "What happened to the dog that was in here last week?" said Mitchell.

"Oh, they gas on Friday mornings, you know. Nobody wanted him."

With a sick feeling welling up inside of him, Mitchell nodded. "I see," he said as he looked at the empty cage. Then, for an instant, he could see the little pointer looking up at him with playful eyes. "They talk about gassing on Friday like some people talk about cleaning on the weekends," he thought.

In the cage next to the empty one, there was a small black dog with pointed ears and a long, fox-like nose. For a moment the little dog seemed to be taken with Mitchell. But he stiffened when Mitchell knelt down next to him, and turning his head away, the dog bared his teeth and began to emit a high-pitched growl. "You don't have to be scared of me," said Mitchell softly. "But it's no wonder," he thought. "I'd be paranoid too." Then, in something like a stupor, Mitchell stared at the dog while his thoughts ran on. "I wonder what it must be like for them. They don't filter everything with labels and talk, like we do. And they're not blinded by wordy, grandiose myths. They might be closer to reality than we are. They can probably smell the death in here."

When he rose up, Mitchell shook his head as if to throw off his thoughts. As he walked on, he knew the sinking feeling in his heart was bringing him to the end of his endurance for this place. Yet, while he wanted to leave, he felt obliged to continue his search. Then, in the last cage in the aisle, he was struck by the gaze of a handsome, reddish-gold dog. The dog was sitting up, and with beautiful, almond-shaped eyes outlined in dark brown, the dog seemed to smile at him. His eyes were knowing, full of life, like a sunrise. He had a lion-like mane with a small white blaze in the middle. For a moment the dog looked demurely back at Mitchell. Then, somewhat nonchalantly, he looked away. A moment later, in a playful, almost coquettish fashion, he glanced back to see if Mitchell was still looking at him. "Well," said Mitchell warmly, "who do we have here?" Then, reaching for the tag that was wired onto the front of the cage, he whispered what he read, "Golden retriever mix, one year old." Letting go of the tag, he bent down to take a closer look at the dog. Still sitting quietly in the middle of the cage, the dog didn't move, and with a furrowed brow, he likewise was studying Mitchell. Then, very slowly, and with apparent deliberation, the dog stood up and moved over to him. Reaching through the chain link, Mitchell rubbed the dog's neck just behind his ears. Seeming to enjoy this, the dog pushed against his hand, but unlike other dogs that whine and fidget when they get attention, this dog was poised, and his beguiling eyes gave only a hint of eagerness or hope. As he stroked the dog, Mitchell began to smile, and deep inside him, he felt a sense of satisfaction and truth that he hadn't felt in years. Then, patting the dog, he said, "I'll be right back."

At the front desk Mitchell told the young girl he wanted to take the dog out of the cage. Moments later Mitchell returned to the cage with an attendant. The attendant was a muscular African American in a beige uniform. His rolled-up short sleeves exposed huge biceps, and he had a big ring of keys chained to his belt. As they walked past the cages, the dogs began to bark, and in desperation some of them threw themselves at the wire fencing. Looking down at them, the attendant's eyes were firm, but not indifferent. Studying him, Mitchell thought it was odd that a black man should be here, a place where another group was being exploited. "It's the oppression," he thought, like Jews being forced to work in the concentration camps. Then, for a second, he remembered a friend, very drunk, in a bar. "The concentration camp is the ultimate metaphor for life," he blurted out, "don't you think." And in his mind Mitchell could see him swaggering, drink in hand. Then the attendant came back into focus.

The attendant's large biceps flexed as he opened the lock on the cage. "Oh, this guy, he's a jumper," he said in a deep voice. "Got outta here one day, jumped that six-foot fence in the back and almost cleared it clean. He's somethin' else, this guy, and he's sure got some shiners, doesn't he." Stepping inside, the attendant snapped a leash on the dog. "This one doesn't like to be caged," he said as he led him out, and kneeling down, Mitchell began to stroke the dog. "You're pretty damned skinny," he said. "It looks like you've been on the run for a while, haven't you?"

As he stood up, Mitchell noticed that the attendant was smiling. He assumed it was because he was talking to the dog. Feeling some embarrassment, Mitchell responded, "I bet a lot of people talk to their dogs, don't they?"

The attendant's smile broadened. "Sure, all the time. Probably talk to their dogs more than they talk to their spouses. Probably more honest with 'em, too."

Mitchell laughed out loud. "Yeah, I can believe that!"

And with a more subdued smile, the attendant seemed to take Mitchell's measure. Apparently coming to a favorable conclusion, he said, "You wouldn't be interested in taking a rabbit, would you? We've got lots of rabbits lately."

Mitchell shook his head. "I don't think so," he said.

"Too bad," said the attendant. "You know, I've been readin' a book about rabbits. It's about a rabbit society, or I guess it's really about our society, but it's pretty interesting."

Still petting the dog, Mitchell looked up at him. "Oh, I think I know that book. I read it a long time ago. *Watership Down*, isn't it?"

"Yeah, that's it."

"And isn't there one rabbit that can tell the future or something?"

"Yeah, there is. They call him Fiver, and he's real frail and sickly all the time."

"Yeah, that's right. I remember him. That was a good book."

With a knowing smile, the attendant pointed down the aisle. "Why don't you walk him a bit, see how he minds." Nodding, Mitchell took the leash and started down the aisle with the dog, but seeing one of their own out of the cage, the other dogs started to howl and bark. In the pandemonium that erupted, Mitchell's fortitude began to fail. As he walked, like Dante descending into the inferno, he felt beseeched by all the condemned and wailing souls in hell. Unable to take any more, he stopped abruptly and turned back to the attendant. "I'll take him," he said. "Let's see if we can get him a reprieve." The attendant gave him a quizzical look, then put the dog back in the cage and closed the metal gate.

"Don't worry," Mitchell said to the dog, "I'll be right back, and then we'll get you outa' here." Seeming to understand, the dog sat back on his haunches, and with eyes that bespoke both hope and curiosity, he watched Mitchell and the attendant leave.

When Mitchell approached the front counter, the receptionist was staring into a fashion magazine.

"I'd like to buy the dog in cage thirty-one."

Putting down the magazine, the young woman reached for the small file box in front of her. While she thumbed through it, Mitchell pondered the sultry, round-hipped blond woman with bright red lips on the cover of her magazine. "She's so made up, she looks like a street walker," he thought with a chuckle.

"Oh, here it is, but he's not eligible for adoption for two more days. Sorry."

"What?" said Mitchell in astonishment, "But today is Tuesday and Thursday is a holiday, and on Friday you kill them!"

"Oh, that's right, they put them to sleep on Fridays."

"But you won't kill him, will you?"

The young woman put the card down on the counter. "Well I'm not..." she began to say, and just then the attendant came in and stood behind Mitchell.

"Give him the dog today," he said forcefully.

"But, Mr. Johnson, the regulations state..."

"Don't tell me about the rules, Marcy," he interrupted. "Just get the paperwork done and tell him about the shots. I'll get the dog."

Taken aback by the exchange, Mitchell gazed with some amazement at the attendant, and for a moment he glimpsed the worn and hard anguish of a man who saw more of life and death than most, a man who made decisions that others couldn't fathom, let alone carry out.

"Be sure he gets his shots," said the attendant, looking back at Mitchell sternly. "They can catch lots of diseases in here." Then, turning away, the attendant muttered, "Someday places like this won't exist, a thing of the past." Then he disappeared through the door, and from behind the counter the young woman brought out some forms.

After signing the papers, Mitchell gave the receptionist twenty dollars. When the attendant returned with the dog, Mitchell thanked him, and with a confident smile the attendant handed him the leash.

"Take good care of Fiver. He's special."

"Fiver?"

"Yeah, you are gonna name him Fiver, aren't you?" With shrewd yet playful eyes, the attendant waited for Mitchell to respond. Looking away, Mitchell paused, thought, and then nodded in agreement. Looking back at the attendant, he smiled.

"Yeah, I suppose I am," he said. "Fiver."

#

Chapter Five

#

It was bright outside, and Mitchell shielded his eyes as he walked to the car. "Come on, get in," he said as he opened the passenger door, and looking up at him with some curiosity, Fiver cautiously touched the seat with his paw, as if to test it. Then, in one graceful movement, he jumped in, and sitting upright on the cushion, he gave Mitchell a trusting glance. "I feel like a chauffeur," thought Mitchell as he closed the door and walked around to the driver's side.

Starting the car with just a flick of the key, Mitchell revved it up a bit. Beside him on the passenger seat, Fiver looked peacefully out through the windshield. When Mitchell glanced over at him, he seemed to smile, the way dogs do when they relax and open their mouths and pull their lips back. As the car pulled out of the parking lot, Fiver looked back at the pound, and letting out a single bark, he seemed to signal both his contempt for the place and his joy at leaving.

Out on the freeway, Mitchell drove with his elbow out the window. As the warm wind rushed past him, it felt good, and looking over, he saw that Fiver was also enjoying the ride. Sitting up and bracing himself with one paw against the dash, the wind buffeted his mane, as he watched the passing scenery. Still marveling at him, Mitchell put a different tape in the stereo. As the music began, he rocked back and forth in his seat while Fiver continued to gaze out the windshield. Then Fiver abruptly turned his head and watched as a hitchhiker at the side of the road shot by them and re-ceded into the past. A moment later, with an acoustic bass slapping out a rhythm, and Elvis singing, "Yes, my baby left me," the two of them, side by side, sailed down the freeway.

A half hour later they exited the freeway, and thinking Fiver might like to go for a walk, Mitchell stopped at a small park not too far from his house. Mitchell lived in one of the older Denver neighborhoods, and the park, along with trees and the stream that ran through it had been there for a long time. With Fiver next to him, he walked along the stream. Then, standing beneath two large elm trees, he picked up a stick and threw it. After a moment's hesitation, Fiver bounded after it and brought it back. Pulling the stick from Fiver's mouth, he threw it again, but this time Fiver didn't move, and lying with his paws out in front of him, he just looked out at the stick and then up at Mitchell. "What's the matter?" said Mitchell with a laugh. "You want me to go get it? It's my turn?" Still not budging, Fiver looked up at him with curious eyes. Shrugging his shoulders, Mitchell knelt and stroked him and through the soft hair fur he could feel every rib. "I guess we better get your strength up," he said. "Or is that fetch business just beneath you? Let's go get some food, huh?"

While they walked back to the car, Mitchell began to worry about how thin Fiver was. Then, ever so quietly, the dying rabbit slipped back into his mind. Staring up at him, the large circles of the rabbit's eyes seemed to question everything about him. Then his thoughts turned to Susan, and she had a foreboding look on her face. Then in his mind Preston looked up from behind his big desk. "It's just business, kid. What's with you," he said. Then, abruptly, Mitchell realized he was back at the car and Fiver wasn't beside him. "Fiver," he said, turning around. "Fiver..." And then he saw him a few steps away on the grass. He seemed to be gagging or coughing, and he had thrown up a green, bilious liquid. As Mitchell looked on, the dog crouched and coughed and gagged, and looking up at him, he seemed em-barrassed. "Aw, that's no big deal," proclaimed Mitchell. "Let's go." Standing up, Fiver backed away from the vomit, and after giving Mitchell a still em-barrassed and apologetic look, he ran past him and jumped into the car.

"Probably just something he ate," thought Mitchell. "I'll get him some good food at the store."

When he came out of the grocery store, Mitchell had two big bags in his arms. As he approached the car, he saw that Fiver was still sitting up in the passenger seat, and for some reason he looked a little sheepish, like he was still embarrassed. Setting the grocery bags down on the hood of the car, Mitchell continued to ponder his expression. "What's the matter?" he asked as he opened the car door, and at that moment he was struck by a putrid odor that made him recoil and turn his head. Then, on the driver's seat, he saw a steamy pool of green vomit. "Yaach!" he said, and seeing Mitchell's discontent, Fiver crouched down. "Shit!" cried Mitchell, and cowering, Fiver shrunk further away. But as he looked up from the vomit, Mitchell saw the dog huddled against the door, and like a child trying to protect himself, Fiver was holding one paw up in the air. Instantly, Mitchell was full of shame and pity. "Aw, it's all right, Fiver," he said, as his anger vanished. "It's OK. Don't be upset." Then, wincing a bit, he leaned across the vomit-covered seat and reassuringly patted Fiver on the neck. "It's no big deal. I'll clean it up," he said. Then, for a second, Mitchell felt something deep inside change, and whatever it was, it yearned for expression. "It's just a car," he said as he patted Fiver. "It's just a damn car."

Chapter Six

Fiver didn't eat much that afternoon and Mitchell was a little concerned when, after taking only a few bites of the canned dog food, Fiver walked away and lay down by the back door in the kitchen. Later, when Mitchell set a bowl of dry dog food in front of him, Fiver raised an eyebrow and then looked away. "Maybe he's traumatized by all the changes," thought Mitchell. Then the phone rang, and he answered it at his desk in the living room.

"Hello."

"Hi there." It was Susan. "Where have you been all day?"

"Well, I went to the pound, and I found a dog!"

"Hmm, what kind did you get?"

"Well, I'm not sure. I think he's a mix, but he's handsome, and I named him Fiver."

"Fiber?"

"No, Fiver, F-I-V-E-R, like a five dollar bill. Fiver!"

"Unusual name. Where'd you get that?"

"Uh, that's a long story, but I like it."

"Well, I'm glad you've finally found a dog. Now you won't have to go out to that depressing place anymore. But, the reason I called, I'm going out to dinner with a client tonight. I wondered if you would like to come along?"

"Uh, no, I don't think I could. Fiver seems like he's a little sick or something. I'd better stay with him for his first night here. Besides, I'm not much good at these social things lately."

"OK, if that's how you're going to be. I'll call you in the morning. Bye." Susan hung up before Mitchell could reply.

"I'll see ya," he said, and as he set the receiver down on the phone his gaze fell upon his baby grand piano. With the afternoon sun shining through the windows that surrounded it, the beautiful mahogany instrument stood quietly in the alcove. A few steps away, on the coffee table, lay two large books, and next to a glass ashtray rested an old rusted metal toy truck. Behind the coffee table sat a brown, overstuffed couch. Above it was a large painting of a sorrowful clown sitting on a park bench, and for a moment Mitchell gazed at him. With his suitcase beside him, and the orange and red leaves of fall rustling and twirling in the wind about him, the clown, white faced and balding, was pondering an old newspaper with great severity. On the back of the crumpled paper, in bold print, the words "All Stocks Down" were just barely visible.

It was dusk when Mitchell decided to take Fiver outside. "C'mon," he said in an enthusiastic voice. "Let's go for a walk." Cocking his head, Fiver jumped up, and trotting down the front steps, he stopped at the bottom and looked back to Mitchell. "Let's go that way," said Mitchell as he pointed up the street, and rising up and whirling, Fiver ran on ahead. Sniffing the ground and everything else that caught his attention, he seemed to delight in exploring the most mundane aspects of this urban environment. Stopping every so often, he would look back mindfully to see if Mitchell was following. "I'm comin'," shouted Mitchell as he waved. "I'm comin'."

When they returned from their walk, Mitchell went straight to the piano. Hopping on the couch, Fiver settled in, and with his head lying on his front paws, he watched Mitchell play. Looking up from the piano, Mitchell smiled when he saw Fiver studying him. Catching Mitchell's gaze, Fiver demurely wagged his tail, and with his eyes shining, he seemed truly fascinated with Mitchell and his music.

Working on some new tunes, Mitchell played the piano for an hour or so. Then, feeling tired, he went to bed. He had just pulled the covers up to his shoulders when he looked over and found Fiver sitting on the floor next to him. Beaming with curiosity, Fiver swept his tail smoothly back and forth across the floor. "OK, c'mon," said Mitchell, and sliding backward across the bed, he made some more room, and in an instant Fiver jumped up and was on the bed. Then, after pawing at the covers as if he were digging in soft dirt, he lay down, and with his back to Mitchell he put his head on the pillow. Draping his arm over him, Mitchell relaxed and drifted off to sleep. Still awake, Fiver raised his head and looked at Mitchell's arm. Then putting his head on the pillow, he too went to sleep.

Chapter Seven

#

Early the next morning, Mitchell felt something nudge his hand. Opening one eye, he saw Fiver sitting on the floor next to the bed. Staring up at him, Fiver's eyes were full of eager anticipation. "Fiver, it's way too early to be getting up," said Mitchell as he fluffed his pillow and tried to return to sleep. Then, just when Mitchell was comfortable, Fiver put his nose under his arm, and flipping it up, waited for a response. "Fiver, you're kiddin', aren't you?" said Mitchell as he rose up on one elbow. "What do you want? It's too early to do anything. What were you, an army dog or something?" Starting to fidget, Fiver nudged him again. "OK! OK! I'll get up," said Mitchell. "I don't know what for, but I'll get up."

With Fiver prancing on the floor in front of him, Mitchell sat on the edge of the bed. "OK, now what do we do?" he said, and looking up at him, Fiver glanced toward the door. Then stepping backward, he let out one restrained bark and glanced toward the door again. "I see. You wanna go outside? You wanna go for a walk? It's six in the morning, and you want to go for a walk?" As he looked back at him, Fiver's ears stood up like those of a puppy. "Don't think it's gonna be like this every day," said Mitchell as he stood up.

It was cool outside, and as he stood on the front porch with Fiver, Mitchell saw that the sun was just coming over the horizon. As the orange light of morning spread across the street, Fiver bounded down the steps and headed up the sidewalk. Then stopping, he looked back to see if Mitchell was behind him. When he saw Mitchell wave him on, he reared up, and in a whirl, he took off again. Smiling, Mitchell followed along, and as he breathed in the crisp morning air, he marveled at the amber colors of dawn.

When they got back to the house, Mitchell was amazed. "I'm awake," he thought, "and I haven't had any coffee." In the kitchen, he whistled as he opened Fiver's dog food. Then, still holding the can in his hand, he watched as Fiver, after taking only a few bites, turned away and lapped up some water. "He ought to be eating more than that," he thought, "and he seems too thirsty all the time."

While he waited for the water for his coffee to boil, Mitchell listened to the news and washed up a few dishes. When the old metal teapot began to whistle, he poured the hot water through the filter into the carafe and made some coffee. Then, with cup in hand, he sank down into his easy chair, and setting the coffee on the small round table next to him, he read the front page and after looking through the financial section, he turned to the comics.

It was nine o'clock when the phone rang, and buried beneath the newspaper, Mitchell woke up with a start. Peering over the top of the paper, he saw Fiver lying on the couch watching him. The tip of his tail wagged subtly. As Mitchell stumbled toward the phone, the paper floated to the floor.

"Hello," he said groggily.

"Oh, I see I woke you up," said Susan, with office machines humming in the background.

"Yeah, I guess you did, but really I've been up for hours."

"What?"

"Oh, nothing."

"Are you coming in today?"

"No, I don't think so. It's a day before a long weekend. It'll be real slow, anyway."

"That's true."

"Tell Preston I finished that prospectus and I'll be in next week."

"What are you going to do today?"

"Ah, I'm gonna' take Fiver to the vet and then straighten up the house. Why don't you come by after work and meet Fiver, and maybe the three of us can go for a walk or something?" Fiver's ears perked up when he heard the word "walk." "No, not now," said Mitchell, waving him off.

"I wasn't coming over now," said Susan somewhat indignantly.

"No, no, I was talking to Fiver. He thinks I want to go for a walk." Hearing the word again, Fiver jumped off the couch, and wagging his tail, he came over to Mitchell. Looking down at him, Mitchell nodded wearily. "Susan, I'll see you when you stop by."

After their walk, Mitchell took Fiver to the vet for his shots, and while he was there he told him about Fiver not eating. After recommending that he try feeding him boiled rice and hamburger, the vet said to bring Fiver back if his appetite didn't improve. On the way home, Fiver sat up in the passenger seat, and with his paw propped against the dash, he took great interest in everything that passed by.

It was after five when Susan arrived, and after some brief introductions wherein Fiver was quite gracious, the three of them went for a walk around the neighborhood. Since it was an older neighborhood, the streets were lined with trees that shaded the sidewalks. Running along ahead, Fiver as usual would stop every so often and look back. When Mitchell waved or said, "I'm comin'," he would rear up, twirl, and bound off like a wild pony. If Mitchell wanted him to come, he would whistle a short, three-note phrase that rose and fell and kind of trailed off gradually. It had natural soothing quality about it, entreating but not demanding, and Mitchell really didn't know where he'd picked it up. It just seemed right.

After they had walked two or three blocks, Mitchell and Susan were passing the neighborhood health food store when Mitchell noticed that Fiver was getting too far ahead of them. In a firm but not loud or hostile voice he called out, "Fiver." Then he whistled, and in the same calm voice, he called out again.

"You'd better yell at him," commented Susan. "He's not coming. He's going to take off and get lost."

Whistling once more, Mitchell caught Fiver's attention, and turning around, he started to trot back toward them. "I don't want to be yelling at him for the rest of my life," said Mitchell. "I'm not gonna train him to just take me seriously when I'm yelling." With a quiet chuckle, Mitchell smiled. "Besides, there might come a time when I really need to get his attention, say a car is coming or something. That's when I'll yell at him. If I yell at him all the time, it won't mean a thing. Besides, I want him to have some freedom. He's not my slave. He's his own man."

"Isn't that a little dangerous?" said Susan, looking hard at Mitchell. "Lots of people send their dogs to obedience school."

"Yeah, I know," said Mitchell. "But I don't buy it. It's a crock. People are supposed to be free and take risks, but dogs, no, dogs are supposed to be servile and better off in cages. Isn't that a crock!" Pausing, Mitchell stared off, and appeared to be lost in his thoughts. Then, looking at him with obvious concern and doubt, Susan took his arm, and they walked on.

When they returned to the house, Mitchell asked Susan to stay for dinner, but she said she was going out for drinks with some of the gals from work. After she left, Mitchell cooked up the hamburger and rice that the vet had prescribed for Fiver, but when he set it out, Fiver sniffed it and took only a few hesitant bites. He ate a little more when Mitchell fed the hamburger to him by hand. But even at that, he didn't eat much.

#

Chapter Eight

#

For the next few days, Mitchell learned to appreciate the importance of getting up early. Every morning he protested, and every morning he and Fiver made the journey around the neighborhood. Fiver still didn't eat much, and Mitchell still thought he drank too much water, but nonetheless, he was always up and eager for his morning walk. Eventually, Mitchell found himself looking forward to it.

It was on a Monday morning, about a week later, when lying in bed, Mitchell felt the sun on his face, and rolled over to avoid it. "The sun," he thought. "It must be late. Why didn't Fiver get me up?" Then, opening his eyes, he heard a raspy wheezing sound coming up over the edge of the bed. It sounded like someone with severe asthma or emphysema. Sitting up, he looked around, and across the room he saw Fiver curled up on the floor. Gazing back at him with drooping eyes covered with dried mucus, Fiver weakly flopped his tail on the floor, and when he breathed, he coughed and wheezed. As Mitchell threw off the covers and got out of bed, he saw that Fiver's nose was running and it was crusted over in places. As he knelt down next to him, he listened to his labored breathing. "Hold on," he said, "you're gonna be all right. I'll get you to the vet."

When they arrived at the vet's office, Mitchell wheeled into the parking lot and brought the car to a sudden stop. Inside, at the counter, he held Fiver in his arms like a shepherd with a lamb, and Fiver's labored breathing was heavy and even raspier than before. The young woman behind the counter took one look at them and quickly opened the door to the examining room. "Bring him back here, I'll get the doctor."

Mitchell laid Fiver on the aluminum table in the middle of the room and he was stroking him when the doctor came in. The doctor was a tall, thin man. He wore black-rimmed glasses, and he was quiet and methodical. He squinted as he listened through his stethoscope. Mitchell told him the doctor about Fiver's lack of appetite and that he came from the pound. The doctor looked over the top of his glasses when he spoke. "You've got a sick dog here," he said gravely. "I'm afraid he's got distemper."

The word distemper made Mitchell grimace, and for a moment he stood frozen in grief and worry. "What can we do?" he said finally. "What can we do?"

Looking back at Mitchell, the doctor shook his head. "There's nothing much we can do. We should put him to sleep and put him out of his suffering."

As the blood rushed to his face, Mitchell stood back, and for a second the white walls of the examining room seemed to emit a sharp glare. Then images of the pound and a shiny, stainless steel gas chamber raced through his mind. "No," he said in a firm but soft voice. "I can't do that. I won't do that."

Seeing Mitchell's determination, the doctor studied him and then nodded. "I see," he said with resignation. Then he wrote something on his chart. Staring down at Fiver, Mitchell ran his hand along his back, and Fiver managed to wag his tail ever so slightly. "I'm sorry," said Mitchell. "If he's gonna die, nature's gonna have to take him. This is too easy, and he's got too much heart."

With a sigh, the doctor shrugged, and for a moment he eyed Mitchell. Then, taking off his glasses, he began to rub them with his handkerchief. "He might suffer a lot, and it'll be expensive," he said calmly.

"I don't care about the money," declared Mitchell. "I know he wouldn't throw in the towel, and I really can't do it for him. That wouldn't be right."

After slipping his glasses back on, the doctor looked askance at Mitchell, as if to take his measure one more time.

"I'd appreciate it if you'd do what you can for him," said Mitchell. "Tell me what I can do to make him comfortable. And there must be something we can do."

Turning to the cabinet over the sink, the doctor reached for a small bottle of pills. "Give him these. They'll help him with his digestive problems. You might steam him at night. That should help his respiratory condition. And give him two aspirin if it looks like he's hurting a lot. Keep trying with the hamburger and the rice. He needs to eat and drink to keep up his strength."

With the pills in his pocket, Mitchell picked Fiver up from the table. As he turned to leave, the doctor gave him a stern yet quizzical look. "Good luck," he said. "If they make it past the onset with the digestive problems, they usually improve somewhat. Then they usually die suddenly when the disease hits their nervous system. Odds are against you. You should know that."

On the way home, Mitchell stopped at another veterinary hospital that was near the entrance to the freeway. The diagnosis was the same. "They're too damn quick to want to put him down," he thought as he pulled the car door shut. "They wouldn't kill humans that fast! They'd have a cure for this stuff if it affected people."

Mitchell squealed the tires as he pulled from the parking lot onto the street, and he didn't ease up until he was well down the freeway. As he drove, he racked his brain, and his thoughts darted in and out between the passing road signs. "How can I get him to eat? What can I do? There must be something!" But his ideas failed him, and like the road in the rearview mirror, they fell behind him and vanished. Feeling trapped and uneasy, he gripped the steering wheel tightly. As he drove on, he searched the recesses of his life for some solution, and up ahead the mountains quietly merged with his thoughts. Then from somewhere in the back of his mind, a memory, like something in the distance, started to come into focus. Before him, he saw his father, and standing at his workbench in overalls, he was holding a shiny bolt up to the light. The threads on the bolt were freshly cut, and a drop of oil on the tip of the bolt fell like blood to the floor. "Son, there are always options," he said as he wiped the bolt with a rag. "Always." Then, gently, the vision faded and the road came back into view. Ahead on the left, he saw the city office building and the old city library. "There it is," he thought, and shifting down, he turned into the parking lot. A half hour later he came out of the library with a load of books in his arms.

Chapter Nine

As he drove away from the library, Fiver was lying beside him on the passenger seat with his head on the armrest. "I've just gotta make one more stop," said Mitchell as he looked down at Fiver. "We're gonna try this." Then, just a few blocks from the house, Mitchell pulled into the health food store. At the counter, he asked a husky and tanned young woman where the powdered protein was. Following her nod, he went to the shelves at the back of the store. When he returned to the counter, he set down a tall can of protein, some multivitamins, some juice, and some thousand-milligram vitamin C. "Going for it, huh," said the young woman as she rang him up.

When Mitchell and Fiver got home, the phone was ringing. Pushing the front door open, Mitchell carried Fiver into the house and carefully put him down on the couch. Ignoring the still-ringing phone, he went back to the car to get the books and the vitamins.

Later that afternoon, he set up a steamer in the bathroom and put a small rug on the floor. Then he picked Fiver up, and carrying him into the bathroom, he laid him gently on the floor. As the steam slowly filled the small bathroom, Mitchell knelt down and stroked Fiver. "It'll be all right," he said. "You'll feel better." When the steam had completely filled the room, Mitchell stood up, and closing the bathroom door tightly behind him, he stepped into the kitchen. Standing by the fridge, he was watching the steam come out from above the bathroom door when Fiver started to bark and scratch. "Fiver, it's OK," he said, and for a moment, Fiver was quiet. Then, with the steam drifting out along the kitchen ceiling, he barked again, and this time his bark was sharper and more intense. "Oh, what the hell," Mitchell muttered. "Probably do me some good," he said as he opened the bathroom door. Then, sitting next to Fiver on the floor, he rested the dog's head in his lap. Twenty minutes later Fiver was breathing easier, and Mitchell was dripping wet. "It's the next part that's going to be hard," thought Mitchell as he took a warm washcloth to Fiver's eyes and nostrils. "How am I gonna get those protein drinks down him?"

The next morning, Fiver was lying on the kitchen floor while Mitchell added eggs and large amounts of vitamin C and other vitamins to a whirring blender. The counter was a mess and Mitchell had protein powder in his hair and on his face, and on his Levi's there were white handprints. "Hmm, I think it needs a little more," he muttered, and as he poured more of the white protein powder into the blender, the creamy liquid foamed up and ran over the sides. Scraping some of it off with his finger, Mitchell tasted it. "Not bad," he said, and from the floor, Fiver watched him pour some of it into a tall glass. Then Mitchell turned his gaze to the book on the kitchen table. In a large diagram, a man was forcing a dog's head back and with the dog's jaw apart, a woman in a lab coat was dropping a pill in his mouth. "Yeah, right," said Mitchell under his breath. Then, with a sigh, he turned off the blender.

With a large glass full of the protein drink in hand, Mitchell stepped toward Fiver, and instantly Fiver apprehensively pulled back, and leaning against the wall, he turned his head away. Beside him, Mitchell set the large glass on the floor and got him to sit up. Then, using both hands, he was able to get Fiver's mouth open. But when he reached for the glass, Fiver quickly and quite naturally closed his mouth. This they repeated several times, and the outcome was always the same. Finally, with much of the protein drink spilled on the floor, Mitchell sat back against the stove and tapped his fingers while he gave the whole thing some thought. Then getting up, he went to the cupboard and pulled a large rubber basting syringe out of the drawer. "This might just do it," he thought, and sure enough, moments later he managed to insert the syringe in Fiver's mouth, and with some coaxing, he managed to squeeze the syringe and get Fiver to swallow most of the contents. "All right! That wasn't so bad, was it?" exclaimed Mitchell as he stroked Fiver's neck, and looking back at him, Fiver puckered his lips and gave him a perturbed but still trusting look. That night, Mitchell steamed him again, and Fiver was breathing easier as he curled up on the floor next to the bed.

#

Chapter Ten

#

For the next few days Mitchell rarely left Fiver's side. Using the rubber syringe, he gave him Fiver his concoction of protein and Vitamin C twice a day, and they steamed together every night. Fiver still wouldn't eat on his own, and even though his lungs seemed to be getting a little better, he was still losing weight. At times, he was too weak to go on walks.

Late on a Sunday morning, Mitchell was at the piano doodling with a new blues riff when out of the corner of his eye he saw Fiver move on the couch. When he looked up he realized that Fiver was quivering and his head was trembling back and forth uncontrollably. He was having a seizure of some sort. In an instant, Mitchell sprang from the piano, and sliding onto the couch, he put Fiver's trembling head in his lap. Looking down at him, he saw a distant look in his eyes. "It's all right," he said in a soft whisper. "It's all right." Still conscious, Fiver's tail thumped weakly on the couch. "You're gonna be alright," said Mitchell. "Don't you go fadin' on me."

In what seemed like an eternity, Fiver continued to quake and tremble for about five minutes. Then suddenly he stiffened, and with his front legs shooting out in front of him, as if he were running, he began to paw frantically. Rolling his eyes, he coughed and choked. Panic-stricken, Mitchell reached in his mouth and tried to pull his tongue down. Continuing to cough and gag, Fiver was now writhing and foaming at the mouth. Then abruptly the tremors stopped, and suddenly he was absolutely still. With every cell in his body, Mitchell listened for breath, and searching the length of Fiver, he looked desperately for any sign of movement. Seeing none, he sank back on the couch, and feeling an angry grief come over him, he was about to shake his fists at the heavens when he saw Fiver's ear twitch. Then slowly Fiver turned his big head and with loving eyes, he looked up at Mitchell. "You son of a gun. You scared the hell out of me!" exclaimed Mitchell, and leaning down, he hugged Fiver like a man who had just found a lost child.

Chapter Eleven

During the weeks that followed, Mitchell spent less time at the office, and did his work at home whenever possible. When he wasn't taking care of Fiver, he worked and read and played the piano. The vet had prescribed phenobarbital for the seizures, and it seemed to help, but Fiver still had more of them, and one seemed to last a long time. In some ways he seemed to be getting better, yet in other ways he seemed worse. He was less congested so his eyes and nose didn't run as much, and he had regained enough strength to go for a walk, at least in the mornings. But he still wouldn't eat, and even though Mitchell force-fed him twice a day, he looked terribly thin.

Mitchell diligently continued to steam Fiver every night, and as a result, the old paint and plaster on the bathroom ceiling was starting to wrinkle and chip in places. In the kitchen, vitamins and protein powder were strewn everywhere. When Susan happened to come over one afternoon, she was visibly dismayed when she saw the mess. When Mitchell laughed and tried to shrug it off, she was not amused, and she told him that he was living like an animal.

That night Mitchell's friend Jerry called and wanted Mitchell to come to the local pub. When Mitchell said he had to take care of Fiver, later in the evening, Jerry and some other friends came over to Mitchell's house for drinks. With Fiver resting beneath the piano, they drank and talked. Jerry was a colorful, quick-witted freelance entrepreneur of sorts. Reckless, yet very intelligent and cunning, he was continually displaying the extremes of his mind with a loquacious and sometimes combative enthusiasm that often baffled and overwhelmed his friends. In college he was an infamous womanizer. After college, while he worked part time with Mitchell at the firm, no one was quite sure what he actually did, but if you asked him, he would tell you about some big deal that was always just about to pan out. Susan dismissed Jerry as a letch, but in his defense, Mitchell saw him as a loyal friend who was a unique mixture of imagination and self-serving malarkey.

Early in the evening, Jerry exhausted everyone with an overbearing entreaty concerning one of his latest projects, which in typical Jerry fashion entailed not only financial success but also world peace and individual spiritual tranquility, a weird mixture of hippy sentimentality and capitalism. In the lull that followed, someone subtly changed the subject to music, and by the end of the night, Mitchell was involved in a discussion about rock and roll and its origins in rhythm and blues.

The next morning Mitchell had a hangover, and he awoke to a crunching noise that sounded like someone walking on gravel. When it didn't stop, he pulled himself out of bed and wandered sleepily into the living room. Getting louder, the sound appeared to be coming from the kitchen. When he got to the arched kitchen doorway, he saw Fiver standing over his dry dog food. Still not quite awake, Mitchell leaned against the doorway. Then, when he realized that Fiver was eating, he straightened up and almost jumped in the air. "Hey, you're gonna make it!" he exclaimed. "You're eating!" Glancing up, Fiver went on munching. Then, wagging his tail, he walked over and nuzzled his head against Mitchell's leg.

Chapter Twelve

In the following weeks, Fiver's condition improved rapidly. With his seizures becoming less and less frequent, he ate heartily all the time. As he put on weight, his reddish-gold coat took on a sheen that sparkled in the sunlight. Mitchell and Fiver continued their daily walks. Occasionally Mitchell would stop at the local health food store, and while he shopped, Fiver would wait outside by the door. Susan came by the house once in a while, but she didn't come as often as she used to. She liked Fiver, but she didn't know how to act around him, and she complained about him being on the couch and the dog hair all over the house.

By late spring, Mitchell's early morning walks with Fiver were routine, and early every morning Fiver would nudge him awake. After their walks, Mitchell fed Fiver and then usually fixed himself a bowl of granola. Sometimes after breakfast he would read the morning paper while he lounged in the tub. Much to Susan's chagrin, Mitchell worked less and less at the office, and he began to spend most of his time reading at home. On his desk, stacks of books grew into miniature skyscrapers, and throughout the house other books lay abandoned here and there. Most of the books were about animals and many were written by naturalists and Mitchell was captivated by them. For him, they seemed to broach questions and paradoxes that as of late, he just couldn't dismiss, questions that were threatening his sense of reality. While the books gave him some validation and a sense of comradery with the authors, they also gave rise to more questions that drove him to read more and more.

For the next few weeks, Mitchell pursued his studies, which were punctuated by breaks at the piano or walks with Fiver. In the afternoons, Fiver liked to lie down by the front door. If the weather was warm, Mitchell would open the door for him, and lying in the doorway, he would look out over the front lawn. After awhile he usually moved to the couch and pawing around a bit at the cushions, he would make himself comfortable. Sometimes when Mitchell was playing the piano, Fiver would hear a loud or strident note and look over at him with a raised eyebrow. If Mitchell happened to catch his gaze, Fiver would wag his tail ever so slightly.

On a Tuesday morning, after one of their routine early morning walks, Mitchell had retreated to the bathtub to soak and relax while he read the paper. He was just finishing the front page when something vaguely disturbed him. He couldn't tell what, but something was out of kilter, and slowly pulling the paper down from his eyes, he peeked around at the bathroom. Squinting, he could see saw small dust particles in the air, and suddenly he felt something hit his shoulder and something else splashed in the tub. Then a cracking sound came from over his head, and when he looked up he saw a jagged line run across the peeling paint on the bathroom ceiling. Before he could move, two pieces of plaster crashed down on top of him. A second later, he was covered with pieces of plaster and white dust. Still holding the newspaper, now torn and shredded, in front of him, he looked up at the hole in the ceiling. Then he heard a bark, and padding across the kitchen floor, Fiver stuck his nose around the bathroom door. Peeking in, he cocked his head and looked at Mitchell and then at the debris floating in the tub and on the floor.

Still sitting in the tub, Mitchell was trying to take in just what had happened, when he heard the front doorbell ring. As the doorbell buzzed impatiently, he shook some of the plaster from his hair and looked around at the mess in the tub. In front of him, like an iceberg in a gray sea, a large piece of plaster was floating in the water. Climbing from the tub, he surveyed the damage and wrapped a towel around him.

When he finally opened the front door, he was in his robe, but there was still some white dust on his nose. In front of him, Susan was on the porch, talking with a friend from work. Turning toward him, she was about to introduce her friend but stopped mid-sentence and stood open-mouthed. "Is the sky falling over at your place, too?" Mitchell said dryly, expecting a laugh. But, instead of a laugh, Susan shook her head in disgust. "My God," she said, "I should have known." And before Mitchell could say another word, she took her friend by the arm and headed down the steps. Puzzled, Mitchell yelled after her. "It's the ceiling. It...it...it fell." But Susan and her friend kept walking, and with clear disdain Susan backhandedly waved him off. As he stood in the doorway and watched them get in the car, Fiver came up and stood beside him. Looking down at Fiver, Mitchell puffed and tried to blow some of the white dust from his nose. "That didn't go well, did it," he said as Fiver raised his eyebrows.

Chapter Thirteen

Susan called later that night, and when Mitchell explained, she said it was just too weird anymore, and she couldn't bring anybody over there ever again. The next day Mitchell repaired the bathroom ceiling, and he spent the next week painting and cleaning the rest of the house. It was late on a Thursday afternoon when he finished the touch-up work. By the end of the day, both he and Fiver were covered with swatches of red, yellow, and gray paint. Sitting side by side on the front steps, they looked like a couple of out-of-work clowns.

In the meantime, Susan got over her exasperation, and with some coaxing she agreed to come to Mitchell's on Friday night for dinner and to watch a video. Cooking up some brown rice and vegetables, Mitchell had the table set with candles when she arrived. Before he answered the door, he put a record on the stereo. When he opened the door, the melodic strain of a violin preceded him. Smiling, Susan gave him a polite kiss.

While Mitchell was in the kitchen putting some finishing touches on the meal, Susan strolled slowly around the living room. On the coffee table, there was a large book lying open. Turning it over, she puzzled at the face of a big gray wolf on the cover. Putting it down, she walked over to the piano, and as she looked at the music, her eyes caught some chord symbols that Mitchell had scratched out. "That's just like him," she thought. "Always wanting to change things."

Susan was sitting on the couch when Mitchell came in carrying a bottle of wine and two glasses. Following behind him, Fiver lay down by the piano.

"Who are we listening to?" said Susan in a decorous voice that bespoke a properly pleasant curiosity.

"You like that?" replied Mitchell. "I think that might be my favorite classical piece."

"Who is it? It's different."

"It's Schubert. It's 'The Unfinished Symphony.' I just heard it myself for the first time a few weeks ago. I think it's incredible! I don't know how I could go my whole life and not hear it!" Standing in front of the coffee table, Mitchell paused, listening for a few moments. Then he said, "You know, in this recording, right in the middle of the second movement, it stops. I don't know why, but it does. I mean, right in the middle of a phrase, nothing. Then it starts again." As he spoke, Mitchell waved the wine bottle in the air, mimicking a conductor. "Life is like that," he said emphatically. "It builds and just goes along, and then it stops, just like that. Without regard to where you are or what you're doing, it just stops!"

Looking up from the couch, Susan smiled. "You'd better stop waving the wine around," she said. And with some playful bewilderment, Mitchell looked curiously at the wine bottle. "Oh...I guess I should open it, shouldn't I," he said, and stepping around in front of the couch, he put the glasses and the wine down on the coffee table.

"Is that how you've been spending your time?" asked Susan. "Listening to music?"

Sitting down beside her, Mitchell rested his arms on his knees. "Yeah, sorta, although I read, too. I read everything I ever wanted to read, and then some, and I play a little piano, too. I guess I'm taking a break from life or something. Anyway, you know, the other day I was playing this little rhythm in the left hand, a boogie-woogie like thing." Mitchell moved his left hand as if he were playing up and down the keyboard. "That stuff's harder than you think," he said, "and there's a feel to it. Anyway, it started me thinking about tempo and rhythm, and how you know how a fast tempo gets us going, dancing and all that. Somehow the tempo is associated with speed or signifies it, and somehow we know it."

"What do you mean?" said Susan. "The tempo's faster because the beat's faster. Isn't that it?"

Mitchell shook his head. "No, here's what I'm drivin' at. What I want to know is why do we get aroused and tap our feet, or generally get going, when the tempo's faster? They're just playing the notes more often. Why should that signal speed or intensity or something like that and get us going?"

"I haven't the faintest," said Susan, and picking up one of the two wine glasses, she frowned ever so slightly when she noticed it didn't match the other one. Taking a corkscrew from his shirt pocket, Mitchell picked up the wine. "Well, I have this theory about it," he said, and as he spoke he twisted in the corkscrew. "I think that, a long time ago, when we were primordial, or maybe when we were ape-like or even older, when you heard pounding sounds coming closer together, it meant you were in trouble. Think of a stampeding herd. The rapid hoof beats would be a danger sign. If you were part of the herd, you'd run. Those that survived ran. Think of something being stalked. As the stalking animal gets closer, it starts to run, and the prey hears the rapid footsteps and flees. I think rapid tempos arouse us to danger because of our primordial programming. That's why we get aroused when we hear rapid beats or beats speeding up or slowing down. What do you think?"

Susan held out her empty wine glass. "I don't know," she said. "I guess that makes sense. But you're going to have a hard time telling the people at the symphony that the composer is scaring them."

As he poured the wine, Mitchell laughed. "But that's precisely it!" he declared. "That's just what a lot of composers do. They take people back to the time when they could feel things, when feeling and thinking were connected. Vicariously, they take people back to nature. The symphony is kind of an urban substitute for a weekend in the mountains. They're sensuous, and in a way, they try to recreate everything that we lost when we climbed down out of the trees. You know, if you don't feel it, you can't know it."

"I don't know," said Susan. "Could be..." And with some discomfort, she looked around the room. "You know, sometimes you really get out there," she said finally. "I don't know what's worse, your bad puns or your theories. Why don't we eat, huh?"

As he looked over at her, a wry smile broke across Mitchell's face. "Why? You think my food will be more palatable than my theories?"

"Oh, please."

At dinner, Mitchell couldn't find a topic that would engage Susan, and nothing he had to say seemed to amuse or interest her. After awhile, everything he said fell stillborn in front of them, and for Mitchell the sparse conversation that remained was mundane if not stifling. Breaking a long silence, Susan asked him if he was going back to work soon. When Mitchell said he wasn't sure if he would ever go back, she put her spoon down and leaned over the table. "Why would you not go back?"

Mitchell filled his wine glass. "I don't know. I guess I feel lonely there. Don't you? Seems like everyone's lonely there, or maybe I'm projecting. I don't know, maybe 'estranged' is a better word."

Susan put her wine glass down on the table. "Lonely? Why do you say that?" she said quizzically.

"I don't know," replied Mitchell. "It just seems that way to me. Maybe it's because of the lying that goes on. Lying is a lonely business. I mean, when you lie, nobody knows you; nobody can, 'cause the real you is not there. It's like being a spy. Can you imagine how lonely that would be?"

Susan shook some salt and pepper on her salad. "It doesn't seem that bad to me," she said, running her fork into a tomato wedge. "You always get so dramatic about everything."

"Dramatic?"

"Yes, dramatic. Saying we're all lying and all that. I don't know what's happened to you lately. You're supposed to think about those things when you're a freshman in college. Then you get serious and grow up. It's a dog-eat-dog world out there.

Mitchell glanced down at Fiver. "She didn't mean that," he said with a laugh. "Hell, the dogs are more honest than we are," he went on. "You know where they're at as soon as you see 'em. A tail wag, a snarl, whatever, they let you know right away."

"See, there you go again. I don't know where you're coming from anymore. You're critical all the time. Why don't you just accept things?" Tilting her head to one side, Susan softened her voice. "Can't you just accept the fact that you're a good stockbroker? You make good money. You're fortunate. Isn't that enough?"

Sitting with one arm resting on the edge of the table, Mitchell fixed his gaze on Susan. Then, forcing his eyes away, he picked up his empty water glass and swirled the lone ice cube around the bottom of the glass. Looking up, he scoffed, "You think I'm a melodramatic buffoon, huh?"

Susan sipped her wine. "I wouldn't go quite that far, but you do get carried away. Look at how you went on about the pound."

"What do you mean?"

"You just let it get to you. I know it's a depressing place. But the way you reacted. Things like that exist. They're necessary. There's nothing you can do about it. People who are together don't let those things distract them. You can't."

Looking down, Mitchell ran his hand across his brow. "I'll have to think about that," he said. "Let's go into the living room and watch the movie."

In the living room, Susan sat down on the couch while Mitchell turned on the TV and the VCR. On the coffee table, there was a big book with a picture of an elephant on it, and next to it there was a copy of *Mechanics Illustrated*. Picking up the magazine, Susan studied the man on the cover. He was wearing bib overalls and holding a saw and a hammer.

"Your place looks great," she said. Then she held up the magazine. "But this doesn't really fit in. You usually see these kinds of magazines in the waiting room at the Minit-Lube."

Glancing over his shoulder, Mitchell saw Susan set the magazine back on the table. "Oh, my father sent me that subscription," he said as he turned back to the television. "He runs a garage in Grand Mesa."

"What do you mean, he runs a garage? You mean a place where they park cars?"

"No. He runs a garage. You know, a place where they fix cars. That's what they used to call them, garages. Somehow, the word has more dignity in it, doesn't it? Funny how it's fallen from use."

Seeming preoccupied, Susan ignored Mitchell's question. "Did you grow up there?" she said in a quizzical voice. "I always thought you were from here."

"No, I didn't come to Denver until I went to college. I grew up in Grand Mesa. We had a little place there. Had a horse when I was a kid." Picking up the three videos, Mitchell turned to Susan. "What do you want to watch?" he said.

"Well, I hope you have something light. You know, last time you got that thing with Kirk Douglas, about the fighter."

"*Champion*! Yeah. The original *Rocky*, the one without the Hollywood ending."

"Yes, that was it all right, and in dreary black and white, and so depressing!"

Slumping with disappointment, Mitchell set the movies on the coffee table. "You know, *Champion* had a good storyline," he declared. "It was like a novel, it developed, it was powerful, it . . ."

Susan interrupted, "I know, it was dramatic."

Looking away, Mitchell stared down at the floor. "No, it wasn't just dramatic, it was true, and it was edifying. It said something about..." breaking off, Mitchell shrugged. "You know, you make me out like I'm some kind of indulgent sentimentalist. Is that what you really think?"

Susan took her cigarettes from her purse. "Well, something like that, but you'd better add a little masochism."

Staring off, Mitchell shook his head. Then, turning back to Susan, he said, "Christ, we're going to spend our whole lives running from one distraction to the next. Is that what you want! Is that all there is to it? Just keep your head down and plow straight ahead. Just go to work, then eat, then catch a movie." As he continued, the words came faster and faster. "Then eat, and eat some more, then go jog it off, then get to work, then go see your shrink, then get back to work. Christ, I'd just like a pinch of reality now and then. I need some time!"

Dismayed, Susan averted her eyes. "I was kinda kidding," she said in a controlled voice.

Mitchell looked back at her with stern eyes. "No, you weren't. You don't tease, not like that."

Exhaling smoke from her cigarette, Susan placed it in the ashtray. Her expression was one of growing irritation and boredom. "Here we go again. Why do you always have to get so serious?" she said in frustration.

"What do you mean," said Mitchell with a sigh. "I just want to get off the damn treadmill for a bit and think about what the hell I'm doing." Starting to pace, Mitchell waved his hands while he spoke. "Granted, I might be a ridiculous fool, but I just can't put the blinders on and get out there and run in lockstep with all your mature, together friends."

From the couch, Susan rubbed out her cigarette and glared up at Mitchell. "Leave my friends out of it," she said. "They at least know what they're doing, and they've got a hell of a lot more going for them than you do. At least they're doing something. Civilized people don't sit around all day and wade into all the crap they can find! Waste their lives away!"

Rising up from the couch, Susan's voice became shriller. "And who the hell do you think you are, criticizing my friends? Leave them out of it. I'm tired of hearing about how rough the animals have it! I'm tired of your silly lectures and your theories." As she spoke, Susan got louder, and as her anger erupted, her face grew contorted and strained. "You're just turning into a freak!" she shouted. "And sometimes you sound like a burnt-out hippie or a damn tree-hugger!"

Setting the videos down, Mitchell stared at her. Then a sense of indignation shot through him. "You think your friends are civilized?" he shouted. "You've been taken in, sister! Anybody can wear one of those suits. Those people aren't civilized! They're just sheltered and pampered by their money! They are on top of the food chain, and they're all huddled there, scared to death that something might happen that would topple everything."

Susan was livid now, and her blue eyes were filled with contempt. "Yeah, well, life is tough, and those people have worked hard, and at least they've made something of themselves. We're not all golden boys with the Midas touch, and we all can't go around worrying about the plight of the world and the seals and every damn stray dog that comes along. Sensitivity is a luxury!" she shouted. "It's only the rich and hypocrites like you that can afford it! The rest of us don't have time to sit on our ass and feel sorry all day!"

The two of them were now squared off, face to face, in the middle of the living room. "Yeah," said Mitchell, with his jaw tightening. "Well..." and as he spoke, he felt something brush against his leg, and before he could look down, like a big bear, Fiver rose up in front of him on his hind legs. Then, separating him from Susan, he laid his paws on Mitchell's chest, and with his big, almond-shaped eyes opened wide, he looked at Mitchell with a deep, entreating gaze. Embracing him, Mitchell was dumfounded. "It's all right," he said finally. "It's all right." Then with amazement, he carefully let Fiver's front paws slip from his chest and back to the floor. Then kneeling down beside him, he rubbed his ears. Still petting Fiver, he looked at Susan. "Maybe you're right," he said softly. "Maybe I am a big, damn fool."

Staring down at Mitchell and Fiver, Susan seemed to pity him. Then, turning abruptly, she went into the kitchen. Gazing distractedly at the toy truck on the coffee table, Mitchell continued to stroke Fiver. Then, rising up, he walked over to the piano. When Susan came back into the room, he was sitting at the piano with his back to her. With her purse in hand, she stood behind him and whispered in his ear, "Let's make this as easy as possible. It's not working with us. We want different things. I don't know what's happened to you. I hope you find what you're looking for, Mitchell."

Chapter Fourteen

#

M itchell couldn't sleep that night, and in his mind, he kept going over the argument with Susan. As he tossed and turned he could see the two of them circling one another like beasts about to pounce. It was three o'clock in the morning when, rising up, the dream disappeared into the silent shadows of the bedroom. Sitting on the edge of the bed, he thought about calling her, but then quickly rejected the idea. "It would probably just infuriate her more," he thought.

That morning, Fiver was up early as usual, and it was about six-thirty when he began to nudge Mitchell. Pulling up the covers, Mitchell rolled over and retreated across the bed. But, undeterred, Fiver jumped on the bed and continued to nudge his arm. "OK, OK," said Mitchell. "I'll get up." Wagging his tail, Fiver looked down at him hopefully. Moments later, with his eyes still heavy with sleep, Mitchell pulled on his Levi's and groped for the buttons on his shirt. As the two of them trudged to the front door, Mitchell stopped, and seeing two empty glasses on the coffee table, he saw what was left of his relationship with Susan.

Outside, it seemed unusually warm, particularly for this time of the morning. As Mitchell closed the front door, Fiver barked and bounded off ahead of him. On the porch, Mitchell stopped and looked about. The sunlight was flat and white, and as he headed down the front steps, everything had the quality of being overexposed, and somehow, it all seemed a little strange and unfamiliar. As he walked, the ground beneath him seemed harder and more indifferent, and with each step, flashes of Susan came and then faded. Unlike last night, he saw her laughing and happy in earlier times, and his heart sank.

As they turned the corner at the top of the street, Mitchell was still mesmerized by the subtle strangeness of familiar things. "I might as well be Robinson Crusoe," he thought, "everything's so different," and as he meandered along, he envisioned the shipwrecked man standing on the beach with a flintlock rifle and a leather bag thrown over his shoulder. Small tools and a sextant protruded from the bag, everything he had salvaged from his sinking ship and the civilization that created him.

When they returned to the house, Mitchell felt a desperate urge to call Susan. But as he reached for the phone, a vague foreboding feeling prevented him from dialing her number. Staring down at the phone, he wrestled with his emotions, and like ghostly figures beckoning him, they appeared and disappeared. Then, with the receiver starting to buzz in his hand, he felt Fiver nudge his leg, and looking down he saw him intently gazing up at him. "Oh, you want some breakfast, huh?" he said as he put the receiver down. "All right, let's go get it."

Mitchell spent the rest of the day trying to read, but thoughts of Susan and pangs of loss punctuated every sentence. On his evening walk with Fiver, the neighborhood still seemed strangely foreign, and Mitchell was trying to put his finger on just what had changed when he noticed a little gray dog sitting on the porch of an old blue house. She was a blue heeler, and she watched them closely as they approached. Coming down the steps, she favored one hip and moved carefully like a little old lady. Nonetheless, she pushed open the wrought-iron gate, and with her nose held high, she spryly marched up to Fiver and began sniffing him. Fiver tensed and wagged his raised tail as they inspected one another. She had an aristocratic aplomb about her, like an elderly queen. When they both had satisfied their curiosity about one another, she sneezed and took a long look up at Mitchell. Kneeling down, he rubbed her lightly behind her ears. "I'll bet they call you 'Duchess' or something like that," he said, and the little dog moved her head so he could rub the other side of her neck.

"Well," said Mitchell as he stood up, "Fiver and I have to go," and when he turned and started heading up the street, the little dog sat back on her haunches. As they walked off, Mitchell could feel her watching them. Glancing back over his shoulder, he saw her, with her head cocked to one side, still sitting in front of the gate. After taking a few more steps, he stopped, and turning around, he took one more look at her, and in an instant, the little gray dog bounded forward and was soon running along with Fiver. She stayed with them for quite a while, and then seeming concerned about going too far away, she stopped and scampered back home.

When they got back to the house, Mitchell was still consumed with thoughts and feelings about Susan. After dinner and two glasses of wine, he dialed her number and listened as the phone rang, and it rang for a long time. But no one answered. "That was a mistake," he said to himself as he put the phone back on the receiver, and he didn't call again. Somehow, it didn't feel right, and now it became a matter of principle.

A few days later, and after a few nights of overindulgence at some of the bars, Mitchell began to immerse himself in his books. He read more now than he did before, and writing extensively in the margins, he merged with them. Sometimes he spent entire days reading, and he would only take a break when Fiver insisted on going for a walk. The walks were usually pleasant and stimulating, and unwittingly, he came to depend on them as much as Fiver did. As of late, Duchess, the little aristocratic blue heeler, joined them for part of the walk.

As the weeks went by, other dogs, one by one, joined Mitchell and Fiver for their walks. The next newcomer was a young English pointer that continually roamed about the neighborhood. His name was "Otis," and on their first encounter, Otis playfully bounded up to Fiver, and after giving him a hesitant lick on the nose, he began darting here and there and jumping and running in circles, inviting Fiver to play. Initially, Fiver pulled back, but then his eyes lit up, and clearly accepting the invitation, he bounded off, chasing after him. From then on, the two of them would frolic and wrestle like two cubs in the wild. Becoming good friends, they always greeted one another with a polite sniff and a rub of their noses.

By mid-July, Mitchell could be seen walking with the dogs at any time of the day, and at times as many as four or five dogs might be running along in front of him. Ambling along behind, he was usually lost in thought about some book he had been reading. He laughed when one day one of the neighborhood children referred to him as the dog man. "King of the dogs," another one said. "King of the dogs."

#

Chapter Fifteen

#

It was after ten in the evening when Mitchell decided to drive down to the local pub. When he walked in, a man over in the corner was speaking loudly and gesticulating with his hands. He was saying something about evolution. Walking past him, Mitchell found Jerry sitting at the bar. "I'd like to buy this derelict a drink," he said as he sat down on the empty stool next to him. "Aw, if it isn't our local broker turned hermit," said Jerry, who, with his tie undone, was clad in a plaid sport coat. "What happened, getting stir crazy? You and Fiver have an argument?"

Smiling, Mitchell nodded cordially. "No, not really. They just won't let him in here, so I didn't bring him."

Looking over the top of his drink, Jerry eyed Mitchell. "I didn't know they still made those denim shirts. You know, with those Kmart ties you used to wear, you always looked like you're teaching night school somewhere."

Mitchell laughed. "Well, you look like you're selling used cars," he retorted, as he turned to the bartender and ordered a bourbon on the rocks.

Slouching down on his bar stool, Jerry shook his head and laughed derisively. He had mischievous blue eyes, sandy blond hair, and a broad, full-toothed grin that at times made him look like the Cheshire Cat from *Alice in Wonderland*. When he flashed one of his confident if not condescending smiles, he told the world that he knew something they didn't, and that someday he would be wildly successful and powerful. "All right," he said, looking over at Mitchell. "So, when are you going back to work?"

Picking up his drink from the bar, Mitchell took a sip. "I've been working a little bit from home," he said with some hesitation. "But I don't know. I might not go back."

Jerry looked surprised. "Right, sure," said Jerry sarcastically. "You're making good money, and what the hell would you do, man?"

Mitchell set his glass on the bar. "I don't know. You know, I'm really not sure."

Jerry threw down the last of his drink. "Is it Susan?" he said. "That really got to you. Breaking up and all that. I mean, was that why you haven't been around? Some people think that's the case."

Mitchell looked away while he gathered his thoughts, and taking a deep breath, he sighed. "Naw," he said. "Breaking up bothered me, all right, but that's not why I haven't been around. I just needed some time by myself."

Jerry shook his head. "Hey man, you dropped off the radar completely. What do you do all day? Are you just by yourself all the time? That would get to me."

Mitchell took another swig of his drink and put the glass back on the bar. "I read a lot, and it's tough at times, but it's been interesting too." Pausing, Mitchell frowned while he thought. Then picking up his drink, he continued. "I've decided that being alone is like losing one of your senses. You feel like something's missing, but you can't quite put your finger on it, and it's kind of scary."

"Well, it's the adjustment," replied Jerry. "People aren't accustomed to being alone like that."

"Yeah, that's part of it, but that's not what I'm trying to get at," said Mitchell, still looking at his drink. "Part of what we call loneliness is really fear."

Jerry smiled. "Yeah, right, I've read some on that. I've got a book on that, fear of being alone."

"No, that's not what I mean," said Mitchell as he set his glass on the bar. "We're just not afraid of being alone," he said. "I mean that puts the emphasis in the wrong place. That makes it seem like a phobia or something like that. Fear's not all bad. In fact, it's kept us alive for thousands of years. It helps us avoid things that are harmful."

Jerry rubbed his forehead. "I don't follow you. So, what do you think it is then? I mean, what's to be afraid of when you're alone?"

Leaning on the bar, Mitchell looked over his shoulder at Jerry. "We're afraid of being cut off from the herd. That's what I think."

Jerry grimaced. "The herd?" he said somewhat scornfully, and nodding, Mitchell returned his gaze. "Yeah, the herd," he replied. "We're basically herd animals, and when we're cut off or separated from it, the pack, the herd, a relationship, whatever? We get frightened because we sense that we are more vulnerable apart from it. We know that intuitively, and it scares us. Deep down we are social animals, right to the core of us."

"OK, we're social animals. Big deal," said Jerry with a shrug. "But you know we're more than that." Then he waved to the bartender for another drink. "Anyway, I don't know how you do it," he said. "I travel a lot, and I hate being alone on the road, in some motel room. That's the worst, man, probably why I come to places like this."

Mitchell nodded. "Yeah, I can imagine," he said. "But there is something to it, being alone. It gives you perspective, and sometimes you need time to think and just stop doing what everyone expects you to do. I mean, sometimes you need to get away from the herd, just to check your hand. But, hell, I'm not alone. I've got Fiver and some good friends."

Squinting, Jerry bit his lower lip. "I don't know," he said. "You're starting to sound like an academic. I think you need to take a break from all that stuff, take the Vette for a spin. Pretty soon you'll be talking about Marx and false consciousness and all that junk."

"I'm not talking about all that," said Mitchell. "But you need to do your own thinking, that's for sure." Then he half smiled and looked off. "At least that's what my dad always told me. 'Never let anyone control your mind,' he used to say. 'Do your own thinking and don't lie to yourself.' Mitchell smiled. Then, shaking his head, he said, "You know he's right, but sometimes I wish he hadn't told me that. Sometimes it's like a curse for me, trying to be so deliberate."

Jerry laughed. "Awe, now you're sounding like Thoreau!" he said triumphantly. "'Live deliberately. Avoid the lukewarm existence.' That I can dig. But it's got to pay, and I've got a plan now, and when it comes to fruition, we can do anything we want, anything, man. I keep telling you that you could come in with me on it. We'll have a yacht and sail around the world, and women and hmmmm..."

As he waved to the bartender, Mitchell, beckoned for another drink. Smiling at Jerry's typical exaggerated enthusiasm, he said, "You mean your big financial planning co-op, the stock offering and all that. What did you call it? 'Utopian Living, Incorporated' or something like that?"

Miffed by Mitchell's mocking tone, Jerry indignantly started to respond, "Well..." But just then the drunken man from over in the corner muscled his way up to the bar between Jerry and Mitchell. "I'll tell you about living and life," he said, staggering back and forth. "There's no purpose to any of it. It's all just a temporary illusion. In this microscopic part of the universe, we're nothing more than a vaporous reflection of some fleeting biological phenomena that we don't understand and never will."

As Mitchell laughed, Jerry grimaced and looked up at the man with obvious displeasure. Drink in hand, the man then aloofly turned and headed to the restroom. "That guy's a professor, or used to be," said Jerry derisively. "Now he's just a damn drunk, and lately he's always here holding court with whoever will listen to his crap. What a load of shit," he went on bitterly. "There's got to be some purpose to all this. It's not just a damn cosmic accident. The guy's a drunk. Bartender, give me another one, will you?"

Sitting with one elbow on the bar and his chin in his hand, Mitchell looked straight ahead. "Hell, I don't know," he said dryly. "The universe and all that, but it does seem like he's stuck on what we don't know, and there might be something to that. Who the hell knows."

When Mitchell and Jerry left the bar later that night, it was starting to rain outside and Jerry asked Mitchell for a lift home. As they walked to Mitchell's car, the yellow light from the street lamps reflected up from the wet pavement. Mitchell was unlocking the driver's door when Jerry spoke. "What's this sticker here on the back window?" he said. And staggering forward, he pressed his face up to the rear side window on Mitchell's car. "Save the seals? What about people? Don't you care about people anymore?"

Looking over the top of the car, Mitchell smiled. "What's so special about people?" he said. "We're all in it together. I'm starting to think that the notion that people are special might be a bad idea." Looking back at Mitchell, Jerry gave him a queer kind of suspicious look. "Aw, I know," he said and then offered his broad playful grin. "People are just the reflection of some vaporous biochemical activity. Just little horny vapors running all around, and then they evaporate."

As the car pulled away from the curb, the two men laughed heartily, but after awhile they slowly fell silent. As they drove, the rain came down in heavy sheets, and the tires hissed when the car went through puddles of water on the street. With the wipers sweeping back and forth across the windshield like a metronome, Mitchell's view of the world was subjective and intermittent, and in the rain and rising mist, the shiny colors on the street quickly blurred and then again took the form of familiar, identifiable objects.

Jerry was the first to speak, and the lights from passing cars seemed to bring him in and out of the shadows. "There has to be something more," he said plaintively. "I mean there has to be!" Then he scoffed. "Aw, it doesn't matter anyway," he said brusquely. "And besides, I've got a solution for all these petty, earthly problems anyway! You'll see."

Mitchell rounded a corner slowly. "You mean that corporate utopian welfare fund of yours," he said, and bristling at his tone, Jerry replied, "It's not a corporate welfare fund." It's a rational approach to satisfying human needs. Don't you get it?"

"But, don't you think it's a bit grandiose?" replied Mitchell.

Jerry scowled as he replied, "It's not grandiose! You have to think big if you want to accomplish anything. It's just that the damned people don't know what's good for them. That's why they need me, and that's why it will go!"

Pulling up in front of the apartment house where Jerry lived, Mitchell brought the car to a halt. "I don't know," he said doubtfully as he looked over at Jerry. "It just seems kind of ambitious to me. But good luck. I hope it goes for you."

As he opened the car door, Jerry shook his head condescendingly. "It'll work," he said forcefully as he got out of the car. Then with his hand on the open door, in the rain, he stooped over and looked back in at Mitchell. "I've got it all set up," he said with utter conviction. "The doctors, the lawyers, the stock, even some architects and even some religious leaders on board. I'll get funding. You'll see, oh ye of little faith."

Leaning across the seat, Mitchell looked up at Jerry and smiled. "And what'll we do when you've saved everybody from themselves?" he asked wryly.

"Hell, we'll be on the yacht, man," Jerry replied exuberantly, and flashing his full-toothed, gleaming Cheshire Cat grin, he went on. "It's the good life! We deserve it, don't you think? You don't want to keep working, do you? We're better than that. That stuff's for the masses."

#

Chapter Sixteen

#

The next day, as usual, Mitchell was in the living room reading in his big, overstuffed easy chair, and with the front door open, a few steps away, Fiver was sitting on the front porch just watching the world go by. From his chair, Mitchell heard growling, and looking over the top of his book, he heard a commotion of some sort. Then suddenly Fiver barked, and a second later he was yelping. Exploding from his chair, Mitchell threw his book across the room and ran to the front door. From the doorway, he saw the mailman at the foot of the steps. He was holding something in his hand, and as if it were a gun, he was holding it out in front of him. Just to the side of the mailman, he saw Fiver rolling on the front lawn, and he was frantically rubbing his muzzle with his paws. Letting go of the doorjamb, Mitchell sprang down the steps. Frightened, the mailman stepped back and fearfully pointed a small aerosol can at him. As he leapt from the last step, Mitchell knocked the aerosol can away, and shouted, "What the hell are you doing?" Then, without thinking, he shoved the mailman backward onto the lawn, and brushing past him, he ran over to Fiver, who was now rolling on his back, pawing desperately at his eyes.

"Fiver!" cried Mitchell, and kneeling down he tried to hold him still so he could look at his eyes. "Fiver, hold still," he commanded, but pulling away, Fiver rolled over and pushing his face along the ground, he tried to rub off the spray. "Son of a bitch!" said Mitchell. Then, looking around, he stood up and ran to the side of the house. Moments later, he returned with a hose spraying water out in front of him.

"He'll be all right!" exclaimed the mailman as he got to his feet. "It's only pepper spray." Glancing back at him, Mitchell bent down and directed the stream from the hose onto Fiver's face and eyes. "You'd better get the hell out of here," he snarled.

"He'll be all right," replied the mailman. "It won't hurt him. He went for me when I came through the hedge."

Laying the hose on the ground, Mitchell inspected Fiver's eyes. "Yeah, I see what happened," he said. "But you're a little quick on the trigger, aren't you?" Then, picking up the aerosol can, Mitchell tossed it to the mailman. "He didn't go for you. You just surprised him."

"Well, I was bitten once," replied the mailman as he put the aerosol can back on the clip on his belt. Then, as Mitchell wiped Fiver's eyes with a towel, Fiver pulled away, and for a moment he stared intently at the mailman.

Visibly shaken, the mailman reached into his bag, and hesitantly, with his eyes on Fiver, he stepped toward Mitchell. "Here's your mail," he said, and bending down, he laid it on the grass a few feet away. As he looked up at him, Mitchell softened. "Hey, I'm sorry," he said. "Are you all right?" The mailman nodded. "I'm fine," he said. I'm sorry too, but you'd better cool that temper of yours; you could get in real trouble." Then turning away and adjusting his mail pouch, he headed up the street. As he left, Fiver watched him intently, seeming to take in every detail, as if to never forget him.

For a while, Mitchell sat on the front lawn and rubbed Fiver behind the ears. "You're gonna be all right," he said. "You'll be OK." Then, motioning for Fiver to go inside, he picked up the letters and thumbed through them as he walked up the front steps. At the top of the steps, he pulled one of them from the bunch. It was from his father. Inside, standing next to his desk, he opened it.

#

Chapter Seventeen

#

Dear Son,

Haven't seen you for quite some time. I think about you often. I hope things are going well for you in Denver. Things are pretty good here. Got lots of business at the garage, and the fishin's been good up on the river. Tom's just as ornery as ever, but he's still the best mechanic in town.

I ran into Jesse the other day, and he told me to tell you hello. He's doing quite well for himself these days. They have a baby on the way. Funny how time flies. It seems like it was only yesterday when you two were raisin' hell, riding those horses all over the place. Everything changes, and things have changed a lot around here lately.

Well, it seems like it's been ages since I've seen you. If you have the time, maybe you could come out for a few days. It might be timely. Got plenty of room in the house. It would be nice to hear some of that boogie-woogie of yours on the piano.

Love,
Pop

When he finished reading the letter, Mitchell pondered the words, "It might be timely." Then, with the letter in hand, he sat back down in his easy chair in the living room. Slumping back, with a sigh, his thoughts drifted back to Grand Mesa and his childhood. Back then his parents' house was still well out in the country. At the end of a lane, off the main highway, it sat contentedly in front of a small pasture. It was a small bungalow, and there were some fruit trees along the south side. The pasture was bordered by a narrow irrigation stream, and beyond that open ground led up to the foothills that fanned out along the base of Silver Mountain.

As a young boy, Mitchell spent his afternoons and weekends riding his horse all over the foothills, and as he sat back in his chair, his thoughts drifted back to the paths and gullies of his youth. As his eyes grew heavy and began to close, he could feel the heat and strength of his horse as they climbed a mountain trail.

It was all an adventure then, and there was always something fantastic just beyond the bend, just behind those trees, just over that rise. Reaching down, a young Mitchell, suntanned and shirtless, not yet in his teens, stroked the neck of his coal black mare as they meandered along the trail. "The pony express used to go by here," he thought as the cool brown dust of the trail wafted about him. Then up ahead he saw something. "What's that clearing up ahead?" he said to himself. "Is that an orchard? That looks like a corral." Then his horse stopped abruptly, and throwing her ears forward, she snorted. Rising up in the saddle, the boy carefully studied the surroundings. He was back at the old abandoned homestead that he had discovered one afternoon while riding on the southern edge of Silver Mountain. "Lets' go," he said finally. Then he made a clicking sound with his mouth, and with a light tap of his heels, he started to ride up to this all but forgotten place.

Just barely visible through the trees, the house was small and quaint, made of smooth river rock. The dilapidated wooden shingled roof was about to collapse, and it hung down over an old wooden porch. To the side of the house there was a big cottonwood tree, and out in the back there was an old barn and a corral. As they approached, the horse whinnied and slowed her gait. Reining her to a stop, young Mitchell swung off the saddle and jumped to the ground. "It's all right," he said as he patted her on the neck. Then, taking her by the reins, he led her toward the house, and following rather reluctantly, the mare looked from side to side as she lumbered along.

Stopping in the shade of the cottonwood tree, the young Mitchell stared at the old house, and for just a moment, he got the strange feeling that the house was somehow looking at him. Then a subtle breeze rustled the leaves of the cottonwood tree, and in an open window, a ragged curtain waved and flapped back and forth. Clutching the reins more tightly, the boy was startled when a leaf scratched its way across the ground beside him. Looking around, he strained as his ears tried to catch the faintest sound. Then, timidly, he stepped forward with the big mare in tow, and as he did, the barn behind the house slowly came into view. Like a cathedral long lost to the ravages of time, it seemed to rise up magically before him, taking all of his awareness. Partially covered in vines and dead weeds that had blown up against it, it stood in silent defiance, making the young Mitchell feel small and frail. As his eyes moved from the barn door to the hayloft above it, and then to a hole in the roof, he stopped walking, and with all of his senses he tried to understand. When finally the horse nudged him, he inhaled deeply and started forward again, and with every step, he anticipated and anticipated.

When he got to the open pine-pole gate at the corral, he stopped again, and looking past the gate, his gaze came to rest upon the barn door. Slightly ajar, it was suspicious, and it caused everything else in view to fall away. As he stared at it, it seemed to pull at him, almost grab him, and he could feel the hair on the back of his neck begin to tingle and rise.

Taking his eyes from the barn, he tied the reins to the pine-pole gate, and then looked guardedly about. Pawing nervously at the ground, the horse turned her ears forward and whinnied. Then, silently, the young boy slipped through the gate and surreptitiously moved toward the barn. But stopping in mid-stride, he saw something protruding from the ground. It was red, and made of metal. Crouching down, he pulled it from the dirt and wiped it off. It was an old, rusted toy truck. One of the wheels was gone, and among the rust, the paint was cracked and flaked. Holding it out in front of him as if it were an offering of some sort, he carried it back to the horse, where he secured it with the leather straps on the back of saddle. After giving the toy truck a tug, he stroked the mare's neck, and he was about to untie her and ride off when a squeaky metal sound came from the barn. Flicking her ears forward, the horse swished her tail as she looked to the old building. "Errwack," went the sound again. "Errwack!" Frightened, the young boy stepped closer to the horse as he gazed at the open barn door. Then, letting go of the reins, he took a breath, and stern-faced, he started toward the barn. As he walked, his eyes darted back and forth, scanning for some sign of movement, some sign of life. Behind him the mare whinnied softly. Then suddenly he was there, and standing in front of the slightly open barn door, he could smell the dry barn wood. As he reached out to it with his hand, the knotholes seemed to swirl about like maelstroms in a stream. Then, placing his hand on the edge of the door, he pulled himself forward, and peering around the door, he looked inside. At first it seemed his eyes wouldn't focus, and he sensed a cool brownness that felt sweet and thick. Then, in front of him, a band of white light cut through the darkness like a pipe. Within the light, bits of dust swirled and danced about, teeming with life. In cautious amazement, with his eyes, the boy followed the light up to its source, and in the roof he saw the diamond-shaped gaping hole where it came in. Then carefully squeezing past the barn door, he stepped inside.

The air was heavy and dank, and it made him cough a little. As he crept about, he felt like he was immersed in another element, almost like water; he could feel it all around him. Then, as if he was opening a curtain, he wiped away some cobwebs, and before him he saw two horse collars and an old bridle hanging on the wall. On the floor, a rusty shovel and some old wooden tools were scattered about. In the back, hidden behind the still-steady beam of light, there was something that looked like an old wagon, or a carriage or some kind of vehicle. Curious, he leaned forward, and he was about to take a step when behind him he sensed something like another presence closing in on him. Spinning around, he felt like an animal caught in a well-set trap, and the barn seemed huge and vengeful. Then, as if he had violated something, his fear mixed with shame as he looked through the shadows. Expecting something terrible to happen, he took a deep breath, and then taking a few well-placed steps, he carefully slipped back out the barn door.

Outside, he stifled his urge to run and headed slowly to the mare. When he reached her, he let out a sigh, and wrapping his arms around her, he buried his head against her huge, muscular neck. Looking out from beneath her, he gazed back at the now-silent barn. Then, from behind him, ever so softly, he felt something touch his arm. In utter panic he spun around, and in the blur he saw a figure moving toward him in the trees. With his heart pounding, shadows danced amid swaying trees and bushes. Then, like something emerging from a cloud, he saw Fiver sitting on the floor next to him. Full of curiosity, he was nudging him with his nose. On his lap, he saw the letter from his father. "I need to go home," he thought.

#

Chapter Eighteen

#

It was dusk when Mitchell and Fiver went out for their evening walk. On a lark, Mitchell decided to take a new route. At the corner, pointing in another direction, he signaled to Fiver. "C'mon, we're gonna go this way tonight," he said, and after studying him for a moment, Fiver ran on in front of him. They had walked two blocks when, up ahead, Mitchell saw Fiver freeze on the sidewalk. Then he heard another dog barking and growling. It sounded like a big dog, and concerned, he broke into a run in order to catch up. When he got to Fiver, he saw a large German shepherd on a chain, and with his teeth bared, he was snarling and snapping. Crouched down, Fiver was backing away. Coming up behind him, Mitchell took him by the collar. As they stepped back, the shepherd bounded forward, and coming to the end of his chain, he was abruptly jerked off his feet and fell backward. Recovering, like someone knocked down in a fight, he jumped up and continued to growl and snap. Standing clear, Mitchell held Fiver firmly by his collar, and side-by-side the two of them pondered the snarling shepherd.

Mitchell went to bed early that night, and with Fiver at his side, he sipped wine and read until he fell asleep. At about two o'clock in the morning he rolled over and realized that he was hungry. Standing next to the bed, he rubbed his neck while his eyes adjusted to the darkness. Then, with his hands groping out in front of him, he found his way to the kitchen. In the light from the open fridge, he put some granola in a large bowl and poured milk over it. Holding the bowl in his hands, he leaned against the stove and ate. When he finished he realized that although he wasn't eating, a crunching noise was still filling the kitchen. With the bowl in one hand, he flipped the light switch on, and standing over his dry dog food, Fiver was crunching away. "Well, I guess we're birds of a feather," he said, and as Fiver glanced up at him, the trust in his eyes confirmed the growing camaraderie between them. Smiling, Mitchell offered him the last of his granola. "You wanna try some of this?" he said as he set the bowl down on the floor.

As always, Fiver had Mitchell up with the sun the next morning, and as they walked, the morning air and the cool colors were unusually exhilarating. They were just rounding the last corner when, up ahead, Mitchell saw Fiver waiting for him in the shade of a sycamore tree. As he walked toward him, Mitchell thought he saw an unusual glint in his eye. Then Fiver tensed and, as if he were about to pounce on something, he crouched down. "What are you up to?" said Mitchell warily, and wagging his tail, Fiver let out a soft bark. "Where'd you get that mischievous..." but before he could finish his sentence, Fiver jumped through the air and landed with his front paws on Mitchell's chest. Catching himself as he fell backward, Mitchell realized what Fiver was up to. "Oh, you wanna play, huh! OK!" And with that, he pushed Fiver away, and hunched over like a wrestler, with his arms dangling in front of him, he began to move toward him. "I'm gonna get you!" he said, and playing along, Fiver again crouched down, and raising his tail in the air, he studied Mitchell with rapt attention. His expression was sly but innocent, and his eyes seemed to invite and then mock. Then he leaped up at Mitchell, and tumbling backward Mitchell fell to the ground, and for the next few minutes the two of them frolicked like puppies.

Chapter Nineteen

#

Later that afternoon, Mitchell was at the piano when the phone rang. Playing a closing riff, he stretched and walked to the desk. It was Jerry.

"Jerry, how you doin'?"

"Oh, all things considered, not bad."

"You don't sound too enthusiastic."

"Aw, things are all right. I called to see if you wanted to go out for a beer tonight."

"Yeah, OK," replied Mitchell after a short pause.

"How about around eight thirty?"

"OK, see ya then."

Mitchell read for the rest of the afternoon. After dinner he gave Fiver a hug and headed downtown. When he got to the bar, he found Jerry sitting in a booth by himself. Looking down at an empty glass, he looked rather glum. "You don't look too chipper," said Mitchell. "That's not like you. What's going on?"

"Hey," said Jerry wearily. Then raising his glass, he waved it at the waitress. "I'll have another scotch, and get my friend here whatever he wants."

"I'll have a draft," said Mitchell. After sitting down, Mitchell leaned back against the booth. "Well, how's business? You put anything together lately?"

Still looking at his empty glass, Jerry shrugged. "No, I haven't," he said somewhat bitterly. "Damned people around here just can't see it! I've got a program, and they just can't get out of their ruts long enough to grasp it."

Looking over at Jerry, Mitchell could sense his friend's frustration. "Yeah, for a lot of people, one rut's as good as the next," he said in a consoling voice. "Maybe you should back off it and try something else for a while."

Shaking his head, Jerry looked away. "No, you've got to have faith!" he retorted forcefully when he looked back around. "This will make it; I know it will. I can feel it. I just need to keep my energy levels up."

Nodding, Mitchell sipped his beer, and looking over the top of it, he gazed up at the large fan that hung down from the ceiling. It made a thumping, whirring sound as it turned. "That fan swings," he said, still looking up at it.

"What swings?" said Jerry. Following Mitchell's gaze, he looked at the fan. "Oh, the fan. Is it loose or something?"

Mitchell smiled. "No, that's not what I mean. I mean it really swings. Some players study for years in hopes of swinging like that. Some never do swing."

As Mitchell tapped out the rhythm on the bar, Jerry glanced back up at the fan. "Oh, that kind of swing. Like Count Basie. It figures that you'd notice that."

"That's what it's all about," said Mitchell. "The good stuff swings." Still tapping the rhythm, Mitchell smiled. "Funny, it's a hard thing to define, yet it's so basic."

Turning back from the fan, with a scoff, Jerry frowned. "Aw, nowadays there's a definition for everything. That's all these academics do, sit around and think up new definitions for things. And music's all calibrated and organized, isn't it? Tempo, meter, time signature, all that stuff. It's all there. It's a science of sorts. No mystery!"

Mitchell paused to consider Jerry's assertion. Then, nodding and shrugging his shoulders, he said, "Yeah, they try, but the definitions don't mean much, and there's more to it than the measurements, really. They can define it, but they all can't do it. Make it swing."

Still scoffing, Jerry shook his head. "Aw, I don't buy that. It can't be that difficult. Not in the twentieth century. Nothing escapes analysis. Somebody will figure it out with some formula or something, a formula for swing, and then they'll have their fifteen minutes of fame."

Staring up at the fan, Mitchell began to snap his fingers. "Well, a lot of 'em call it 'playing behind the beat.' That's part of it. Listen to 'Satin Doll.'" With Jerry watching, Mitchell hummed a few bars, still snapping his fingers. I think it's the surprise that makes it work, that makes it cool and sensuous."

"What surprise?"

"The surprise of being off the beat a little, and changing the emphasis here and there. Well, I mean...I think...well, I think all music preys upon the element of surprise." Mitchell laughed at his own words. "Hmm, it sounds like I'm talking about ambushing somebody, doesn't it. But that's kinda what it is."

"What? What are you talking about?"

As he sat back in the booth, Mitchell thought for a moment. "I think basically we've survived because we could see or maybe feel the changes. I mean that was one of the things that promoted our survival. It's the way we're built. It's like our eyes. You know, they're constructed, or at least they've evolved, in such a way that they detect movement, right? Same same for our ears, and probably for what's left of our sense of smell. Anyway, it's just like a leopard when he sees something in the grass, or a rabbit when he hears something behind him. I think our senses are set up to notice anything out of the ordinary. They react to the changes, the surprises. I mean our eyes notice when something moves, when something changes, when something is out of place. So do our ears. We're all set up to react to changes, and that's why it's the changes in a piece of music that make it interesting, make it good or bad, for that matter, and the tension comes from the changes and then resolving it. I bet a composer would agree with that. And it's those same changes that affect the leopard and the rabbit. An animal tenses when he senses a change. It could be a threat. Then when it's gone, he feels better. We do the same thing, right? That's what they create in music, tension, and it's from the changes."

With a thoughtful and skeptical frown, Jerry rubbed his brow before he replied, "Hmm, that's kind of interesting, except we're not just animals. I mean we're more than that." Jerry's tone became more serious. "We're more intelligent than they are. I doubt they can even hear it, let alone understand it or relate to it. Music is abstract, and it requires some degree of intelligence to appreciate it. Animals just don't have that."

Looking somewhat disheartened, Mitchell rubbed his chin. "Well, obviously, I would differ with you there, about the animals not getting it, but..."

Interrupting, Jerry's voice was suddenly much more forceful. "We're more than animals!" he declared with strained conviction on his face. "We don't just run around in the woods preying on things! C'mon, you don't think we're just predators."

Struck by Jerry's outspokenness, Mitchell leaned on his elbow and thought. "Boy, as far as I can see, we are," he said finally. "I mean, most everything in nature is either prey or predator, or maybe both."

Jerry drew back from the table. "Ah, come off it, we're not just another predator! How can you say that?"

"It's obvious," said Mitchell rising up. "We're the most vicious, powerful predators on the earth. We prey on everything. Hell, we've almost exterminated every other species on the planet!"

"Ah, c'mon," said Jerry, waving him off. "That's crap."

Mitchell rubbed his forehead while he thought. Then he said, "You and I don't kill anything because we're sheltered. We're part of the great middle class. We're too bourgeois for that. We let other people do our killing for us. We kill politely from a distance, and we have machines to do it, way out on the edge of town."

Jerry threw up his hands. "Where do you get this off-the-wall stuff? You're up in the night, man."

Unphased, Mitchell smiled. "It's not off-the-wall," he replied. "We're so good at it, and we don't even see it. We kill while we're asleep, and then we let someone else, some big company, package it up and disguise it. Hey, we live in a dream world, and it isn't even our own dream. We let these hacks on TV supply us with the illusions and distractions, but we kill, and we're as heartless and savage about it as any so-called beast. We just don't cop to it. We're in denial all the time."

Throwing down the last of his scotch, Jerry gave Mitchell a frustrated and very condescending look. "No, there's more to us than that. I mean we're not here just to scratch around and try to survive. But I don't want to get into all that....What does all this have to do with music, anyway?"

Mitchell laughed. "I don't know. All I was saying is that it seems to me that music is composed of changes, you know, different cadences, harmonies, things like that, and it's the animal in us that senses the changes, because the changes imitate life. And they're the same changes that musicians talk about when they talk about groovy chord changes and things like that. See what I mean?"

Jerry was still skeptical. "Well, I don't know," he said sternly. "According to that, I can get those changes by just walking down Main Street. Lots of things going on there, but it's chaos, and you wouldn't call that music, would you?" Taken off guard, Mitchell had to stop and think. "Hmm, he mumbled, "harmony and structure, yeah?" Then with a wry smile, he said, "Well, I guess it depends upon what part of town you're in. Some songs are better than others."

"And I still think you're up in the night, man." replied Jerry, shaking his head ruefully.

"Aw," said Mitchell, hoisting his beer, "up in the night. There might be a song in that somewhere." And with that, they both laughed and rocked back and forth in the chairs.

Then, flashing his big Cheshire Cat grin, Jerry raised his glass. "That's your song, all right," he said. "Here's to being up in the night."

Chapter Twenty

For the next few days it rained on and off, and during that time Mitchell and Fiver enjoyed their reclusive existence. While Mitchell devoured his books and played the piano, Fiver would lie by the front door and with apparent curiosity watch robins hunt for worms in the lawn. From the piano, Mitchell marveled at how Fiver seemed to enjoy just watching them, and more than once he left the piano bench just to see what was holding his attention. The mailman was the only creature that ever seemed to disturb Fiver's composure, and when he would see him start up the front steps, he always stood up, and eyeing him carefully, he would back off a few paces and then lie down again. Since there were different mailmen, Mitchell assumed that it must be something about the uniform or the mail pouch that caused Fiver to maintain his distrust of them, and considering what had happened, it was only natural.

One afternoon, when the rain was lightly tapping on the windows above the piano, Fiver came up, and sitting next to Mitchell, he gently nudged his right hand from the keyboard. "Whoa," said Mitchell. "What's the matter, you don't like that song?" Slipping his nose under Mitchell's hand, Fiver again flipped it up from the keyboard. "What, you wanna talk?" Then, sliding off the bench, Mitchell knelt down on both knees in front of him. "What's up?" he asked, and still sitting, Fiver carefully put one paw and then the other on Mitchell's shoulders. "What's the matter? You got the blues or something?" And like a smiling Buddha, Fiver flashed his big, almond-shaped eyes. Gazing back at Mitchell, he seemed happy or thankful, in a way that only someone who loves someone can be. "I love the Fiver," said Mitchell, squeezing him close. "I don't know what I'd do without you."

Later in the afternoon, Mitchell was pulling a book from the shelf when the phone rang. It had been a long time since he had a call, and for a moment he looked at the phone with some apprehension. Fiver raised an eyebrow as he watched him walk across the living room to the desk. "Hello," said Mitchell in a questioning if not surprised manner.

"Hi, is this Mitchell?" The voice on the phone was vaguely familiar, but there was an urgent tone to it.

"Yeah, this is Mitchell. Who is this? Is it...is it Tom?"

"Yes, Mitchell, this is Tom from the garage. Ah, I have some rough news for you, and I'm not much good at this sort of thing, so I'll just give it to you straight out, man. Your father's in the hospital; he's had a heart attack."

For a second, Mitchell felt as if he were falling, like in a dream. "Oh, hell," he said in a choked voice. "How bad is it?"

The man on the other end paused, and Mitchell braced himself. "I don't know, Mitchell. He's stable, but it's not good. He went down pretty hard."

Taking a deep breath, Mitchell sighed. "Thanks, Tom, I'll be on the next plane. If anything happens in the next little while, call me."

"OK, we'll see you when you get here."

Within the hour Mitchell was waiting for a cab to take him to the airport. He wanted to drive and take Fiver, but under the circumstances, he couldn't take the time. Fortunately, Jerry was home, and when Mitchell called, he agreed to come over and stay with Fiver while Mitchell was gone. When the cab pulled up out in front, Mitchell knelt down and hugged Fiver. "I'll be back," he said. "You stay here. I love the Fiver."

On the plane, Mitchell sat next to the window, and pulling back the blind, he watched the ground crews scurry about like busy little squirrels. Absentmindedly, he moved his arm when a rotund man in a brown suit sat down in the seat next to him. The man's breathing was heavy and labored, and with the flesh on his neck spilling over his collar, he gave Mitchell a perfunctory nod. "You didn't happen to see the pilot, did you?" he asked in a voice that seemed small for his incredible size.

Looking around, Mitchell was struck by the way the man seemed to gasp with each breath. "No, I didn't," he said, looking back out the window. "I didn't notice."

Rolling down into his seat, the man coughed and began to loosen his tie with his chubby fingers. "I always like to know who I'm flyin' with," he said. "You never know who's in command up there."

Looking askance at the man, Mitchell just nodded, and the man continued to talk, as if Mitchell had replied. "I'm told that someday some airlines may let...well, damn near anybody fly these things. So, I just like to know who's up there in front, don't you?

"Well," said Mitchell, "I can't help you, but you know the pilot's not really flying this thing all by himself. He's got lots of help. By the time you figure in the air controllers, the mechanics, and the engineers, there are probably hundreds of people flying this machine. People you'll never see."

Pulling himself up in his seat, the rotund man gave Mitchell a doubtful look. "Well, I just wanna know who's drivin', that's all."

Nodding reluctantly, Mitchell began to buckle his seat belt. Turning away, he looked out the window, and as the plane taxied down the runway, its huge engines began to whine. "My God, this thing has a lot of power," he thought, and leaning forward, he unconsciously tried to overcome the thrust of the plane's acceleration.

When they were airborne, Mitchell undid his seat belt. As he leaned back in his seat, his thoughts immediately drifted to his father, and he could see him in his overalls, standing in front of the garage in Grand Mesa. Back then the garage was located at what was then the edge of town. Originally it was a blacksmith's shop where Mitchell's father had worked as a young man. His father took it over when the advent of automobiles left the blacksmith with a dwindling business.

Everyone called the blacksmith Red, and after Mitchell's father bought the place, he kept him on, and as wagons and carriages of an earlier time began to rust and deteriorate in fields and barns, Red spent more and more time welding car frames and trailer hitches. In his later years, Red had cultivated a strong disdain for automobiles. "Those things will be the ruination," he used to say. "We shoulda stayed with horses and buggies."

For years, Red was the only one who still used the old forge and bellows, and now and then, at the insistence of a local farmer or rancher, Mitchell would see him pounding on his anvil, fashioning out a set of horseshoes or a part for a tractor.

Red was a tall, thin man. At the garage he always wore dirty brown overalls and a greasy skullcap. Most of the time his face was blackened with soot and grease that made his teeth and eyes seem extra white, and when he laughed he howled. To the young boy Mitchell, Red was a frightening specter, and to this day Mitchell could still see him standing there in the darkness, a great, dirty giant, grinning through the flames as he fanned the bellows. At the time Mitchell thought he seemed like the devil himself, laughing demoniacally as he stoked the fires of hell.

Mitchell's father installed gas pumps in front of the garage, and not long after that, a large sign appeared on the roof that said "Mitchell John's Automobile Repair." Inside, he replaced the old horse and wagon stalls with three hoists and a cement floor. Over the work benches, and surrounded by an array of fan belts and water hoses, a wagon wheel and a harness still hung on the wall. Eventually, the old bellows and forge were replaced by a shiny lathe, a pneumatic tire changer, and a drill press.

From the road, the garage almost looked like a little cottage. The front of it was done in small windows, and the white paint went nicely with the wood shingles on the roof. Two rock columns held up an overhang that extended out from the office. Originally, two sets of old wooden doors opened up into the shop area. But, over the years, the workers complained about them, and in the early 50s Mitchell's father installed new overhead doors. From the road the place still had a quaint charm about it, and two large willow trees in the back added to the picture.

When Mitchell was growing up, his father insisted that he work at the garage. At eight years old, he was sweeping up every night, and by the time he was fifteen, he was replacing clutches and brakes and doing tune-ups. For his age, he was a decent mechanic, but for some reason, he always managed to smear grease on his face, and the other workers teased him about it. Nonetheless, he enjoyed the camaraderie, and over time he grew to love the older cars that came in. Sitting back in his seat on the plane, Mitchell smiled as he envisioned them, Fords and Plymouths and Chevys. A lot of them, particularly those from the 30s and 40s still had running boards and flowing fenders with teardrop headlights and beautiful nickel grills. When he was young, Mitchell felt honored just to be around them. To him they were beautiful, and he marveled at his father's way with them. His father wasn't just a mechanic. To Mitchell, he was more like an artist or an alchemist. His understanding of automobiles was intimate and bespoke his knowledge of physics and chemistry. "He could fix or build anything," thought Mitchell, and then he heard the strident voice of the man next to him.

"Look at all that land out there," he said as he pointed out the window. "You know, these environmentalists are always squawking about save the land, save the wilderness. Look out there! There's more land than we'll ever need. We got all kinds of land, all kinds of resources. Why, this planet could hold ten times as many people as we have now. There's no population problem. Look at it!"

Sitting up in his seat, Mitchell turned to see the man waiting for a response, and something about his presumptiveness caught Mitchell, and he paused a moment before he spoke. "You can't see much from ten thousand feet," he said. "You know, on every inch of that land, somebody, some creature is trying to make a living. You just can't see it from your frame of reference. You just see property. What about the coyotes and the rabbits and the deer and the wolves? Don't you think we ought to give them some thought? I mean give 'em some space?"

Looking as though he had just swallowed something tainted, the man's expression grew sour. "Aw, we've got plenty of zoos and national parks for the animals," he retorted, "and besides, there's already too many of them. Every year we have to thin the deer herds in Utah. If we don't, they just starve to death."

Taking a deep breath, Mitchell looked down pensively, and he could feel the man arrogantly waiting for some confirmation of his proud declaration. Shaking his head, he thought for a moment and finally looked back at him. Then he spoke. "You know, we thin their herds because our herd has overrun all the land. Maybe we ought to thin our own herd, don't you think?"

Fidgeting in his seat, the man acted as if Mitchell's words were now infesting him like vermin. "Look out there," he protested. "There's plenty of room for the damn animals. Besides, the planet was put here by God for us. That's the way it was meant to be. And besides, we've got technology... technology that can do anything, solve any problem. I'm an optimist; scarcity is a myth. You have to think abundance...abundance!"

"Well..." said Mitchell, but before he could get another word out, the stewardess came by, and looking up, the man waved a large, rounded, fleshy arm and asked her if they were serving lunch on this flight, and could he get a bloody Mary with celery. For a moment, Mitchell wanted to ask him if technology wasn't part of the problem, but thinking better of it, and seeing the likely futility of it, he said nothing and reached for a magazine. On the cover, a large, shiny-white nuclear power plant sat surrounded by a lush forest.

#

Chapter Twenty One

#

At the small airport in Grand Mesa, Tom was waiting at the gate when Mitchell arrived. Tom had worked at the garage almost from its inception, and Mitchell had known him since childhood. He was a quiet man and the deep lines in his leathery brown skin said more about him than he ever did.

"Well, how are you, Mitchell?" he said extending a big, dark hand with protruding knuckles and blackened nails.

"I'm fine, Tom. It's good to see you."

"It's good to see you, too. Hell, you look more like your old man every day."

"How is he?"

"Well, he's stable. You know, he's strong and a stubborn old goat."

Mitchell smiled. "Yeah, he is, isn't he? Have you got something at the garage I can drive while I'm here?"

"Well, I brought out the tow truck. I...uh...thought you could get around in that. Your dad's Caddy was gettin' so old, he was havin' a hard time gettin' parts, and he was trying to convert it over to run on natural gas or something. Can you believe that? Anyway, he's been drivin' the truck back and forth to work. You could just drop me off back at the garage and use it while you're here."

The tow truck was a '37 Chevrolet, complete with running boards and teardrop headlights. In the back of it there was a large crane that shot up like a rooster's tail, and the passenger door screeched as Mitchell pulled it open. "The old gal needs a little work, doesn't she?" he said as both men climbed in and shut the old heavy metal doors with two loud clangs.

"She needs to be retired out to some junkyard," said Tom from behind the wheel. "That's what she needs." Then, reaching with his foot, he tapped the starter button on the floor. "She's long overdue to be scrapped, but you know your old man. Says as long as she can be fixed, there's no need wastin' money on a new one." With a grind and a bit of a rumble, the truck started up, and the old engine knocked a bit as they pulled away.

"Yeah, that's my dad all right," said Mitchell. "If you got the right tool, you can fix anything." Glancing around the cab, his eyes came to rest on the dash. "But, you know, she is a classy old gal. Look at that dash! Look at the chrome on it! Look at the way it's sculpted!"

It was a short ride from the airport to the garage, and as he rode along, with his elbow out the window, Mitchell looked out at the countryside. The mountains in the distance seemed almost dark blue, and the fields next to the road were flowing with alfalfa. Not far from the airport, there was an old bi-wing crop duster parked at the edge of a short landing strip. As they passed, Mitchell leaned forward, and turning his head, he kept it in view as long as he could. "Beautiful!" he exclaimed to himself.

When they pulled up to the garage, Mitchell was surprised to see relatively new cars parked out in front. Unwittingly, he had expected to see older cars, cars with flowing fenders and big, oval-shaped grills. The new ones all seemed out of place.

"Take it easy on her. She's about that far from throwing a rod," said Tom as he slid out of the truck and slammed the door shut. "Tell Mitch that everything's OK down here."

The clutch in the old truck was heavy and stiff, and the transmission whined and howled when Mitchell pulled away from the garage. Bouncing up and down as he drove, he could feel the coil springs pushing up from the old leather seat, and with the engine sputtering and popping between gears, the big weathered steering wheel jumped and strained with every bump in the road. Leaning forward, Mitchell gripped it with both hands, and as he drove he felt every contortion the old truck went through on its journey.

Chapter Twenty Two

The new hospital was on the edge of town, next to the main highway. Only a few miles from the garage, it was across the street from a new shopping center, which had killed the downtown area, leaving only two or three old buildings vacant and deteriorating. Next to the shopping center there was a new fast food restaurant that had a huge, round, brightly colored plastic clown out front. Beckoning to people on the street, the clown's large round head rolled back and forth while his short arms moved up and down, and to Mitchell he looked more than a little insane. As the old truck turned into the hospital parking lot, it kicked out some blue smoke, and passing through a field of parked cars, it looked like a derelict from the past trying to find a port in the modern world.

When Mitchell asked the woman at the front desk what room his father was in, he began to truly face the reality of his father's condition. Alone in the elevator, he watched the numbers light up as he ascended. When it stopped and the elevator door began to open, he felt his throat tighten. In the bright hallway, a biting antiseptic smell permeated the air. As he moved along the hallway looking for his father's room, he whispered the room numbers. "Two-ten, two-twelve." Glancing into a room on the left, he saw an old woman. With her mouth open and her arm dangling off the side of the bed, she was staring up at a television. In another room, a man and a woman held each other as they looked down at a young child in bed. "Two-twenty, two-twenty-two."

Standing in front of his father's room, Mitchell grimaced, and gritting his teeth, he fought back his first impulse to cry. "Get mad," he said to himself, and with the muscles in his jaw rippling, he opened the door and went in. His father's bed was close to the window, and he was gazing out at the mountains. Without saying anything, he rolled his head and looked up at Mitchell. His hazel eyes were peaceful and serene. A little choked up, Mitchell's voice was higher than normal when he spoke. "Hi, Pop."

Slowly, his father raised his hand from the edge of the bed and reaching out, Mitchell clasped it with both hands. Still silent, Mitchell senior looked him up and down, and his eyes were full of approval. "Hello, son," he said in deep, relaxed tones.

"How do you feel?" Mitchell replied.

"About as good as can be expected, I guess. I guess I'm all worn out. It's a good life if you don't weaken."

Mitchell flicked a tear from the corner of his eye. "Aw, Pop, you're gonna' be all right."

Rolling his head on his pillow, his father looked out the window again. Silver Mountain stood high in the distance. There was a sad but tranquil quality in his father's voice. "You know, Doc Jenson was just in here. You'd think he'd know better than to try to con me after all these years."

Mitchell squeezed his father's hand. "Pop, they've got new techniques; they can fix you up."

Still gazing out the window, his father sighed. "You know, I haven't done much with my life. I mean I've really never left Grand Mesa. But it was enough for me. I loved it here. The garage, your mother, and all those damn grease balls down at the shop."

Mitchell pressed hard on his father's hand. "Pop, you're gonna be all right. I mean..."

Taking his gaze from the mountain, Mitchell's father looked up at him. "You look good. Better than the last time I saw you. How's business? How's livin' in the city?"

Looking a little chagrined, Mitchell let his eyes fall. "Well, actually, I'm, uh, pretty much unemployed right now."

His father lifted his head from the pillow. "The hell ya say," he said with a laugh. "Well, you still look better. Looks like you needed it." Gazing off again, his father squinted into the light coming in from the window. "You know, you've always got options. Don't forget that, ever, and you gotta be honest with yourself, and with everybody else..."

"I know," said Mitchell, finishing his father's statement. "They'll respect you for it."

"And you'll respect yourself," his father added. "That's more important."

"I know, Pop."

Grabbing a chair that was next to the bed, Mitchell spun it around, and with the back of it facing his father, he sat down, straddling the chair.

"You know," his father went on, "the Bible says that man shall live by the sweat of his brow, and there's something to that. I was wondering how you'd fare in the city. It's another world, and it's pretty fast." For a moment, Mitchell's father just looked at him with eyes full of pride and relief. "But you'll be all right. You're a good man, and its down deep. I know that. I'm glad you came. We've got a lot to talk about. But first, why don't you go out and get us a couple of malts? I mean real ones. Get 'em from Randy's place, not that new plastic joint."

"OK. That sounds good," said Mitchell. "But will they let you have that? I don't..."

"It'll be all right," his father replied bemusedly. "You know you're really old when ice cream sounds about as good as anything else. At my age, it's better than sex, and it's a hell of a lot easier to get, and it doesn't melt as fast, either."

Smiling at his father's joke, Mitchell fought back the tears and nodded. As he headed for the door, his father turned away and looked out the window at Silver Mountain. "Everything melts after awhile," he muttered softly, "everything but that damned beautiful mountain."

When Mitchell returned with the malts, the sun was just setting, and when he came through the automatic glass doors at the entrance to the hospital, the nurse at the front desk gave him a surprised look. Setting her pen down, she came out from behind the counter. Her eyes were pained. When she took his hand, Mitchell knew that his father was gone.

"I'm sorry," she said. "Your father passed away. He's still in the room if you'd like to see him now." With his gaze falling to the floor, Mitchell nodded. Leaving the malts on the counter, he headed empty-handed to the elevator.

In his father's room, they had pulled the blinds, and for a long time, Mitchell stood in the shadow next to the bed. Except for an amorphous pain that seemed to be waiting like a cloud in the distance, he felt empty and bereft of life, and the few words and thoughts that came to his mind seemed petty and futile. Like a blind man trying to force himself to see, he stood in the shadow and groped for meaning. Finally, realizing that his words would fail him, he moved to the window and opening the blind, he let the last of the afternoon sun flood the room. When he turned around, he saw his father bathed in a sea of warm, orange light. Then, with a tear sliding down the cheek of his clenched face, he stepped back over to the bed, and softly picked up his father's tan, weathered hand. "I love ya, Pop," he whispered.

Chapter Twenty Three

Mitchell left the hospital at about five in the afternoon. The old truck left a trail of blue smoke as it pulled out of the parking lot. With his face still tightly clenched, Mitchell pushed the tall floor shift from second to third, and as he drove his eyes remained fixed on the road ahead. Still numb, and lost in a sea of wondering thoughts, it wasn't until after he had turned onto the main highway that something caught his attention. Up ahead, on the left side of the road, he saw a large, modern-looking building with an office in the front. It was surrounded by smaller rectangular buildings with shiny metal roofs, and the entire area was enclosed by a tall fence with three strands of barbed wire running along the top. Two Dobermans sat at attention by the office entrance.

As he eased off the gas, the old truck popped and backfired. "What's this?" he wondered. "It looks like a makeshift prison. It wasn't here last year." As he passed, he read the sign over the front gate: "SNYDER'S SCIENTIFIC PACKAGING AND PROCESSING." "What the hell is that place?" he thought. Then, stepping down on the gas, he sped on.

It was dusk when Mitchell passed the road that ultimately wound up Silver Mountain and ran along the Eagle Gorge. His father's house, the house that Mitchell grew up in, was just up ahead at the end of a short lane that ran out to the highway. As he shifted down and turned down the lane, the engine in the truck groaned. On the sides of road, he noticed how tall and green the fields were. In a field next to one of the houses, a horse stood quietly next to the fence.

Mitchell's house was at the end of the lane. Feeling some strange doubt that it might not be there, he unconsciously pulled on the steering wheel and peering out over the hood of the old truck, he searched the road ahead. Then he sensed that something was wrong. "The Sorenson place ought to be there," he thought. "It's gone. So is Jesse's place. What's this white brick wall doing here?" he wondered. "What the hell," he said aloud, and stepping on the brakes, he stopped in the middle of the road. Leaning forward, with both hands on the steering wheel, he found himself staring at a huge mansion. Surrounded by a white brick wall, it resembled something you might see in the Old South, but more garish and obviously new. Where once there used to be small, humble country homes, there was now a square two-story mansion, and it was sitting on a hill, a hill that wasn't even there before. In front of it, a well-manicured lawn ran down to the front gate. "My God," said Mitchell, and following the circular driveway from the gate to the side of the mansion, he saw a new four-car garage. Parked next to it, there was a thirty-foot boat, a cabin cruiser, and staring at it, he wondered where such a boat could be used around here. In front of the boat there was a big, shiny, black four-wheel-drive Chevy Suburban, all jacked up with huge chrome wheels. "Hmm, I'll be damned," grunted Mitchell, still taken by the spectacle of it. Then, shaking his head, he pulled the shift lever into first, and startled, the old truck lurched forward like a horse someone had given the spur to.

As he drove on down the lane, Mitchell watched the endless white brick wall pass by. Then abruptly, at his father's house, it finally ended. Turning off the road, he brought the tow truck to a halt in front of the house. With a sigh, he pulled the key from the ignition, and leaning over the steering wheel, he closed his eyes and fought back the tears. Then a gust of wind rustled the leaves on the big cottonwood tree in the front yard, and through teary eyes Mitchell looked at the old place. Behind a frail picket fence that ran across the front yard, the house looked smaller and more vulnerable than he had remembered.

As he closed the truck's rusted door, his sadness was soothed a bit by a warm sense of being home, a sense of peace. When he closed the small wooden gate behind him and headed up the little sidewalk that led to the front porch, for a moment he felt like he had left all of the bad in the world on the other side of the gate, locked it out. As he walked, the sweet smell of decaying apples toyed with his nostrils, and looking over to the south side of the house, he saw that the leaves on the fruit trees were still green but starting to yellow just a bit. In front of the apple trees, he saw the garage that his father had made out of an old shed, and on the side there were gaps where pieces of wood had just rotted away. In the field where he used to keep his horse, the grass was high, and the water trough had just a puddle of brown mud in the bottom of it. Except for the new white brick wall that now ran along the south side of the property with puritanical perfection, everything was old, and to Mitchell the honest humility of it gave it grace and beauty.

When he opened the front door, the living room was just as he had remembered. In front of the fireplace there was a braided rug lying in the middle of the hardwood floor. To the side of the rug there was an over-stuffed couch, and across from it, close to the fireplace, sat a matching easy chair. A floor lamp and a small round table stood beside the chair. There was an open Bible lying on the table, and his father's pipe, with a bit of tobacco spilling out, rested next to it. The rich aroma of the pipe still permeated the room. Over the fireplace there was a large painting of a farmer walking behind a plow and two big, muscular white horses. In the painting, the sky was gray and turbulent, and the farmer was dwarfed and humbled, first by the massive horses, and then by the fierce sky and the wind.

Along the wall separating the dining room from the living room, the bookcases were filled with old dog-eared books that looked as if they'd been read with interest and reverence. In the dining room on the far wall, he saw his mother's upright piano, and like a pulpit in a church, it seemed to overlook the rest of the room. Walking over to it, he noticed that the keyboard cover was closed. Tapping his fingers on the piano, he looked over at a bowl of brightly colored fruit that sat on the dining room table. "Aw, Pop," he whispered as his head dropped.

Chapter Twenty Four

Mitchell slept in his old room, and the next morning he awoke to the chirping and singing of birds, and in his grogginess, he reached out for Fiver. Then, opening his eyes, he realized where he was. "Birds," he thought as he looked around the room, "I'd forgotten." He muttered, "Aw, I wish Fiver were here."

In the kitchen, the morning sun was coming in the window, and like a fairy dancing from flower to flower, it gave color to everything it touched. Standing in front of the old stove, Mitchell could feel the cool linoleum on his bare feet. As he lit the gas burner with a long wooden kitchen match, his thoughts turned to his father, and somewhere in the flame, he could see him looking out the window at Silver Mountain from his hospital bed. Then the image faded. "I guess I'll go for a walk," he said, blinking, and in a few minutes, with a cup of coffee in his hand, he was standing on the front porch. As he went down the steps, he inhaled the crisp morning air, and the cool sharpness of it distracted him from the grief that was growing inside him.

At the front gate, he noticed that the latch needed to be repaired. "I'll have to fix that," he thought, and as he started walking up the lane, he was entertained by fresh new fragrances at almost every step. Even the manure smelled pure and clean. But then all too soon, he couldn't avoid the estate next door, and looking through the large iron gates in front of it, he saw a dark-haired man get into the big suburban. Then the gates slowly swung open, and stepping back, Mitchell watched the huge truck leave and head up the lane. Down the lane a piece, an old army-issue jeep with no top or doors was headed toward him, and although it was too far away to tell, Mitchell had an odd feeling that the driver was staring at him. Moments later, in a cloud of dust, the jeep came to a jerking stop next to him. Inside, a handsome, dark-complected man with long, jet-black hair sat behind the wheel wearing a western shirt and Levi's. For a moment, he gazed with contemplation at Mitchell, then he smiled, and in one flowing step, he was out of the jeep. "Well, how the hell are ya, Mitch?"

"Jesse!" said Mitchell as he threw out the last of his coffee on the road. "I was wondering where the hell you were." Then after a brief handshake, the two men embraced and hugged one another.

"I'm sorry about your dad," Jesse said as they pulled apart. "I heard about it from Tom down at the garage."

"Yeah, thanks," said Mitchell as he stepped back. "I guess he went peacefully, not a lot of pain." Then, for a moment, the two men just studied one another silently. Having been longtime boyhood friends, they didn't need words to communicate their appreciation of one another. Mitchell spoke first. "So what have you been doin'? I like the jeep. I didn't think you could find 'em like this, except in museums."

"It gets me around," said Jesse as he patted the front fender. "It'd crawl right past that big showboat you just saw go by."

"You mean that black thing with all the chrome and balloon tires? Who the hell is that?"

"Ah, that's Snyder," said Jesse, "your new neighbor. He's got a lot a toys, and he likes to deck everything out."

"It looks like it's set up to climb on the moon," said Mitchell. "Does he go anyplace where he needs those big balloon tires?"

"No, not really," said Jesse. "It's all show, but he does take it on the Jeep Jamborees that he sets up every year on the mountain. You know, lots of guys drinkin' and braggin' on their trucks."

Mitchell smiled, but then his countenance took on a more serious quality. "What happened to your folks' place? I thought you were livin' there."

Looking away, Jesse seemed bothered by the questions. "Aw, things have changed around here, man," he said, looking around. Then, in a way that signaled his own questions, he looked Mitchell directly in the eyes. "Why don't we talk later?" he said. "Things have changed quite a bit for me. I've gotta work right now."

"OK," said Mitchell in a tentative tone. "Why don't we meet down at Lucille's later, say around nine, all right?"

With a wave and broad smile, Jesse hopped back in the jeep. "See ya then!" he shouted as he drove off.

#

Chapter Twenty Five

#

When he returned to the house, Mitchell plopped down in the overstuffed chair in the living room. On the little table next to him, the Bible still lay open. Curious about what his father had been reading, he picked it up and, holding it in his lap, he read the first verse that caught his eye: "And the earth and the works therein shall be destroyed by fire." The phrase echoed in his mind, and like a meandering cloud of smoke, it began to mingle with his grief.

After breakfast, Mitchell made arrangements for the funeral, which he set for the day after tomorrow. Then he called Jerry in Denver and made sure Fiver was OK. By noon, he was on the highway headed downtown. Up ahead, with the sun glaring off the metal roofs of the buildings, he saw the strange, compound-like place that he had first seen the day before. As he went by, he watched a yellow truck slow down and then turn in.

When Mitchell arrived at the garage, there were lots of cars and trucks parked out in front. On the steps in front of the office, Tom was talking to someone. Mitchell parked the tow truck next to a big yellow truck, similar to one that he had seen on the highway. As he climbed down from the cab, he read the sign printed in big red letters on the side of it: "SNYDER'S STOCK AND PACKAGING INC."

As he walked toward the office, Mitchell glanced back at the yellow truck. When Tom saw Mitchell coming, he dropped some keys into the hand of the man he was talking to and then walked over to meet him.

"I'm really sorry about your dad," he said as he extended his hand.

"Yeah, thanks," replied Mitchell, and without saying anything else, he looked around and studied the garage and all the cars.

"I didn't know what you'd want to do about the garage," said Tom. "I guess it's yours now. Anyway, you can see all the cars to finish up. We had a lotta' work, so I opened up anyway. I..."

"Dad would've liked that," interrupted Mitchell, and just then one of the mechanics leaned out of the office door. "Tom, you're wanted on the phone."

Mitchell followed Tom into the office. Sitting down behind a desk that was cluttered with papers and repair manuals, Tom answered the call. On the desk, there was a shiny round ashtray made out of a large ball bearing. Next to it, there was a note on a piece of scratch paper. Leaning over, Mitchell saw that it was in his father's handwriting. "Order parts for Mercedes, and don't forget driving lights and speakers." Mitchell was still studying the note when Tom got off the phone. As he put the scratch paper back on the desk, he asked Tom if he had seen much of Jesse lately. Tom was looking for something, and with his head down, he was pulling the desk drawer open. "Oh, yeah, I see Jesse all the time. You know he works for Snyder now."

Mitchell looked puzzled. "Who is this Snyder?"

Taking a pen from the desk, Tom closed the drawer, and pointing to the window, he said, "He owns those trucks out there. Gives us a lot of business. He owns that slaughterhouse out by the highway, too."

"Ah, I saw that place," replied Mitchell with some visible consternation. It's a slaughterhouse, huh?"

Tom was writing something down on a scratch pad as he replied, "Yeah, sure is. But he runs a lot of stock out there, too."

"Stock? I didn't see any stock."

Frank J. Page

"That's because most of 'em are inside. He's got chickens and veal, and I think he's got some pigs. He's the new wave of ranching. Big corporate man." Mitchell nodded knowingly. "And Jesse works for this guy?"

"He sure does."

"What does he do?"

"I don't know exactly what he does. He calls here on the trucks now and then, and I see him all over the place. Sometimes he's in the Suburban, and now and then he brings in the Mercedes."

"I see," said Mitchell, and for a moment his thoughts drifted back to his childhood with Jesse. From atop his horse, he had his hand extended to a very young Jesse with flowing black hair. Beaming, Jesse took hold and swung up behind him. Then Tom spoke, and the image dissolved. "What do you think you're gonna do with the garage, Mitch?" he said, and Mitchell was a little befuddled when he looked up. "Ah, I don't know," he replied. "I mean, I don't see any reason to shut it down. I know dad wouldn't like that. If you would, why don't you just keep on runnin' it for a while? Think about what you need for a salary and that, and we'll work somethin' out with what's left over and see what comes. Whad'ya think?"

Tapping his pen on the desk, Tom nodded. "Sounds good to me. It's not like I've got some place to go, and I'm sure the other guys will be relieved, too. I know they've been worried."

Mitchell smiled reassuringly. "Well, that's good. That takes a load off me, too. Listen, I'm gonna head over to Noah's. The funeral's the day after tomorrow. I guess it will be Friday before I have to get back to Denver."

# #

Chapter Twenty Six

# #

Noah Webster was a lifelong friend of Mitchell's father, and to Mitchell, he had become something like a favorite uncle. He was also an attorney, and for years he had handled all of the family's legal matters. With dark eyes that sparkled behind round wire-rim glasses, he was a short man with curly black hair and some graying at the temples. For a man of his era, he kept his hair rather long, and there was something rebellious about the way he let it curl up on the back of his neck. Sitting behind his desk, he looked a little bit like Teddy Roosevelt, but there was definitely something about him that was more like a painter or a jazz musician. When he looked over the top of his glasses and saw Mitchell standing in his doorway, a confident smile broke across his face, and his eyes beamed.

"Mitchell, it's good to see you," he said, standing up from behind his desk.

"Hiya, Noah," replied Mitchell, and with respectful but almost boyish shyness, he extended his hand.

"I can't tell you how sad I am about your father," said Noah in almost a whisper. "He was like a brother to me."

"Yeah, I know. I guess you were closer to him than anybody. I imagine it won't be the same around here without him."

"No, it sure won't. He was special, your dad." Letting go of Mitchell's hand, Noah sat back down in his chair. "Well, have a seat, Mitch. Have you made any funeral arrangements yet?"

Pulling up a small chair in front of the desk, Mitchell sat down. "That's what I wanted to talk to you about," he said. "I'd like you to speak at the funeral. You knew my father probably better than most anybody else."

Leaning back in his chair, Noah rubbed his chin. "Hmm, I see," he said thoughtfully. "Well, I guess I could do that, all right. It would be an honor."

Leaning forward in his chair, Mitchell rested his arm on his thigh. "Good, I'd sure appreciate it. I don't know who else I could get. Say, you know I ran into Jesse this morning."

"How's he doing?" replied Noah, and then looking puzzled, he began to shuffle some papers on his desk.

"He looks good," Mitchell replied. "What are you lookin' for?"

"Can't find my pipe. Your father gave me some good tobacco awhile back. You know Jesse works for Snyder, and Snyder just put in that new slaughterhouse, a big operation out there."

"That's what I hear. Who is this Snyder?"

Finding his pipe under a yellow legal pad, Noah tapped it on the palm of his hand. "Oh, he's a hotshot from back East, and he's brought some jobs into the area, so most people think a lot of him. He made some money in the seventy's real estate boom, and he has a business degree from some prestigious school..."

Mitchell interrupted. "And what do you think of him? Noah."

Looking over his wire-rim glasses at Mitchell, Noah smiled and then scooped some tobacco out of his tin and pushed it down in the bowl of his pipe. "He's not too personable," he said. "As businessmen go, I'd say he's that new breed, everything has to be big, economies of scale and all that, a sign of the future. I assume you know he owns that palatial spread next to your place."

"Couldn't miss it," said Mitchell, looking aside. Anything else I should know about him."

"No, that's about it," replied Noah as he took a match to his pipe and puffed. "For a while there, he was buying everything in sight. They say he wants to build a ski resort over on Silver Mountain. People say it will bring in a lot of money and jobs. For a while he and Jesse were coming in here every day, asking me about zoning and this and that. But to make a long story short, I couldn't work for the man. He's overbearing, and it got so I couldn't stand to see him come in the office. I don't know how Jesse does it. But, anyway, the guy has the city fathers in his back pocket."

"Aw, I get the picture," said Mitchell with a sigh. Then, putting his hands on his knees, he stood up. "Well, the funeral's at eleven. I sure appreciate your agreeing to speak. I know my father would want you to. You're his closest friend, and he always told me how much he respected you. I guess I'd better be going. Call me if you have any questions, huh."

Outside, Mitchell climbed into the truck and shut the door with the usual clang. With his arms resting against the steering wheel, his thoughts went back to his childhood, and again he could see young Jesse swing up behind him on the horse, and he could feel him holding on as they rode off. Then he was sitting in a bus, and it was hot, and much older, he was going away to college. Looking down from the bus window, he saw Jesse waving and forcing a smile, and then he saw his father smile. "It's a good life, if you don't weaken," his father said. And suddenly, Susan was shouting, "The sixties are over!" And then Fiver rose up between them and Mitchell could see Fiver's pleading eyes, and he felt the shame of that moment. Then, gritting his teeth, he shook off the images, and with his foot, he felt around on the floor for the starter button. Finding it, he stepped down on it hard, and the truck started with a rumble.

As he drove down the highway, the town passed by as if it were part of a dream. Lost in his thoughts, Mitchell was oblivious to driving, and before he knew it, he had passed his father's house and was well out into the country. With pastures and fields rolling by on both sides of the road, he saw hills and then mountains in the distance. He drove on with his elbow out the window, and he smiled unwittingly when a horse in one of the fields raised his head and, swishing his tail, watched the truck go by.

Soon he was in the mountains, and there was a sign at the side of the road: "Connor's Lookout Point, 5 Miles." As he shifted down, the gears whined and clanked, and bouncing and clattering, he drove up an old dirt road. Behind him, the truck left a billowing stream of dust. For a ways the landscape was covered with sagebrush and scrub oak, but soon aspen trees were passing on both sides. Up ahead groves of dark-green pine trees seemed to march down the side the mountain. As the road got steeper, it wound around and around, and the air that wafted through the window was sweet and pungent with the smell of pine, and it got cooler and fresher as they climbed. The old truck, like an old horse that had something to prove, responded well to the workout.

At the end of the road, there was a small parking area next to a grove of pine trees. A sign by some picnic benches said, "Connor's Lookout Point, 2 Miles." Stepping down from the truck, Mitchell took a deep breath, and the fragrant mountain air seemed to cleanse his lungs and his soul. "Damn, I wish Fiver were here," he thought. "He'd love this."

The trail to the top was narrow, and the surrounding foliage was lush and green. As he started walking up a trail, he noticed how rich and black the soil was. Under his feet the leaves and twigs crackled in the rich mulch. From the top of a large rock, a squirrel stared down at him, and then with a wink, scampered away. Smiling, Mitchell walked on. Not far up the trail he stopped, and in the distance he could hear the cry of a hawk and some other birds that he didn't recognize. He continued on for a while. Then, as he came around a bend in the trail, he saw a small mule deer drinking from a tiny stream that trickled across the trail. The deer raised her head as he approached, and with her ears forward and her gentle eyes shining with a shy curiosity, she pondered him. Then she twirled, and in one graceful leap, she escaped into the underbrush without a sound.

Mitchell was breathing hard when he came to the small clearing at the end of the trail. The scent of the pines was even stronger now, and with his lungs tingling, he looked up at the lone pine tree that stood at the edge of the lookout. In the background, the sky was deep blue. In the distance, snowcapped peaks pointed up to the heavens. When he got to the edge, a cold breeze blew past him, and like a child, he was awestruck as he looked out at the expanse of mountains and valleys in the distance. As he marveled, he asked himself how he had come to live without it. "What's happened to me?" he wondered out loud. Then he closed his eyes, and as if the wind could somehow baptize him and reestablish his faith in things beyond him, he leaned into it.

Chapter Twenty Seven

#

It was dark when Mitchell parked the truck in front of Lucille's Bar and Grill. As he headed up the front steps, a warm yellow light emanated from the windows. Inside, a man in a plaid jacket was hunched over a cup of coffee at the counter. Jesse wasn't there yet, and since Mitchell didn't recognize any of the people there, he sat down in one of the booths that ran along the wall opposite the bar. In the back there was an old jukebox, and each of the booths had a dome-shaped chrome wall box mounted on the wall containing the song titles on the juke box. They looked like miniature cathedrals done in an art deco style.

In the booth next to him there were four robust men in various types of hunting attire, and they were all laughing and grinning. One of them sneered proudly while he exhaled the smoke from his cigarette. As he settled into the booth, Mitchell found himself listening to their conversation.

"Shot that sucker right through the neck," the man said. "Goddamn arrow went right through him, and the son of a bitch didn't even break stride. Just kept on runnin'. Had to follow him for a mile, and then I still had to shoot him when I found him."

Sitting with his back to the wall, Mitchell dropped his head and looked down at the wooden table. He tried not to listen and think of other things, but bits and pieces of the conversation caught his attention, and gradually his eyes turned dark, and while he wanted to disengage from the conversation, the threat of it, and its ugliness, kept him fast.

"Shit, I shot one, one time, with a thirty-thirty," said the other man in the booth. "Blew the guts right out of him, and he kept on runnin' too. Didn't hardly have to clean 'im. Bastard had a good rack on him, too."

Mitchell was rigid now, and the words fell on him like a whip. Grimacing, he fought an urge to climb over the top of the booth and tell them how depraved they were, but just then a husky woman's voice interrupted him. "Can I get you something? You!" Befuddled, Mitchell looked up, and two bright-red lips and a pair of blue eyes set beneath ratted blond hair pulled him back to reality.

"What can I get you?" said the waitress one more time, and her tone made it clear that she had her doubts about him.

"Oh," said Mitchell, sitting up and turning around. "Uh...why don't you bring me a pitcher and two glasses. I'm expecting someone."

Still seeming to question him, with raised eyebrows, the waitress smiled, and then turned on her heel and started back to the bar. As she left, she said something to the men in the next booth, and grinning, they laughed and guffawed. Mitchell's eyes fell downward, and when he looked up, he saw the chrome wall box. Leaning to one side, he reached down and pulled a quarter from his pocket. Dropping it in the slot, he looked at the old yellow title strips, and pushing two of the square buttons, made a selection. As he sat back in the booth, the conversation of the men in the next booth gave way to the twang of an old Hank Williams tune. A moment later, Mitchell was turning the chrome knob that rotated the selections on the wall box when he felt someone standing next to the booth. Looking up he saw Jesse wearing a western style sport coat and a traditional cowboy tie.

"Well, you still like Hank," said Jesse with a grin.

"Sit down!" exclaimed Mitchell. "Good old stuff on the jukebox, Hank and Tex Ritter." As he scooted into his seat, Jesse glanced at the men in the next booth. Then the waitress brought over the pitcher and glasses.

"You look prosperous these days," said Mitchell as he poured out the beer.

"It's part of the show," replied Jesse with a touch of embarrassment. "I guess by now you know I work for Snyder, but hell, you're the one who went to the big city and made it big. That's what they say."

As he replied, Mitchell's gaze fell toward the table. "Yeah, I was doin' all right," he said. "I did make some good money for a while, at least enough to take some time off."

"I wish I could do that," replied Jesse. "Ellie's wanted to get away for months. We haven't been out of here in two years."

"Well, why don't you get some time off?" said Mitchell with inquiring eyes.

"Ah, we can't right now," replied Jesse. "You know we just had our first child awhile back, and now Ellie's expecting again. We need a bigger place. Ellie's got her heart set on a new house over in Brookdale. And we need it, and I'm makin' decent money now, more than I ever thought I'd make around here. I've got to stay with it."

Sitting back in the booth, Mitchell held his beer in front of him and smiled. "Well, that's good," he said. "I'm glad for you. Man, you deserve it." Then he looked down at his beer glass. "So tell me," he said as he looked up. "What happened to your pa's place?"

"You mean, how did Snyder end up with it?" replied Jesse, clearly not liking the question. "Well, he offered five times the going rate, that's all, and we needed the money. You know, the little spreads and farms don't make it anymore. He'd already bought out Sorenson's, and it gave Ellie and me a chance, and you don't get many chances around here."

Seeming to prepare for Mitchell's disapproval, Jesse's face became rigid as he waited for a response, and returning his gaze with an equally stern expression, Mitchell didn't smile, but then he laughed. "It's all right," he said with a chuckle. "Hell, I just wondered how it was that the Hearst Castle had been moved so I get to wake up to it every morning."

As if he was about to reproach Mitchell, Jesse leaned forward. Then, dropping his shoulders, he smiled as he too started to laugh. "The Hearst Castle?"

Then Mitchell laughed, and soon they were both rocking back and forth, and like two sly little boys, mischievously glancing at one another, they laughed harder and deeper.

Chapter Twenty Eight

#

The funeral was held in a small church in the center of town. With Noah on one side, and Jesse and Tom on the other, Mitchell sat in the first row. Mitchell spoke first, and somewhat overcome, he spoke of how his dad encouraged him to read and taught him how to ride and how to work, and told him "work was a privilege." Then he spoke of how much his dad loved his mother and the farm. Tom spoke next; he recounted stories about working with Mitchell senior at the garage, and how he always helped the workers when they needed a little extra money. Noah was the last to speak. Stepping up to the podium, he was visibly shaken, and staring up at the ceiling, he gathered his composure. Then, wiping a tear from his cheek, he said, "You know, it's for ourselves that we weep, and I will suffer without the presence of this man. I will miss him very much."

Placing both hands on the podium, Noah looked out at the people in the small church. "I have known Mitchell John Black virtually all of my life. He was like a brother to me. Sometimes he was more than that." Noah's voice was shaky, but tempered. "When we were young men, I remember a time...a time when we were out hunting deer. You know, we all grew up learning to hunt back then. You learned to hunt just as sure as you learned to ride a bike. On this particular day we were over on the north end of Silver Mountain, way up in the high country. There was myself, Mitchell John, Bill, and two other guys. We were all sporting rifles. Mitchell and I had hunted pheasants together, and I can tell you, Mitchell was probably as fast and true with a shotgun as anybody I knew, but neither of us had done a lot of deer hunting."

Taking a moment to compose himself, Noah closed his eyes and swallowed hard. "I remember," he went on. "We were all standing on the side of a hill overlooking a gully when suddenly someone yelled, 'Cougar!' And across from us, on the other side of the gully, no more than say fifty or sixty yards away, there was a big cat. She was gorgeous, the only mountain lion I've ever seen in the wild. I'll never forget her. But anyway, in an instant, one of the guys, I think his name was Rich, drew down on the lion. Then I heard someone else cock his rifle and slam a bullet into the breach. Then a shot rang out, and we were all stunned for a second, and we all watched the cat, and it must have jumped about ten feet. Then it disappeared into the brush. When we looked around at one another, Mitchell John was standing there with his gun pointed in the air. I remember the smoke was still curling up from the barrel, and he didn't say a word. Just stood there lookin' at us."

Pausing, Noah looked down at Mitchell. Then he continued. "Now, Rich, the guy who first drew down on the cougar, was a crack shot, and he was mad! Before anybody could say anything, he turned on Mitchell and started cussin' him out, and I remember Mitchell didn't say anything. He just looked back at him and didn't say a word. Some of the men wrote it off as buck fever, but I knew better, and a while after that, I asked Mitchell about the cat, and I told him I didn't buy the bit about buck fever, and you know what he said to me, he said, 'I just didn't like the way everybody was so quick to want to kill that cat. It was just blood lust. We weren't hunting for cats. We had no business shooting it. She's just out there like us, trying to make a living. And nobody gave it any thought.' Then he said something I've never forgotten. He said, 'The least you can do in this life is think about what you're doing. Everybody's obligated to do that, aren't they?'"

Dropping his head, Noah pulled the back of his hand across his forehead. Then, like a preacher bearing down from the pulpit, he searched the faces of the people before him. "That was the kind of man Mitchell John was, and you only have to pick up a newspaper to realize that there aren't many men like that around anymore." Then, falling silent, Noah wiped a tear from behind his round glasses and looked out at the small crowd in the church. "I'll miss you, Mitchell John," he said. "We'll all miss you. We needed you."

#

Chapter Twenty Nine

#

They buried Mitchell John next to his wife in the old cemetery north of town. Afterward, Mitchell invited everyone over to the house. Some of the people who came were relatives and friends, and many of them were long-time customers from the garage. It was dark when they left, and from the window, Mitchell watched the headlights of the last car as it headed up the lane. Then, with a sigh, he collapsed in the overstuffed chair in the living room. In the silence, he tapped his fingers on the arm of the chair. Then standing up, he walked into the dining room and pulled the bench from beneath the piano. Sitting on the bench with his head bowed, like someone at confession, for a long time he didn't move. Then, hesitantly raising his hand, he caressed the smooth mahogany lid that covered the keys. Sliding his thumb down the curve of it, he started to lift it up, but then with the keys still unexposed, he stopped, and ever so slowly, he set it back down and withdrew his hand.

Mitchell's plane left at seven the next morning, and he looked haggard when he got up. Standing in the front doorway, about to leave, he looked back and surveyed the house. On the table next to his father's easy chair, he saw his father's Bible still sitting open. His shoes clicked on the hardwood floor as he walked over to it. Lifting it from the table, he ran his hand across the grainy leather cover. Then he tucked it under his arm like a newspaper and went outside and waited on the front porch for Tom to pick him up and take him to the airport.

Shortly after takeoff, with the Bible lying in his lap, Mitchell was fast asleep. He didn't awaken until the elderly woman next to him tapped him on the shoulder.

"Young man," she said, "we're landing soon. You'd better fasten your seat belt."

"Oh, thanks," said Mitchell, and yawning, he sat up and rubbed his neck. He was tightening his seat belt when the woman spoke again.

"I see you carry your Bible with you. I always take mine everywhere I go," she said proudly. Surprised, Mitchell looked at the Bible on his lap. "I sat down to read it nine years ago," said the woman, "and my life has been blessed ever since. You know, I really couldn't face life until I was reborn, and now every day is a wonderful miracle. I mean, look at this airplane. Isn't this wonderful, flying and everything?"

Hoping to avoid the conversation, Mitchell nodded. "I guess it is," he replied, and eagerly the woman spoke again.

"How often do you read it? Your Bible there."

"Oh, not much lately," Mitchell stuttered. "It was my father's. It's more of a keepsake."

"Oh," said the woman, and the wrinkles around her mouth seemed to deepen a bit. "You seem like a nice person," she said. "But, you seem sad. Is everything OK? The Bible might help you. Have you been saved?"

In mild frustration, Mitchell closed his eyes. The response, "I didn't know I was drowning," flashed across his mind. "No, I'm not saved," he said. "I guess I'm really not much of a Christian."

"Oh, I see," said the woman in a deflated tone. "What religion are you? If I might ask."

Mitchell measured his words. "Well, I'm not formally a card-carrying anything," he said. "I mean, I like a lot of the principles, particularly the Golden Rule, but I'm not what you'd call a believer. I'm..."

The woman interrupted, "I know, you're a humanist or something like that, right?"

Mitchell shook his head. "These days, I don't know if I'd say that," he said, forcing a smile. "Let's just say I love life, and to me, in a way it's all kind of sacred. I mean everything, not just the people. I mean the trees and the mountains and the animals and all the other creatures, it's all connected."

Smiling, the woman scrutinized Mitchell, and then with a condescending smile, she said, "You know the animals are part of God's creation, but technically they don't have souls."

In disbelief, Mitchell stared at the woman, and in the back of his mind, he saw the men at Lucille's in the booth next to him. "I shot the sucker right through the neck," said one of them, and feeling his stomach tighten, Mitchell closed his eyes to rid himself of the image.

"We're made in God's image, you know," the woman went on, and still hearing the voices of the men at Lucille's, Mitchell blindly stared at her until, embarrassed, she looked away. Then he spoke. "I really have to doubt that," he said firmly with a quiet restraint. "To me it's a bit self-serving, don't you think? I mean to afford souls only to ourselves and not other creatures. I mean, how can that be?" Then, as he tried to contain his growing anger, he thought, but didn't say, "If you ask me, it's the religious zealots and true believers that don't have enough soul. It's been scared out of them." But then, seeing the woman's eyes widen, he wished he hadn't spoken at all. "I was cruel," he thought, and looking away, the woman clutched her purse on her lap and looked out the window. "I've got to learn to shut up," he thought to himself. "Just shut up!" Then, before he could consider making amends, a stewardess announced the landing over the intercom: "We are now in our final approach."

Chapter Thirty

Mitchell took a taxi from the airport. As they drove across town, the cab driver smoked indifferently while he adjusted the radio. With the cars in the oncoming traffic whizzing by like bullets, the city seemed bigger and more strident than before, and on the radio, a man with a frantic voice screamed out the prices of TVs and stereos.

When they arrived at Mitchell's home, the cab pulled up directly behind Mitchell's car. As he stepped from the taxi, Mitchell noticed a layer of soot on it. Looking up, he saw the brown cloud of pollution that shrouded the city. Anxious to see Fiver, he whistled his special call as he went up the steps. When he put his key in the door, he heard Fiver. Then, pushing it open, he saw him in the hallway, and his tail was wagging so hard that it rocked him from side to side. "Hey, how's my sunshine?" exclaimed Mitchell, and kneeling down, he wrapped his arms around him. "I missed you, Fiver. Boy, did I miss you." And for a long time they hugged and embraced, each one looking into the eyes of the other.

After he carried his bags into the house, Mitchell saw a note from Jerry on his desk. Sitting down, he rubbed Fiver's ears while he read.

Mitch,

Sorry to hear about your father. I enjoyed staying in your house. Had a lady friend over last night. Good stuff. By the way, Fiver's a trip. We went for walks, like you said. Kind of enjoyed that. I don't think Fiver likes mailmen. In fact, he gets real quiet when anyone in a uniform comes around, and that includes the guy who delivered the pizza last night. Oh, and that reminds me, the lady two houses down the street called. She said Fiver growled at her. I find that hard to believe, but that's what she said. Anyway, I'm off. Got a new deal coming together.

Jerry

P.S. You've got to teach him not to get up so early in the morning.

Mitchell smiled as he read the last part of the letter. Then he looked again at the part about Fiver growling at the neighbor woman. "Naw, Fiver wouldn't do that. It's impossible. Not Fiver," he thought, and he was still shaking his head when, looking up, he saw his piano in the alcove. Its patience and tranquility left him transfixed for a moment, and like a leaf, the letter in his hand fell back to the desk. Then Fiver nudged his leg, and looking down he saw his beautiful almond eyes shining with anticipation. "Ah, whad'ya say we go for a walk?" he said, and jumping up, Fiver let out a sharp bark.

After their walk, Mitchell fixed dinner, and later in the evening he sat in his easy chair and tried to read. But finding himself staring at the page and unable to concentrate, he set the book on his lap. With a sigh, he looked over at the piano. Then, putting the book aside, he pulled himself out of his easy chair and sat down at the piano, and for a long time he just stared at the keys. Then, slowly and carefully, he spread his hands over the keyboard. When he began, his touch was soft but deliberate, and after playing a rich but plaintive C-minor thirteenth chord, he listened to it resonate, and when the last of it was about to float away, he instinctively used a descending phrase to resolve it to a B-flat ninth chord. Then, in another key, in the upper register, he played a simple little riff that echoed the melancholia of the first two chords. As he became immersed in the making of the music, he played the progression again and again, and each time he added another echoing phrase in the upper register.

As he played, the unabated sorrow within him came forward out of the shadows like a wounded animal, and feeling its presence, Mitchell abruptly stopped playing and dropped his head. Aroused by the sudden silence, on the couch, Fiver raised his ears and looked over. When Mitchell raised his head his eyes were filled with a sad resolve, and with his right hand he repeated the melody. Then with his left he played a slow but bouncing stride in the bass. When he put them together, he had a bluesy, more syncopated variation of the opening theme. Playing it again, he took it back to the beginning, and as he played, the corners of his mouth began to turn down. When he got to the bridge, tears were starting to fill his eyes. As they rolled down his cheeks, he smiled forlornly, and by the time he returned to the main theme he was sobbing. Continuing to play, with his hands floating above the keys, his growing sadness drove the music to a dark angry crescendo and a final chord that he struck with almost brutal finality. Then as he turned away from the piano, his crying gave way to uncontrollable wailing and sobbing.

By this time Fiver was watching him closely from the couch. Wrinkling his brow, he gracefully slipped from the couch and went over to him, and sitting down, he raised up one paw. As Mitchell wiped away his tears, he looked over and saw Fiver's beautiful eyes filled with concern. Still sobbing, Mitchell tried to say something, but the words wouldn't come. Then Fiver set his paw on his knee, and looking down at him, Mitchell continued to cry. Then, as if he were struck by an idea, Fiver's eyes began to shine, and with his gaze fixed on Mitchell he stood up, and in slow measured steps he began backing away. Then, crouching down with his tail high in the air, he started to bark, and each bark was more insistent than the last. Finally, Mitchell raised his head, and with red cheeks and quivering lips, he pondered Fiver. And when Fiver saw that he finally had Mitchell's attention, he jumped backward and barked even louder. Sniffling, Mitchell pulled the back of his hand across his nostrils and wiped his cheeks with his sleeve. "You're tryin' to lighten' me up, aren't ya," he said with a faint smile. "You're right. That's enough grievin' for now. Maybe we'd better go for a walk."

#

Chapter Thirty One

#

For the next few days, Mitchell settled back into his routine of reading and playing the piano, but he spent a lot of time thinking about Grand Mesa and his father. One afternoon while walking Fiver, he was considering the garage and Tom, and what he ought to do, when he heard a woman shrieking in a high, shrill voice, "Get! Get out!" In the yard next to him, he saw an old, white-haired lady standing on her porch furiously waving a broom at Fiver. "Get! Get out of here!" she screeched. "Get, get!" On the lawn, a few feet away, Fiver turned, and with considerable indignation, walked slowly away. Still waving the broom, the woman kept yelling, "Get! Get!" Then, when he was safely off her property, Fiver stopped and looked back at her, and in what could only be described as disgust, he growled faintly and then barked at her. Mitchell couldn't believe his eyes. "He's telling her off," he thought, and then he laughed as the woman stomped into her house and slammed the door behind her. "So that's it," thought Mitchell. "That's what Jerry was talking about in the note. Fiver's telling people where to get off."

Two days later, while sitting at his piano, Mitchell saw one of the trucks from the pound pull up in front of the house. Climbing out of it, a heavy-set man in a blue uniform headed for the front door. "Those bastards," said Mitchell, and before he answered the door, he put Fiver in the bedroom. "You stay here. I'll be back, and be quiet." The man at the door was holding a clipboard, and after asking Mitchell if he had a dog, he proceeded to tell him of the complaint filed by the woman two doors down.

"She says your dog growled at her and tried to bite her."

"No, that's not true," said Mitchell.

"Well, he was on her property, correct?"

Looking down, Mitchell nodded. "Yeah, I suppose he was."

"Well, you know your dog has to be on a leash at all times."

"At all times?"

"Unless he's on your property, it doesn't matter where you're at. In the park, here, any place in the city."

Feeling himself tense up, Mitchell lowered his voice as he tried to control his anger. "That's not much of a life for them, is it? How would you like to go around on a five-foot rope?"

Looking bored, as if he'd heard it all before, the man in the doorway tugged on his belt. "The laws are made to protect the dogs," he said. "You know how easy it is for them to get hit. You know how they can run after something! Besides, I don't make the laws. Just keep him on the leash from now on."

Closing the front door, Mitchell stopped and sighed. "The laws are here to protect the animals," he thought. "Yeah, right." Then he let Fiver out of the bedroom, and kneeling down, he petted him. "These people want you to suffer just like they do," he said as he rubbed his ears, "in one of their damn cages. What are we gonna do?"

#

Chapter Thirty Two

#

A week later, Mitchell was reading at his desk when the phone rang. It was Jerry, and he wanted to go out for beers.

"I shouldn't tonight," said Mitchell. "I'm kinda beat. But how have you been?"

"I've been real good. Workin' on the project again. I think it's ready to go, and I've got another thing goin', too, bigger than this one!"

"That's good. You sound like you've been busy."

"Yeah, I guess I have. It's like I've been unconscious. Too busy to think about things. It feels good. But you sound a little out of it. What have you been up to?"

"Oh, the usual stuff, just reading and a little piano, and some work now and then."

"Mitchell, sometimes I think you read too much. That might be your problem. You read too much, and you think too much."

Mitchell smiled. "That could be," he said. Then he changed the subject. "You know, lately I've been thinkin' about goin' back to Grand Mesa for a while. Might work at the garage or something."

"What for?"

"I don't know, maybe just to appreciate the difference."

"Well, there's not much to appreciate, is there? You're not going to make any money, and those small-town rednecks will get under your skin."

"Yeah, well, there's always a trade-off. This place has disadvantages too, and besides, there are plenty of rednecks here. They just drive BMWs instead of pickups. They might be a little smoother, but they're just the same. I just need fewer people for a while. I'm starting to feel like a misanthrope. You know, people aren't everything that they're cracked up to be. I mean, they're really not so damned special. Sometimes I think the animals are a lot more beautiful. People are just ugly, hairless creatures. Sometimes they're disgusting."

Jerry laughed. "You sound like you need a drink. When was the last time you got laid? You sure you don't want to come down to the pub? One of the waitresses thinks you're cute."

Mitchell laughed. "No, not tonight."

"All right, then, but I'll be there, and I think we ought to talk about you going back to Grand Mesa. What are you thinking?"

"OK."

"See ya."

When he hung up the phone, Mitchell leaned back in his chair, and just then he felt Fiver's paw on his knee. Looking down, he saw Fiver smiling up at him. "How's my sunshine?" he said softly, and Fiver raised his ears and narrowed his eyes as he listened to Mitchell. "I don't know what I'd do without you, Fiver," Mitchell went on, and sliding off the chair, he got down on both knees and rubbed Fiver behind the ears. "You wanna have a talk?" he said, and as if to give his undivided attention, Fiver sat back on his haunches and put one paw on Mitchell's shoulder. "What do you think?" said Mitchell. "You wanna go to Grand Mesa? I think you'd like it. How about a walk?"

As they left for their walk, Mitchell stood on the front porch for a moment. It was early afternoon, and as he looked about, his gaze came to rest upon his car. There was a small dent in the front bumper, and for a split second he saw the rabbit that he hit in the canyon. Like always, it was pawing in the air. "It's time to let go of that too," he thought bitterly. Then Fiver barked, and jumping up and down, he urged Mitchell to get on with the walk.

They had walked about three blocks when Mitchell heard the grating noise of a buzz saw. Up ahead he saw a utility truck with a long extension reaching up to the top of a huge, old tree. A man in the basket at the end of the extension was using a chain saw to cut off the uppermost part of the tree. Calling Fiver over to him, Mitchell held him by the collar, and they watched the big branches tumble and twist to the ground. Avoiding the falling limbs, Mitchell spoke to a man in gray work clothes and a yellow hard hat standing next to the truck.

"Why are they cutting the tree down?" Mitchell asked.

Taking off his hat, the man brushed his hair back as he spoke. "The roots are lifting up the sidewalk."

As he replied, Mitchell held Fiver close. "Damn, that's a shame to cut down a tree like that. It's ancient!"

"It is old," the man replied somewhat quizzically.

"Why don't they just run the sidewalk around the tree," Mitchell asserted. "Then they wouldn't have to kill the tree, and it's probably cheaper too. Even if it's not cheaper, it'd still be better than killing the tree."

Smiling incredulously, the man laughed. "Hey, I just work here," he said as he fired up the chain saw.

Up the block, Mitchell was still thinking about how easy it would be to move the sidewalk when he saw the old woman who owned the little gray dog that often came with them on their walks. Sitting on her porch in an old metal chair, the woman had a grim, downcast expression on her face. "How are you?" said Mitchell. "Where's Duchess?"

As she looked down at him, the old woman's face seemed to harden, and above her flaccid cheeks, there was a hateful look in her eyes. "That man up the street killed her," she said scornfully. "Said he didn't see them! Said he was going to work and just ran over them. Killed the brown and white one too. Right there!" Like an accuser pointing out her assailant, the old woman pointed to the road.

"Oh, that's terrible," said Mitchell, visibly saddened. "Otis too?" he inquired, and standing up, the old woman glared defiantly out at the road. Then, without a word, she went into the house, and the screen door slammed behind her. As they left, Mitchell called Fiver over to him, and he kept him at his side as they walked the rest of the way home.

Chapter Thirty Three

The next morning Mitchell took the Corvette to the carwash, and it was shiny and clean when he pulled into Strong's Exotic and Classic Auto. On the front row of the lot there was a Ferrari, a Maserati, and two Jaguars. Behind them were some Corvettes and three or four Porsches. The car that caught Mitchell's eye was parked on the back row. Sitting next to a new Porsche, it was an old 1955 Austin Healey with its top down. Covered in dust with a little rust here and there, it had a small dent on the front fender, and the rear tire was flat. Mitchell was leaning over looking at the dash when the salesman addressed him.

"That's a nice Vette you've got there. Thinking about trading it?"

"Yeah," said Mitchell, "sure am. How much is this one?"

The salesman looked at the Healey and then over at the shiny Porsche. "Oh, the Porsche, that one's in..."

Mitchell cut him off. "No, the '55 Healey." Somewhat bewildered, the salesman stared in disbelief at the Healey. "She could use some work and some wax," said Mitchell.

"You want to trade your car on that?" said the salesman incredulously.

"That's right."

"Do you collect them?"

Leaning over the fender, Mitchell inspected the two leather belts that held the hood down. "No, not hardly," he said with a chuckle.

"But you are familiar with them?" asked the salesman. "You know there's no air, and no fuel injection, and it doesn't even have roll-up windows. It needs a lot of work, and no power steering, drives like a truck."

Mitchell smiled. "Yeah, that's what I like about them. You can still feel things, and I understand them. I had one something like this in college, an MG, British."

After giving him another skeptical look, the salesman glanced back at Mitchell's shiny red Corvette. "Well, I don't see why you'd want to trade that for something like this. It's pretty unusual."

Turning away from the salesman, Mitchell bent over the door of the old red-and-black Healey, and reaching under the dash, he pulled the lever that released the hood. Then moving to the front of the car, he unbuckled the two belts that held it down.

Perplexed, the salesman glanced around the lot. "If you really want to trade down, I can put you in a new Datsun Z for a song. Probably under ten thousand."

With the hood up, Mitchell pulled out the dipstick. "Naw," said Mitchell, "I don't want something that new. I'm goin' the other way, and I can't buy Japanese right now. You know they kill whales over there, and dolphins too."

Somewhat surprised by Mitchell's comment, the salesman paused. "I see," he said awkwardly. "Well, if I remember correctly, this car is a one-owner, but it's set for a long time. With that many miles and just sitting, you might end up going through it, rebuilding it. Do you want to do that?"

Mitchell closed one eye as he read the level on the dipstick. "These guys are heartier than you think. But that's OK if I have to rebuild her. That way I'll get to know her."

With the salesman rubbing his chin, Mitchell closed the hood. Then, leaning over the fender, he started to buckle one of the leather belts on the hood. "God, they feel good," he thought. "It's like pullin' the cinch on a saddle." Then he turned to the salesman. "How much do you want for her?"

Chapter Thirty Four

#

It took Mitchell most of the day to conclude the sale and get the Healey up and running well enough to get home. When he pulled up in front of the house, he revved the throaty sounding engine before he turned it off. As he got out, he patted the door with his hand, as if it was a trusty horse. He was smiling as he headed up the steps, and when he opened the front door, as usual, Fiver greeted him exuberantly. Kneeling down, Mitchell gave him a hug. "We're gonna be outa here pretty quick," he said. "We're gonna head out to the mountains. We got enough in our poke. What do you think about that?" Sitting back on his haunches, Fiver seemed to study him. Then, throwing his head back and rolling his eyes, he let out a sharp bark. "I thought you'd like that," said Mitchell.

It took Mitchell a few days to get the Healey in shape for the road. After taking it to the car wash and steaming off the engine, he parked it in front of the house. Then, with the engine and the car all cleaned, he put in a set of plugs and points, and after adjusting the valves, he set the SU carburetors as best he could. It drove reasonably well and it shifted well; even the electric overdrive worked. By Thursday evening, it was all tuned up and waxed, and the black curving fenders contrasted nicely with the red hood and trunk. All the gauges worked, and the freshly oiled black leather seats were soft and clean, and in case of an emergency, Mitchell had a bag of important tools in the trunk. On Friday morning he made sure the knock-off hubs were tight and that the spoked wheels were sound and true. In front of the house with the top down, the Healey stood proudly, ready for the trip.

With Fiver watching from the front lawn, Mitchell strapped the last suitcase onto the rack on the trunk. As he finished he saw a concerned almost fearful look in Fiver's eyes. "What's the matter?" he said as he walked around to the passenger door. "I'm not leavin' you again. You're goin', too. C'mon, get in." Then, leaning over the door, he reached for the cord inside the door that would open it. There was no latch on most old British sports cars, just a cord. But before he found the cord, Fiver ran, and in one graceful leap, he cleared the door and lit on the passenger seat. Sitting up proudly, his eyes sparkled with happy anticipation. "Nice move," said Mitchell. "Nice move." Then, smiling back at him, Mitchell walked coolly around to the driver's side, and placing his hand on the top of the door, with a heave, he too jumped over the door and lit in the seat. "See, I know that move," he said as he slid down onto the cushion. Then, after he buckled his seat belt and put the key in the ignition, like an aviator starting an old bi-plane, he pulled the starter button on the dash, and with a deep rumble, brought the Healey to life. As they pulled away, Fiver looked over at Mitchell, and with one paw resting against the dash, he looked ahead.

The skies were clear and blue that day, and as they drove, Fiver blinked when he looked into the wind, and now and then, as if to give his approval, he glanced over at Mitchell. When they reached the Interstate, Mitchell put on a cassette tape, and rocking in his seat, he sang along with Lightnin' Hopkins and a variety of other blues players.

They had been on the freeway for about half an hour when up ahead, on the side of the road, Mitchell saw a huge metal wing of an old airplane sticking straight up from the ground. Painted white, it had big red-and-blue letters that, marching downward, spelled "Army Navy Surplus." Shifting down to third, Mitchell slowed, and with the engine popping and growling, he turned into the parking lot. "I'll be right back," he said to Fiver as he got out of the car. "You stay. I just wanna see something, if they still have them."

As he walked toward the old, dilapidated store, Fiver looked through the windshield and traced his every movement. When Mitchell returned to the car, Fiver was still sitting up attentively. As he opened the door, Mitchell tossed a heavy wool navy pea coat on the small jump seat in the back. "It might get cold up there in the mountains," he said, and looking up at him and then over his shoulder, Fiver gazed back at the pea coat. "It's got brass or some kind of metal buttons," thought Mitchell as he closed the door. "Never see many like that anymore."

As they pulled back onto the freeway, Fiver braced himself against the dash with his paw, and the two of them looked like a happy couple out for a Sunday drive, and more than one passing driver did a double take as they passed by. An hour later, they came to the cutoff from the Interstate that led up into the mountains. As he took the exit, Fiver again put his paw on the dash, and braced himself, and soon Mitchell was following the old road along the foothills. As the road got steeper he shifted down, and beneath him the old Healey felt solid and powerful. After a pleasant ride through the countryside, they were just nearing the first summit when, happening to glance at the gauges on the dash, Mitchell saw that the ignition light was on, bright red. "Damn! I'll be in trouble out here if she needs a generator," he thought. "Maybe she just threw a belt. Naw, she'd be getting hot if she did that."

The next town was about ten miles up the road, and the Healey was starting to miss when Mitchell pulled into the only gas station. Stopping next to the pumps, he hesitated and then turned the engine off. Then, looking over at the station, he saw a man in bib overalls leaning against the doorjamb.

"What is that?" the man said. "Some kind of small Jaguar?"

"Boy, I'm in trouble," thought Mitchell, and with a sigh he reached down and pulled the hood latch. "No, it's a '55 Austin Healey. I think she's got generator problems."

Shaking his head, the man in the doorway watched him get out of the car and raise the hood. "You'll play hell findin' parts for that around here," he said, and nodding ruefully, Mitchell looked down into the engine compartment.

A half hour later, with its hood still up, the car was parked at the side of the station, and using the tools in the trunk, Mitchell had removed the generator. Inside the station, he was talking to the man in the coveralls. "I don't suppose you have a generator that would fit any kind of British car, do you?" The man in overalls smiled sardonically, and then shook his head to the contrary. Rubbing his forehead, Mitchell groaned. "Well, I think I could get away with a set of brushes. Have you got any of those?"

"Naw, we haven't carried those things for years, you know everything runs alternators now. And you don't rebuild 'em, anymore. You just replace 'em."

"Yeah, I know," thought Mitchell, "it's a throwaway society." "Is there a junk yard around here?" he asked.

Nodding, the man in the overalls pointed down the street. "Yeah, Ted's got a place down there. He's got a lot of cars, but most of 'em are newer. But some are old, might even find a Jag down there."

Lifting the generator to his shoulder, Mitchell turned to the door. "Well, it's the only game in town," he said. "We'll give it a try." Outside, he yelled to Fiver, and after jumping from the Healey, Fiver began to trot along beside him.

The junkyard was an old place with a wooden fence around it. Behind it, wrecked cars were scattered here and there all over the mountainside. Some of the cars were stacked one on top of one another next to the fence. With their windshields and headlights just above the fence, from the road it appeared as if they were trying to get a look over the fence and maybe escape.

As they walked through the big gates that opened up into the yard, Mitchell wondered if they'd have anything at all that he could use. "This could be bad," he thought. Then suddenly, he saw Fiver freeze, and it was only then that he noticed the other dogs.

The closest one was on the porch directly in front of them. A big, short-haired pointer with pinkish eyes rose up slowly, and with his lip curled back like a villain in a movie, he began to growl and snarl at Fiver. In the doorway behind him, a smaller dog with pointed ears and sharp, spindly teeth, stood stiff-legged with his tail in the air. Then from around the side of the building, a big brown shepherd with a dirty, mangy coat stopped dead in his tracks, and dropping his head menacingly, he began to take slow, guarded steps toward them.

Keeping his eye on the shepherd, Mitchell bent down and set the generator on the ground. Then, ever so carefully, he reached for Fiver's collar, and he could feel him tense for the fight. In front of him, the pointer began to carefully descend the stairs, while the shepherd continued to snarl. "Now take it easy, you guys," said Mitchell. But the dogs seemed to have already passed some primordial point of no return, and ignoring him, with their eyes locked on Fiver, they edged forward like wolves moving in on their prey. Then a loud voice came from inside the old shack. "Chief, go over there and lie down. Blue, you go find a place." Then, with Mitchell and Fiver still poised for the worst, the shepherd stood menacingly in front of them, while the Blue Heeler turned away.

"Chief, I said go lie down!" the man yelled again, and this time the shepherd, after giving Fiver one of those 'next time' looks, turned and flopped down in front of a big Dumpster. Still holding Fiver tightly by the collar, Mitchell pulled his eyes from the shepherd. On the porch, he saw a thin man in Levi's with a short, white, stubbled beard, who looked down at him and smiled.

"What were you gonna do if they got into it?" the man said mockingly.

Taking a deep breath, Mitchell patted Fiver on the neck. "I don't know. I was thinkin' about picking my dog up and throwin' him in that Dumpster over there," replied Mitchell with half a smile.

The man on the porch laughed. "That mighta worked," he said with a chuckle. "Not bad."

Feeling somewhat relieved, Mitchell rubbed his forehead. "Yeah, and I was gonna be right in after him," he said.

"Is that right?" said the man on the porch, and still smiling, he looked over at the shepherd. "They wouldn't a fought anyway. Old Chief was bluffing. He just wanted to test his mettle, see who he was dealing with. They always greet strangers that way. I just keep him here to protect the place.

Between the bunch of them, they do a pretty good job of it. That's about all they're good for anymore. All a bunch of bluffers."

By late afternoon Mitchell returned to the gas station with two generators and three different sets of brushes. Neither of the generators worked, but fortunately one set of the brushes, with some modification, seemed to fit. Hoping that the bushings in the old generator were OK, Mitchell carefully put it back together. By dusk, he was tightening the last bolt on the bracket that held the generator. Then, dropping down behind the wheel, he fired up the Healey, and watching the red ignition light flicker and then go out, he breathed a deep sigh of relief. "Well, Fiver, we're back on the road!" he exclaimed, and from the passenger seat, Fiver seemed puzzled and cocked his head as he looked back at him. Later, when Mitchell was washing up, he saw the object of Fiver's curiosity. Looking in the mirror over the sink, he saw black grease smeared across his forehead and cheeks, giving him the look of a combat soldier.

It was dusk, when they pulled away from the gas station, and the mountain air was getting chilly. With his pea coat on, and the collar up and buttoned around his neck, Mitchell flipped on the driving lights, and sliding down in his seat to avoid the cold, he guided the Healey along the mountain road. With the black mountains in the distance silhouetted against the sky, looking out over the hood, he watched the road pass beneath his headlights. When he saw the fluorescent eyes of a small animal, he tapped the brakes, and shifting down, he saw a rabbit at the side of the road stare and then, turning away, scamper off into the brush. Slowing down to almost a crawl, he patted Fiver on the back of his neck. Then, reaching to the dash, he pulled a knob and turned on the heater. With the hot air from the heater rushing past his legs and then colliding at his neck with the cold air that was rushing in over the windshield, he began to accelerate. Overhead, the stars seemed to get brighter as the night got colder. As he pulled on the wheel to round a sharp bend, he was content, and his machine felt warm and strong. Together they cut through the darkness with power and precision.

It was well after midnight when Mitchell idled the Healey up the gravel driveway in front of his father's house. The deep-sounding engine, like a racehorse breathing heavily after a sprint, loped and popped as the light from the headlights glided across the front yard. Asleep on the seat, Fiver didn't move until Mitchell turned off the engine. Then, noticing the sudden silence, he sat up, and like a sleepy child, he looked around. "This is it," said Mitchell as he pushed the button on the dash that turned off the headlights, and for a second Fiver sniffed the air. Then both of them, like two pilgrims deep in the forest, listened as the wind rustled the leaves on the big cottonwood tree.

#

Chapter Thirty Five

#

Mitchell and Fiver slept in the next day, and Mitchell awoke when he felt the warmth of the morning sun coming in through the bedroom window. Raising an eyelid, he saw Fiver lying next to him. After breakfast, they went for their usual morning walk, and delighted with the new smells and aromas, Fiver barked enthusiastically as he romped along. But when he saw a black mare standing next to the wire fence that ran along the side of the road, he stopped dead in his tracks. With his ears cocked, he rolled his head from side to side. Amazed, he studied the horse for a long time. Then he jumped the ditch that ran along the fence between them, and with his tail wagging timidly behind him, he cautiously approached her. As if to satisfy her own curiosity, the horse leaned over the fence, and with her round nostrils pulsing in and out, she lowered her huge head to him. With his eyes cast cautiously upward, Fiver sniffed her large nose. As if she had expected more, the horse snorted, and then raising her head, she walked off. Puzzled and still curious, Fiver looked back at Mitchell. "Big, aren't they," said Mitchell. "C'mon, let's go."

Mitchell spent the rest of the morning settling into the house. In the afternoon he took Fiver out for a drive, and stopping by the garage, he talked to Tom about working there, what he could do, and how he could help out. Tom welcomed the idea, and Mitchell told him that he'd be there bright and early the next day. On the way home, they stopped by the supermarket and Fiver sat in the Healey while Mitchell went inside.

Mitchell needed to stock up on a lot of things, and his cart was brimming over with food when he got to the checkout counter. Aside from vegetables and cereal, a good portion of it was dog food. The pretty girl at the checkout laughed when Mitchell started unloading all the dog food. "Looks like the dog's eating better than you are," she said, smiling.

Noticing her long auburn hair and pretty green eyes, Mitchell grinned and nodded. "Yeah, it looks that way, doesn't it? Listen, I wanted some good granola and some real whole wheat bread, but I couldn't find anything but the commercial stuff here. Is there a health food store around here?"

The young woman laughed mockingly. "No health food stores around here. You have to go to the city for that. Real cowboys don't eat granola."

Still smiling, Mitchell looked back at her, and something about her eyes caught his fancy.

"Well, maybe you can get your dog to share some of his food," she said, laughing. "He's doing pretty well."

"He likes granola too," said Mitchell.

Smiling, the young woman began to put some apples and cheese into a large grocery bag. Mitchell marveled at how playful and hopeful her eyes were, and as he handed her his money, he glanced furtively at her hands for a ring.

After dropping his receipt into one of the bags on the counter, the young woman cheerfully handed him his change.

"Do you need some help with those?" she asked.

"Ah, no, I can manage," said Mitchell as he leaned over and scooped up the two bags. "We'll see ya, now," he said, and for a second, the young woman seemed to ponder him. Then she laughed mischievously. "You look like the proud father of twins," she said, beaming, and looking down at each of the bags, Mitchell saw that there was some broccoli protruding from the top of one of them.

"These aren't mine," he said as he bounced the bags up and down in his arms. "Look at this one; he's got green hair. I don't know anybody with green hair."

Smiling, the young woman leaned flirtatiously on one arm on the counter. "Likely story," she said. "Probably some creature from a disco one night."

Mitchell conceded the touché with a grin and turned to leave. As he pushed open the glass doors, he looked back toward the counter and watched her put money in the register. When she looked up, he looked away, but just then one of the doors swung back and hit him, and stumbling forward, he let the doors close behind him. Not looking back, he wondered if she had seen him trip.

Chapter Thirty Six

Mitchell arrived early at the garage the next morning, and he parked the Healey next to the old tow truck. Inside, Tom and the other men were all drinking coffee and eating donuts.

"How was the drive over?" asked Tom. "A little cool with the top down, wasn't it?"

Mitchell held Fiver by the collar. "It wasn't bad. But I ran into generator problems comin' over the summit. I was lucky, though. I scored some parts in a junk yard."

Tom sipped his coffee, and with a donut in his hand, he pointed toward the other two men who worked at the garage. "This is Glen Austin and Rick Davis. They've been workin' here for a couple years now."

"Glad to meet you," said Mitchell. "This is Fiver. He goes everywhere I go. He makes all the big decisions."

Setting his coffee down, the worker named Glen stepped over and began to pet Fiver. "He's a beautiful dog, isn't he? I'll bet he weighs in at eighty or more."

Lighting a cigarette, the other worker looked out the window at the Healey. "What kinda sports car is that?" he said. "It looks like it's damn near as old as the tow truck."

Mitchell followed his gaze out the window. "It's a '55 Healey."

"What's it got for an engine?"

Mitchell broke off a piece of one of the donuts and gave it to Fiver. "Oh, it's got a four banger."

As he turned around, the worker blew some cigarette smoke in the air. "I'll bet we could drop a little V-8 in there in no time," he said. "A 327 Chev would make that thing really scream."

Still feeding Fiver, Mitchell knelt down and gave him the last of his donut. "She's not real fast," he said. "But that's all right, she feels fast. It's the sensation that counts. I mean, it's all relative, don't you think?" When he stood up, Mitchell noticed the puzzled looks on the faces of the other workers. Trying to make his point clearer and avoid seeming strange, he said, "Horses aren't as fast as cars, but they still have horse races, don't they? And what about the Olympics? Humans are slower than hell on foot!"

Mitchell spent the morning changing tires and pumping gas. During a break, he told Tom that he wanted him to run things just like he had been. "I'll just do some of the menial work for a while," Mitchell said. "And I'll do the books and things like that. It's been too long for me. The cars have changed. Maybe you can break me in slowly, and you just tell me what you need done."

Mitchell also did some oil changes that morning, and they broke for lunch at 12:30. As he washed up in the men's room, he shrugged when, in the mirror, he saw a black smudge across both cheeks. "I gotta stop rubbin' my face," he said to himself.

By five o'clock, Mitchell was genuinely tired, but he felt good, and he felt right about going home and relaxing. On the way, he thought about the young woman at the market. She had hopeful eyes, and he thought about stopping to see if she was working. But then, seeing grease beneath his nails, he decided not to. Then an image of Susan scolding him about his clothing, popped into his mind. He was thinking about what to say back to her when, out on the highway, the shiny roof of the slaughterhouse came into view. As it drew closer and closer, the high chain link fence that surrounded it gave it the look of a concentration camp. As they passed, Mitchell noticed Jesse's jeep parked next to the gold Mercedes in front of the main building. At the front gate, the Dobermans were lying down, and when Mitchell glanced at them in the rearview mirror, they seemed forlorn and bewildered.

When Mitchell and Fiver got home, Mitchell cooked up some vegetables, and then for a while he read in the living room. Before retiring, he went into the dining room and sat down at the upright piano. After a brief hesitation, he lifted the lid, and with his right hand he ran his scrubbed but still oil-stained fingers up the keys, stopping here and there to play a note. The piano was a little out of tune, but the tones were nice and round, and none of them were harsh or metallic like they are on a lot of old pianos. After a bit, he eased into some blues, and with Fiver lying down beside him, he played for an hour or so before going to bed.

When Mitchell and Fiver left for their walk early the next morning, the light outside was amber and cool. Fiver's step was spry, and he rushed ahead while Mitchell stood on the porch and sipped his coffee. Walking down the sidewalk with his coffee still in hand, Mitchell smiled as he listened to the murmurings of the birds, and he was just about to close the front gate behind him when he saw Fiver take off on a dead run. From the street, he saw him dart through the big iron gates in front of Snyder's mansion. Sloshing and spilling his coffee, Mitchell ran to catch up.

"Fiver!" he yelled. "Get back here!" And when he got to the gates, beyond them, he saw Fiver running in circles, nose to the ground. To the side of the huge house, a garbage can was turned over, and cans and bottles were strewn everywhere.

"Fiver, come here! You get out of there!" he yelled. But Fiver was onto something, and oblivious to Mitchell, he continued to run back and forth, sniffing the ground.

"Fiver, you get back here!" cried Mitchell, and in vain, he shook the iron gates with his fists. Finally, with a frustrated glance, Fiver acknowledged him, and still smelling everything in his path, he started to work his way back. As he padded casually up to the gates, he looked back longingly at the garbage. Then, after deftly slipping through the iron bars, he started to meander on up the lane.

"You gotta stay of there!" exclaimed Mitchell as he followed along behind. "You're gonna get us in trouble goin' over there."

Mitchell and the other men went to lunch at Lucille's that day, and on the way back to the garage, Mitchell stopped at the market, but the young woman wasn't there. After browsing around for a while, and unable to find anything that he really needed, he left without making a purchase. When he got back to the garage, the gold Mercedes from the mansion next door was parked out front. Inside, Tom was sitting at his desk.

"You work on that?" said Mitchell, pointing out the window at the Mercedes.

"Oh, yeah, we work on that one all the time. Snyder brings it in every other week. He's always complaining, and he's got so much stuff on it, something's always down. Now he wants some new speakers installed. Five hundred dollars' worth. Can you believe that? I guess we'll get on it tomorrow, and he wants the air conditioning charged, too. Seems like we just did that for him."

Mitchell stared at the car for a moment. "People shouldn't have air conditioning," he said. "It's bad for the environment."

"What if they live in Phoenix?" replied Tom.

"If they can't take the heat, they shouldn't be there," replied Mitchell. "That place won't support all those people. They've already screwed up the water table."

Sitting back in his chair, Tom gave Mitchell a skeptical look. "It's a little too late to worry about that, isn't it?"

As he stared out the window at the Mercedes, Mitchell nodded. "It's probably later than we think," he replied. Then, shaking his head, he turned back to Tom. "You still want me to put that pinion seal in the blue Ford?"

Studying him, Tom hesitated. "Yeah, I guess you better," he said. "Why don't you borrow one of Glen's brake tools. Sometimes those covers can be a bitch coming off. It's been on there a long time."

Mitchell smiled. "It's a piece a cake," he said, and a few minutes later he and Fiver went out back where, behind the garage, the Ford was already raised up on an old hoist.

Tom was right about the seal, and Mitchell had been prying at it for thirty minutes before it finally gave, and when it did, a huge gush of gear lube flooded out behind it. For a moment, Mitchell seemed to be standing in a virtual waterfall of heavy, brown oil. As he stepped back, he wiped it from his eyes. Then, patting the top of his head, he realized that it was in his hair, too. Pulling his hands down across his T-shirt, he looked over at Fiver, who was lying on his side on the ground a few feet away. Raising his head, Fiver looked Mitchell up and down and then lay back down.

A while later, Mitchell came through the back door, and after throwing his tools on the workbench, he grabbed a rag and began to wipe his face. Looking up from under the hood of one the trucks, Tom started to laugh. "What happened?" he asked. "Was that piece of cake more than you could chew?"

"Aw, I thought I had the rear end drained," said Mitchell, pulling the rag down below his eyes, "but I guess I didn't."

Looking away, Tom tried not to laugh anymore, but just then Glen came around the side of the truck. Seeing Mitchell, he stopped abruptly, and waving a wrench the way a school teacher wields a piece of chalk, he said, "You know, when you're workin', you always look like you just walked away from a train crash or something." Chagrined, Mitchell chuckled a little, and then they all laughed together.

Moments later, Mitchell went to the washroom, and peeling off the oily T-shirt, he leaned down into the basin. With the water running over his head, he washed off as best he could. Then reaching blindly to the towel dispenser, he dried himself off. When he finished, he opened his eyes and saw one of his father's red flannel shirts hanging on the door. Lifting it from the hook, he held it up and examined it, and seeing it was clean, he slipped it on. Standing in front of the mirror, he noticed that it was a little big, but he liked the feel of it, and it looked good when he got the sleeves rolled up.

As he came out of the washroom, Mitchell saw Tom talking to a tidy-looking bald man in a brown suit. In a pleading voice, the man said, "Can you fix it? My wife is fit to be tied. Every time we get set to go somewhere, it won't start. We could end up stranded somewhere."

Tom set a wrench back on the workbench. "I'm sure we can find the problem. But you'll have to leave it for a while. When it won't start, does it turn over? Does it click? Or does it make any noise at all?"

The man in the suit scratched the back of his head. "I don't know. I mean, nothing happens. It just won't start the way it's supposed to."

Seeing the man was incapable of any useful description, Tom gave him a consoling nod. "I'm sure we can fix it," he said.

"Oh, that'd be wonderful," said the man in an ingratiating voice. "I didn't know what we were going to do."

Still standing in front of the washroom, Mitchell watched the man in the suit find his way out of the garage. He was very careful not to touch anything, and outside, he brushed his hands together as if he had just concluded a deal. "That was our illustrious mayor," said Tom. "They say he's a real tyrant downtown."

Mitchell pulled on the collar of his red flannel shirt. "He didn't look like a tyrant to me," he said. "He was damn near on his knees."

Tom smiled. "Yeah, I guess he was. He's got no clout here, and he's a boob when it comes to anything physical or mechanical. I guess that's why he sucks up to me so much. Just like a politician, isn't it. He probably thinks he just worked us pretty good."

Mitchell spent the rest of the day putting a set of brakes on a Dodge truck. After closing, he stayed to work on the books. With everyone else gone, he'd been at it for a couple hours when, looking up from the desk, he saw Noah bend down to rub Fiver behind the ears.

"Is this guy with you?" asked Noah, and smiling, he looked over the top of his round, metal-rimmed glasses.

"Yeah, he sure is," said Mitchell. Then, laying his pen down, he stood up from behind the desk. "That's Fiver. He's my best friend."

As he rubbed Fiver under his chin, Noah seemed to ponder him. "He's got an intelligent look in his eyes, doesn't he," he said as he stood up.

"He's smart, all right," replied Mitchell. "He's taught me a lot. More than I ever learned in school."

"Is that right?" said Noah. "That either says a lot for the dog, or it's quite an indictment of the schools."

Mitchell smiled. "I guess it's a little of both."

Reaching into the pocket of his sport coat, Noah pulled out his pipe. "Say, where is everybody?" he asked. Then, taking his tobacco from another pocket, he dipped the pipe into it.

"Oh, they've all gone home," said Mitchell. "I'm just doing a little book work."

As he lit his pipe, Noah began to puff. "Say," he said, looking through the smoke, "why don't you come over to my place Friday night? I'll cook something up, and we'll drink a little wine, and you can tell me how things are in Denver. You can bring him along, too." Noah looked down at Fiver. "If he's everything you say, he'll add to the conversation."

Mitchell smiled. "That sounds good. What time?"

Taking his pipe from his mouth, Noah exhaled some smoke. "Oh, about seven thirty or so. How's that?"

Still smiling, Mitchell looked down at Fiver. "All right, we'll be there," he said as he looked up. "We'll look forward to it. Won't we, Fiver."

Taking another puff off his pipe, Noah waved it as he spoke. "Oh, and can I bring in my Olds? The damned automatic choke isn't working. I've fought that thing ever since it was new. Maybe you guys can fix it. I just don't have the time to fuss with it."

Mitchell nodded. "Yeah, bring it in on Monday. I think we can get that without too much trouble," he said.

"That's great," replied Noah. "Hey, maybe you can fix my neighbor's, too. He's a doctor. He's got a new Buick. Does the same damn thing as mine.

Chapter Thirty Seven

#

Mitchell wore the red shirt to work the next day. When they broke for lunch he went to the washroom, and looking in the mirror, he made sure there was no grease on his face. Then he and Fiver piled into the Healey and drove over to the market. As he had hoped, the young woman was working that day, and she smiled demurely as she watched him set some vegetables and decaffeinated coffee down on the counter.

"I like your shirt," she said.

Mitchell averted his eyes. "Aw, thanks," he said. "It's actually pretty old. It was my father's."

Still smiling, the young woman rang up the vegetables and set them in a bag. "How's your dog?" she said.

"Oh, he's fine," replied Mitchell. "That's him sitting up out there in the car." Mitchell pointed out the window, and standing on her toes, the young woman looked over the register.

"Oh, he's a handsome one, isn't he?"

"Yeah, he is. His name's Fiver."

"Fiver. Oh, what an unusual name. I like that."

Mitchell put his hands in his pockets. "Yeah, I named him after a rabbit in a book called *Watership Down*."

Stopping to think, the young woman's face lit up. "Oh, I read that. I liked it," she said. "But it was sad."

After giving him a gentle, inquiring look, the young woman rang up the coffee. Pulling out his wallet, Mitchell watched her total up the register. When she handed back his change, her expression was warm and welcoming. Wanting to seize the moment, but afraid of seeming too assertive, Mitchell smiled and then looked away. But, feeling the opportunity start to fade, he spoke up abruptly. "You...uh...Do you live here?

"Yeah, I left Kansas a long time ago," she said with a laugh. "And I don't have a boyfriend."

"Well," said Mitchell with an embarrassed smile. "Way ahead of me, huh? Was I that obvious?"

With unpretentious confidence, the young woman struck a thoughtful pose. "Well, I just thought we'd best get to the point before you run out of things to come in and buy. They told me you've been in a couple of times without buying anything. But don't worry, I told them you were just a discriminating shopper, that's all."

Rolling his eyes, Mitchell was chagrined. "I knew I should have bought some gum or something," he said with a laugh. Then, smiling, he regained his composure somewhat. "OK," he said gamely. "So how about a picnic? Maybe on Saturday. You, me, and Fiver."

Teasingly, the young woman gave Mitchell a critical look. Then she laughed. "That sounds like fun," she said. "Why don't you pick me up here at eleven?"

Mitchell nodded. "That's great. And, oh, my name's Mitchell. What's yours?"

Bracing herself with her arm, the young woman leaned on the counter. "Nancy. Nancy Rawlings."

Chapter Thirty Eight

\#

When Mitchell got back to the station, the other men were already hard at work. Rising up from under the hood of a white Dodge sedan, Tom motioned him over. "Mitch, before you get dirty..." Tom interrupted himself with a laugh. "Would you take that Mercedes and drop it off out at Snyder's packing house? They've got a truck out there with a bad miss in it. You can drop off the Mercedes and drive the truck back."

Instinctively wanting to avoid the slaughterhouse, Mitchell hesitated. But then seeing the curious doubt on Tom's face, he shrugged. "Sure, I'll take it out," he said. "Keep an eye on Fiver, will ya?"

The Mercedes had smoked glass windows, and inside it was replete with all the latest glistening technology. As he closed the door, Mitchell marveled at the phone mounted on the console. When he put the key in the ignition, he heard a chime-like bell ring as the engine started up. As he pulled away from the garage, he noticed how smoothly it accelerated.

Out on the highway it was absolutely quiet inside the car, and Mitchell had to consciously listen to even hear the engine. With the windows rolled up, there was no road noise at all, and the outside world was completely blocked out. Gliding along in what seemed more like a hotel room than an automobile, he couldn't feel a thing. When he tried to roll the window down, he pushed various buttons that only moved the mirrors back and forth and made the antenna go up and down. Finally, when he pushed a button on the door, the window beside him clicked, and as it descended, the real world seemed to rush back in to him.

When he got to the plant, the two Dobermans by the front gate jumped and snarled as he passed by. He parked next to the big suburban four-wheel drive with balloon tires, and went inside the main building. He was walking down a long hallway that led to the office when he stopped to read a silver plaque over one of the doors. "Trophy Room and Reception Hall," it said, and although the lights were off, the door was open. Without thinking, he peeked in, and reaching around the doorjamb, he flipped on the lights. Then, almost instantly, he jerked back and scowled. The room was as big as a gymnasium, and it was filled with all sorts of exotic animals that had been killed and stuffed. To his amazement, he saw that there were literally hundreds of them, in all sizes and shapes, and like a child who had come across a dead person, Mitchell stood frozen in the doorway. Then slowly, with his eyes darting back and forth, he was drawn into this macabre menagerie. Taking a few cautious steps forward, he looked up at a huge polar bear that was standing on his hind legs. With black and shiny eyes, the towering bear seemed angry and humiliated. At his feet, a brass sign said, "Bagged 1971, by Bob Snyder, in Alaska." Still looking up at him, Mitchell stepped back, and then just to the right of the polar bear, he saw a mountain lion and two cubs, and following behind her, the cubs seemed to be looking to their mother for direction. Mitchell winced as he stared at them. Then, turning slowly, just across from the mountain lion, he saw a rhinoceros, and next to him there was a huge water buffalo.

Stunned by what he was seeing, Mitchell moved about like a man in a trance, and everything around him seemed frozen in time. Stopping in the middle of the room, he found himself surrounded by an incredible number of animals and birds. In abject silence, as if some alien force had suddenly left them in suspended animation, they seemed to plead with their eyes for someone to release them. Aghast, Mitchell whispered to himself, "For Christ's sake, he even shot a zebra, and there's a seal and a sea lion and a walrus and, I don't believe it, there's an African elephant. You can't shoot them, can you?"

Like a man privy to his own private hell, a man whose illusions had suddenly been stripped from him, Mitchell continued to gaze around the room in a stupor. In cases and displays he saw rabbits and ducks, and even little mice and squirrels, and in one glass enclosure there was a big gray wolf. To make him look more fierce and menacing, they had bared his fangs. Then, just as his disgust began to overtake his bewilderment, from somewhere behind him, Mitchell heard a voice. "It's quite a spectacle isn't it," he heard Jesse say, and with his face flushed with anger, Mitchell turned and saw him standing in the doorway.

"Spectacle?" said Mitchell incredulously. "Hell, it's an abomination."

Jesse was wearing a light-beige suit, and seeing Mitchell's distress, he took a deep breath and sighed. "Yeah, I didn't think this would set well with you. Let's get out of here." Still thunderstruck, Mitchell couldn't move. Then, shaking his head, he followed Jesse out of the room.

Out in the hall, Jesse leaned up against the wall and shook his head. "I know what you're gonna say," he said. "My boss is..."

Mitchell cut him off. "I know what he is," said Mitchell with contempt.

Looking down, Jesse signaled his resignation. "You haven't changed, have you," he said flatly. "Well, let me tell you that isn't the worst of it. And you know there's thousands of guys, millions of guys, just like him. Are you gonna hate the whole human race? C'mon, I'll take you out to the truck."

As they started down the hallway, Jesse put his hand on Mitchell's shoulder, and Mitchell shook his head as they walked. Then, stopping abruptly, he took Jesse by the arm. "What did you mean when you said this isn't the worst of it?"

Turning, Jesse closed his eyes and shrugged. "Look," he said. "There are things in the world, things that go on, things that most people don't see. Things they don't want to see. You know that. You know what goes on here. Why don't you just take the truck and get the hell out of here? If you want, we'll talk about it some time."

Still filled with angry contempt over what he had seen, Mitchell looked up at Jesse with determined eyes. "Hey, I know what goes on here," he said defiantly. "It's a slaughterhouse, what they call a factory farm. I've read about it. Why don't you show me around? Give me the real tour."

Closing his eyes, Jesse groaned. "Mitchell, you don't want to see this place," he said. "Believe me!"

"Yes, I do!" declared Mitchell with even more determination, and for a moment Jesse looked down at the floor. Then, raising his head, he said, "OK, tough guy. I'll show you around. I'll show you what it's like for the other half. I'll show you the stuff that civilization is built on. C'mon!"

With Mitchell a step behind him, Jesse looked straight ahead as they walked up the hall.

"Did he really kill all those animals?" asked Mitchell.

"Yeah, he did," replied Jesse curtly. "He calls the trophy room 'Noah's ark.' They used to bring school kids out here to see it. Kind of like a petrified zoo."

Mitchell frowned. "You're kidding. They bring kids out here?" he said incredulously. "Do they tell 'em that people like Snyder are sinking the ark? Do they tell 'em that once it's gone, that's it?"

Not responding, Jesse opened the door that led out into the yard. Waving his hand, he motioned for Mitchell to go first. "It's out here," he said.

Outside, the sun was glistening off the metal roofs in the yard, and shielding his eyes, Jesse pointed out the different buildings. "They house the chickens over there," he said. "And the pigs and the calves are in those buildings up there. In that small building they raise rabbits and mice."

"Rabbits and mice?"

"Yeah, Snyder sells them to companies for experiments. He keeps a calf or two up there, too. They've been using them to test artificial hearts." Seeing Mitchell take a deep breath, Jesse paused. "Are you sure you want to do this?"

Screwing up his courage, Mitchell nodded. "Yeah, I'm sure. And they sell the rabbits to companies to do tests for cosmetic companies, and they put chemicals in their eyes, right? You ever see them do that? They tie them down," and looking away, Mitchell imagined a man in a white lab coat using an eyedropper to put a scalding chemical in the eyes of a flinching rabbit.

"The calves have it worse than the rabbits," said Jesse as they walked up the steps to the first building. "The guy that picked the last one up said they put an artificial heart in him, and I guess the computers can't regulate an artificial heart as well as our brain does. Anyway, the calf exploded from inside. Can you imagine that?" Stopping at the top of the steps, Mitchell stared wide-eyed at Jesse. "You're the one who wanted the tour," said Jesse. Then, turning away, he opened the door, and holding it, he waited for Mitchell to go inside one of the buildings.

To his surprise, Mitchell found himself in almost total darkness. "There's about a hundred head in here right now," said Jesse as he flipped on the lights.

"Why were the lights off?" asked Mitchell, and then with a grimace, he shrank back from the unusually foul smell of the manure and urine.

"The calves are kept in darkness twenty hours a day," replied Jesse. "It keeps them quiet, and when they're quiet, they burn fewer calories. They get bigger faster that way."

Glancing skeptically at Jesse, Mitchell started to walk down the aisle between the stalls. "You keep them in these cages for twenty-four hours a day?" he said in disbelief. "And most of that in darkness? Do you know what that kind of sensory deprivation does to an animal?" Stopping in front of one of the stalls, Mitchell looked down at a small calf. As he watched, it seemed to rock back and forth like an autistic child. "These stalls are too small," he said. "They can't hardly lie down. How come I don't see any hay or food for them?"

"They're mostly on a liquid diet."

"Why?"

"The liquid diet and the confinement give the veal that tender pink quality that your gourmets want. We grow anemic calves here. That's what the consumers want."

Moving down the aisle, Mitchell stopped in front of another stall, and with his face twisted with consternation, he watched as one of the calves nibbled at a board that ran along the side of his cage. "This one's starving!" he cried out. "'He's eating the wood!"

"A lot of 'em do that," said Jesse as he wrote something on a clipboard that was hanging by the door. "I guess it's the closest thing they can find to a blade of grass. Maybe they're just bored. Anyway, they're gonna make the stalls completely out of metal in the future."

The next building housed the chickens, and when Mitchell stepped inside, he was immediately taken aback by the acrid smell of ammonia. "The gas comes from the droppings," said Jesse as he flipped on the lights.

"My God, how can anything live in here!" exclaimed Mitchell, and waving his hands in front of his face, he tried to brush away the rank smell. Then, looking through bleary eyes, he saw piles of wire cages stacked one on top of another in tiers. Blinking, he saw that the lower ones were covered with droppings from those above, and inside each of the small cages, cages that were about two feet in diameter, were six to eight chickens.

Putting his hand over his mouth, Mitchell moved closer, and as he did, there was suddenly a great commotion. Shrieking and squawking, the chickens frantically attempted to flap their wings, and in desperation, they tried to flee to the back of their cages. Bewildered, Mitchell leaned forward, and when the noise finally subsided, he saw one chicken was standing fast in his cage. "Aw, hell!" he exclaimed. "His claws have grown around the wire mesh. He's rooted there, and he's beakless. They're all beakless!"

"C'mon, Mitch, we've got to go," said Jesse, and standing up straight, Mitchell backed away from the cages.

Outside, Mitchell coughed and took several deep breaths. "What happened to their beaks?" he said.

"They remove them so they won't peck each other to death," replied Jesse. "They do that when they're overcrowded like that."

Jesse waited for Mitchell to catch his breath. "Are you sure you wanna see more?" he said tersely.

After taking a moment to think, Mitchell nodded. "What's left?" he said, and looking back at him, Jesse rolled his eyes.

"Well, there's the pigs and the plant. But I haven't got time to show you both of them. I'll show you the plant, and I'll tell you about the pigs on the way over."

With Mitchell at his side, Jesse talked about the pigs while they headed back to the main building. "They keep 'em up in that long building over there," Jesse pointed. "Most of 'em never see the light of day," he started.

Then Mitchell interrupted. "And the sows spend their lives in their stalls, in a metal contraption that's kinda like a stockade. I've seen pictures. It keeps them immobile while they're nursing, and to keep them producing, they give them drugs that keep them fertile all the time. As soon as they quit nursing, they're pregnant again."

"That's pretty much the story," said Jesse with flat resignation.

As they walked, Mitchell looked down at the ground. "So that's how they spend their lives, right, pregnant all the time, and constantly in the dark, and when they can't produce anymore they kill them, right?"

"They call it harvesting," said Jesse.

"Harvesting?" replied Mitchell derisively.

"That's what they call it," retorted Jesse. "Around here, if you're not productive, you get killed. These guys don't have retirement programs. They're not race horses, and they don't get put out to pasture."

Standing in front of a door on the side of the main building, Mitchell took a deep breath. "This isn't farming, he declared, it's a damn holocaust, and we're the Nazis."

"You wanted to see it," retorted Jesse resolutely, and then turning, he opened the door to the plant. Inside, in a small office, a woman sat behind a typewriter. "Hi, Sally," said Jesse. "This is a friend of mine. I've been showing him around." Giving Mitchell a perfunctory smile, the woman put some paper into a copy machine. Then Jesse walked across the room and opening a big metal door, beckoned Mitchell to go through it.

Inside the room there was a network of conveyer belts, and on an overhead cable a long row of hooks looped and meandered across the ceiling. Closing the door behind him, Jesse pointed to the conveyer belts. "The chickens come down there on belts," he said, "and the men hang them on those hangers up there. In the next room a machine-operated knife cuts their throats and guts them." Mitchell flinched as he imagined the chickens flailing upside down as they approached the knife.

Glancing down at his watch, Jesse seemed impatient. "C'mon," he said. "We'd better hurry. That's it for today. I've got some work I have to do."

Still staring at the row of hooks meandering across the ceiling, Mitchell seemed not to hear Jesse. Then, turning toward him, he said, "You sound like there's more. Is there?" Taking some keys from his pocket, Jesse opened another metal door on the other side of the room. "Yeah, there is," he said as he held the door open, "but the tour ends here. Let's go."

Outside, Jesse pointed to a truck. "There's the truck," he said, nodding toward it. "The keys are in it." Stepping toward him, Mitchell extended his hand. "Thanks," he said. "I know that was hard for you, and I appreciate it. I've only read about these places."

"Most people don't even read about it, let alone think about it," retorted Jesse as he turned and walked away. "We need the truck back as soon as possible, huh?"

Standing alone in the yard, Mitchell looked at the truck and then over to the last building, the one he hadn't seen. The sign over the door said, "DANGER! DO NOT ENTER! DANGER! POISONOUS GAS PRESENT!"

As he walked toward the truck, Mitchell paused. "No, I want to see it all," he thought, and impulsively he changed course and headed to the building with all the danger signs over the door. When he pulled on the door it opened, and inside, there was a small room. On one side of it, a large glass window ran the length of the room. On the other side of the glass there was long metal trough that paralleled the window. Above a small platform that protruded from the wall, there were some valves and two round lights, one green and the other red. "This is where they gas the pigs," thought Mitchell, and in his mind he could see the pigs squealing frantically in the trough on the other side of the glass. Then the gas came billowing in, and one of them jumped, and with its flat nose pressed against the glass, it pawed frantically. Then, from behind him, Mitchell heard someone yell. "Mitchell, what are you doing? You can't be here!" A second later, he felt a hand take his shoulder and turn him away from his dark imaginings. Then Jesse's face came into focus.

"You were right," said Mitchell in almost a whisper. "I wasn't ready for that. I'm sorry."

Reassuringly, Jesse patted him on the shoulder. "You're incorrigible, you know that?" he said. "But, it's all right. Just take the truck and get the hell out of here, will ya? I shouldn't have done this. Anyway, now you know what civilization is really all about."

Still a bit dazed, Mitchell felt angry and yet ashamed as he climbed into the big truck. When he started it up, the engine was rough, and in addition to a miss, he thought he could feel a knock and a vibration that wasn't good. "There's something really wrong here," he thought to himself, "this is not just a miss." Then, after taking a long look around at the place, he put the truck into gear, and jerking forward, he headed off. At the gate, the Dobermans leaped toward the truck, and hitting the end of their chains, they growled and snarled. Out on the highway, grotesque images of what he had seen and imagined swirled in his head, and when he could take no more of them, he switched on the radio and let the music blare. When he arrived back at the garage, he parked the big truck off to the side. When he went up the steps to the office, Fiver greeted him in the doorway, and kneeling down, Mitchell petted and gave him a long hug.

"What took you so long?" asked Tom from behind the desk. "Fiver and I were just about to leave without you. Everyone else is gone for the day."

Without replying, Mitchell walked over to the water fountain, and leaning over, he splashed some cold water on his face. Looking up from his desk, Tom studied him. "You look a little out of it," he said. "You feel OK?"

As he wiped his face with a paper towel, Mitchell took a deep breath. "Yeah, I'm fine," he said. "I think I'll stick around and work for a while."

Giving Mitchell a skeptical look, Tom closed the desk drawer. "We're not behind," he said. "You don't have to stay."

"I know," replied Mitchell as he dropped a paper towel in the wastebasket. "But there are some things I wanna get done."

Mitchell worked until after ten that night, and with every turn of his wrench he methodically tried to push the events of the afternoon from his mind. When he was too tired to keep at it any longer, he put his tools away. After he washed up, he turned off the lights and called to Fiver. "C'mon, Fiver, it's time to go home."

As they pulled away from the garage, Fiver looked on with his usual Buddha-like composure. On the highway, Mitchell hit the overdrive switch, and when the Healey dropped into fourth and over, he instinctively reached for a tape. But sensing that nothing was really appropriate, that in fact the music would be something of a lie, he drew back, and with both hands on the wheel, he listened to the deep sound of the exhaust. Like a chant, it was smooth and repetitive, and soon nothing but white lines and headlights crossed his mind on the way home.

When he turned onto the lane, the sight of Snyder's mansion aroused him from his almost semiconscious state, and seeing a light on inside, he wondered what this Snyder must be like. Then suddenly, the image of the pig scratching at the glass loomed up before him, and with a grimace, he revved the Healey and pulled it down into second. As the car abruptly slowed, Fiver rocked forward, and putting his paw against the dash, he braced himself while Mitchell turned onto the gravel drive in front of their house. After he pulled up to the mailbox, Mitchell turned the car off, and lost in his thoughts, he collapsed back in his seat. When he finally looked over at Fiver, he marveled at his wonderful countenance. Then, leaning over the armrest, he hugged him. "I love the Fiver," he whispered. "I don't know if I could make it without you."

#

Chapter Thirty Nine

#

Mitchell spent the next morning changing tires and greasing trucks. With the grease gun attached to a long hose, he was standing under the hoist when Tom motioned to him from the office. Letting the grease gun slip back into the rack on the ceiling, Mitchell wiped his hands.

"What's up?" he said cheerfully as he stepped into the office, and looking back at him, Tom smiled sardonically. "What's the matter, I got grease on my face again?" asked Mitchell as he shook his head. Nodding a yes, Tom held back a laugh. Then, rolling his eyes, Mitchell pulled the rag across his cheek. "Well, what's up?" he said. "You didn't call me in here to give me a hard time, did ya?"

Tom smiled. "No, not really. It's the tow truck. She finally threw a rod. She's dead in the water. I was thinking, maybe we ought to get rid of that old pig and buy a new one. We've got enough in the account for a down payment."

When he heard the word "pig," Mitchell grimaced as the image of the pig with his nose against the glass flashed through his mind. Then, blinking, he threw off the image. "Isn't a new tow truck gonna be awfully expensive?" he said, and looking up at him, Tom sat back in his chair.

"Well, they're not cheap, but we could make the payments."

"What about fixing the old one?" said Mitchell as he continued to wipe his face with an oily rag. "Can we get the parts?"

Leaning forward, Tom rested his elbow on the desk. "Yeah, we could get the parts, or make some of 'em, but it's a damn old truck. She belongs in a junkyard. She's all wore out, and the new ones have so much more power."

Mitchell looked down at the floor while he thought. "I tell you what," he said when he looked up. "You help me, and I'll rebuild her."

Tom moaned and shook his head in disbelief. "You're just like the old man, aren't you."

"I don't know about that," retorted Mitchell. "But think about all the energy that goes into making a truck. If the parts are around, we ought to use 'em up, don't you think? We ought to use up the truck, for the planet. Besides, that old sixbanger gets pretty good mileage for a truck. Pop had it set up pretty good."

Picking up a pen, Tom began to tap it on the desk. "For the planet?" he said dryly.

Mitchell thought for a moment. "Yeah, and if I do most of the work, we'll be money ahead."

Staring curiously at Mitchell, Tom continued to tap his pen on the desk. "OK," he said. "I'll order the parts...for the planet."

Mitchell smiled, and as he turned away, he said, "Besides, the old trucks have better lines. You have to admit, she's beautiful."

Chapter Forty

#

It was dark when Mitchell and Fiver arrived at Noah's for dinner Friday night. Switching on the porch light, Noah came to the door with a bottle of wine in hand.

"Come in, come in," he said jovially, and behind his round, metal-rimmed glasses, his eyes seemed to sparkle. "It's good to see you," and bending down, he stroked Fiver. "And you too, Fiver. Right this way."

Noah's house was small but well furnished, and there was a fire burning in the fireplace in the living room. Mitchell and Fiver stood in front of it while Noah poured the wine.

"I know it's a little early in the year for fires," said Noah, "but sometimes I just like to sit there and watch the flames."

As he handed Mitchell a glass of red wine, Noah sniffed the air. "Oops. I better go check the oven," he said. "If I didn't burn it up, we're having Eggplant Parmesan." Then, turning on his heel, he headed to the kitchen. "Make yourself at home," he said, "and tell me what you think of the wine. I'll be right back."

As Noah disappeared into the kitchen, Fiver sniffed around, and after circling a bit, he laid down in front of the fireplace. Sipping his wine, Mitchell wandered about in the living room. On the wall adjacent to the fireplace there was an old, glass-enclosed bookcase. Leaning forward, he peered through the glass at the books. Some of them were on philosophy, and there were a lot of classics, and some classic novels, but many of them were historical, *Fall of the Roman Empire, Spangler, Woodrow Wilson, The Renaissance.* On the other wall, a large mahogany desk faced out into the room. For a lawyer, it was not too cluttered, except for a pipe, a can of tobacco, and a pile of books. Most of the books were weighty-looking law books, but one, lying open face down, was obviously of a different bent. Leaning over the desk, Mitchell read the title of the cover: *Great Dialogues of Plato.* Picking it up and turning it over, he began to read Noah's handwritten comment in the margin. "Allegory of the cave," it read, "reality versus illusion."

Holding the book in front of him, Mitchell paused. "Yeah, whose reality?" he thought dismissively. Then, laying it back down, he meandered slowly around the room. On the wall next to one of the bookcases there was a large, vivid painting, and holding his wineglass to his lips, he gazed at it intently. Done in a surrealistic vein, at first glance it seemed truly bizarre, like something by Salvador Dali. In the lower right-hand corner there was a very ornate violin setting on a pedestal, and lying next to it there was a beautiful, large, long-stemmed red rose. In the background, which was all done in dark blue and shades of purple and reddish black, a shiny guillotine sat menacingly in the upper-left corner. Winding down from the guillotine across the center of the painting, a twisting trail of mundane tools and appliances ended with the violin on the pedestal. Following it down, Mitchell pondered the items...a hammer, a saw, a toaster, a camera, a pistol, the wheel off an old Model T, a telephone...

Mitchell was still fixed in front of the painting when Noah came back into the room. "Is that how you see it? " asked Mitchell without taking his eyes off the painting.

Noah was carrying a large casserole dish. "See what?" he said.

Mitchell gestured to the painting with his wineglass. "Is that how you see life? Somewhere between the strains of a violin and the drop of the guillotine?"

Laughing, Noah set the casserole on the table in the dining room. "Whew, not exactly. Actually, I really don't know what that painting's about, but there's something there, isn't there." Then, leaning over the table, he inhaled the aroma of the casserole. Glancing at Mitchell, he said, "Interesting take, though. You remind me of what William James said, ' For most of us life is like a man hanging on the side of cliff clinging to a vine. Not knowing what's going to happen and fearing the worst, he still takes a moment to appreciate the view.' Smiling, Noah laughed. "Ah, but that's all too existential," he declared, "particularly on an empty stomach. Existentialism's not for the hungry or the poor. It's a luxury for the well-off. So, let's eat."

When Mitchell sat down at the dining room table, Fiver curled up on the floor next to his chair. Across the table, Noah smiled contentedly as he dished out the casserole.

"Well, how are things down at the garage?" he asked. "I imagine that's quite a change from what you were doing in Denver?"

"You know, I really enjoy it," said Mitchell as he reached for a piece of garlic bread. "I even look forward to going to work for a change. How's that!"

As he listened, Noah heaped some casserole on a plate and handed it to Mitchell. "Well, that's certainly unusual these days. What do you like about it?"

Mitchell set his napkin on his lap. "Well, I guess it's what my dad used to call honest work," he said. "We really do something worthwhile, and I think I like the problematic side of it. I mean, every job is different, and I learn so much. You know, it's all interrelated, and it's all physics and chemistry and engineering and electricity." Mitchell reached for his wineglass as he went on. "And you have to use your head and your muscles. That's what I really like about it. Everything's hooked up, and it seems like they all have a purpose. I mean my hands and my head. It's like that's the way it was meant to be, thinking and working as one operation."

Noah set his fork down on the table. "Oh. Now you're going to get existential on me again, aren't you? You'd better have some more wine." With a self-deprecating smile, Mitchell held out his glass, and Noah continued to talk while he poured. "But you're right," he said. "That's what Marx was talking about when he wrote about alienation and the assembly line and all that mindless work. For Marx, our minds were essentially social and meant to solve problems, and we feel good using them that way, and we're lost when we don't, and it all seems meaningless."

While Noah poured himself some more wine, Mitchell rested his arm on the table and thought. "I read some of his stuff a while back," he said. "He made some good points about class and stuff." Mitchell's brow wrinkled as he spoke, and his thoughts, having been trapped in his head for so long, were pressing hard for expression. "Marx was right when he said that the class a man's born into pretty much determines the quality of his life, and he was right when he said that people ought to be paid according to how much labor they put into something. That's only right."

Setting his wine on the table, Noah wiped his mouth with his napkin before he replied. "Ethically he was right, but economic systems aren't always ethical. You know that."

"But the system should be ethical," asserted Mitchell. "It was made by people, and people could change it."

"Ah, but they don't know that," replied Noah forcefully, "and they're too busy scratchin' to stay alive and feed their kids to know better, and that's just how the powers to be want it, and they do everything in their power to keep it that way, believe me."

"I see that," said Mitchell, "but..."

"Here's the hell of it," interrupted Noah. "Just giving everything to a bunch of old, stodgy, Russian bureaucrats still leaves the people cut off from their own livelihood, and the elites still took the cream. They turned out to be just as exploitive as the corporations, and the masses aren't any better off, either way."

"So, what's the solution?" asked Mitchell as he put his fork down.

"I don't think there is one right now, not on the horizon," replied Noah, and as he spoke, his bushy eyebrows popped over the top of his metal-rimmed glasses. "Big forces are in place," he went on, "and you're not going to stop it right now. That sounds cynical, I know, but I think that for the next while, it's just going to be a great battle to see who gets the resources and who gets screwed in the process, seems unavoidable. Of course the rich have the advantage, at least for now. They have the power and the money and the technology."

Mitchell broke off another piece of garlic bread. "What about fewer people?" he said earnestly. "I think that would at least eliminate some of the conflict, and it would take the pressure off the planet."

Noah pursed his lips as he thought. "Well, some industrialized countries are approaching zero-population growth," he said. "But all these underdeveloped countries are still growing, and they want a piece of the action. They want their new cars and their televisions. And they want the medicine and the air conditioning. It's only natural, and think about China, all those people."

Mitchell stared at the table for a moment. "But I've read some of the books on the environment, and some scientists are saying that there just isn't enough to go around, that we've already surpassed the carrying capacity of the planet. They're saying that if we industrialize the whole world, we'd need a planet four or five times bigger than the one we have. They say it just isn't there, the resources, and think of the pollution. We can't all live like this. There are too many of us."

Noah set his napkin on the table. "People can't think that far ahead, and try and sell that to the third world," he retorted. "Try and sell it to Africa. Try and sell it to Americans. Not gonna fly. It's not an issue, and it's really not even on the table."

Looking forlorn, Mitchell glanced away while he thought. "If it were me," he said finally, "I would at least tie our foreign policy and our aid and trade agreements to some kind of population control, and I'd set aside some places and just give back to the animals."

Shaking his head, Noah reached in his pocket and took out a small cigar. "What an idealist you've become. Hell, that's not what the corporations want," he said as he lifted the cigar to his lips. They're gonna run the country, and for them it's all about cheap labor and more demand for their products. They're not gonna push for population controls; they want the sales, and if you ask them, they'll tell you we'll always have a technological fix for everything. You know that's what they say, and so far they've got everybody to believe it."

Mitchell set his fork down by his plate. "I don't know," he said, looking up. "Hell, I work on machines, technology, and they are marvelous, but sometimes I think we've created a Frankenstein monster, and I think the 'technological fix' stuff is a scam, stops people from seeing the obvious."

Exhaling the smoke from his cigar, Noah smiled. "It's hard to say, isn't it? Maybe we're coming to the end of a cycle. Things in the industrial democracies have been decadent now for quite a spell, and the historians say that decadence usually precedes the demise of a country, like the Roman Empire and all that. But it doesn't seem like there's a hell of a lot we can do about it. Big forces at work, bigger than you and me. I wouldn't lose too much sleep over it."

"Maybe so," said Mitchell, "but I think we have an obligation to try to fix things. We can't just eat, drink, and be merry, and dump everything on the next generation."

"You're right, of course," retorted Noah with a playfully sarcastic smile. "But, let's go in the living room and have another glass of wine while we talk about it."

As they moved to the living room, Mitchell stopped and stared at the painting of the guillotine and the violin and the string of appliances flowing between them. Standing behind him, Noah looked over his shoulder and puffed on his cigar. "I'll tell you what grabs me about that painting," he said. "It's certainly not the style or the beauty of the thing, but the contrast..."

"They're both machines," Mitchell interjected, still staring at the painting. "That's what it is. They're both machines, the guillotine and the violin. People don't see musical instruments as machines, but they are. They're machines, pianos, trumpets, guitars, all of them machines!"

Taking the cigar from his mouth, Noah too studied the painting. "You might be right," he said finally. "I didn't see that, and it was there all the time."

After Noah threw a log on the fire, the two men sat down in the big easy chairs that sat in front of it. Behind them, Fiver curled up by one of the glass bookcases. For a while they both gazed at the flames. Then Mitchell spoke. "Fire is one of the basic things, isn't it? I mean, it's a profound primordial process, the source, in a way. That's where the energy comes from. Almost everything is burning up one way or the other."

Noah lit his cigar and smiled. "It certainly is," he said, looking at the glowing ash. "It's one of Aristotle's main elements." Then, reaching behind him, he turned off a lamp next to his chair, and in the darkness, the warm glow of the fire filled the room with orange and gold tones. "I had my wife cremated," he said. "That's what she wanted. Funny, how it made things more final. Death's an inscrutable thing. Religion, philosophy, all that, all those explanations, and still an honest man has to admit he really knows nothing about it, except what he sees at the moment."

Holding his wine in front of him, Mitchell looked over at Noah. "I don't think we really know any more about death than Fiver does," he said. "At least I don't."

As he exhaled the smoke from his cigar, Noah looked askance at Mitchell. Then both of them watched as the fire caught and devoured the fresh log. As it burned more furiously, the fire cast large willowy shadows on the wall, and the room took on a new and more brilliant orange hue. Then suddenly Fiver started to bark and growl. Looking around, Mitchell knew that he was alarmed about something. As he set his wineglass down, he saw Fiver crouched down and backing away from the bookcase, growling and snapping. At first it seemed bizarre. Then he realized what was going on. He was growling at the reflection of the flames on the glass doors of the bookcase. "It's OK!" Mitchell said as he stood up and then knelt down next him. "It's only a reflection. It's all right." Then, from his chair, Noah smiled and raised his glass as if to make a toast. "Smart dog," he said. "Interesting."

After Mitchell got Fiver calmed down, the two men went on sipping wine and talking for another hour or so. For a while they reminisced about Mitchell's father, but as they drank more of the wine, the topic changed back to politics, and Noah was going on about Marx, capitalism, and private property. "In the main," he said, "capitalism has worked to some degree. Things get produced and traded, clothing, a toy for a child. But, it hasn't solved all the problems. It's not a panacea. But we've got to face facts, it's gonna be the dominant system, and the capitalists are in charge now.

Who knows, maybe at some point they'll realize that taking care of the planet is in their own interest. But for now, it's the little guy who'll get hurt, who'll end up losing his property. You know, big monopolies and the end of small businesses and mom and pop stores, and small farms and all that. You see it happening everywhere."

"Yeah, I do see that all the time," interjected Mitchell. "But what you're implying is that, in some basic way, people need property."

Noah rose up in his chair. "That's right!" he said. "It's implicit in all the economic writings and in political thought. People need community and they need property. They feel powerless without them. People need something constant they can hang on to, something to build on. Jeffersonian democracy, that was the dream. Everybody works, everybody has their own place, and we produce and trade, and people get food and clothing and camaraderie."

Mitchell nodded in agreement. "We all need to feel like we have some control over our lives," he said. "That's for sure."

Noah leaned forward. "Exactly!" he exclaimed. "And if you're powerless and you've got no choice, it doesn't matter if you're working for GM or the state, you're still a slave. That's why we drink so much, and that's why the Russians drink all that vodka! You'd think the academics would see that by now."

Mitchell set his empty wineglass on the floor. "Well, you can't expect too much from academia," he said. "As a friend of mine told me, the sixties are over, and besides, nowadays academics depend on the system too. They can't afford to question things too much, and in reality, most of them have been trained not to. Now the universities just train you to be something, like trade schools. You know, a doctor or a psychologist, an engineer, a dental hygienist. I don't think they educate as much anymore, not in the broad sense of the term. It's all just job training."

Now a little drunk, Noah threw down the last of his wine and stared deeply into the fire. "And the lawyers, they train us to do property. That's what we do, property. Lawyers and dogs, we work for the man. That's what we do, defend property, and neither of us really care to know why!"

Laughing hard and ruefully, Mitchell rose up from his chair. "On that note, I think we'd better go. It's late, and Fiver gets me up early."

"Well, thanks for coming over," said Noah as he put out his hand. "I guess it's time to call it a night. It's like being in college again, talking about politics and fate and all that. You know at my age it's easy to be cynical. This has been good. I've enjoyed it. But, be careful, you can't change things overnight. It could be a long time before people really see what's happening to them. Maybe we never will, and we'll go the way of the dinosaurs. Just don't let it break your heart. As they say, keep the faith."

As he let go of Noah's hand, Mitchell smiled and nodded. "Thanks," he said, "I really enjoyed myself." Then, with Fiver trotting along at his side, he turned and headed for the front door, but on the way he stopped and took one last look at the dark painting. "One creates and the other kills." he mused, "that's it."

Chapter Forty One

Early the next morning, Fiver jumped on the bed and began to paw at the covers. "Naw, it's too early," said Mitchell as he rolled over, and sitting back on his haunches, Fiver seemed frustrated by Mitchell's lack of enthusiasm. Then he pawed more eagerly at the covers. "Just let me sleep for a little while. It's too early!" cried Mitchell. But like a persistent parent forcing a lazy child out of bed, Fiver put his nose under Mitchell's exposed elbow and flipped it up. When Mitchell didn't respond, he did it again, and again, and each time his nudge became more forceful. "All right, all right," said Mitchell finally, and as he rolled over, he saw Fiver smiling at him. "OK, I'll get up," he said. "You'll get your walk. I don't see why you're in such a rush this morning."

Standing on the porch with his coffee in hand, Mitchell was only half awake. As he went down the steps, his coffee trailed steam. When he closed the gate behind him, suddenly Fiver took off like a shot and headed up the lane. Taken by surprise, Mitchell saw him dart through the big gates in front of the estate next door. "Fiver, get back here!" he yelled, and with his coffee sloshing and spilling over the edge of his cup, he ran after him. When he reached the gate, he slid to a stop, and the last of his coffee splashed to the ground. Through the gate, he saw Fiver with his nose to the ground, running in frantic circles like he did the other day. At the side of the mansion, two large garbage cans were lying on their sides, and as before, the garbage was strewn everywhere. "Fiver, get over here!" he shouted. "Fiver, you get back here!"

Completely distracted, Fiver was oblivious to Mitchell's call, and in frustration, Mitchell yelled again. "Fiver! You get over here right now!" Finally hearing his shouts, Fiver glanced back at him, and after taking one last look around, he nonchalantly trotted back and stepped through the gates.

"Damn it, Fiver. You're gonna get us in trouble. Now, c'mon, let's go. We've got some things to do this morning. Why'd you do that with the garbage? C'mon, we're goin' on a picnic today."

When Mitchell and Fiver pulled up in front of the store, Nancy was standing in front. With a bag swung over her shoulder, she was wearing Levi's and a plaid cotton blouse. Reaching across the seat, Mitchell pulled the cord inside the door that opened it.

"Fiver, you'll have to get in the back," he said, and jumping in the back behind the seats, Fiver made himself comfortable and then looked on while Nancy got in.

"Got the top down and everything," she said as she closed the door. Then, smiling, she leaned over the seat and began to stroke Fiver. "Oh, isn't he beautiful," she said as she petted him. "And look at those eyes." As she turned back around, she looked at Mitchell and then at the dash. "And look at this car. It's beautiful. So ornate, and not a straight line on it."

Mitchell smiled. "I know. It's like a piece of art, isn't it?"

"It is," replied Nancy, still marveling at it. "You know," she said with emphasis, "there aren't many straight lines in nature. That's why it's so beautiful. All those curves."

"Curves are good," said Mitchell with affect. Then he bounced his eyebrows up and down like Groucho Marx. Then what Nancy said struck him at a deeper level. "You're right," he said as they drove off. "The straight lines are things that men have dreamed up, aren't they. I mean geometry and all that. They're utilitarian things, it's all about organization and efficiency. That's what you see in the city, a bunch of straight lines all measured out."

"I never thought of it that way," said Nancy, looking back at Fiver. "I just know when I paint they're more the exception than the rule."

"You paint?" said Mitchell as he put the car in gear.

"Yes, I do," said Nancy demurely. "I really love it."

As he pulled away from the curb, Mitchell cranked the steering wheel. "What kind of stuff do you do?" he said.

"Oh, I have my own style. Most people would call them still lifes, but somehow that always bothers me, like I'm freezing things or painting sedentary things."

Mitchell shifted into second. "Aw, I like that," he said, as they headed down the road. "A bothered painter with curves, and sensitive."

Still gazing at Fiver, Nancy stroked him. "My, isn't he magnificent!" she exclaimed. "That would be hard to catch on canvas. His eyes say so much."

Mitchell had already turned onto the main highway when, looking over, Nancy asked him where they were going.

"I was thinking about Connor's Lookout," he said. "Or, if you don't mind, we could try to find an old place that I used to go to when I was a kid. It was an old homestead over on Silver Mountain. It's just off the road that goes up over the gorge."

With the wind drawing out her auburn hair, Nancy sat back in her seat. "Oh, let's go there," she said. "Maybe it's something I could paint someday."

As she buckled her seat belt, she saw Mitchell's cassettes in a box on the floor. "Oh, do you mind if I look through your tapes?"

"No, pick something you like," said Mitchell, and moments later, they were listening to Paul Desmond's mellow saxophone. In the distance they saw the slaughterhouse. When they passed, Nancy turned in her seat and stared at the two Doberman's out in front.

"Poor things," she said, "being tied up like that. It's no wonder they're mean. I would be too."

Looking over at her, Mitchell responded with a question. "You know that is what makes 'em mean?" he said. "It's being chained up. It takes away all their options. A dog, all of us for that matter, have a strong instinct for flight or fight. When you chain a dog up, in terms of instinct, he can't flee, and fighting is his only option."

Seeming lost in her thoughts, Nancy didn't reply. "It's just so sad, so sad," she said softly.

Down the road a piece, Mitchell geared down, and turning off the highway, they headed up the road that led up to the gorge on the south side of Silver Mountain. As they drove the mellow pitch of the exhaust rose and then fell as Mitchell went through the gears. "It's not far," he said. "There used to be a trail that took off from the road. It kind of wound around, and the old homestead was at the end of it."

Moments later, Mitchell shifted down and turned onto a gravel road that soon became little more than a rutted dirt road and then nothing more than a trail. Pulling off into some aspen trees, he parked, and the three of them headed up the trail, and as they rounded a bend, the old homestead suddenly came into view. The wooden roof was bowed with age, and many of the pine poles that once made the corral were strewn about the ground recklessly. In the back, the old barn, with its sloping roof half covered in vines, sagged and leaned like an old marooned schooner.

"It's beautiful," said Nancy as the three of them stood in front of the car. Magnificent."

Still in awe, Mitchell stammered a bit. "Uh...I wasn't sure if it would still be here," he said wistfully. "I thought maybe I imagined it. How 'bout that." Then, taking a few steps, Mitchell stood on the porch and looked in through the crack in a boarded-up window. In the darkness and shadows, among cobwebs and debris, he saw some objects that he really couldn't make out, maybe a table and something large against one wall. Then he saw that the door was partially open, but his impulse to investigate was muted by something deep inside him that made him hesitate.

"Shall we picnic here?" said Nancy, still standing by the car. "I don't know," replied Mitchell in a doubtful voice, and for a moment he continued to stare at the partially open door. "Maybe not," he said finally as he looked back at her. "Let's drive further on up the mountain. There's a stream up there. I know a place, it's nice."

"Oh," said Nancy as they turned back and headed to the car, "you know my grandfather has a farm over that way, on the other side of the ridge. It's nestled right up to the cliffs, on the backside of Silver Mountain, a beautiful place."

"Someday I'd like to see that farm," said Mitchell as they got back to the car, and as they climbed in, Fiver jumped over the door to the small seat in the back. When they drove off, Nancy talked about her grandfather's horses, and how he worked the farm with them, and how he was defiantly old fashioned, wouldn't even get a tractor. Mitchell was impressed, and started talking about the horse he had as a kid, and how he rode all over the foothills on this side of Silver Mountain. "Probably one of my first big mistakes," he said with a frown, "selling my horse and buying a car."

"But you seem like the kind who likes his cars," replied Nancy, in a puzzled voice, and Mitchell nodded with a smile. "Yeah, that's true," he said. "I can't deny that." Then, shifting down, he said, "You know, I think out here in the west, cars replaced horses, and we just haven't realized it yet. You know, we have race cars, just like there are racehorses, and some people have show cars, just like other people have show horses, and instead of having a wagon and some workhorses, most people have trucks."

Nancy laughed when she replied, "And we have station wagons instead of buckboards and buses instead of stagecoaches."

"And I'm not sure the change has left us any better off," said Mitchell belatedly, and looking over at him, Nancy smiled. "You're going to like Gramps, all right," she said. "You two will get along." Then, ever so lightly, she leaned over and kissed him on the cheek.

The road up the canyon was narrow and steep, and only the small frail guardrail separated them from the steep cliffs that plummeted to the gorge below. They were almost to the top when Mitchell slowed down and pulled off to the turnout that overlooked the gorge. "You stay in the car, Fiver," he said as he and Nancy got out, and together they walked over to the railing and looked down at the deep gorge below. At the bottom of the canyon, the river rumbled and the trees looked like tiny specks of black and green.

"Boy, I'd forgotten how treacherous the gorge is," said Mitchell. "It looks like it would just swallow you right up, doesn't it?"

Holding his arm tightly, Nancy looked over the edge. "It makes me dizzy," she said. "It scares me. It always has."

It was well after lunchtime when they pulled into the little campground, and Fiver barked enthusiastically when Mitchell turned off the Healey. In a clearing not far from the car, Nancy set the wine and the sandwiches on a picnic table surrounded by tall pine trees. There was a small stream on the other side of the trees. With Fiver standing beside him, Mitchell was looking down at the stream when Nancy came up to them.

"What you looking at?" she said playfully.

"I was just looking to see if there were any fish," replied Mitchell as he looked over at her.

"Do you fish?"

"No, but I used to." Mitchell stood up as he spoke. "I got so I couldn't kill them anymore. But I miss getting out. I used to sit by this one lake for hours, just watchin' my bobber. It was like a natural way to Zen out."

Looking down in the water, Nancy seemed to be thinking aloud. "It's nice to just clear out your head, isn't it?" she said, seeming almost hypnotized by the water. "Sometimes the words get in the way. There's so many of them, and they complicate things so. That's one of the things about painting I really like. No words."

Taken by what she had said, Mitchell glanced thoughtfully at Nancy. Then, turning away, he looked back at the stream. "Music's like that too," he said. "It seems closer to the truth, and you can't hardly make it lie. Sometimes I envy other animals. I wonder if they don't really have more music than we do. I wonder if they aren't happier without words. I mean more at peace."

Bending down, Nancy hugged Fiver. "I know what you mean," she said as she rubbed his ears. "Some of those little words can cause so much trouble." Rising up slowly, she took Mitchell's arm. "C'mon, let's go have some lunch."

While Mitchell sipped his wine from a plastic cup, Nancy broke out the sandwiches. "So, are you all settled in yet?" she asked as she handed him a sandwich.

"Pretty much," said Mitchell, and peeking under the top layer of bread, he inspected the makings of his sandwich.

"It's all vegetables," said Nancy.

Mitchell nodded. "Oh, that's good. Are you a vegetarian?"

"I try, but I'm not full-time," said Nancy, looking over the top of her sandwich. "But I avoid the red meats."

Mitchell reached for the wine bottle. "Me too, although lately, I'm really thinking of getting more serious about it. Anyway, so what makes you ask if I'm settled in?"

"Oh, they told me all about you at the market," she said in a teasing voice. "Small town, you know. And my grandpa, the one with the farm, it seems he used to know your father, and some guy named Red that owned the garage before your dad did. I'm sorry to hear about your dad."

Mitchell set his plastic cup back on the picnic table. "Yeah, thanks. He was a wonderful man. So what about you? You don't seem like a local."

Nancy smiled. "Oh, I'm not. I was teaching art at a prep school outside of Boston, and, well, I just tired of it, and the students were...well, it just wasn't what I expected. So, anyway, they didn't renew my contract, and I was having problems with my boyfriend, so I came out here to paint and sort things out. I'm staying with my aunt. My mother grew up here, and we used to come here in the summer."

With his eyebrows pulled down, Mitchell bit into his sandwich. "And?"

Studying his eyes, Nancy caught his unspoken question. "Oh," she said, "that. Well, the guy I was with worked for a big company back East, a subsidiary of IBM. He wanted to get married and have kids right now, and I, well...I didn't. Then he called last week, said he had met someone in San Francisco, a model." Blinking rapidly and raising her chin, Nancy began to mimic a haughty, condescending model, and Mitchell smiled sympathetically. "Well, that's too bad," he said almost sarcastically, and with her elbow on the table, Nancy ended her burlesque.

"Aw, it's all right," she replied. "I know everybody says this, but I think it was for the best. We really didn't have much going on. And what about you, Cowboy?"

Resting his arm on his lap, Mitchell rubbed his chin with his other hand. "Well, let's see," he said. "My first wife was...then there was Hilda and the kids..." Mitchell started to laugh. "No, I was just kidding. I just got the boot, too. I guess we really didn't have much either. Now that I think of it, it's amazing how long we stuck it out. I think she thought I was an under-achiever who was really going to bloom someday, a good investment. When I didn't, she just bagged it. In a way, I don't blame her. I was difficult, to put it mildly. At least she had the gumption to do something. I was just in a weird holding pattern. Anyway, we broke up, and then my father died, and Fiver and I came out here. We're gonna stick around, at least for a while, maybe longer." Breaking off part of his sandwich, Mitchell gave it to Fiver.

"Is he a vegetarian, too?" asked Nancy.

"No, but you'd be surprised," said Mitchell with a smile. "They eat a lot more vegetables than you'd think. He likes apples and eats my granola, and, by the way, I still can't find any good granola at the market. It's all sugary stuff."

Drinking the last of her wine, Nancy set the empty cup on the bench. "Hum, I'll have to see what I can do about that," she said. "It's not like the health food stores in the city where you can buy in bulk."

"Guess not," said Mitchell as he stood up from the table, and when he asked, "How far's your grandfather's farm from here?" Nancy started to beam.

"Oh, you want to see it?" she replied, trying to hide her enthusiasm. "Actually, it's just down the road a piece. It's beautiful. If you want, maybe we could go riding."

#

Chapter Forty Two

#

It was about a half hour's drive to Nancy's grandparent's farm, and pines lined the road as they wound down the other side of Silver Mountain. In between the trees they caught glimpses of the green farmland that covered the valley below. Gradually, the pines gave way to groves of slender aspens and small blue ponds. When they reached the valley floor, Fiver seemed to anticipate some destination, and began to inch his way forward between the seats. With a little nudging, he got Nancy to move over and share the front seat. Then, sitting almost on her lap, he seemed to smile as he looked out at the surrounding farmland. Reaching across in front of him, Nancy pointed. "That's it up ahead, at the base of the mountain," she declared happily. "See the little two-story house and the barn? Isn't it a sight!"

"It sure is," replied Mitchell. "It sure is."

Gearing down, Mitchell turned off the highway, and a little cloud of dust trailed after them as they headed up the long gravel road that led to the house. "Boy, it smells good out here," said Mitchell with an unrestrained smile. "And look how tall that alfalfa is, and look at those horses, aren't they something!" Sitting almost on Nancy's lap, Fiver leaned out and sniffed the air, and turning his head, he looked back at the two horses standing in the field.

When Mitchell brought the Healey to a stop in front of the house, Fiver, unable to contain his enthusiasm, barked excitedly. As they got out of the car, from inside the house an older woman with white hair pulled back a curtain, and with gentle but somewhat apprehensive eyes, she looked out the window. Then, recognizing Nancy, a joyful smile lit up her face. A moment later, opening the front door, she rushed out on the porch. "Oh my land!" she cried, wiping her hands on her apron. "It's my favorite grandchild come to visit." And, grinning, she came down the steps with open arms.

"Oh, it's so good to see you, Granny," exclaimed Nancy as they embraced, and Mitchell smiled when, over Nancy's shoulder, her grandmother cast an eye on him. Then, still beaming, Nancy took her hand and turned to Mitchell. "Granny, this is Mitchell, and that's Fiver over there." Mitchell extended his hand.

"My name is really Isabelle," said Granny, "but she's been calling me Granny for so long, it feels like my Christian name."

Mitchell glanced approvingly at Nancy. "Hi, Isabelle. I'm glad to meet you."

Smiling warmly, Granny looked down at Fiver. "My, he's a handsome one, isn't he? He reminds me of Ben. Josh nearly died himself, when old Ben died." Then, pausing, as if she had forgotten something, she glanced back at the house. "I'm baking some bread," she said as she looked back around. "Josh is out by the barn working on something. Why don't you go say hello, and I'll get the bread out of the oven. Oh, and I'll throw in a pie. I've got some apples. You can stay for dinner, can't you?"

With a shrug, Mitchell looked inquiringly at Nancy.

"Sure, we'd love that," she said as she took Mitchell by the arm. Smiling gratefully, Granny turned and headed up the front steps. "Isn't she wonderful?" said Nancy as they walked to the barn, and with his tail wagging ecstatically, Fiver ran along in front of them.

Arm in arm, Nancy and Mitchell were laughing when, coming around the corner of the barn, they saw Nancy's grandfather leaning over a large plow. With his back toward them, his curly gray hair was spilling down over the collar of his green plaid shirt. Sensing their presence, he straightened up, and when he turned around, Mitchell was struck by his large, soft blue eyes, and his smile was broad and unassuming.

"Well," he said with a hammer in one hand, "it's our long-lost grand-daughter." And throwing her arms around him, Nancy gave him a squeeze.

"Grandpa, this is Mitchell Black," she said as she stepped back, and after he stuffed his handkerchief back in his pocket, Grandpa extended his hand.

"Glad to meet you," he said. "I knew your father. He was a good man. I was sorry about his passing."

Pursing his lips, Mitchell nodded. "Thank you. It's good to meet you. Should I call you Josh?"

That'd be fine," he said. "You know, I used to go to your father's garage years ago. Old Red used to do a little work for me every once in awhile. He was a hell of a blacksmith. He used to work magic with that fire of his."

Mitchell put his hands in his back pockets. "I remember him from when I was a kid, but I never really knew him."

Seeming distracted, Grandpa looked over Mitchell's shoulder. "Now, who's that over there by the water trough?"

"Oh, that's Fiver!" exclaimed Nancy, and turning around, Mitchell called him over."Fiver, come here."

"Fiver? Is that like in a five-spot?" said Grandpa, and wagging his tail, Fiver came over and sat down by Mitchell.

"That's it," said Nancy. "Isn't he handsome."

With a warm sigh, Grandpa bent down and stroked Fiver's head. "He's a gentle soul, isn't he? Reminds me of old Ben a little."

Mitchell smiled. "Yeah, he's a great dog."

"I'll bet he is," said Grandpa. Then, standing up, he looked down at the plow.

"What are you working on?" asked Mitchell. "Maybe I could give you a hand."

Grandpa pushed on the handle of the old plow. "Oh, just a broken bolt."

Stepping closer to the plow, Mitchell ran his hand along the old wooden handle. "Do you still use this? You don't have a tractor?"

Grandpa laughed. "Aw, I had one once. But I got rid of it. The damn wheels where always packing the ground down when I tried to plow. And I didn't like chasin' after parts and gas all the time. Old Trix and I do a better job with the plow." Grandpa pointed to a big workhorse standing in the corral with two other smaller horses. "Don't have enough acreage here to use those big machines. You know, they're not really very efficient. Those things are made to mine the land, not farm it." Kneeling down, Grandpa inspected the old plow.

"You really don't have a tractor?" exclaimed Mitchell.

"Nope. You get too far away from the land when you're atop one of those things, and they belch out all that damned smoke. The stuff that comes out of old Trix is a lot better for you and the land!"

Mitchell smiled. "You use the horse manure for fertilizer?"

"Sure do. It comes with the horse. It's free, horse shit is one of God's gifts. He moves in mysterious ways, you know." Grandpa's eyes sparkled as he laughed irreverently. Then, picking up his hammer, he tapped on the plow. "Listen," he said between taps. "Why don't you kids saddle up Gypsy and Sunny, and take them for a ride. By the time you get back, it'll be evening, and Isabelle will have some dinner ready."

Mitchell at Nancy. "Sounds good to me."

Smiling, Grandpa stood up and set his hammer on the plow. "You ride, don't you?" he said to Mitchell.

"Yeah, I do. I grew up on a horse."

Grandpa squinted as he scrutinized Mitchell for a second. Then he said. " The horses are in the barn. Why don't you ride Sunny, he's a chestnut gelding, and Nancy, you take Gypsy. The saddles are in the tack room."

In the barn, still uncertain but curious about horses, Fiver watched intently while Mitchell put the saddles on. Always keeping a safe distance, he studied them from every angle. When finally he seemed satisfied that they were just big and not something to be particularly frightened of, he lay down on the ground, and he was calm when Mitchell led the horses out of the barn. But moments later he was completely surprised when Mitchell swung up into the saddle. Crouching down, he began to bark, and before Mitchell realized what was happening, he ran, and with a great leap, tried to jump up to him. Mitchell caught him with his free hand, and as the horse spun and reared, he pulled Fiver close to his side. "Whoa!" he yelled, pulling the reins in tight. "Whoa, easy." Then, with the horse still shying and sidestepping, he swung down and set Fiver on the ground. "You can't ride," he said as he knelt down. "No, you stay on the ground."

"That was something!" yelled Nancy from atop the palomino mare. "What was that about?"

"Oh, Fiver just thought we were both gonna ride," replied Mitchell as he put his foot in the stirrup. "This is all new to him."

Sitting on his haunches, Fiver watched Mitchell swing back up into the saddle. Then, relaxing, he seemed to understand and accept the situation. As they left the corral, he ran along in front of them, and out in the pasture, he was soon engrossed in the new world before him. Occasionally he'd look back and seem to still question the relationship between Mitchell and his horse. Then, whirling, he would run on ahead of them.

On the other side of the pasture, a gate opened up to a trail that led up from the base of the mountain. Swinging down from his horse, Mitchell got off and lifted the wire noose that held it shut.

"There's a little lake up there," said Nancy as she rode through the gate. "If we just follow this trail, we'll be there in about half an hour. It's kind of steep. Do you wanna go?"

With his horse behind him, Mitchell closed the gate and dropped the wire noose back over the pole. "Yeah, let's go," he said as he swung back up on his horse. "C'mon, Fiver."

At first, the trail was wide and well worn, but soon it got rockier as it got steeper, and after a while the horses had to be careful where they stepped. With their shoes clicking on some of the rocks, their heads bobbed up and down as they climbed. Running along in front, almost skipping like a child, Fiver jumped over the larger boulders. "Isn't it wonderful?" said Nancy as she looked back over her shoulder at Mitchell. "I mean, the air is so clean and fragrant, and the horses, aren't they great!"

Smiling, Mitchell leaned forward in his saddle. "Yeah, it's good to be here," he said as they approached a flat place where the trail widened a bit. "I haven't felt this good in a long time." Looking back over her shoulder, Nancy smiled as she passed a huge boulder lying just off the trail. Seeming to be wary of the boulder, her horse shied, and then with a quick step went on up the trail. Behind them, sniffing the air, Mitchell's horse whinnied nervously, and with his head falling from side to side, he followed along.

The trail got even steeper as they approached the top, and the horses were pulling hard when they climbed the last fifty yards. Then suddenly, from beneath some overhanging trees, the trail seemed to burst upon a small pond that was surrounded by deep grass and tall, white aspens. Reining her horse to a halt, Nancy waited for Mitchell to catch up.

"Isn't it beautiful," she declared, and with Fiver trotting along beside him, Mitchell brought his horse up beside her.

"It sure is," he said. "I'm glad you brought me up here."

As they sat on their horses at the edge of the clearing, Mitchell and Nancy looked on while Fiver trotted down to the pond. After taking a drink, he put one paw in and then the other, and then taking a few steps, he gradually eased into the deeper water. About thirty yards out in the water, there was a duck.

"Is he going after the duck?" asked Nancy.

"I don't think so," said Mitchell as he swung down from his horse. "I think he's just cooling off. Shall we stretch our legs a bit?"

Mitchell tied the horses to one of the aspen trees, and then hand in hand, he and Nancy headed down to the pond. When they got to the edge of it, Fiver was just getting out, and the water was still pouring from his coat when he approached them.

"Uh oh," said Mitchell. But before he could say or do anything else, Fiver shook, and cold water sprayed all over them. In shock, Nancy screamed, and for a moment she pouted while Mitchell laughed. Then, chagrined, she began to laugh. Then Mitchell moved closer, and looking up at him, she put her arms around his neck. Falling quiet, Mitchell looked down at her. "It is nice up here," he said. And slowly, with searching eyes, they kissed. When their lips parted, Nancy looked away for moment. Then softly pushing on his chest, she stepped back.

"Aw, you're all wet, Cowboy," she said. "C'mon, we'd best get back to the bunkhouse. They'll have the grub on pretty soon."

On the way down, the trail seemed steeper than before, and the horses rocked back and forth as they found their way along. With Fiver a few steps in front of him, Mitchell rode in front, and they were just coming to the place where the trail flattened out when hearing Fiver growl, Mitchell rose up in his saddle. Before him, he saw Fiver fall into a low crouch with his teeth bared. As he reined his horse to a stop, he motioned to Nancy behind him. Then Fiver, still crouched, as if he were stalking something, took a step forward and then froze. Motionless, with the hair on his back standing up, he was locked onto something, and whatever it was, it seemed to be behind the large boulder just off the trail.

Searching the trees for any sign of movement, Mitchell felt a surge of potential danger race through him. Whinnying, his horse stepped backward, and behind him Nancy held her reins tightly as the palomino began to prance. Sensing the threat, Nancy's eyes got big and round. Then Fiver began to inch forward, and his growl got louder as he approached whatever it was that was behind the boulder. With his horse shying and stepping to the side, Mitchell reined him tight.

"Whoa, take it easy," he whispered. Then, swinging down, he led the horse toward the boulder, and peering over the top of it, he saw Fiver crouching down, and there was something in the bushes in front of him, something brown and red. Then, with a grimace, Mitchell realized what it was, the bloody carcass of a deer. Its neck and belly had been torn open, and some of his entrails were exposed and pulled out. Most of the hindquarter was gone. "It's a fresh kill," thought Mitchell. "It's not more than a few minutes old."

Continuing to growl and bare his teeth, Fiver seemed less occupied by the deer than he was by something that he seemed to sense in the surrounding trees. Then Mitchell felt the hair on his arms stand up, and like Fiver, instinctively, he too searched the trees for any sign of movement. When he saw no movement or evidence of anything in the trees, he turned back to his horse, and lifting the reins over his head, he quickly swung up in the saddle.

"Fiver, let's go!" he said sternly, but Fiver ignored him, and with his eyes still locked on the surrounding trees, he bent down and sniffed the dead deer. With a look that was filled with primordial questions, he glanced up at Mitchell. Then slowly, still scanning the trees, he backed away, and while Mitchell stared down at the mutilated deer, Fiver padded off down the trail. A few yards away he stopped, and sitting on his haunches, he waited patiently for Mitchell and Nancy to catch up.

Bewildered, Mitchell kept looking at the awful spectacle in front of him. When he finally looked up, he saw Fiver down the trail, and looking back at him, he seemed perplexed by Mitchell's inability to move on, and cocking his head, he let out a sharp bark. A moment later, reining his horse back onto the trail, Mitchell rode past the big boulder, and looking over his shoulder, he waved to Nancy to come on behind him.

"What is it?" she whispered as loud as she could.

"There's a dead deer," said Mitchell in an intentionally calm voice. "It's an ugly sight. If it will upset you, don't look at it."

Giving her horse some rein, Nancy edged forward. "Why didn't we see it on the way up?" she asked more loudly.

"It wasn't there then," shouted Mitchell. "It's a fresh kill. I don't know what got it, maybe a bear or a cat or something. But I didn't think there were any mountain lions left up here."

Gripping her reins tightly, Nancy prodded her horse, and coming to the boulder, she saw the legs of the deer protruding out from behind it. Almost instinctively, her eyes followed them up to the bleeding belly. "Oh my God!" she cried out. "How terrible!"

"Watch the trail," yelled Mitchell. "Watch the trail. The horses could panic if there's a cat or a bear around here."

With tears welling up in her eyes, Nancy forced herself to look away, and prodding her horse, she wiped her eyes and rode on.

When they got back to the pasture at the base of the mountain, the sun was just about to set. Swinging down from his horse, Mitchell opened the gate. "That's too bad about the deer," he said as he watched Nancy ride through. "Nature's beautiful," he said, "but she's a cold-hearted bitch."

Looking down, Nancy watched Mitchell close the gate, and forcing an acknowledging smile, she leaned forward in her saddle. "C'mon, I'll race you home."

Swinging up in his saddle, Mitchell gave his horse some rein. "Let's go," he said in a sharp whisper, and in an instant his horse bolted forward, and with Fiver barking as he ran along beside them, Mitchell and Nancy galloped across the pasture.

After they had watered and unsaddled the horses, Mitchell and Nancy brushed them down. Then Mitchell let them loose in the corral. As they came up the front steps to the house, Mitchell was boasting about winning the race across the pasture. Granny greeted them at the door.

"Hurry up, you kids," she said, smiling. "The food will get cold."

"We'll be right there," said Nancy, and with Fiver a step behind them, they walked through the doorway hand in hand. "Kids, huh," laughed Mitchell with a smile, "nice to be a kid again," and then from behind them, Fiver barked. When they turned around they saw Granny still holding the door open. On the porch, with a concerned expression on his face, Fiver was sitting back on his haunches.

"You too," said Grandma, gesturing with her head. "Come in," and looking to Mitchell and then back to Granny, Fiver stood up and proudly trotted through the door. "Now that's one sensitive dog," said Grandma as she closed the door. "He's got better manners than most of the men around here."

At dinner, Granny was the last one to sit down, and like a cornucopia, the table was overflowing with a variety of brightly colored vegetables. In the middle of it, a heaping bowl of mashed potatoes stood next to a red serving plate stacked high with yellow corn. Next to the corn there were some rolls, hot out of the oven.

"It's the best I could throw together," said Granny as she straightened her apron on her lap. "But we've got apple pie and ice cream for dessert. Josh, why don't you start by passin' the biscuits."

Grandpa set two of the rolls on his plate. "Well, how was the ride?" he asked as he held the plate of biscuits in front of Mitchell.

"It's beautiful country up there," said Mitchell, lifting one of the rolls from the plate. "The leaves are just startin' to turn up on top." Taking the plate of rolls, Mitchell held them while Nancy set one on her plate. "Good horses, too," he said. "Climbed right up there."

Grandpa poured some gravy over mashed potatoes. "Did you see any deer? There's usually a few up there by the pond."

Dropping his head, Mitchell glanced over at Nancy. "Well, we saw one, but he was dead."

Grandpa looked up from his plate. "Dead?"

"Yeah, it was kinda strange. It looked like he'd just been killed. I guess we scared off whatever got him. But he was pretty chewed up."

Grandpa's long gray eyebrows pulled down. "It's that cat. Goddamn! I told ya there was a big cat up there, Isabelle! I heard him cryin' the other night. I've seen his tracks!"

Waving the big spoon from the mashed potatoes, Isabelle rebuked him. "Josh, you watch your language."

Mitchell smiled at Granny's injunction. "I didn't think there were any cats left around here," he said. "Maybe it's a bear, huh?"

Grandpa took a bite out of his corn. "Naw," he said. "A bear wouldn't take down a healthy deer. Those were cat tracks I saw. I bet she's a beauty."

Sitting next to Mitchell, Nancy's expression was becoming increasingly troubled as she listened to the conversation. "Well, whatever it was," she said somewhat defiantly, "it was terrible what it did. If I were God, I might have stopped making creatures when I got to things like deer, and rabbits, and horses, and maybe elephants, and chipmunks. Nice, kind vegetarians would have sufficed."

Smiling, Grandpa set his ear of corn down. "You know," he said, "without predators, all those nice vegetarians would've devoured the planet in no time. This place'd be like the surface of the moon. There'd be nothing growing."

Nancy popped her chin forward. "Well, if I were God, I could have gotten around that problem. I'd be all-powerful, you know."

Grandpa chuckled. "All-powerful? Well, I've never seen anything like that around here. Not in my time. Everything I've ever laid eyes on always had to give way to something else eventually, the rain to the sun, the summer to winter. It's always that way. Nothing's all-powerful, everything changes." Grandpa set his fork down. "If God's all-powerful, he must be a lonely old devil. What the hell would you do with nothing to come up against, nothing to push against!"

Mitchell smiled as he looked to Grandpa and then to Nancy. "That's how some people define him," interjected Nancy somewhat playfully, "all-powerful and all-knowing."

Grandpa eased back and wiped his mouth with his napkin. "Ah, that's just those Sunday mornin' television preachers. They offer you all that so you'll drop all your change when they pass the hat."

Isabelle scowled at him. "Someday that blasphemous mouth of yours is going get you in real trouble! God is all-powerful, and wonderful," she said curtly.

Grandpa shrugged. "Now, Isabelle. It could be that he just did the best job he could with what he had. I mean, how do we know? The rest is up to us."

Standing up, Granny shook her head. "You know, he always talks about God like he's just another guy living down the road a piece," she said. "I'm surprised he doesn't get struck by a bolt of lightning. God's certainly more patient than I am. I'll go get some more rolls."

With unquestionable love in his eyes, Grandpa watched Granny leave the room. Then, breaking open one of the rolls, he said, "Maybe he is all-powerful. If he is, and omniscient and all that, he probably created us just to kill the loneliness. Can you imagine what that would be like? Knowing everything, everything that was and will be. Hell, you'd go mad. Maybe that's why he created us the way are, just to kill the loneliness and boredom. Lots of people have children for the same kinda' reasons." Hearing his final world on the matter, Mitchell couldn't help but laugh aloud, and Grandpa chuckled while he buttered his roll.

Still smiling, Mitchell looked down, and at his feet he saw Fiver curled up on the floor. As he looked up, Nancy passed him the corn. Then, coming back into the dining room, Granny put some more hot rolls on the table. After setting a piece of corn on his plate, Mitchell held the plate for Grandpa, and as Grandpa reached up to take one of the smaller ears, Mitchell noticed a jagged scar that ran along the underside of his arm. "Boy, that's quite a scar on your arm," he said. "How did you get that?"

Turning his arm over, Grandpa looked at the scar. "I got that in Germany. A jeep I was in hit a mine."

Mitchell buttered his corn. "Were you hurt bad?"

"No, just blew me out and tore up my arm and my leg," said Grandpa as he shook some salt on his corn. "You know, I served under Red, the guy who used to work at your dad's place. He was our company commander. He's the one that told me about this place. That's how I came here. You know, he hated Patton. Said Patton didn't care about his men, and he got a lot of 'em killed that didn't have to."

Grandpa took a bite of his corn. Then, wiping his mouth with his napkin, he said, "Red always let the tanks and the planes do most of the fighting. He never sent you over the top if he didn't have to. He was a good man, a smart man. Kinda' lonely, though." Grandpa raised his eyebrows. "You know, it was our machinery that won the war," he said flatly. "It wasn't guts or any of that John Wayne stuff. Christ, the Japanese had guts. They were fanatical as hell."

Isabelle frowned. "Josh, you mind your language!"

Glancing at Isabelle, Grandpa waved his fork as he went on. "We had better planes and better tanks, better ships, better flamethrowers. We blew them out of the water. Then we ended the thing with the bomb."

Nancy set her napkin down on the table. "Do you think that's how the world will end?" she said plaintively. "In war, maybe a nuclear Armageddon?"

Pouring some more gravy over his biscuits, Grandpa shook his head. "I don't know, maybe. But, I'd like to think we learned something."

"The Bible says the world will be destroyed by fire," replied Nancy.

"I know. A lot a people make that connection," said Grandpa as he cut a biscuit with the side of his fork. "But if you want my opinion, I think a slow burn is more likely. Maybe that's what they're predicting in the Bible, pollution and smoke killing everything." Leaning back in his chair, Mitchell marveled at the rush of ideas that suddenly collided in his mind. Interjecting, he said, "You know, they say we're depleting the ozone layer, and it could have disastrous effects. They say we'll have more skin cancer, and there's the greenhouse effect. It really is a slow burn, and if it goes too far, there'll be no way to stop it."

Setting his fork down on his plate, Grandpa sat back from the table. "People think with all this new technology you get something for nothin', and you don't. It's like a guy who invents a new labor-saving device, a high-powered can opener or something. Then, in the next breath, he says that this new labor-saving device will create jobs. Now think about that! A labor-saving device that creates jobs, more work!"

Staring at Grandpa, Mitchell grinned. "It's an oxymoron, isn't it, and what you're saying is that the machines really don't make us more efficient, do they."

"Hell no!" said Grandpa. "People confuse efficacy with speed. In reality, speed takes more energy. Efficiency is all about how much energy consumed. Hell, the animals are more efficient than we are. They don't waste anything. We consume energy all day long. We have to have hot water and heated homes and airplanes..." Grandpa threw his hands in the air. "And air conditioning. We use more energy just getting up in the morning than an animal probably uses in a month."

When Isabelle set the apple pie on the table, it was piping hot. "Boy, doesn't that smell good!" exclaimed Mitchell.

"I'll get the ice cream and the silverware," said Nancy as she stood up.

Then Grandpa looked over at Mitchell. "Were you ever in the service?"

With some apprehension in his eyes, Mitchell shook his head. "No, I wasn't. I was in college during Nam. When they finally had the lottery for the draft, my number didn't come up."

Rubbing his chin, Grandpa looked thoughtfully at Mitchell. "That's good," he said finally. "That was a bullshit war. Were you a radical back then?"

Wondering how loaded that question was, Mitchell studied Grandpa's eyes before he replied. "Well, I did demonstrate against it," he said flatly. "And I did campaign for Eugene McCarthy. I liked him. Then they killed Robert Kennedy and it was all over."

In an accepting silence, Grandpa nodded at Mitchell, and then Nancy came up behind him and set some pie à la mode on the table in front of him.

"The twentieth century's not everything it's cracked up to be," Grandpa said wryly. "Families get knocked around, torn apart. You ever read Steinbeck's *The Grapes of Wrath*? He had it down, farmers caught between the big companies and the government, and preyed upon by the banks. Then the land gave out, and the big companies and the banks didn't give a shit about the land, let alone the people. Those big institutions don't have any respect for the land."

Listening intently, Mitchell interjected. "The land?" he said inquisitively.

"Right, the land," said Grandpa outspokenly. "Those politicians are always tryin' to make a religion out of the government, patriotism and all, and yet they don't respect the land. A religion or a government that's got no concern for the land is barren, literally. Without it, they're just a sham, a lot of hustlers selling snake oil. It's like a family without parents. There's no real authority. The authority comes from the land. From dust to dust, that's what it says!"

As he stared down at his pie, some things that Mitchell had wondered about for a long time started to merge into a new clarity. "Some of the Indians had a deep respect for the land," he said when he looked up.

"Sure they did!" said Grandpa with a laugh. "Hell, even the cavemen knew that. They at least had enough sense to worship animals and the land, and the water. That's the real mystery in life. That's the miracle."

Mitchell was about to say something when Nancy stood behind him and put her hands on his shoulder. As Mitchell looked up at her, Grandpa leaned over and pointed down at Fiver. "Look," he said, "he's dreaming." On the floor, Fiver was sound asleep, and with his feet twitching, he was making little moaning noises. "Old Ben used to do that," said Grandpa. "I think he was always chasin' rabbits or something. It's amazing, isn't it? They're just like people sometimes."

"It's not that they're like us," said Mitchell. "What's important is that we're like them, and we don't realize it, or we just forgot it. It's amazing how we fail to see that." Then, ever so lightly, Nancy softly stroked the back of Mitchell's neck. "And life is the stuff that dreams are made of, and 'tis rounded by a sleep,'" she said softly.

Later in the evening, while Nancy and Isabelle chatted in the living room, Grandpa and Mitchell were in the kitchen doing the dishes. Almost like a museum exhibit, the walls were adorned with pots and pans and all kinds of old-fashioned hand-operated kitchen gadgets and appliances that were clearly still in use. "What plans have you got for the future?" asked Grandpa as he rinsed off a bowl.

Mitchell was wiping off a plate when he replied. "You know, I'm not sure," he said, "but it's been good here so far. I came out here to get away from the city for a while. I guess I was starting to burn out. You ever live in a good-sized city?"

Grandpa was attacking a pan with a scouring pad. "Yes, I tried it for a while," he said. "When I was younger. Then I went to college for a time. But when I got back from the war, I'd seen all the cities I cared to, or what was left of them." Scrutinizing the pan, Grandpa continued to scrub while he talked. "I'm better off here," he said. "I make a difference here. I'd be nothin' in the city. Out here I have some clout, and I couldn't take one of those jobs where you do the same thing over and over again. That's not right." Grandpa held the pan up and then set it in the rinse water. "And workin' for somebody else, I couldn't handle that. Out here, it's up to me, and every day's different. I think that keeps me alive. And all the work in the city is paperwork and sales and on phones, people, people, people. I tried some of that too. Just got fat, and sicker and weaker.""I know," said Mitchell sympathetically. "That's why they have those spas and gyms that people belong to."

Grandpa laughed and shook his head. "Wouldn't I be a sight in some of those tights, running in place on a treadmill? That all seems so damned ridiculous to me, to stand there and work and sweat and really not get a damn thing done, not produce anything, it's unnatural, never heard the likes of that."

Mitchell laughed. "Well, I don't know," he said. "That's about all you can do when you're at a desk somewhere or in an office all day."

Nodding, Grandpa let the water out of the sink. "You know what else bothers me about the city?" he said as he dried his hands with a towel. "All you really see there is your own reflection. I mean, everything there is man-made. Man, man, man, that's all you see. Television, movies, buildings, it's all man, man, man. I guess some people like that. But out here you get to see things that are nonman, and to me that's a hell of a lot more interesting. The city's kinda artificial, like the food you get there."

After the dishes were done, everyone retired to the living room, and as they sat down, Mitchell marveled at an old upright piano that sat against the wall. Built out of African mahogany, it was quite striking. "Nice piano," he said. "I think they call this tigerwood, don't they?"

"Sure do," said Nancy. "It's the black stripes." Then she asked him if he would play.

"Oh, I don't know," he said, but after some prodding, he sat down and played a ballad, then some blues, and a little bit of stride, and finally an up-tempo boogie-woogie that Grandpa really liked. Nancy beamed when he finished.

It was late in the evening when Mitchell and Nancy decided to leave. When Mitchell fired up the Healey, Isabelle and Josh were standing together on the porch. "Aren't you going to put the top up?" yelled Granny. "You'll freeze going over the mountain."

"No, she's got a good heater," yelled Mitchell, and with Fiver sitting between them, they waved as they pulled away.

"Your grandpa is somethin' else," said Mitchell as he turned on the heater. "You know, they say you can't make money farming like that. They say you have to have a big place with lots of big machinery."

"Oh, they do OK," said Nancy as she slid down in the seat to avoid the cold. "Granny told me that Grandpa was raised on an Amish farm. But I guess he really was a hell-raiser when he was a kid. His parents didn't know what to do with him. She said he left home when he was eighteen, and he was too proud to go back. Made his fortune after the war, in mining or something like that. Nobody really knows, but he made a stash and then moved here."

"That makes sense," said Mitchell as they turned onto the highway. "The Amish are the only ones that can make a go of farming like that. Did you see all those old utensils in the kitchen? Nothing electric in there, not even a toaster."

"I know," said Nancy, and then, looking first at Nancy and then at Mitchell, Fiver eased into the backseat and laid down. As they drove, Nancy took Mitchell's arm and snuggled up against his shoulder. "It was quite a day, wasn't it. Granny says that Grandpa writes during the winter. Holes up in a room upstairs in the attic."

Chapter Forty Three

Mitchell and Fiver slept in on Sunday morning, and the sun was well up in the sky when the two of them headed out for their morning walk. As they walked, Mitchell was thinking about the farm and Grandpa and Isabelle. Then suddenly, Fiver, who had been trotting along at a leisurely pace, took off like a shot, and much to Mitchell's frustration, again he darted through the gates in front of Snyder's mansion. Mitchell cussed as he ran to catch up. "Dammit, Fiver, come back here." When he got to the gates, the scene was the same as before, and with garbage strewn everywhere, Fiver was smelling the ground and running in circles. "What the hell is it?" thought Mitchell as he looked through the gate. "Fiver, get over here!" he yelled, and then hearing a door open, he saw someone at the side door to the mansion. Still in his pajamas and a robe, a dark-haired man appeared on the porch. He grumbled bitterly when he saw the garbage strewn about the grounds. Then, seeing Fiver, he jumped from the porch, and looking around, he grabbed an empty beer bottle.

"Get out of here!" he shouted as he tossed the bottle, and, bouncing, the bottle broke just to the side of Fiver. Flinching and jumping sideways, Fiver turned and looked toward his assailant.

"C'mon, Fiver!" yelled Mitchell from the other side of the gate. "Get out of there!"

When he saw Mitchell, the man in the robe stopped and stared. Then, as if the sight of Mitchell added to his fury, he stooped over and grabbed another bottle. Then Fiver broke and ran toward the gate. "Get out of here!" yelled the man again, and then, just as Fiver stepped through the gate, another bottle crashed and broke on the driveway behind him. Wincing, Mitchell felt the broken glass and what smelled like beer splash across his pant leg, and in disbelief he looked at the incensed man. Standing beside him, Fiver addressed a bark and then a growl to the man. "Keep your damn dog out of here!" screamed the man, and then he turned and went back into the house, slamming the door behind him.

"You can't do that!" Mitchell said to Fiver as they headed up the lane. "What am I gonna do with you? He thinks you're getting into his garbage."

It was almost one o'clock when, after lunch, Mitchell knelt down and gave Fiver the last of his granola. While he watched Fiver eat, his thoughts returned to the day before, and he smiled as he envisioned the horses standing by the lake. Then the thought of Grandpa expostulating about the virtues of horseshit and Isabelle admonishing him increased his fondness for him. Then he could hear Nancy's laugh, and for a second, he could feel her head on his shoulder as they drove home. When Fiver finished the granola, he licked his chops. Then, coming over to Mitchell, he rubbed his head affectionately against Mitchell's leg. Bending down to him, Mitchell hugged him. "I love the Fiver," he said. "It's good, here, and we've got a lot to do, don't we."

On Monday, Mitchell started work on the old tow truck. "I wanna do her all up," he said to Tom. "I wanna strip her down and paint her while we've got the engine out. Do the whole bit."

Tom rubbed his forehead. "That's a lot of sanding."

"That's all right," replied Mitchell. "I'll do that part. I'll have her ready for Glen by the end of the week."

With a somewhat paternalistic smile, Tom gazed at Mitchell. Then, patting the rusted fender of the old truck, he said, "All this for the planet, huh?"

With some help from Tom, Mitchell unbolted the hood of the truck. By lunchtime, they had the engine sitting on the workbench. At the end of the day, there were parts stacked everywhere, and the old tow truck, bereft of its hood and engine, stood naked without bumpers or chrome. "I think maybe black fenders and a tan body," said Mitchell as he stood back and assessed the rather helpless-looking truck. "Whad'ya think? They used to paint 'em like that, didn't they?"

Tom tapped the palm of his hand with a wrench. "Yeah, she was two-toned when she was new."

For the rest of the week, Mitchell worked hard on the truck, and he met Nancy for lunch or dinner almost every day. On Saturday evening they went to a movie, and afterward they went to Mitchell's to listen to records. In the kitchen, Nancy pulled open the cupboards in search of some wine-glasses. "Oh, that's good," she mumbled.

"What's good?" said Mitchell as he twisted a corkscrew into a bottle of red wine.

"None of your glasses match," said Nancy.

Mitchell stopped turning the corkscrew. "Why is that good?" he said as he began to pull on the cork.

"Oh, I just never get along with people who have glasses and dishes that are all in perfect sets. You know, where everything matches."

Smiling, Mitchell popped the cork from the bottle. "Well, you don't have to worry," he said. "It's all mix-and-match around here. Shall we go listen to some music?"

In the living room, Fiver was lying down on his side in the middle of the floor. While Mitchell thumbed through some albums, Nancy sipped her wine from an old Coca-Cola glass and perused the bookcase. Coming to a large volume of Shakespeare, she stopped and ran her finger down the back of it. "Have you read much of the Bard?" she asked.

Mitchell was pulling an album out of its jacket. "I've read some of the major plays, but it's been a while," he replied as he set the record on the turntable.

"I think he's wonderful," said Nancy, still gazing at the bookcase, "and I love the language."

When Mitchell rose up from the stereo, a soft, muted trumpet began to play in the background. "Sometimes I think he said it all," he said. "At least, existentially, you can't go much past *Hamlet* and *King Lear*. If I could only take one book with me to a desert island, it would be Shakespeare."

"My favorite was *The Tempest*," said Nancy. "I always thought it was wonderful that Prospero could be so old and tired and yet have so much faith and still see so much beauty in the world. I think that was Shakespeare's final statement."

"Boy, you do know your stuff," said Mitchell as he picked up his wineglass. "I couldn't remember that name."

As he watched Nancy carefully scan the bookcase, Mitchell sipped his wine. "I guess I just read the tragedies," he said. "But it always struck me how the theme and the plot usually revolved around some character telling a lie, a lie that gets hatched out of someone's unchecked ambition."

Turning away from the bookcase, Nancy looked thoughtfully at Mitchell. "Hmmm," she said. "I can see that."

Sitting down on the arm of the couch, Mitchell poured himself some more wine. Then staring out past his glass, he said, "It's all in the language, or how we use it, good and evil, I mean." And, standing in front of him, Nancy watched Mitchell pause and think. "Earth to Mitchell," she said finally. "This is Earth to Mitchell. Come in."

"Oh...I'm sorry," said Mitchell, looking up at her. "Sometimes I do that. Lately, I mean when I'm here, I sit around and read and think and drift off sometimes."

Flashing her eyes over the top of her glass, Nancy sipped her wine. "And why does a man who thinks so much about language and truth work with his hands all day?"

"I don't know," replied Mitchell. "Maybe it keeps me grounded, and I get some peace of mind from it." Pausing, Mitchell looked down at his wine, and in his mind, his thoughts seemed to bicker and battle among themselves. Then, almost to himself, he said, "When you're doing one thing and thinking about something else, you're off center, estranged from yourself, alienated. That's how I was when I was a broker, and you know when you're like that, you're living a lie, and no amount of money can get you past it. You know it's all bullshit, and deep down you know you're bullshit. Then it's just like in one of Shakespeare's plays, and pretty soon the screw turns, and no matter what you do, it haunts you. You know, like Macbeth or any of those characters. Then one day you realize that you're trapped, and that you made the cage yourself."

With her eyes growing sad, Nancy looked down at Mitchell. "Everybody does that to a certain degree," she said.

"I know," replied Mitchell. "But, it's no good, and besides, I just wasn't good at it."

Holding her wine at her waist, Nancy looked at Mitchell with a sorrowful curiosity. "I think you're a little hard on yourself."

"Not really," said Mitchell, looking back at her. "You just can't be anything, and you sure can't be free, if you're not honest, at least with yourself. That's all I'm saying. No big thing."

Nancy sighed. "It sounds very lonely, living a lie, I mean."

"Yeah, that too," replied Mitchell in a soft voice. "Can you imagine what it would be like to be a spy, how lonely that would be? You know, that's how it is for some people. That's how it was for me. I mean, nothing was ever spontaneous. That was too risky. After a while, you play the role so much that you don't really have any self of your own." Looking down, Mitchell laughed ruefully. "How the hell can you be spontaneous if you don't really exist, if it's all a façade?"

Finishing the last of his wine, Mitchell set his glass down on the coffee table. "What gets to you," he said dryly, "is that in the end, you start to fear the truth, and that's the nightmare of it. That's when it gets hellish. That's why some guys kill themselves when they go broke.""Oh, the tangled webs we weave," said Nancy, smiling down at him. Then, setting her glass on the coffee table, she bent down, and placing her hands under Mitchell's chin, she raised his head and kissed him. "To thine own self be true," she whispered, and kissing him again, she took his hands, and moving to the couch, she pulled him to her. "You should lose the guilt," she said tenderly. "You're OK. You're just my cowboy in King Arthur's court, all troubled and tortured."

Later in the evening, after more wine and music, and lots of intimate laughter, Nancy rose and, taking Mitchell by the hand, headed to the bedroom. "I don't supposed you have some extra pajamas?" said Nancy, and lying on the floor, Fiver's eye's narrowed as he watched them leave.

In the bedroom, Mitchell smiled and opened the closet door. After a pause, he pulled out one of his freshly pressed blue work shirts. "How's this?" he said, and taking the shirt, Nancy stepped into the bathroom. When she came out, she pulled the large shirt down over her nakedness and tiptoed over to the bed and slid in beside Mitchell. "Perfect," she whispered. "Perfection."

In the morning, Mitchell awoke with Nancy intertwined in his embrace, and for a long time he luxuriated in the warmth of her presence. Moving closer to him, she kissed him and pulled him close. Then he noticed Fiver sitting up next to the bed looking on curiously. Nodding back at him, as if to say, "all right, we'll get up," he looked back at Nancy. Then, lightly kissing her forehead, he said, "You know, making love with you like this, it makes me...well, it makes me want a big bowl of granola, what do you say?"

Laughing, Nancy pushed him away and looked over at Fiver. "He's impossible, isn't he," she said. "How do you put up with him? Or is this your idea?"

In the kitchen, Mitchell brewed some coffee and made some toast. Then he put another record on the stereo. As the three of them ate granola, the slow, heavy cadence of an old blues song filled the room. The singer's voice was rough but rich and resonant. "Well, so long, oh, how I hate to see you go," he sang.

"Who's that?" asked Nancy as she reached for her granola.

"That's Elvis," said Mitchell with barely disguised pride. "He had some pipes, didn't he."

Looking up at him, Nancy listened carefully. "Sexy stuff, I didn't know he could sing the blues like that.""Well, that's not his commercial stuff," replied Mitchell. "You know, rock 'n' roll is basically rhythm and blues mixed with country and gospel, and a little jazz, and Elvis helped it happen. I remember the first time I saw him. I was a just a kid, but suddenly I knew there was something that people weren't telling me, something deep and magical.""He was beautiful," said Nancy, "but he made some bad movies."

"That's true," said Mitchell as looked over at Nancy. "He did get lost. But that happened to lots of them, didn't it. A lot of 'em didn't make it. But, the music, the blues, rock 'n' roll, jazz, that's America's contribution to the world. The world owes us big time for that. The music was more honest and real."

Chapter Forty Four

Glen painted the tow truck on Monday of the following week, and by the end of the day, Mitchell had the bumpers and the chrome back on. On Tuesday morning they lowered the rebuilt motor into the engine compartment and it was after ten at night, when rising up from under the hood, Tom gave Mitchell the sign to start her up. "Here goes," said Mitchell as he stepped down on the starter button, and laboring against the physics of a virgin engine, the starter whined and moaned. "I don't think she's gonna do it!" yelled Mitchell. "She's too tight!" And just then the engine seemed to give, and suddenly, with a great commotion and a clattering of valves, it sprang to life. Holding onto the steering wheel, Mitchell beamed as he felt the power vibrate all around him.

"Check the oil pressure," said Tom as he leaned over the engine, and looking past the steering wheel, Mitchell's eyes fell immediately onto one of the old round gauges on the dash. As he watched, the heart-shaped needle trembled and then rose up.

"She's got thirty pounds at idle!" he called out.

Stepping back, Tom set his wrench on the workbench. "That's just right," he said. "Let her idle a bit, and we'll set the timing and the carburetor tomorrow."

Climbing out of the truck, with his hands in his back pockets, Mitchell marveled. "That's really incredible, making it come to life like that. Damn, that's something."

"Yeah, it's kind of like delivering a baby, isn't it?" said Tom as he wiped oil from his forearms.

Turning his head, Mitchell gave him a quizzical look. "Yeah, it's just like that. It's miraculous, isn't it?"

As he looked back to the truck, Tom pulled his cigarettes from his pocket, and tapping the pack on his palm, he spoke. "Sometimes I like working on the older ones. You have more to do with it. You know what's goin' on. With the new ones you have all that electronic stuff, and you're always following directions. Half the time you don't really know what you're workin' on. You just follow the instructions, you know, replace this or that. It used to be that a good mechanic could fix anything on a car, even make a part if he needed it. I mean, he knew it from stem to stern. Now we have technicians that just fix certain things." Stopping to lift a match to his cigarette, Tom exhaled and then shook the match. "I guess everything's more abstract nowadays. Even the lines on the new cars are all geometrical now. I've heard they're starting to design 'em with computers, you know."

Turning away from Tom, Mitchell gazed at the truck. "Not this one," he said proudly. "This one looks like a big puppy dog sitting here panting."

With the smoke from his cigarette drifting over his head, Tom smiled at Mitchell's fascination with the truck. Walking around it as if it were a priceless museum piece, Mitchell leaned over the front fender and gazed down in wonderment at the idling engine.

"It was kind of fun to resurrect the old gal," said Tom.

"And when we started her up, it was like magic," replied Mitchell, still gazing down at the engine. "Like that, you've created all the power." Mitchell snapped his fingers. "That's really incredible!" he exclaimed as he stood back. "That's the romance of it, isn't it? It's the power."

Chapter Forty Five

With Fiver on the seat beside him, it was cold on the drive home that night, and the warm air from the heater was gone before it got to Mitchell's arms. Fall was definitely just around the corner. Shutting off the engine in front of the house, Mitchell noticed something unusual on the front porch. From the car, it looked like a big bag of dry dog food. "Maybe somebody left me some potatoes," he thought as he climbed the front steps, and as he approached the bag, Fiver ran ahead of him and began to sniff it. Bending down beside him, Mitchell read the label: "Sunshine Granola," it said in big letters that were arched like a rising sun. "There must be twenty pounds of it," he thought, and standing up, he saw a small card sitting on top of it. Flipping on the porch light, he pulled the card from its envelope and read.

> I thought we might need this.
>> Should do us for a week or so!
>>> Ooo la la!
>>> Nancy

On their walk the next morning, Mitchell held Fiver by the collar until they were well past Snyder's mansion. Later, when they were on the highway heading to work, Mitchell noticed an unusual grinding sound coming from the engine of the Healey. "The throw-out bearing's getting bad," he thought, and when he pushed in on the clutch, it felt weak. Then something gave, and suddenly it was gone. There was nothing. With the pedal falling limply to the floor, he knew the clutch had had it. "Dammit!" he shouted, and revving the engine, he tried to push the shift lever out of fourth. From the passenger seat, Fiver looked over to see what was the matter.

As they went down the highway, Mitchell continued to fiddle with the shifter, and after some experimentation, he found that by revving the engine to just the right rpms, he could still shift without the clutch. They used to call it dry shifting, something he hadn't done since high school. As long as he didn't have to stop, he could make it to the garage, and by running two stop signs he did just that. When he got to the garage, unable to use the clutch, he turned off the key and brought the Healey to a bucking halt. Looking over from the gas pumps, Tom gave him a look. "Lost the clutch on the way in," said Mitchell as he got out. "I was hoping to get a few more miles out of her."

Opening the car door, Tom reached in and pushed on the limp clutch with his hand. "Yeah, she's gone, all right," he said as he closed the door. "You'll be driving the tow truck for a while."

"She needs tires, too," said Mitchell. "Actually, I'm surprised I got this far. I guess I've been running on imagination for a long time."

After Mitchell and Tom got the Healey inside the shop, Mitchell worked the rest of the day and then closed up. With keys in hand, in front of the station, he admired the old tow truck. "Pop would like this," he thought as he looked at the shiny new paint. Then, pulling the door open, he gestured for Fiver to jump in, and with Fiver situated on the passengers seat, he stepped up on the runningboard and slid behind the wheel. Inside, the sweet odor of the new paint mingled with the rich aroma of the old leather seats. "Yeah, Pop would like this," he whispered.

As he drove down the road, the image of his father stayed with him, and almost without thinking, he headed to the cemetery. Before he knew it, he found himself standing at the grave, while Fiver remained in the truck. As he looked down at some flowers that had long since wilted, he felt a deep ache of loss flow over him. He had the urge to say something, but nothing true came to him, no words to salvage things. Finally, after standing there for a considerable time, he shrugged his shoulders and said, "Hi, Pop. I hope you like the truck. I, ah...I know I got off course there for a while, and I knew you knew it. But you were patient, like you always are. So patient. I guess that's from working isn't it, fixing things. I didn't really appreciate that till now. It's a sign of strength. There's always options, huh. Anyway, I'm trying to get back to it. I really am. I don't know how it's going to work out. I miss you, Pop."

#

Chapter Forty Six

#

The next day Mitchell met Nancy for lunch at Lucille's. He arrived at the café before she did, and he left Fiver sitting in the cab of the truck. Mitchell was in one of the booths when she arrived.

"Where's the Healey?" she said. "I see Fiver's guarding the truck."

"Oh, she blew a clutch on the way in to work," said Mitchell. "I'll be driving the truck for a while. You like the paint job?"

"Yeah, I like the colors," she said as she slipped off her Levi jacket. "Warm earth tones. My compliments to the painter." Nancy smiled as she slid into the booth and grabbed a menu. "You guys always refer to your cars as 'shes.'"

Mitchell looked over the top of his menu. "It's true love," he said, smiling, "and it's a matter of respect. Makes 'em more than an 'it,' doesn't it?" Nancy glanced at her menu and then laid it down. "Could be," said Nancy playfully. "It's like putting a title on a painting, makes it more intimate and alive."

Putting his menu down, Mitchell sat back in the booth. After a thoughtful pause, he said, "Maybe if we made a habit of showing more respect for all the inanimate things, it might rub off on how we deal with the animate things."

Nancy turned her head slightly. "I know what you mean," she said. "Sometimes I get that feeling when I paint. When I paint, I get a sense of how sacred everything is, the simplest object, or the most mundane subject. Everything has a story in there somewhere."

"That's the way Native Americans see it," replied Mitchell. "Everything has a soul, everything is sacred."

"Ah," said Nancy excitedly, "you know, sometimes they have a farmer's market over in Thompson, and sometimes they have Indian powwows there."

"That would be fun," said Mitchell.

"Well, maybe we'll go," replied Nancy. "I've heard they had a good harvest this year, there'll be lots of fresh veggies."

"Hum," replied Mitchell, and for a second his countenance darkened, and reacting, Nancy said, "What's the matter?"

"Oh, nothing," said Mitchell, looking away.

"No, it's something," replied Nancy, "What is it?"

"Ah, it was just a word," said Mitchell. "'Harvest.' When I was at the slaughterhouse that day with Jesse, I told you about that—that's the word they use for killing the animals. They call it harvesting. Can you believe that?" With his eyes narrowing, Mitchell paused and thought for a moment. "I'm starting to see how that works," he went on, "you define something as different, not feeling, as an object, I guess, and then you can abuse it. The labels, they facilitate the abuse and carnage. You see it in racism and sexism and war; they all work on the same principle. Define something as 'the other' or as some kind of a threat, and then you can abuse them, kill them, and take their property, and still feel good about yourself."

"I know, I know," said Nancy, looking up. "I remember once I was reading a book about a bear, and in the book they described it as an 'it.' They said 'it' went down the river, not he or she, but 'it.' It's all built into the language, the prejudice, I mean."

"Boy, that's it, you're right!" Mitchell exclaimed excitedly. "It's built into the language, and it makes them the other."

Nancy tilted her head to one side while she thought. "It does depersonalize them, doesn't it, and it's built right into the grammar, and you don't even see it. The rules become automatic." Pausing, Nancy wrinkled her nose while she thought. "Painters have to fight that too, you know," she went on. "There are rules and techniques for painting, but if you're not careful, they'll stop you from painting what you see, and what you feel. The rules can blind you, limit your creativity. I've seen some perfectly executed paintings that said nothing, didn't move you at all."

Mitchell nodded. "Yeah, I can see that. There are musicians who are great technicians but can't put any soul into it. I guess it's about soul, isn't it, and some language can take the soul out of things, everything. The very word 'animal'—people use it as a put-down. And pig and chicken, they're used the same way, as put-downs, and all those stories about the big bad wolf. Hell, the wolves never killed anybody, and we wiped them out."

"Boy," said Nancy, looking lovingly at Mitchell, "you have been thinking a lot, haven't you, Cowboy." But before she could say any more, the waitress, who apparently had been waiting for an opening, finally intervened and asked if they were ready to order.

"I think so," said Nancy cheerfully. "I'll have a Coke and a cheese sandwich."

"And I'll have dead cow with a bun," said Mitchell wryly.

"What?" replied the waitress.

"Just kidding," said Mitchell, cocking his head. "No hamburger. I'll have a grilled tuna and a Diet Coke."

After she finished scribbling on her pad, the waitress raised an eyebrow and looked doubtfully at Nancy and then Mitchell. Then, shaking her head, she turned toward the kitchen.

"I think she thinks I'm a little weird," said Mitchell with a chuckle.

With a playful smile, Nancy raised her eyebrows. "Well?"

"I guess she's right," replied Mitchell with a laugh, and then slowly he became more somber. "I didn't mean to get carried away on all that stuff," he said. "Most of the time there's no one I can talk to about this stuff, and I guess I lay it on you pretty heavy. I'm sorry. I've got to learn to shut up."

"It's fine," said Nancy, and her eyes were warm and confident. "You know, you can tell me anything. That's one of the great things about us. We can talk about anything, anytime. We're free. Besides, I know your heart is good."

Unable to reply, Mitchell gazed back at her in silence. "Have you started anything, a new painting?" he said finally.

"I haven't painted for a while," she replied, "but I'm sketching in something. I think you'll like it. And I'm reading a book on van Gogh. Did you know he started out as a preacher? But the ministry threw him out when he really started living with the poor, you know, like Christ. Can you believe that?"

Mitchell was about to reply when he felt someone standing over them, and looking up, Mitchell saw his neighbor, Snyder, the man on the porch. Heavyset, in a suit and tie, with narrow, dark eyes set close together, he peered down at them.

"That your dog out there?" he asked forcefully. "You better keep him out of my yard or else."

Looking up at him, Mitchell's face started to redden, and his words were measured. "Listen," he said, "I don't think he's the one tearing up your garbage. He just sees it there on the ground and has to check it out. I think he can smell another animal, that's all. Maybe it's a raccoon or something."

"I don't think so," said Snyder. "You know, I can shoot him if he's on my property. That's the law."

"I don't care about the law," said Mitchell, and then suddenly he pushed himself up from the table and looked Snyder in the face. "But I'll tell you this," he retorted, and as he spoke he clenched his fist, and the rage in his eyes was undeniable. "You do that and you'll wish you were never born, you...and that'll be the last thing you do, got it? Don't you ever lay a hand on him!"

Truly surprised, Snyder stepped back, but his eyes were calculating and contemptuous, and for a moment the two men stared at one other like two dogs about to fight. Then Snyder smiled confidently. "Don't threaten me. I'll sue you for battery," he said coolly. Then, smiling condescendingly, he turned away, and straightening his tie, he headed to the door. After he left, Mitchell went to the doorway, and with a number of stunned patrons watching him, he looked out to see if Fiver was OK. In the truck, Fiver was looking out the window, while next to him, the gold Mercedes slowly backed up and then left. Then Mitchell felt Nancy tug at his sleeve. "Are you all right?" she said, and as he turned toward her, he saw an apprehension in her eyes that he had never seen before.

Chapter Forty Seven

When Mitchell got back to the garage, Tom was going over some bills in the office. Standing in the doorway, Mitchell studied him before he spoke.

"Well, I just had a run-in with one of our best customers," he said abruptly in a straightforward voice. "I don't think it's gonna help business."

Setting the bills on his desk, Tom leaned back in his chair. "Who was it?"

Mitchell shrugged. "It was Snyder."

Tom raised his eyebrows. "What happened?"

Looking down, Mitchell leaned against the doorjamb. "He got after Fiver," he said laconically, "and we got into it."

Tom picked the bills back up from the desk. "He'll be back," he said as he began to thumb through them. "He's a business man. We give him the most for his money, and the nearest shop is a hundred miles away. He's not going to let his pride cost him money. Besides, he might not even know who you are." Nodding, Mitchell turned to leave. Then Tom set the bills on his lap and shook his head.

At the end of the day, Mitchell moved the Healey into the garage. After everyone left, he removed the hood and started undoing the bolts that held the radiator. By ten o'clock, the radiator and the carburetors were lying on the workbench, and except for the bolts on the motor mounts, the engine was ready to come out. "I'll pull it in the morning," he thought as he cleaned his tools. Then the phone rang, and setting a socket wrench back in a tray of tools, he wiped his hands with an oil-stained rag and walked over to the phone.

"Oh, there you are," said Nancy in a playful voice.

Smiling, Mitchell leaned against the wall. "Yeah, I'm here. But after what happened at lunch, the question is, am I all here?"

Nancy laughed. "That's what I like about you. If you were together, I probably wouldn't have called. Those really squared-away types intimidate me, and that makes me lonely."

Looking down at the greasy rag in his hand, Mitchell chuckled. "So we'll be together in our un-togetherness. Yeah, we really make a great couple."

"I think so," said Nancy, still laughing. "Who else would tolerate all these horrible puns?"

Pulling the rag across his cheek, Mitchell chuckled. "You've got a point there," he said as he examined the rag. "Oh, and I meant to tell you, thanks for the granola. I think that should last us for a while."

Nancy laughed. "I hope not."

Laughing, Mitchell looked down at the floor, and then growing quiet, he said, "I do apologize for all that. I...uh...I lose it when somebody threatens Fiver. I'm not like that very often, but that guy Snyder gets to me. He's everything I detest, everything that's wrong with the world."

"I understand," said Nancy. "Don't worry about me. I just have one question."

"What's that?" asked Mitchell.

After a silence, Nancy laughed. "I wanna know if there's grease all over your face."

Chapter Forty Eight

I t was unusually dark outside when Mitchell locked up and climbed into the old tow truck. With Fiver curled up on the seat beside him, he started her up. Then absent-mindedly, he turned the worn chrome knob on the radio, and he was surprised when the pinkish-blue light behind the dial started to glow. "I didn't think it would still work," he thought, and crackling and screeching, the old radio sounded just like it should. Hearing the twanging voice of a country singer, Mitchell turned the knob in search of another station, and as he did, a strident collage of American culture spilled out from the radio. "Today the Russians announced...Get your Chevrolet at Thompson's...And when we get behind closed doors...With science the future is...The Yankees won today...Give your life to Christ, and the power of God can be yours."

When he arrived back at the house, a preacher on the radio was talking about the end of time, and how the cities were dying and full of sin, and how the day of reckoning was coming. With a click, Mitchell turned the radio off, and as the light in the dial faded, the preacher's voice slipped into oblivion. "It's all about power," thought Mitchell. "Everything's for sale, God, baseball, the future."

In the house, Fiver immediately jumped on the couch and lay down. Tired, yet somehow bothered, Mitchell tried to play the piano, but finding he wasn't really in the mood for it, he grabbed a magazine and sat down in his father's easy chair. As he thumbed through the magazine, his eyes fell on a stunning aerial photograph of downtown Los Angeles, replete with skyscrapers and a grid of busy streets. Minutes later he dozed off, but when the magazine fell to the floor, he woke up. "Let's go to bed," he said groggily to Fiver.

Following him to the bedroom, Fiver hopped up on the bed, and with his head lying on the pillow, he watched Mitchell get undressed. Then, sliding in from the other side, Mitchell pulled up the covers and gave him a hug. "I love the Fiver," he said. "Don't you think it's better here?" Raising one eyebrow, Fiver seemed to listen intently. "I love the Fiver," said Mitchell again, and as he drifted off, he heard a plane flying overhead, and soon after closing his eyes, he was flying high in the clouds above a city.

As the plane descended to the airport, the buildings got taller and taller, and to Mitchell's amazement, they seemed to multiply and grow even taller. Then, having somehow left the airport, he found himself standing on a downtown corner. With Fiver at his side, he was in a crush of people and streaking automobiles. The horns and screeching brakes made it almost impossible to think. Looking up at him, Fiver seemed to wonder why they were there, and wanting reassurance, he nuzzled Mitchell's leg. "It's all right," said Mitchell, stepping off the curb. "C'mon, we'll get outta here." But as they crossed the street, the crowd suddenly got thicker and more strident. Glancing up at Mitchell, Fiver's eyes were worried. Then, out of nowhere, a yellow bus, belching out black smoke, careened around a corner, and with the driver frantically motioning for them to get out of the way, it headed straight for them. Like a mother picking up her child, Mitchell scooped Fiver up and jumped to the opposite curb. As he held him in his arms, he felt the heat of the bus as it shot past them.

Turning around, Mitchell was panting as he watched the bus fly up the street. Then, before he could catch his breath, he heard a siren, and looking past the crowd, he saw the flashing lights of a shiny yellow truck coming toward them. Setting Fiver on the ground, he began to recognize the undulating sound of the siren. It was a truck from the pound, and there were two men inside. One of them was pointing at him. "You, with the dog," said a voice over a loudspeaker, "stay where you are!"

With the sea of people in front of him going by like a bulging river, Mitchell recoiled as he watched the truck pull to the curb. "Don't you know there's no room for animals anymore!" shouted one of the men as he got out of the truck. Then, behind him, another man in a blue uniform pulled a long pole from the rear of the truck, and Mitchell recoiled when he recognized what was on the end of it. It was a noose, a hangman's noose.

Glancing desperately back and forth between the sea of people and the approaching men, Mitchell grabbed Fiver by the collar, and pulling him, he fled into the flow of the crowd. In the midst of it, an old man with white hair stumbled and fell backward. He cussed as he went down, and then, like a wave, the sea of people swarmed over him. Then Mitchell tripped, but quickly he caught himself, and then, from the side, someone shoved him, and for a second he balanced precariously on one foot. As he fell backward, he pulled on Fiver's collar, and feeling the rough texture of cement scraping against his shoulders, he realized that he had fallen against a wall. When he looked up, he saw the incredibly tall concrete building that had stopped his fall. Without windows, completely nondescript, and only one huge, stainless-steel door, it shot up above the other buildings like a massive sepulcher.

As he looked down at Fiver, Mitchell nervously stroked him while he desperately tried to think. Then, from somewhere in the crowd, he heard the voices of the men from the pound. "There they are. Hey, you! Don't you know you can't resist?" one of them shouted, and an in instant, Mitchell grabbed Fiver by the collar and headed toward the steel door. Behind them, with the hangman's noose waving like a flag, their pursuers pushed and shoved their way through the teeming crowd.

Reaching the door, Mitchell pulled the handle down, and when the door flew open, he and Fiver tumbled forward into a cavernous room. It was then that he heard the deafening churning racket everywhere, gears grinding and shrill bells and buzzers going off at odd random intervals in the distance. Before him there was a tall metal structure that looked like another metal building inside the building. Along the outside of it, a labyrinth of ladders and scaffolding ran every which way. "It looks like a fire escape for the insane," thought Mitchell, and high over his head he saw something move, and looking up, he saw a man on one of the scaffolds. Wearing a white lab coat and a hard hat, the man was writing on a clipboard. Then a bell rang, and suddenly there were lots of men, and wearing white lab coats, they were all scurrying about in a maze. Like mice, they stopped here and there, and raising their noses up, they methodically read dials and gauges and then wrote down figures on their clipboards.

Backing away, Mitchell took Fiver by the collar and started to walk. Beside him, Fiver gazed back at the door where they had come in. Pulling back, he signaled his doubts to Mitchell. "No, we can't do that," said Mitchell as he dragged him on, and walking faster and faster, the two of them were soon running. Coming to the corner of the structure, Mitchell slid to a stop, and peering around it, he looked down a corridor that seemed like a narrow street between two giant skyscrapers. At the end of it there was a door with a green light flashing over it. "C'mon," he said to Fiver as he started to run down the corridor, "let's get outta here."

Mitchell was out of breath when they reached the door. Glancing at the flashing light, he frantically pulled on the handle, but the door wouldn't open. Turning in each direction, he saw more corridors, and each one was nondescript and identical to the other. "My God! We'll never get out of here," he thought, and feeling his heart pound, he was starting to panic when a ladder from a scaffold directly above them started to rattle and descend toward them. As he stood back he watched it shake and come to a stop just inches from the ground. Then, in front of him, he saw shoes and then a white lab coat. It was one of the men that worked there. Hopping to the floor, the man turned from the ladder, and without acknowledging them, he started to walk off.

"Pardon me," said Mitchell, pulling on the man's shoulder. But when the man turned around, Mitchell drew back. To his amazement, his face was flat and perfectly round, like a child's drawing, and his eyes were nothing more than two dots, his mouth merely a straight, black line. "Yes, what do you want?" he asked, and when he spoke, his words came out in bursts, like Morse code. "What are you doing?" said Mitchell. "And what is this thing?"

The man in the lab coat let his clipboard fall to his side. "We're tending the machine, of course," he said, and his words popped out like bubbles. "What does it do?" yelled Mitchell, realizing that the noise was getting louder. "It doesn't matter," said the man. "I just tend to this part of it. I don't know what the rest of it does. It's not my job."

Mitchell held Fiver's collar tightly. "I don't understand," he cried. "Why is it so noisy?" With the dots of his eyes becoming bigger circles, the man seemed perplexed by Mitchell's question. "It's not noisy," he said, and then he pointed to a small box on his chest. On it there was a button and the outline of a human ear on it. "What's that?" yelled Mitchell, but after giving him a queer, frustrated look, the man turned and started to walk away. Grabbing him by the arm, Mitchell caught him and brought him back around. "I don't understand!" he yelled. "What's goin' on here?"

With his round, balloon-like head rocking back and forth, the man seemed puzzled by Mitchell's questions. "It's all very complex," he said. "That's the way of the modern world. The twentieth century is very abstract."

"But we want to get out of here," Mitchell retorted loudly.

"There is no way out," said the man as if he thought the question was absolutely bizarre. "Why would you want to do that? It's unthinkable!"

"But there must be a way!" cried Mitchell. "There must be."

Shaking his head, the man in the lab coat brought his clipboard back up to his chest. "Maybe you should look back the way you came," he said.

"But we're lost," said Mitchell.

"I'm sorry," said the man. Then, stepping into a metal cage, he started ascending the structure. "You might follow that yellow line on the floor," he yelled down. "That's from another time, but then, you know any more time doesn't really exist."

Pulling his eyes from the ascending cage, Mitchell looked down at the line on the floor, and he was just about to start following it when behind him he heard voices and footsteps. When he turned around, he saw the men from the pound. "There they are!" one of them shouted, and backing up, Mitchell bumped against the door with the green light over it. Seeing the men start to run toward them, he shook the handle and the lock gave. Flinging the door open, he grabbed Fiver by the collar and jumped through it. Behind them, the door slammed shut with a great, echoing bang. Then there was a biting smell, and as he tried to regain his bearings, he heard more footsteps, and now there were hundreds of them. Looking up, he saw a glass barrier and pigs racing along in a trough coming straight toward him, and now he could see the gas. "No! No!" he screamed, and then suddenly everything went black, and in the darkness Fiver was barking, and he could feel his paw on his arm. Then slowly Fiver came into focus, and with raised ears and intent eyes, he was on the bed gently nudging Mitchell.

Chapter Forty Nine

When they went for their walk the next morning, Mitchell held Fiver firmly by the collar. "I don't want any trouble this morning," he said as they went out the front gate, and walking along beside him, Fiver seemed calm and carefree. But when they got to the big iron gates in front of Snyder's mansion, Mitchell felt him tense and try to pull away. "No, you're not goin' in there today," said Mitchell. Then Fiver barked, and out of the corner of his eye, Mitchell thought he saw something move. Through the gate, it looked like it darted behind the big mansion, and seeing it too, Fiver whined, and twisting, he tried to get free of Mitchell. "Now, settle down," said Mitchell as he knelt down in front of him. "You can't go in there. I don't know what that was, but you'd never catch him." Looking away from Mitchell, Fiver kept searching the yard with his eyes. "Now c'mon," said Mitchell, "we've gotta go."

An hour later, the two of them pulled up to the garage in the old tow truck. Inside, Tom was standing next to the Healey with a cup of coffee in his hand. "How much more do you have to do before you put the clutch in?" he asked.

"Oh, not too much," replied Mitchell. "She's all undone. I just have to lift out the engine."

"Hmm. We've got two transmission jobs to get done, and Glen needs the hoist. Do you think we could move her outside and use the A-frame to pull the engine?"

Mitchell looked at the Healey. "Sure. The parts aren't here yet, anyway."

Mitchell and Tom pushed the Healey outside, and later on, while the morning air was still cool and crisp, they rolled the A-frame over to the Healey. Then they began to hook up the chains that connected the pulleys to the engine. With one of them on each side of the car, they were both bent over the engine when Mitchell said, "Tom, it seems like you've always been here. Ever since I can remember. Is that right?"

Groaning, Tom pulled on his wrench. "No, I traveled a little. I went to Detroit. Went to a GM school there. I guess I could've stayed there and gone up the ladder, as they say."

Mitchell spun a nut off one of the head bolts. "Why didn't you stay?"

Tom set his wrench on the fender. "I don't know, just didn't feel right. You ever watch them slap horses with a belt to break 'em? You know, they just stand there and slap 'em, not hard, but all the time, and they do it until the horse stops flinching. That's what it felt like to me. I felt like they were trying to break me like that."

Rising up, Mitchell pulled on the chain. "They were trying to make you slap-happy, huh?"

Tom put his wrench on another bolt. "Something like that. You know, I remember one day I was talkin' to your old man." Tom pulled on the wrench. "He was making something on the lathe. Your old man liked to do that. He'd rather make somethin' than go buy it, even if it cost him money. Anyway, I asked him why he never left, and I remember he said to me, 'Tom, I've got the elements right here. It's all the same. I don't need to go traipsin' around the universe.'" As he pulled on the wrench, Tom clenched his teeth. "Anyway, I've been here ever since."

Leaning over the fender, Mitchell stared down at the engine, and for a moment, in his mind he saw his father stooped over the lathe in the shop. He was grinding on something, and sparks, like those of a sparkler, were shooting out from the spinning wheel. Behind him, old Red was holding up a piece of white-hot steel that he had just pulled from the fire with his tongs.

"Well, she's ready," said Tom, interrupting Mitchell's vision. "Let's pull her out."

At lunchtime, with his feet up on the desk, Mitchell was eating a sandwich when the parts came for the Healey. With his sandwich in one hand, he picked up one of the boxes and examined it closely. "Dammit!" he exclaimed. "These are the wrong parts. These are for a Three-Thousand Series. They won't work on a One-Hundred-Four." In disgust, he tossed the box down on the desk and looked out the window. In the yard, the engine, hanging from the A-frame, looked like a gallows from time past.

"You look tired," said Tom as he closed his lunch bucket. "You've got that world-weary look. Why don't you take the afternoon off? We're caught up around here. In fact, we've never been so damned caught up. Take a couple days off, if you want."

Mitchell lifted his feet from the desk and rocked forward in his chair. "I think I will. Maybe Fiver and I will get out, go for a walk in the hills." Lying down by the desk, Fiver raised his head when he heard the word "walk."

An hour later, on a dirt road that led up to a dry wash on Silver Mountain, the two of them were bouncing along in the tow truck. With his paw on the dash, Fiver barked when Mitchell parked the truck in front of an old, barren-looking cottonwood tree with leaves that were starting to turn to fall colors. "C'mon, Fiver, let's go for a walk," said Mitchell as he got out of the truck, and jumping to the ground, Fiver immediately began to pick his way up the wash. With his hands in his pockets, Mitchell followed along behind him, and as they walked, he took in the view and the pristine air. As always, Fiver continued to run ahead, and stopping here and there, he would look back to check on Mitchell.

They had been walking for the better part of an hour when, coming around a sharp bend in the ravine, Mitchell saw Fiver stop in his tracks and, like a lion about to pounce, crouch down. Ahead of him, growing out of the ravine, there was a tall tree with big orange leaves, and there was something about it, the way it just was there all by itself. Hurrying to catch up, Mitchell hopped from rock to rock, and with eyes pinned on the trail, he heard Fiver start to growl the low-pitched growl that bespoke danger. Finally, coming up behind him, Mitchell stopped and scanned the dry stream bed. Then he saw it. Just below the tree there was a dog, a big, dark-colored Great Dane. He was huge, and with his large, square head lying on his front paws, in mummified silence, his round eyes looked straight ahead like an Egyptian sphinx. Then, as Fiver's growls seemed to fade away, Mitchell realized that the Dane was dead, and that he'd probably gone off by himself to die. His stone-like stare evidenced his courage, and to Mitchell, who stood mesmerized next to Fiver, it was as if, unflinchingly, this proud dog had faced death straight on, alone.

As Mitchell gazed at him in utter reverence, a lone leaf fell from the tree, and swirling silently downward, it came to rest in front of the dog. Then seeming to follow it, came another, and then another, and suddenly the leaves were showering down like a waterfall. Behind them the tree seemed to shudder, and everywhere there was red and yellow. Then, in almost the blink of an eye, the tree itself was barren, and with its black skeleton standing naked against the blue sky, it seemed to reach up and beseech the heavens. Below it the dog was now graced by a magnificent blanket of orange and red leaves, and staring out, he seemed to look through time itself.

Trying to fathom the sight in front of him, Mitchell gazed at the now-entombed dog for a long time. Then, hearing Fiver bark, he looked away. Up on a trail that left the streambed and headed up the mountain, he saw Fiver had gone ahead. From atop a large flat boulder, he was intently looking down at him with shining, demanding eyes. Then, letting out two short impatient barks, he seemed to say, "that's enough with death. Let's move on!" Completely taken by the moment, Mitchell nodded reflectively. "All right, I'm comin," he said. "I'm comin."

Chapter Fifty

On the way home, visions of the dog and the leaves raining down from the tree bedeviled Mitchell. He was still thinking about them and shaking his head when he got out of the truck and took some letters out of the mailbox. As he thumbed through them, he noticed a postmark from Denver. It was a postcard from Jerry. Inside the house, Mitchell threw the other letters on the table and began to read Jerry's note.

Dear Mitch,

I suppose you've been wondering why you didn't hear from me. Well, things have been up and down, but they're wonderful now. It's absolutely amazing how things have turned out. I've got a lot to tell you. This time it's the real thing. It's amazing. I was so down, and now it's all so right. It's a miracle. It all came together like I knew it would. I'll write soon and fill you in. I have some books I want you to read. Could change your life. Give me a call when you're in town. I travel a lot, but I'm around, and I'm flexible. Hope to see you soon.

Have faith, Jerry

Smiling, Mitchell shook his head. "You're incredible," he thought. "You never quit." But, something about the card, he didn't know exactly what, bothered him, and leaving it on the table, he went into the dining room and sat down at the piano. As he played some soft blues, images of the Great Dane looking out from the fresh blanket of leaves haunted him. A few minutes later, he was still playing when the phone rang, and from the floor next to him, Fiver raised his head and watched him leave the piano and pick up the receiver.

"Hello," said Mitchell, in a somewhat forced voice.

It was Nancy. "Boy, do you sound distant. Were you takin' a nap?"

"No, I was just playin' the piano."

"Is anything wrong?"

"No, it's just been an unusual day. How are you doing?"

"Oh, I'm just fine. I called the garage. Tom said you were taking the day off. Maybe tomorrow too, huh?"

"Yeah, I might. There's not much going on, and I'm waiting for parts for the Healey."

"That's great. I've got tomorrow off, too. How would you like to go out to Grandpa's? He's been asking about you. He thinks a lot of you, and he's bringing in a late crop of alfalfa. We could give him a hand."

Mitchell leaned against the fridge. "Yeah, I'd like that."

"Oh, good, they'll be pleased. See you about nine-ish, huh?"

"OK, see you then."

Chapter Fifty One

The sky was cloudless and blue the next day, and it was about ten when Mitchell and Nancy arrived at the farm. Since Mitchell was going to work with Grandpa in the afternoon, they decided to go riding before lunch. When they got back, both of them were red from the sun, and with Fiver running along beside them, they came loping up to the corral. They were laughing and teasing as they unsaddled the horses in front of the barn.

"Oh, sure," said Nancy, loosening the cinch on the palomino. "I had to let you win. If I didn't, your male ego would've been so wounded, all that testosterone and stuff, you'd never be able to face me. Anyone could tell my horse is really faster."

"Oh, is that right?" said Mitchell as he carried his saddle toward the tack room in the barn. "Maybe you should tell her that," he said over his shoulder.

"I did," replied Nancy, and catching Mitchell's attention with a sly smile, she patted her horse on the back. "She understands. In fact, she knows just exactly how heavy the male ego can be."

In the afternoon, Nancy and Granny decided to bake bread while Mitchell helped Grandpa clean out some irrigation ditches in the fields. After the men had been working for about an hour, taking a break, Mitchell leaned on his shovel. On the other side of the ditch, Grandpa took a hanky from his pocket and smiled as he wiped his face. Then, with a nod, he looked over to where Fiver was lying in some tall alfalfa. "I'd swear that dog's taken in my every move. I don't know if he's wonderin' what I'm doin' or why I'm doin' it, but it sure seems like he's givin' it some thought. Pretty soon he's gonna come over here and tell me where to dig. Never seen a dog that seemed so contemplative all the time."

Still leaning on his shovel, Mitchell glanced over at Fiver. "Oh, he's always thinking. You can see it in his eyes."

Grandpa put his handkerchief back in his pocket. "It makes you wonder, doesn't it. I suppose that they have to be able to put a lot of things together or they wouldn't survive, would they?"

Mitchell picked up his shovel. "Oh, they think, all right," he said as he stepped over to the ditch. "To me, they're just more metaphorical than we are; maybe they think in images that they associate, something like that. If the scientists weren't so stuck on pointing out the differences between us and them, and looked at the similarities, I think they'd see that."

"Could be," said Grandpa, with his blue eyes shining. "Could be. You sure think about a lot of things don't you."

Throwing a shovel full of mud over his shoulder, Mitchell nodded. "When I'm not workin' I do."

"It's good we have the work," said Grandpa. "Without it, we'd go mad just thinkin' about things."

After another sumptuous dinner filled with Grandpa's philosophizing and Isabelle's admonishments about his language, Mitchell and Nancy piled into the old tow truck. As they left, Fiver was sitting between them while Grandpa and Granny waved good-bye from the porch.

"Isn't a wave a funny thing," said Nancy. "I guess it's our kind of sign language, isn't it," she said, and holding her hand up and watching her wrist rise and fall, she mused at the odd motion.

"It's our way of wagging our tails," said Mitchell. "It's a long-distance pat on the back," he continued as he reached over and patted Fiver. "Same thing when a mother pats her child or a dog licks her puppies."

"Hum," replied Nancy as she leaned over and lightly kissed Mitchell on the cheek. "Same as a kiss, huh?"

It was dark when they rolled into Grand Mesa. When they came to a stop at the intersection by the new shopping center, Fiver was asleep with his head on Nancy's lap. On the other side of the street, the big neon clown in front of the fast food restaurant rocked slowly back and forth, and his rolling eyes distracted Mitchell. Then a metallic-blue '62 Chevy with chrome side exhausts rolled to a noisy stop beside them. With his tattooed arm hanging out the window, the swaggering young driver revved the engine. Music was booming out the windows. In the backseat, two teenage boys and a girl with ratted, bleached-blond hair were smoking cigarettes and swilling beer. You could hear the boy's macho raised voice, and his speech was filled with proud cussing about something or someone.

Nancy flinched with displeasure at the swearing. "They don't have much of a vocabulary," she said finally with a laugh. "I thought that macho trip with low-slung cars and hot rods went out in the fifties," she said as they turned onto the main street.

"No, that'll be around for a long time," said Mitchell. "Till they run out of fuel. That's the only power kids like that have, cars and cussing and being cool. It's not much of a start is it."

"Well, they like to strut their stuff," said Nancy. "They remind me of peacocks." Mitchell chuckled as he shifted. "That's pretty much it," he said. "It is a mating dance of sorts."

As he turned a corner, Nancy leaned over and hugged Mitchell. "Maybe you should go into psychology," she whispered, "put all that thinking to work. You'd be good at it."

Mitchell smirked. "No, not me," he retorted. "A psychologist is supposed to be a wise person. They should be experienced and deep, like an old Indian chief. But they're really not, and I just don't trust them. Most of them come from privilege, and then they come out and tell the rest of us that we have personal problems, something in our genes or our childhood!" Mitchell shook his head, and going on, he said, "And they never tell some guy who's rotting at some dead-end job that the system is screwing him! They're comfortably apolitical. I guess I think a lot of 'em are just poverty pimps! They're like some of the guys I knew in the sixties, they were gonna go out and help the poor, but only if they could get a grant and make fifty grand a year doing it."

With a contemplative and slightly troubled look on her face, Nancy didn't respond, and in the silence, Mitchell was wondering if he had gone too far when slowly a coy but affectionate smile crossed Nancy's lips. "Ooh, so radical. You make me feel young again," she whispered in a flirtatious voice. "It seems like nineteen sixty-eight. Shouldn't we smoke a joint now, and then go make love on the floor somewhere? I've got an old Mateus wine bottle somewhere. It's still got the candle in it. We just need some beads and some grass."

"I don't know how your aunt will deal with that," said Mitchell with a laugh.

"Might do her some good," said Nancy, smiling.

#

Chapter Fifty Two

#

On Saturday morning, Mitchell and Nancy loaded up the old tow truck with her easel and an overnight bag. "Boy," said Nancy as she climbed in and slammed the truck door behind her, "that Mrs. Martin came over this morning. She lives across the street, and she just comes over to chat, and she talks and talks, and never stops. I couldn't get her out of there."

Stepping down on the starter button, Mitchell brought the old tow truck to a rumbling start. "What did she talk about?"

"Nothing really," said Nancy as she petted Fiver. "I mean just gossipy stuff about her relatives, people I don't even know. It's amazing how she can turn it all into these big issues. But I guess that's what gossip's for, isn't it?"

"Could be," said Mitchell with a smile. "Maybe it just fills the void for her, huh?"

When they arrived at Mitchell's, Nancy set her easel up on the back porch. On the canvas, she had sketched a rough outline of Mitchell's garage with an old car parked in front of it.

"It's a thirty-six Ford," said Mitchell as he looked at the work in progress. "It's got great lines, doesn't it." On Sunday, they went out to Grandpa's, and while Mitchell and Grandpa made some repairs on the barn, Nancy and Granny cooked up a big Sunday dinner. On Monday, Mitchell went into work, but he came home early in the afternoon, and for the rest of the week, the two of them spent most of their time together at Mitchell's. As the days passed, they seemed to grow closer and closer. When they weren't teasing one another with a barrage of battered puns, they talked about serious things, and even on the things they disagreed about, their affection for one another seemed to reduce their differences to interesting speculations. For the next while, their only time away from one another came when retiring to their respective arts; Nancy would paint while Mitchell played the piano.

Nancy was meticulous and diligent in her artwork, and Mitchell was awed as he watched the painting unfold beneath her brush. "I keep thinking it can't get any better," he said one afternoon, standing in the doorway behind her. "But it does, and it's already a masterpiece. I mean it. It really is."

With Fiver lying beside her, Nancy laughed, and touching the brush to the canvas, she highlighted the curved slope of the front fender on the car. She had painted the Ford a dark green, and at Mitchell's suggestion, she surrounded it with orange and red leaves falling from the big cottonwood tree that in the painting towered over the garage.

"You didn't tell me you were this good!" said Mitchell, still standing in the doorway. "What am I going to do when you're famous?"

Nodding and then looking back at him, Nancy fell strangely silent, and not saying a word, she again lifted her brush up to the painting. But then her hand started to tremble, and without a stroke, she pulled it away, and as her head dropped to her chest, she started to cry. Stepping quickly from the doorway, Mitchell knelt down beside her. When he looked up at her, the tears, already welled up in her eyes, were starting to trickle down her cheeks.

"What's the matter?" he pleaded, and Nancy's lower lip quivered as she tried to compose herself.

"I don't know. I guess I just can't stand compliments."

Mitchell looked at the painting. "The painting's terrific. You should have your own studio and quit the market."

Averting her eyes, Nancy looked down at Fiver and started to sob.

"Hey, what is it?" said Mitchell, taking her by the shoulders, and she sputtered as she tried to respond.

"I...I can have a studio...in Boston. They offered me a job there. I interviewed last spring, and they said there were no funds, and...and now they tell me there are."

Leaning over, Mitchell tried to catch her gaze. "Who offered you a job?" he said softly, and continuing to cry, Nancy gasped as she tried to talk.

"Boston...Boston University. Last spring they told me no, and now suddenly they want me to come. Why now?" Raising her head, Nancy wiped the tears from her cheeks. "School starts in three weeks. I'd have to leave soon. In two weeks at the latest."

Rising from his knees, Mitchell gently drew Nancy from the chair. "Hey, we'll work this out," he said, and still sobbing, Nancy laid her head on his chest. "It's not the end," declared Mitchell. "Fiver and I aren't gonna let you just walk out of our lives. Are we, Fiver?" Aroused by Nancy's crying, Fiver was sitting on his haunches, and he swished his tail when he heard Mitchell mention his name. "I know we can get around this," said Mitchell. "We've got options. We'll work through it. There're always options."

Looking down from Mitchell's shoulder, Nancy saw the affectionate concern in Fiver's eyes. "There are, huh?" she said with a reluctant smile.

"Of course. Why don't we just enjoy the next few days and we'll talk about this on the weekend? We'll come up with something by then."

In the days that followed, Mitchell and Nancy spent as much time together as possible, and as it dwindled it became more precious and seemed to bond them more deeply. In the evenings, while Mitchell read or played the piano, Nancy continued to work on her painting. At night they talked and drank wine by the fireplace, and for a while, except for the fact that it made their lovemaking more passionate, the thought of their pending separation seemed less pressing.

On Sunday, Mitchell was still asleep when he heard some black gospel music coming from the stereo in the living room. Then, wearing one of his blue work shirts as a nightgown, Nancy appeared in the doorway, and the sight of her made him smile.

"I thought we'd better get some religion after all this delicious sinning we've been doing," she said playfully as she leaned against the doorjamb. "I just love the way they do it. Their music is so alive."

Raising up on his elbows, Mitchell pulled back the covers. "OK, come show me your religion," he said, laughing. "You show me yours and I'll show you mine."

Shaking her head, Nancy climbed in bed. "Oh, you're so bad," she said as she pulled the covers up, and with his hand sliding under the shirt, Mitchell kissed her lightly on the neck. In the background, a gospel group sang out, "Rock me, Lord. Rock me, Lord. I got a home on the other side."

At breakfast, Nancy, still clad in Mitchell's blue work shirt, was sitting at the table when Mitchell set a plate of light-brown pancakes in the middle of it. "There they are," he said. "My one and only specialty. Mitchell's banana whole wheat pancakes." Smiling up at him, Nancy took her fork and set one of the pancakes on her plate. As she buttered it, Mitchell saw her demeanor begin to change. Pouring the syrup, she was visibly sad, and sitting across the table, Mitchell was hit by the weight of the moment. "Listen, I've given this a lot of thought," he said abruptly. "And I think you'll agree with what I propose."

Nancy's eyes were heavy when she looked up, and Mitchell took a deep breath before he went on. "I'm just gonna tell it like it is and keep it simple. I don't want to lose you, and I'm torn between that and how important your painting is." Mitchell looked down while he gathered his thoughts, and his face was strained when he continued. "Now, we haven't had a lot of time together, but the time we have had has been good. At least for me, and I know it's only gonna get better." Mitchell pushed his plate away. "Anyway, it seems to me that you have to go. If you don't, if you stay here, you might regret it, and it could ruin things for us." Nancy searched his eyes as he spoke. "I know we'll make it," he went on. "To me, what we have is truly special, and I think we both know it. So we can survive nine months apart, and then we'll go from there next summer, and we'll have times together in the meantime. Thanksgiving's coming up and Christmas." Surprised at how intense his own emotions were becoming, Mitchell paused awkwardly. "I mean, if we want to, if we decide to, we can make it. Besides, we'll probably get a better sense of what to do after we're apart. That would be good and..."

Nancy interrupted, "What about you coming to Boston to live?" she said straightaway.

Mitchell sat back on his chair. "I could do that. But not right off. I just got out of the city, and it's no place for Fiver. I couldn't subject him to that. It's no place for a dog."

Nancy set her hands on her hips. "Then what am I doing there, if it's not fit for a dog?"

Mitchell smiled sadly, but he didn't reply.

"Well, I don't have to go," retorted Nancy in an adamant tone. "I have something to say about this. It's my decision. I still have a couple of days."

Mitchell nodded. "Yeah, that's true, but I think you should give it a lot of thought. I've told you how I feel." Feeling still more dread and apprehension, Mitchell looked down at the floor. "I mean, you know how I feel, don't you? I mean, about you. I've really never felt this way before." As she looked back at him, Nancy's eyes fell, and then starting to cry, she turned her head away. "I don't like this," she whispered faintly. "It's so hard, so awfully hard."

After breakfast, Mitchell and Nancy took Fiver for a long walk, and they hardly talked. When they returned, Nancy began to pack up her things.

"Here, you better take this," said Mitchell, handing her his blue work shirt. "It looks a lot better on you than it does on me."

Wiping a tear from her eye, Nancy took the shirt, and unable to bear her tears, Mitchell turned away. "I'll get your easel and stuff from the porch," he said.

"No, you don't have to get that," said Nancy with a sniffle. "I haven't made up my mind yet, and even if I go, I can't take the easel." Turning back around, Mitchell saw the sad defiance in Nancy's eyes. "I always leave that one at my aunt's, anyway," she said tersely. "And the painting's for you, and it's not quite done, anyway."

Mitchell looked perplexed. "It's not?"

Nancy lifted her suitcase from the bed. "No, it's not. I'll finish it next time I'm here. I'll finish it when we're together. If Schubert can have his unfinished symphony, I can have my unfinished painting!" Nancy forced a smile. "Sometimes paintings take years to finish. They're like poems. They're never done, they're just abandoned."

Chapter Fifty Three

It was late Monday night when Nancy finally called. When he heard the phone ring Mitchell knew it was her, and the sad tone in her voice confirmed his suspicion. "What time does the plane leave?" he asked, and Nancy paused before she replied, "It leaves at nine tomorrow morning. Could you and Fiver take me to the airport?"

Mitchell exhaled slowly. "Of course."

Then, after another long pause, Nancy burst out, "And don't be surprised if I'm back here in a week, and you take care of Fiver, and be sure that he's the only other one that gets any of my granola, and it's all your fault. Yours and Fiver's, and I love you, both of you, and I don't know why I'm doing this. It seems crazy."

Mitchell laughed softly. "We love you, too, and it'll work out. I know it will," said Mitchell, trying to conceal his dread. "We'll see you in the morning." Then, putting down the receiver, he looked around at the empty house and then to Fiver, and seeing his gaze, Fiver swished his tail.

Mitchell picked Nancy up at eight o'clock the next morning, and on the way to the airport, Fiver sat between them. As they went down the highway, Nancy stroked him. "I'll' miss you," she said, pulling him close. "You and those eyes of yours. I swear you could stop a train with just one look." Smiling at Nancy's comment, Mitchell glanced over at the two of them. Then, looking back to the highway, he gazed at the old biplane that was still parked in the field by the airport. He was about to say something about a book by de Saint Exupery, when, thinking better of it, in silence, he turned onto the road that led over to the airport.

Nancy was pensive but businesslike while they waited for the man at the counter to process her ticket. But as they walked to the gate, her eyes started to well up with tears. "I don't know why I'm doing this," she said, whisking a tear away. "It doesn't seem right."

As he turned to embrace her, Mitchell looked into her eyes. "We'll be right here, waiting," he said. "You check it out. Soon you'll know for sure."

Rising up on her toes, Nancy kissed him. "I love you, Mitchell Black."

"I love you, too, and I don't want our relationship to be like one of your paintings." Nancy cocked her head. "You know, never finished, just abandoned."

Nancy stared up at Mitchell. "I do love you," she said after a long silence. "And try to keep clean, will you? You're the only guy I know who can get dirty just thinking."

Mitchell smiled. "I guess I just have dirty thoughts."

As he walked out to the truck, Mitchell heard the whine of the plane's big jet engines. Moments later, with Fiver sitting next to him, he pulled the truck off to the side of the road, and leaning out the window, he watched the plane taxi down the runway. When the plane finally vanished into some clouds, he turned from the window, and stepping on the starter button, he fired up the truck. Then, feeling numb and speechless, almost as he did when his father died, he drove straight to the garage. He parked the truck next to the Healey, and as he got out, he saw the engine sill swinging from the A-frame.

Inside, Tom was sitting at the desk. "Well, if it isn't our absentee owner," he said when he saw Mitchell come through the door. "It's good you're here today. We've got plenty of work, and we need the truck."

Putting his hands in his pockets, Mitchell leaned against the wall. "How's that?"

"Well, Snyder's got two trucks down," said Tom as he shuffled through some papers on the desk. "One's got a blown rear end, and it looks like a tranny's out in the other. We've got some other jobs comin' in too. We'll be busy."

"Well, I guess you were right about Snyder," said Mitchell. "His pride doesn't get in the way, does it?"

"Nope, didn't expect it would," said Tom with a chuckle. "It's not cost-efficient for him to do that."

Smiling at Tom's matter-of-fact indictment, Mitchell looked around at the office. "Did the parts come in for the Healey?" he said, and standing up from behind the desk, Tom put his pen in his pocket. "Some of them came," he replied. "But the rest will be here soon. Lately everything is back-ordered."

As he often did when he was troubled, Mitchell engrossed himself in work for the rest of the day, but nevertheless, in between projects and difficult tasks, and particularly at lunch, thoughts and images of Nancy danced across his mind. By quitting time, he was in the middle of putting some brakes on a Plymouth.

"You can finish that tomorrow," said Tom as he washed up, and without looking up from his workbench, Mitchell shook his head. "Naw, I'll get this done tonight. It won't take me too much longer."

It was after eleven when after finishing up the Plymouth, Mitchell and Fiver climbed into the truck to go home. "I guess it's just you and me again," said Mitchell as he looked over at Fiver, and as they pulled away, Fiver put his paw on the dash of the old truck.

#

Chapter Fifty Four

#

For the remainder of the week, Mitchell put in long days down at the garage, and he usually came home exhausted. On Friday night, he was asleep in the chair by the fireplace when the phone rang and startled, the book in his lap fell to the floor. Hoping the call was from Nancy, he rushed to the phone. "Hello," he said eagerly.

"Well, how's my cowboy?"

"Oh, we're doing pretty good." Mitchell tried not to sound drowsy. "How's Boston?"

"It's fun. But I'm not settled in yet, and I miss you and Fiver a whole lot."

"Yeah, we miss you, too," he said. "It's not the same around here. Have you found a place yet?"

"No, not yet, but I'm living with an old girlfriend of mine. You could still come out, you know, and we could find a place together."

"I'd like to," replied Mitchell. "Believe me, I've thought about it. Maybe if we found the right neighborhood. How's your painting going, and how's the teaching?"

Nancy sighed. "You know, you're a stubborn one, Mitchell Black. But it will be a while before I have time to find a place. You still have time to think about it. How's Fiver?"

Mitchell nodded. "Oh, he's fine. He's already gone to bed. So, tell me, how is the painting coming?"

"Actually, it's going well. They like my stuff now. I don't know why. They didn't like it that much last year. I think maybe it's because I'm so far from the contemporary stuff that my traditional style seems new. I really don't know. Is my painting still on the porch?"

"Yeah, I haven't touched it. I was thinking I might move it into the living room, but I haven't."

"That's good. Don't touch it 'til I get back. What have you been reading lately?"

"Oh, not too much." Mitchell glanced at the book lying open on the floor. "I was reading a little paperback about Einstein and physics. Most of it's beyond me, but they say he was a practical thinker. So, what the hell, I'm wrestling with it. I guess it's the stuff about time and speed that I don't get. As far as I can tell, the idea is that if you go fast enough in a circle, you could run into yourself. That boggles my mind. How can you be in two places at once? They also treat time like it actually does things, when to me it's just an abstraction, a measurement, you know, like a yard stick."

Nancy laughed. "So you don't think time exists?"

Mitchell paused. "Hell, I don't know," he said with a chuckle. "If it does, maybe you should try to paint it sometime. Now there's a project for you. You'd be famous."

Nancy laughed, and then fell silent. "You know, you're wonderful," she whispered. "A little crazy, but wonderful. I love you."

#

Chapter Fifty Five

#

The next day, about eleven, at the garage, Mitchell was putting gas in an old Datsun when he saw Jesse pull up to the pumps in Snyder's big four-wheel drive. Jesse smiled as his window came down. "Well, it's about time you came by," said Mitchell. "What have you been up to?"

Jesse rested his elbow in the open window of the truck door. "Oh, things have been busy. This ski resort business is a full-time proposition. How have you been?"

"Oh, not bad." Feeling the pump handle click off, Mitchell pulled the nozzle from the tank of the Datsun. "I've been doing all right," said Mitchell. "What's this about a ski resort? I've heard the rumors. Is it real?"

"Could be," replied Jesse. "Let's get a beer sometime and talk. It's been too long."

"So, how about tonight?" asked Mitchell as he put the gas cap back on the Datsun.

"I can't tonight," replied Jesse. "I've got to work. We've got some pro-posals that have to be in to the city tomorrow."

"Well, maybe next week," said Mitchell with a nod.

"Sounds good," said Jesse as he drove off, and just then another car pulled up to the pumps.

In the following weeks, business picked up at the garage, and Mitchell found himself working longer and longer days. He called Jesse once or twice, but they never could get together, and Jesse always seemed a little awkward on the phone, as though something were eating at him. Mitchell mentioned it to Noah at lunch one day.

"It's hard to say," replied Noah. "Maybe things aren't too good at home. Maybe it's something at work. I honest-to-God don't know how he puts up with Snyder. I hear he's hard to work for."

"Could be," said Mitchell. "I guess we'll just see what happens."

Searching in the pocket of his sport coat for his pipe, Noah eyed Mitchell. "Have you heard from Nancy lately?"

"Yeah, she writes all the time, and we talk on the phone. Although lately we haven't talked as much."

Noah loaded his pipe. "How is she?"

"Oh, she's fine."

Noah gave Mitchell a subtle, questioning look. "Have you guys decided what you're going to do? It's kind of hard to have a long-distance relationship."

Mitchell nodded. "Yeah, I know," he said, and his voice trailed off as he spoke. "It's damned hard."

Noticing that Mitchell was a little uncomfortable with the questions about Nancy, Noah changed the subject. "Say, what happened to your sports car? I saw it parked on the side of the garage with the engine out."

Mitchell picked the bill up from the table. "Oh, the clutch went out," he said as he studied the bill, "and they keep back-ordering the parts. It's just as well, I guess. I've been too busy to put them in. They should be here soon, though."

Setting the bill back on the table, Mitchell looked off into the distance. "Well, I might drive back and see Nancy," he said as if he were trying to convince himself. "It'd be fun to drive cross-country." Smiling, Noah puffed on his pipe.

On Saturday, Mitchell spent the day with Grandpa working around the farm. When he got home there was a letter from Nancy in the mailbox, and he flopped down in the easy chair to read it.

Dear Mitchell,

Well, I've finally got my apartment set up. It's not much, but it's clean and there's a little coffee shop across the street. The people at the university are nice, although they tend to be a little too serious sometimes, and I really don't care for all the schmoozing that goes on. Cliques and that sort of thing.

Last week my old friend Marsha called, and we've kicked around a bit. And it looks like I'm going to have a showing. How about that! My own show, here in Boston, and maybe one in New York.

Well, I hope things are good for you and Fiver, and I think about you every day. I miss you terribly. Please think about coming here. It's not the same without you. Give Fiver a hug for me.

Love,
Nancy

As he finished the letter Mitchell drew a deep breath and put it on the table. In the kitchen, he grabbed a glass and poured some wine out of an already open bottle. Wine in hand, he went out on the porch and stood in front of Nancy's painting. Some of her small and delicate brushes lay in the tray at the bottom of the easel. "Looks abandoned to me," he thought as he looked at the painting, and lost somewhere in the dark green of the car and the falling leaves, he didn't hear Fiver come up and sit down beside him.

Later that night, Mitchell dozed off in his chair in front of the fireplace. Lying beside him, Fiver seemed to sense something, and rising to his feet, he sniffed the air. Then, padding over to the window, he pushed the curtain aside with his nose and looked out and began to whine. Still whining, he returned to Mitchell, and started to bark and nudge Mitchell's arm. Then he ran to the front door and barked again, and his bark was sharp and urgent. "What is it?" said Mitchell as he looked around, and barking more excitedly, Fiver started to growl. "What's the matter?" said Mitchell as he set aside his book. "We just went out a while ago." But, growing more frustrated by the second, Fiver started to cry and moan, and throwing his head back, he rolled his eyes as he barked. Then, with a soft-pitched sort of wail, he began to howl, and in between howls he scratched at the door. With pleading eyes he looked up to Mitchell. "OK," said Mitchell as he stood up. "If it's that bad, we'll go out, but we'll do it together, and I'm gonna put the leash on. You can't take off."

After he secured the leash on Fiver, Mitchell opened the front door, and jumping forward, tugging and pulling, Fiver dragged him across the porch. At the bottom of the steps, Fiver's nose immediately went to the ground, and with Mitchell behind him, he moved in small circles in the front yard. Then, seeming to follow an invisible trail, they went out the gate, and moments later they were in front of Snyder's mansion. With his head through the gate, Fiver was pulling at the leash with all his strength. "No. We're not goin' in there," said Mitchell as he peered into the darkness, and it was all he could do to restrain him, and then drag him back to the house.

Chapter Fifty Six

#

When they got to work the next day, Mitchell was downhearted and tired, but his spirits picked up some when on the front desk he saw the parts for the Healey. "Well, they finally got here," said Tom. "It's about time."

"It sure is. I'll stay late tonight and get things straightened around. Maybe I can get it put in tomorrow."

From behind the desk, Tom sat back in his chair. "You know, you've worked late ever since Nancy went back East. I never realized that there was so much to do around here."

The garage was unusually quiet when Mitchell finished up that night. As he washed his hands with the abrasive powdered soap that spilled out from the small barrel-like container above the basin, a sinking feeling nagged at him. When he finished rinsing his hands, he splashed some cold water on his cheeks. "Aw, I'm gonna call her," he moaned as he pushed his face into the towel hanging down from the linen machine. "What the hell. I'll call her."

As he stood in the doorway of the washroom, Mitchell buttoned his shirt. Then, looking up at the round clock high on the far wall, he saw that it was after nine. "I don't care!" he thought as he walked over to the phone. "So what if it's late." Then he lifted the receiver. "Operator, I'd like to make a long-distance call, and I'd like to charge it to my home phone."

239

While Mitchell was waiting for the operator to dial Nancy's number, Fiver appeared in the doorway that led into the office. Looking curiously at Mitchell, he seemed to wonder why they weren't leaving. Then, through the receiver, Mitchell heard Nancy's number begin to ring. "She must be home," he thought. "It's after midnight back there." But continuing to ring and ring, the phone betrayed his expectations, and in the doorway, Fiver cocked his head when he saw Mitchell's eyes fall. "I'm sorry, sir, your party doesn't answer," said the operator.

"Thanks, operator," said Mitchell, and still holding the phone, he stared off. "Maybe she's gone to a show," he said to himself. "It's not that late." Then, sitting on his haunches in the doorway, Fiver barked as if to say, "Let's go home."

As they left, Mitchell had just turned off the outside lights and was locking the front door when, from behind him, headlights flashed across the front of the station. Turning around, he saw a truck come to rest by the pumps. Stepping off the front step, he recognized the giant chrome rims of Snyder's four-wheel drive. Then the driver's window came down. "Hey, fool, what you doin' workin' this late?" yelled Jesse.

Smiling, Mitchell shook his head. "I might ask you the same," he said, walking toward Jesse with Fiver by his side. "I bet you still have your damned tie on, don't you."

Jesse grinned. "Maybe we'd better go to Lucille's and have that beer, huh?"

Mitchell took Fiver by the collar. "Yeah, it's about time. I'll meet you there."

When Mitchell arrived at Lucille's, Jesse was already there, and the big four-wheeler sat in the parking lot by itself. Stopping next to it, Mitchell pulled on the emergency brake, and with Fiver sitting up on the seat, he gazed through the yellow glare that came from the window of the café. Inside, he saw the waitress light a cigarette and then sit down on a stool at the end of the counter. "You stay here," he said to Fiver as he opened the door, and just as he was about to slide off the seat, Fiver put his paw on Mitchell's shoulder. "Naw, you can't come in here," said Mitchell. But Fiver was insistent, and again he pawed at Mitchel's shoulder. "OK, OK, I'll go see," said Mitchell with a shrug. "Maybe she'll let you in. I'll go see."

Seeming to understand, Fiver watched intently as Mitchell walked up the steps. Through the window, he saw the waitress look up from the counter, and taking a puff of her cigarette, she looked at Mitchell and then out at the truck. Then, smiling, Mitchell nodded in the direction of the booths. A moment later he opened the truck door. "OK," said Mitchell. "She said it's all right. Just this once."

As he followed Mitchell into the restaurant, Fiver's tail wagged enthusiastically. Inside, the waitress gave them a knowing smile, and together Fiver and Mitchell stepped over to the booth where Jesse was already pouring a beer for Mitchell. "Well," said Jesse, and reaching down he gave Fiver a pat. "How are you doing, Fiver?" Then sliding into the booth, Mitchell sat down and cupped his hands around the beer. Beneath the table Fiver curled up by his feet. "And how about you, Mitch?" said Jesse. "How are you doin'?"

"Oh, not bad. How about yourself?"

Jesse smiled complacently. "Oh, I'm all right."

As he sipped his beer, Mitchell peered over the white foam and scrutinized Jesse. "It's been so long," he said, setting the beer back down, "I thought you were mad or something."

"That's funny," replied Jesse with a raised eyebrow, "I thought you were mad. I thought me workin' for Snyder and the plant and all that was getting to you."

Mitchell pursed his lips while he thought. Then, with the corners of his mouth pulled down, he shook his head. "Naw, I don't like that place, but, uh, I wasn't gonna to let it get in the way of friends."

Seeming to relax, Jesse leaned back in the booth, but his eyes were still heavy with doubt. "I'm glad to hear that. I didn't know what you'd do after that day out at the plant. I didn't know what you'd think of me after that."

Looking down at his beer, Mitchell stopped to think. "That's your business," said Mitchell. "Besides, it was good for me to see all that, for real."

Taking a sip of his beer, Jesse eyed Mitchell. "Listen," he said, "this is my grubstake. In a few years I'll have enough to get away and do something on my own, get away from it. This is my only shot."

"That's great," said Mitchell. "I'm glad for you, and you know I understand. Hell, you're working hard. After I left here, I went right after the money, completely sold out."

"What happened to you?" Jesse asked sympathetically. "The last I heard, you were going to grad school, and then I heard you went to Denver and hit it big, making lots of money in the market or something."

"I don't know what happened exactly," said Mitchell. "It was the end of the war, and I got out of the draft by going to school for a while. When my number on the lottery finally came up, it was so high, they didn't call me. In the meantime, you went in the marines, and you made it through, but I know Billy got killed. And Sammy came back, but he was never right after that."

"Yeah, those were hard years," said Jesse. "And Sammy just couldn't put himself back together. He'll probably drink himself to death."

"I know," said Mitchell sadly. "How'd you get through it, man? I know you had tough duty."

Setting his glass down, Jesse looked away. "Aw, funny, I got through all the killing, but it does change you," he said as he looked earnestly at Mitchell. "You know what I learned. I learned that you hurt people the most when you're trying to kill your own pain. That's it. When we're scared and hurt, that's when we're really dangerous. Damn wars, they oughta make the damn politicians that vote for 'em go fight 'em, and they shouldn't let any eighteen-year-old kids be doin' that. It's criminal, man. There should be a law that only adults, adults who have made it, do the fighting. The whole thing's a travesty."

"I agree," said Mitchell, nodding.

But then Jesse interrupted. "Funny, how that went, me fighting and you protesting and things like that. It's like two brothers, one fighting for the south and the other the north, isn't it," he said with a shrewd smile.

"Pretty much," said Mitchell, leaning back against the booth. "But then the war ended, and it was over, and everybody I knew got jobs selling insurance or whatever. It all changed, and suddenly to me everything seemed so pointless and corrupt. I just couldn't figure out what happened." Shaking his head, Mitchell paused. "So, well, I guess I gave up and went for the money," he went on. "Then after I made a pile, had new cars, and all the damned steak dinners I could eat, I realized I was lost, that's all. I didn't know who the hell I was or what I was doing. So then Pop died and I packed up and came back here with my tail between my legs. That's about it, for me."

Looking over at him, Jesse smiled warmly and ran his hand through his dark black hair. His eyes were sympathetic. "I get it," he said. "So much for the sixties. I guess we both sold out in a way. It's hard not to, if you want to make it. You know, when I got out in sixty-nine, that's when reality hit me. There was nothing for vets, particularly if you were messed up, and after a while I figured that the only way I was going to make it was doing things that nobody else would do, you know, dangerous, shitty jobs. For a while I cleaned sewers, and I worked in a mine in Wyoming until one of the men got killed in a cave-in. Anyway, I guess that's how I ended up working for Snyder. It's not a pretty story, but I'm gonna do something with my life."

Touched by Jesse's summation, Mitchell looked at him admiringly. "You're a better man than I am," he said firmly. "That's for sure."

"Ah, nonsense," Jesse said, laughing. "You remember when we were kids, we had a good time, didn't we. We were wild as hell!"

"Yeah, I know," said Mitchell smiling. "Do you remember when we used to go see your great aunt way out on Creek Road in that little cabin by the river? To me, she was like a fortune-teller. Your father used to drop us off there, or sometimes we'd just ride out there on the horses."

"Sure," said Jesse. "You mean Wynona. That was her Indian name."

"Do you remember all those stories she used to tell us about the animals and spirits," asked Mitchell, "the ones about the eagles and the wolves and the bears and the rabbits?"

"Yeah, the power animals. Those stories," replied Jesse, "they were something to hear in front of her fireplace, weren't they."

"Funny, I haven't thought about that for years, and now I remember it like it was yesterday," said Mitchell. "I can see the flames reflected on her face, and her hair all pulled back. She had strong eyes. She was a handsome woman."

"She was," said Jesse. "She was Cherokee. When my great uncle left Philadelphia to make his fortune out West, he met her in Oklahoma and brought her out here. She could tell stories, couldn't she. You remember how she'd get down on her knees in front of the fire, and right in your face, she'd whisper as she talked, all those Indian dreams."

"She was amazing," said Mitchell, and then his face tightened. "Say, you ever see a tree drop its leaves all at once? I mean, in a second, just like that, gone, all of them."

"No, I haven't," said Jesse, quizzically. "But the Indians have a word for that. I don't remember what it was." Then he looked hard at Jesse. "But it's a bad omen of sorts. I know that."

"Really?" said Mitchell with surprise in his voice.

Then Jesse smiled. "Same old Mitchell," he said. "You always see the mystery in everything. Let's have another round, what do you say? Or do you want to go home and chase your girlfriend around the bedroom?"

Mitchell smiled. "Well, she had to go back to Boston," he said. "She's a painter. It was a big opportunity for her."

Setting his beer aside, Jesse gave Mitchell a penetrating look. "She's really got you, doesn't she? Why'd you let her go?"

Mitchell reached for his beer. "We talked..."

Interrupting, Jesse shook his head derisively. "You talked?" he said with raised eyebrows. "What does your gut say, man? If you want her, you better damn well go get her. Don't give me this 'we talked' crap."

"Is that right!" said Mitchell with lighthearted indignation. "Just like that, huh?"

"Yeah, that's right," declared Jesse. "For once stop thinking and just go get her, for hell's sake. She's supposed to get under your skin, man. That's the way it is! You don't go to a shrink every time you get a hard on."

Laughing, Mitchell almost choked on his beer. "I get it," he said. Then for the rest of the evening, the two of them swapped stories about riding horses and fishing, and girls they used to like, and girls that didn't like them. As they laughed and reminisced, the rekindled camaraderie was comforting, and Mitchell was grateful for the friendship. It was midnight when, with a laugh, Jesse paused and stood up and said he had to get home. Then, shaking Mitchell's hand, he smiled and left.

With no one in the café except Mitchell and the waitress, Mitchell called Fiver up from beneath the table and patted him on the head. Then he glanced at his watch. "It's two o'clock in Boston," he thought. "Why not," he said to himself, and standing up, he slid by Fiver and headed to the pay phone on the wall.

On the phone, the operator was terribly businesslike, and as the phone began to ring, Mitchell unconsciously held his breath. "She'll understand," he thought, but the phone just kept ringing and ringing. "It's two o'clock," he thought. "Where could she be?" Then, slowly, he set the receiver back on the phone. "Come on, Fiver. Let's go home."

#

Chapter Fifty Seven

#

The next morning, Mitchell was dead asleep when Fiver nudged him and tried to wake him up. "Aw, c'mon, Fiver, I can't get up this morning." Sitting next to the bed, Fiver seemed to muse on Mitchell's laziness. Then he jumped up on the bed, and standing over Mitchell, he began to paw at the covers. "OK, OK," said Mitchell, finally. "I'll get up." After he jumped back to the floor, Fiver wagged his tail, and rising up, Mitchell moved to the edge of the bed. "What's the matter? You need to go to the bathroom?" he said groggily, and emitting a sharp enthusiastic bark, Fiver looked anxiously toward the door. "OK. But you wait 'til I get dressed. You can go out in the back."

Mitchell rubbed his neck as he stood up from the bed, and as he pulled on his Levi's, Fiver continued to bark. "OK, OK. Let me find my shoes." With his shoes in hand, Mitchell followed Fiver through the kitchen, and out on the back porch he stopped to ponder Nancy's painting. "It seems to change," he thought, and as his eye traveled from the car to the leaves that were scattered around it, a pang of loneliness and apprehension swept over him. Then Fiver barked demandingly and pawed at the screen door. Still thinking about the painting, Mitchell absently reached over and opened the door without looking. Brushing past him, Fiver ran through the door and down the steps. "Just do your business and get back here!" yelled Mitchell without taking his eyes off the painting, and for some reason unknown to him, the dark-green Ford suddenly seemed heavy and rooted like a tree. In his mind he could hear the door closing shut, and like an echo, it shut again and again.

When Mitchell finally turned away from the painting, he opened the screen door, and leaning out, he yelled for Fiver. "Fiver, c'mon!" But Fiver was nowhere to be seen.

Running at full stride past the side of the house, completely indifferent to Mitchell's calls, he crossed the front yard, and with his paws reaching out far in front of him, in a smooth, graceful arc he jumped the little picket fence. Then, without breaking stride, he headed for the iron gates in front of Snyder's mansion. Seeing they were open, he rounded the corner like a racehorse, and with the muscles rippling on his shoulders and thighs, he ran even faster.

Ahead of him, there was an animal that looked like a good-sized black dog of some sort. With something in her mouth, she ran swiftly away, and Fiver barked as he pursued. But then, just as quickly as she had appeared, she was gone, and coming to a stop against the wall in back of the mansion, Fiver sniffed at another iron gate that she had somehow managed to pass through or over. Wagging his tail and crying, he scratched at the cement below the gate, and then, looking through the bars, he searched the foothills that lay just beyond the houses. Still intent on following, he sniffed every inch of the ground along the wall.

Completely engrossed in his pursuit, he didn't notice the man with black hair standing on the porch, and he didn't sense the danger, either. He couldn't smell the gun, and completely distracted, he didn't see the dark squinting eyes that looked down the long barrel of a large hunting rifle. Had he sensed the danger, he wouldn't have stopped to try to decipher a particular scent. Had he not been so involved in his own pursuit, he might have heard the click of the rifle as the cartridge was forced into the firing chamber. But just then he did hear a voice, and it sounded familiar. When he looked up, he saw Jesse reach over Snyder's shoulder, grab the barrel of the rifle, and pull it skyward.

"You can't do that!" Jesse said with calm defiance, and pulling back, Snyder tried to yank the rifle free from Jesse's grip. But he held on, and when Snyder tried to hit him with the stock, Jesse caught it, and with one hand on the barrel and the other on the stock, he turned, and twisting, he forced Snyder to fall to his knees. Then, yanking the rifle from Snyder's grasp, he began to eject the shells.

Snyder was wild-eyed when he got to his feet. "You know you're through, don't you!" he shouted. "You damned half breed!"

Hearing the threat, Jesse froze and stopped ejecting the shells. "What did you call me?" he said grimly as he stepped toward Snyder. Then suddenly, with fear in his eyes, Snyder scrambled to his feet and ran back into the house, slamming the door behind him. Shaking his head, Jesse sighed, "What a fool." Then he ejected the last shell from the gun, and after removing the bolt, he carefully set the gun against the wall.

Fiver, who had watched the scuffle like a curious spectator, was now sniffing the ground over by the big four-wheel drive. Jesse called his name as he walked toward him. "Fiver! Here, boy. You remember me." Looking up, Fiver paused while he placed Jesse. Then, like someone happy to see an old friend, he padded slowly over to him. Kneeling down, Jesse stroked him. Then, taking him by the collar, he stood up. "Let's get you out of here," he said, and just then Mitchell came up the drive.

"I'm sorry," he said in a flustered voice. "What happened?"

"Better take him home," replied Jesse as he gestured to Fiver to go to Mitchell.

"But what happened," said Mitchell, and bending down, he took hold of Fiver's collar.

"Well, I don't know where to start," replied Jesse, and as he spoke his darkening countenance bespoke his growing awareness of what he had done. "Snyder was in a rage about the dog," he went on, "had a gun, and... and...aw, he'll get over it."

Before Mitchell could reply, Snyder reappeared on the porch holding a phone with a long cord that trailed through the partially open door. "The hell I will!" he shouted. "You're fired! Now get off my property. I'll deliver the Goddamn rabbits myself, and I'll see you both in court. I'll sue the hell out of both of you. Now get off my property!" Then, while shouting orders at someone on the phone, Snyder turned and disappeared into the mansion.

Briefly, Mitchell and Jesse stood silent. "I don't know what to say," said Mitchell finally, and with his head held high, Jesse just grimaced and stared out at the distant foothills. For a moment, taken by Jesse's grief, Mitchell was overcome with disbelief and sadness. But just then Fiver pulled away, and with his nose sniffing the air, he padded directly over to the big four-wheel drive. Then, rearing up on his haunches, he tried to look in the back of the SUV, where a large wire cage housed a dozen rabbits, some white, some gray, and some that were black and white. Next to them, in a bigger metal cage, one of the Dobermans looked menacingly out. As Mitchell grabbed Fiver by the collar, he looked in and stared at the rabbits until the Doberman bared his teeth and began to snarl.

"We'd better get of here!" yelled Jesse. "Who knows what Snyder will do. He goes crazy when someone crosses him."

Chapter Fifty Eight

Inside Mitchell's house, still in something of a daze, Mitchell and Jesse tried to sort through things for a while, and after much consternation and grief, Mitchell was offering Jesse another beer when the phone rang. It was Tom from the shop. "Mitchell, where you been? We've got a call. Some guy is stranded up on Silver Mountain, and we need you to take the tow truck and go get him. He's towing a boat, lost a wheel, and they've been waiting a long time. They're just over the summit, not far from the lookout." Mitchell sighed and looked woefully at Jesse. "OK, OK, I'll go get 'im," he said before he hung up, and then turning from the phone he looked at Jesse.

"It's all right," Jesse interjected, "I need time to think anyway. Don't know what I'm gonna tell...aw hell. Anyway, we'll talk later, huh? But can you give me a lift over to my place?"

"Sure," said Mitchell dejectedly. "But tell me one thing, what's with the rabbits?"

"Oh, yeah, the damn rabbits," said Jesse. "Well, they're going to the experimental lab over in Denton. Sometimes Snyder likes to deliver them personally. He does a lot of business with them. I usually go with him, and he always takes the shortcut over Silver Mountain. He takes the dog along for protection, so nobody will steal the rabbits out of the truck when we stop to eat. Paranoid, isn't it."

"I see," said Mitchell, "but will he really fire you?"

"Are you kidding," replied Jesse with a morbid chuckle. "I'm dead meat, and so are you. Dead meat. He's a vengeful son of a bitch."

Before they left the house, Mitchell knelt and hugged Fiver. "I'll be back," he said as he rubbed his ears. "I love the Fiver. You stay here this time. I love the Fiver."

After he dropped off Jesse at his home, Mitchell headed up Silver Mountain, and with the engine whining, he had just shifted into third when in his rearview mirror he saw Snyder's big four-wheeler gaining on him rapidly. Top heavy, the lifted truck, with its huge tires, was tipping on the corners. Moments later, with the driver hidden behind the black-tinted windows, it passed Mitchell and accelerated. Shifting down, Mitchell slowed and watched the truck continue to barrel up the road, and he wondered if Snyder was driving. As the road got steeper and the cliff along the gorge came into view, the gears in the old truck started to whine. In the distance, Snyder was already well up the mountain, where the switchbacks were very tight. "We're getting close to the summit," thought Mitchell, and with one hand on the shifter and the other on the steering wheel, he studied the road ahead.

Then, a few minutes later, as he came around the last tight curve, in the middle of the road, the crippled boat trailer suddenly came into view, and then a truck and a man waving frantically and pointing to a gaping hole in the guardrail. "Oh, hell," thought Mitchell as he looked at the skid marks and the broken railing. As he pulled up to the boat trailer, the man ran up to the truck. "He went over!" he cried. "Right there!"

"Take it easy," said Mitchell as he got out of the truck. Then, stepping over to the broken railing, fearing what he might see, he looked down at the cavernous canyon below, and there below him, about twenty-five yards away, he saw the four-wheeler. Mangled and twisted, with its rear wheels still spinning in the air, it was dangling precariously on the edge of a large flat rock that hung out over the gorge.

Holding onto the torn railing, Mitchell looked for any sign of life or movement in the truck, but all he saw was a rear wheel still spinning ever so slowly. Then, looking over at the tow truck, he decided what to do, and moments later he backed the tow truck up to the opening in the railing. After setting the emergency brake, he ran to the back of the truck, and glancing down at the wreck below, he pulled the lever that let out the cable from the boom.

While he was wrapping the cable around his waist, he heard a noisy but familiar-sounding car pull up, and when he looked around, he saw Jesse hop out of his jeep. "What are you doing here?" yelled Mitchell with critical surprise.

"Tom called me from the shop, gave me some jacks to bring up, sent me up here to give you a hand. Said he didn't have anybody else available, and said he just thought I should come."

"He went over," said Mitchell, looking down at the suspended truck. "I need a hand, need you to let me down on the cable. It's that lever right there. Toward the cab is down, the other way is up. Got it?"

"OK," said Jesse, and stepping to the railing, his eyes widened as he looked down at the truck. "My God," he said. "I'd better chain the truck to something." And in instant he pulled a large chain from the back of the jeep, and after wrapping it around the post on the guardrail, he secured it to the tow truck. "I guess that's better than nothing," he said doubtfully.

As he climbed over the broken railing, Mitchell turned his back to the canyon and gave the cable a tug. "OK, let her out," he said, and like a rappelling mountain climber, he edged slowly down the steep slope, and with each step, the rocks that he loosened with his feet began to rain down toward the destitute vehicle. As the cascading rocks gained momentum, they bounced, hit the huge flat rock under the truck, and flew out into the oblivion of the gorge. Up above, Jesse leaned over the torn railing, and with one hand still on the lever, he watched Mitchell silently descend.

When he reached the flat outcropping where the truck was hanging, Mitchell waved for Jesse to stop letting out the cable. Then, with the cable still around his waist, he turned and crawled toward the truck on his hands and knees. The glass in the rear door was broken, and inside he heard the Doberman whimpering. Carefully, he pulled the latch and tugged at the door to see if it moved the truck at all. When it didn't, he pulled harder and then jerked at it until it popped open. Suddenly everything before him was a moving, scampering cloud of gray and white, and flying past him, the rabbits were everywhere, running and jumping over his head, bounding off his neck and shoulders. Then everything was quiet. When he looked back he saw the rabbits running for shelter on the steep mountain. As he turned back to the truck he saw the open rabbit cage and the Doberman still in his cage, and still whining. Behind the dog, in the front seat, Snyder was moaning and semiconscious.

As Mitchell wondered what to do next, what he could do, if anything, Snyder's moaning changed to a shrill scream. "Get me out of here! Help me! Get me out of here!" he shrieked as he twisted to look back over his seat at Mitchell.

"Take it easy!" shouted Mitchell. "Don't move, and I'll get you out of there. Just let me get this cage out of the way." Then quickly, with Snyder still crying and yelling, Mitchell pulled the empty wire rabbit cage forward and out of the truck, and once he had it on the ledge, he kicked it away with his foot. Then, edging forward on his hands and knees, he reached into the back of the truck and carefully opened the Doberman's cage. "Come on, boy," he said softly as he gestured to the dog. But, frightened and shocked, the Doberman pulled back and bared his teeth. "Oh, hell," thought Mitchell, and just then, white with fear, Snyder began to pant like a wounded animal, and in a daze he turned and looked out the broken windshield. Seeing nothing but blue sky and the small trees on the other side of the canyon, he drew back and screeched, "Oh, God! Oh, Goddamn it!" Turning back around, he grabbed and clutched at the back of his seat, and diving between the front seats, he pulled himself into the backseat. "Get me out!" he shrieked as he extended his arm and lunged. "Get me out!"

"Don't move, for hell's sake!" shouted Mitchell, and at that second, the truck shuddered. Before him, in something like a blurred dream, Mitchell saw the Doberman snarling and Snyder's terrified angry face and his flailing extended hands. In an instant, Mitchell reached out, and grasping, he felt nothing; then suddenly, he did feel something, and grasping, he pulled.

Then, before him, he saw the Doberman's eyes grow wide. He had him by the collar, and yanking him forward, Mitchell rolled over on his back and with both arms threw the Doberman toward the mountain. Then he felt the rock beneath him tremble, and there was a loud, deep, scratching sound, and spinning back around toward the truck, he saw nothing, nothing, nothing but the other side of the gorge, rock, and cliffs. The truck was gone, taken, taken without a word, snatched like some kind of unsuspecting prey.

Unable to fathom things, Mitchell gazed at the now-barren rock, and then for a moment he looked at his hands, as if to admonish them. "What the hell happened?" he mumbled. "Why didn't he stay still?" Then slowly, he turned away from the gorge, and behind him, up on the steep slope, he saw all the rabbits scattered here and there. Sitting silently next to a bush or a rock, like jurors in a court, they seemed to be watching him, studying him, pondering what had happened, what he had done. Then the Doberman whimpered, and taking his eyes from the rabbits, Mitchell took a deep breath. "It's OK, kid," he said. "It's all right." And moving closer, without hesitation, he petted him and rubbed his ears. Then, standing up, he adjusted the cable around his waist and took one last look at the now-empty cliff.

Moments later, with the Doberman under his arm, Mitchell yelled to Jesse, "Take us up," and with the taut cable in hand, he and the Doberman made their way up the steep slope, step by step. Behind them, a cascade of rocks, like dirt thrown onto a coffin, showered down into the gorge.

As they neared the top, Mitchell heard voices and a pulsing siren. Just beyond the railing a crowd of people had gathered. Grimacing at the pain coming from the arm that held the Doberman, Mitchell could hear people talking. Then abruptly, the siren stopped, and somewhere in the back of the crowd a man was talking loudly, "I don't know. It looked to me like he just let him go. I was watching through my binoculars. Coulda saved him, but he just grabbed the dog!"

As Mitchell approached the twisted railing, the crowd went silent, and an officer with firm blue eyes reached down and helped pull them up.

"Hang on," he said as he grabbed Mitchell's arm, and a second later they were on level ground. Turning to the crowd, the officer shook his head. "Now listen, Officer Thompson will take your statements," he said, pointing to the other officer. "If you saw what happened, please give us a statement, and we'll need all your names." Then Mitchell felt Jesse's hand on his shoulder. "You all right?" he said.

"I'm fine," said Mitchell, as he carefully set down the Doberman, "and... Snyder?"

Without responding, Jesse tipped his head toward the canyon and shrugged. "Not good." Then the officer spoke. "We've got some men on their way down there. But there's not much chance. Not after a fall like that. Never had one make it out yet. The gorge doesn't give 'em back. You know, you'll have to come into the station," he concluded. "Both of you, and it's gonna take some time."

"What do you mean?" said Mitchell as he looked in amazement at Jesse.

"Well," said the officer, it seems Snyder had filed some complaints against both of you."

"What complaints?" said Jesse, cocking his head.

"Well, what they told me back at the station was that there were complaints of assault and trespassing against Mitchell Black, and assault and battery against Jesse Littlefield. Just came in an hour ago or so. That complicates things, so you'll have to come in, boys. Sorry, but we'll get this straightened out."

#

Chapter Fifty Nine

#

Sitting in the backseat of the squad car, Mitchell put his head in his hands while Jesse just looked out the window at the passing trees. As they headed down the mountain road, the sheriff lit a cigarette. Then a detached voice came over the radio. "Sheriff Larsen, they found the driver of the truck. It looks like he was crushed on impact. He's dead." Exhaling the smoke from his cigarette, the sheriff lifted the mic from the dashboard. "Thanks, Ed," he said, holding the mic to his mouth, and as he spoke a cloud of smoke hovered around his head. "We'll be there in a few minutes." After he put the mic back on the dash, the sheriff looked at Jesse and Mitchell in the rearview mirror. "Well, that's that," he said. "You wouldn't know it, but there's about six cars and trucks down there. Can't get 'em out. Eventually, you can't even find them. The canyon just sort of swallows 'em up."

When the sheriff got to the bottom of the mountain and turned onto the highway, Mitchell lay his head back on the seat and closed his eyes, and for a bit the darkness was a relief. But then, from out of nowhere, he saw Snyder screaming, "Get me out of here!" and opening his eyes, he jolted forward and looked confusedly over at Jesse. Then, looking past him out the window, he saw that they were passing the garage, and with not a soul around, the Healey was sitting outside with the engine still dangling from its chain on the A-Frame.

At the station, a woman in uniform handed the sheriff some papers as he sat down behind his desk. "Have a seat," he said to Mitchell and Jesse, and as they sat down, they saw the sheriff's expression change as he shuffled through the papers. "Well," said the sheriff, throwing the papers on the desk, "it looks like this thing is going to get complicated." Then he looked directly at Mitchell. "Did you have an altercation with Snyder a while back, at Lucille's? Did you threaten him?"

"We argued," said Mitchell, surprised. "We argued, but I don't remember exactly what I said."

"I see," said the sheriff. "And have you been on his property, and has your dog been getting into his trash?"

"Well, that did happen," said Mitchell, "but it was an innocent..."

"Uh-huh," said the sheriff, interrupting. "So there was some bad blood between you and Snyder." And then he looked to Jesse. "And did you knock Snyder down?"

Without replying right away, Jesse frowned. "I wouldn't say I knocked him down," he said finally. "I...ah...I disarmed him. He was gonna shoot Mitchell's dog. Not much else I could do."

Sitting back in his chair, the sheriff reached into his pocket and took out his cigarettes. "Well, you'd better call your attorney, or let me get you one," he said casually. "You're going to be here for a while, at least until you get bail or some kind of representation."

Sighing, Mitchell dropped his head. "How long?" he inquired without looking up.

"Well, it depends on whether or not they file more serious charges," said the sheriff as he pulled some forms from the desk. "It's not likely, but someone could make more out of this. Anyway, you'll be here for a while, maybe a few days, or...well, we'll see."

"I was trying to save the man!" cried Mitchell, rising up in his chair. "This is ridiculous!"

Then Jesse took Mitchell's arm. "Settle down," he said calmly. "It's all right."

"And what about my dog?" asked Mitchell. "I'll have to get someone to take care of him."

The sheriff scratched the side of his neck. "Sorry, he'll have to go to the pound. For the time being, he's evidence, and that makes him property of the state for now."

Mitchell fell back in his chair. "Isn't there any alternative to that? He hates to be caged!"

The sheriff shook his head. "No, I'm sorry, there isn't. After I get you booked, I'll have to take him over."

"You're gonna book me?" said Mitchell.

"Both of you," replied the sheriff.

"Oh, hell," said Jesse as he dropped his head to hands. "What's going on?"

"I wouldn't worry too much," interjected the sheriff as he looked straight at Jesse. "From what I see, there aren't any witnesses to your little tussle with Snyder. You could be out pretty soon." Feeling some relief at hearing that, Mitchell's thoughts turned to Fiver and the first time he saw him in the cage at the pound. His eyes were so magnificent and beguiling. "Can I see him before you take him away?" he asked as his heart sank. "It's important."

Standing up from behind the desk, the sheriff gave Mitchell a long, pitiful look. "I doubt it, but I'll see what I can do."

Chapter Sixty

#

After the booking and the fingerprinting, the sheriff handed Mitchell the phone. "You'd better call someone before we get you situated," he said as he lit another cigarette. Taking the phone, Mitchell dialed Noah at his office. "I'll be right there," said Noah without asking any questions. "You hold tight, and don't say anything!"

As he reached across the desk to hang up the phone, Mitchell's eyes followed the sheriff's nod toward a steel door across the room. A sign above it said, "Restricted Area. Do Not Enter Without Guard."

"Is this really necessary? Our attorney will be here in a few minutes."

"Sorry," said the sheriff, exhaling his cigarette smoke. "He can't get you out of here today. It's late, and it'll take a while to unravel this thing." Then, standing up, he put out his cigarette and motioned for Mitchell and Jesse to walk in front of him.

Taking a key from the ring on his belt, the sheriff unlocked the metal door and started walking Jesse and Mitchell down a long hallway with barred cells on each side. As they walked, curious but indifferent faces peered out at them from behind the bars. In a cell on his left a man in rags was huddled in the corner like someone in an asylum. In the next cell there was a hard-faced Indian with long braids sitting on his bunk, and his eyes were narrow and distrustful as he watched them pass.

"You're down at the end," said the sheriff, and at that moment, a Mexican man in Levi's and a T-shirt was pointing at the sheriff and yelling in Spanish. When Mitchell caught his eye, he glared at him and bared his teeth, and then, still yelling, he grabbed and pulled at the bars of his cell. "Hey, gringo, you want to fight me?"

The next cell was empty, and hearing the sound of his own footsteps, Mitchell tried to keep his eyes to the floor. But on his right, he saw some brown wing-tipped shoes. Following them up, he saw a man with light red hair and albino eyes. Muttering to himself, he was methodically pacing back and forth in his cell like a cat. In the cell next to him, two guys in T-shirts and beards were playing cards, and next to them, a black man looked over the top of a magazine. "Hey, sheriff," he said. "You call my wife yet?"

The sheriff smiled. "Yeah, she's on her way. But from the way she sounds, if I were you, I don't know if I'd want to get out or not."

Coming to an empty cell that was the last one in that block, the sheriff opened the door and waved for Jesse and Mitchell to go in. After they were in, the sheriff locked the door, and the sound of it made Mitchell queasy. Behind him, Jesse sat down on a bench next to a bunk bed. "With a little luck, you won't be here long," said the sheriff. Staring back at the sheriff, with reticent frustration, Mitchell shook his head and sat down on the bench next to Jesse. Across the aisle in another cell, they saw a man lying on his bunk. He was wearing headphones, and they were connected by a long cord to a small stereo that sat on a shelf at the head of his bed. Next to the stereo there was a miniature TV, a clock, and another set of headphones. Immersed in whatever he was listening to, he seemed aloof and his face was expressionless, and judging by how far his feet were from the end of the bunk, Mitchell put him to be no more than five feet tall. On the floor by his bed there was a paper plate, and it was filled with bread and bits of cheese. "Been here a while," thought Mitchell, and then looking around their cell, he noted the sink and a small toilet, and the barred window above it.

#

Chapter Sixty One

#

Noah arrived at the jail within the hour, and Jesse and Mitchell both stood up and shook his hand. "Thanks for comin'," said Mitchell. "I hope we didn't ruin your day."

"My day's been all right," said Noah as he let go of Mitchell's hand. "Now you, you've had a day!"

"Yeah, it was a beaut. Did they tell you anything?"

Slipping off his glasses, Noah rubbed his eyes with his fingers. "Yes, they did, and you know Snyder's dead?"

Closing his eyes, Mitchell nodded. "Yeah, I know," said Mitchell.

Noah slid his glasses back on. "Evidently, the love-loss between you and Snyder wasn't a private matter, and one of the witnesses at the scene is saying that you might have or could have saved him, but didn't, that maybe you let him go over. That's the bad news that opens Pandora's box. I suppose if they pushed it, they could investigate it as a possible homicide, but that's really not likely. If they do anything to muddy up the waters, it's more likely we'll have to deal with the Good Samaritan laws. Pain in the ass."

"Homicide? That's absurd!" cried Mitchell.

"Of course, that's not likely," replied Noah, "but with all this circumstantial evidence, they'll look into it, and the Good Samaritan law could be a factor. They could push you around with that."

"Exactly what is it?" inquired Jesse.

"Well, it's designed to help someone who, in helping someone in distress, ends up being sued for doing the wrong thing, you know, hurting them," replied Noah. "But here's the thing. It can also work against you if they can prove negligence or malice. You see my concern with the bad blood and all. But, don't worry, I'm sure we'll get it all settled within a day or two. And Jesse, I don't think the assault and battery will hold with you. From what I've read, they have no witnesses, no evidence, just an unsubstantiated charge over the phone, so I should be able to get you out of here sooner. They don't have anything. Mitchell, yours is gonna take some more time. I'll try to arrange a hearing and bail as fast as I can."

With his mind swimming with images, Mitchell winced and then sagged. "I didn't touch him," he said, shaking his head. "It all happened so fast, there wasn't any time to think. I just did what I did, and...and then he went over. When Snyder started moving, he set it all loose...and, hell...I, I don't know...maybe, maybe I could of done it differently, but the dog was in front of me."

Taken back, Noah squinted through his glasses while Mitchell continued.

"I was gonna hook the cable on the truck if I had too, but that seemed risky, and it all happened so fast. Hell, I don't know! Maybe I didn't do enough, maybe I did..."

With a deep sigh, Noah looked away, and his face was strained when he looked back. "I know, it's hard now," he said. "Don't be hard on yourself. You're a good man. I know that. We'll get through this. I'll be back when your head's clear, and we'll go through the details. It should be pretty much routine."

After Noah left, Jesse and Mitchell talked and tried to think through things. When Mitchell got visibly upset, Jesse calmed him down. Then, early in the evening, a guard came and opened the door, and stepping past Mitchell, he addressed Jesse. "You've got bail," he said, "and it looks like they're not pressing charges on you. Noah always gets the job done. You're lucky to have him. Before he left, Jesse and Mitchell hugged. "I'm sorry," said Mitchell, "for the whole damn mess."

Chapter Sixty Two

Noah came back the next day at noon, and he was about to go over things when immediately Mitchell asked him if Fiver was OK, and if they put him in the pound. Shrugging, Noah responded, "They did pick him up, and he's in the pound, but I had Tom from the garage go over and check on him. He told me he's OK, fine, and I'm gonna try to get him out of there, maybe have Jesse or Tom take temporary custody. It's a long shot, but I'll try, but I have some pull, and we'll see. What about your girl?" Noah went on. "Nancy, isn't it? Could she take care of him for a while?"

"No, she's gone," said Mitchell, visibly saddened, and in his mind he recalled his last failed phone call. "So where are we at?" he said finally, and it was then that Noah's expression changed. "What is it?" asked Mitchell. "What's going on?"

"Well, it's too soon to tell for sure, but it looks like they're going to pursue something," said Noah, "and we'll have to have a hearing to set bail and with some luck get the whole thing dismissed. But it seems Snyder's family is pretty upset and vindictive about the whole thing. They've lost lots of money and there's talk that they want to bring in some high-powered investigators and attorneys and not leave a stone unturned. It seems your dislike for Snyder has become local folklore."

Closing his eyes, Mitchell sighed and nodded disparagingly. "They're pushing it as a homicide?"

"Don't know yet," said Noah, "but I doubt it. More likely they will push the Good Samaritan case, and if they can't get criminal charges, they'll go for a civil case. Then, even if they can't win, they'll try to bury you financially with court costs and ruin your reputation. That's the legal way of slaughtering people."

Shaking his head, Mitchell looked away. "It's like a nightmare. I can't believe it," he said, and drawing a long, slow breath, he looked to Noah and searched his face. "So I'm gonna be stuck here, aren't I," he said.

"Not really, not if I can help it," replied Noah, "but there's one thing we have to discuss right now. You may want to get a real good defense attorney."

Surprised, Mitchell raised his head and turned back around. "You mean you don't want to defend me?"

Gazing back at him, Noah looked dejected. "Listen, you might want to consider getting a pro. I've been doing estates and trusts and wills for farmers, and if I can't get this thrown out quickly, it could be very serious. We know you're innocent, but you can't fool around with this. If it comes to that, you'd need the best."

"I've got the best. You know you're the best around here. Everybody knows that."

Noah shook his head. "I'm just a big fish in a small pond. I could put you in touch with somebody from Denver. He's a good man, and he's handled thousands of serious criminal cases."

"I can't afford him. I can't afford bail. I don't have that kind of money. I'd lose the garage and everything, and I'd be taking Tom and everybody with me. I've got some money saved, and I could pay you on time, and you know I'd be good for it."

"I'm not worried about the money. You know that. You just ought to have the best. It can make the difference."

Turning away, Mitchell looked up at the small window over the bed. Then, after a long silence, he said, "Please do what you can. Some big-city lawyer, that wouldn't work. He wouldn't understand. You know me. Hell, you know the town. That makes a difference, doesn't it?" With his eyes falling from the window to the bed, Mitchell fell silent. "Maybe I'll defend myself. That might be the solution. What the hell."

"Listen, you can't do that!" declared Noah, and taking Mitchell by the shoulder, he turned him around. "Now, that's out of the question! Just forget that. People around here aren't all that sophisticated. If you want me to defend you, I will. But you think about it first. This could be one of the most important decisions you'll ever make. Now I'm gonna go. Do you want me to stop by your house and get you anything?"

Mitchell rubbed the back of his neck, and nodding at Noah, he said, "Yeah, I guess I'll need some things, won't I? If you could grab me some clothes and things, and my mail, and maybe some of my books, I'd appreciate it. The back door's open."

"Sure, I'd be glad to," said Noah, and picking up his briefcase, his eyes caught Mitchell's. "Have you called Nancy?" he said, and at the mention of her name, Mitchell slumped.

"No...No, I didn't."

"I can call her, if you'd like," said Noah, "or I can arrange for you to, or if you want, you can send a telegram if that's easier."

Mitchell shook his head. "No, that's OK. Maybe I'll write her." Then he laughed. "Hum, wouldn't that make a great postcard: 'In jail. Indicted for homicide. Wish you were here.'"

Shaking his head at Mitchell's dark humor, Noah motioned to the guard to let him out of the cell. "I'll see you in the morning. I'll get this hearing set up. There's a judge I want to handle it," he said as the guard rolled the bars back, and watching him leave, Mitchell thought of something. "Noah, could you see if you can get someone to walk Fiver? He needs to do that at least twice a day. He'll go crazy if they don't do that."

Leaning against the bars, Mitchell watched Noah head up the aisle between the cells, and when the big metal door echoed shut behind him, Mitchell's eyes fell to the floor. Then, looking up, he saw the little man in the cell across from him. Lying on his side on his bunk, with his headphones still on, he was watching his tiny television. But, noticing Mitchell's gaze, he reached up and turned the television off. Then, pulling the headphones down to his chest, he sat up on the edge of the bunk. With his feet dangling above the floor, he studied Mitchell. Then in a high but clear voice, he said, "I can tell by the look in your eyes that you're smart."

Looking back at him, Mitchell raised his eyebrows. "Right, that's why I'm here."

With his legs swinging back and forth like those of a child on a park bench, the little man continued to scrutinize Mitchell. "I have some magazines over here," he said. "You can borrow one when you're ready, after you settle down and get adjusted. That'll take a while, but some guys even like it here after a while. They don't wanna leave."

"You sound like you've been here before."

"It's an occupational hazard with me. That's why I come prepared."

Mitchell smiled. "I'll take a magazine. And by the way, what's the food under your bed for? You have a cat or something?"

Like a cocky leprechaun hopping down from a branch, the little man jumped from his bunk. Then, bending over, he began to poke through the pile of magazines on the table next to his bed. "Oh, this one is good," he said, holding up an issue of *Time* magazine. "I've got a *Harper's* if you'd rather."

Mitchell replied, "The *Harper's* is all right. What do you do with the food? I mean on the plate there?"

Kneeling down, the little man rolled up the magazine, and then reaching through the bars, he tossed it toward Mitchell. "It's for the mouse," he said after the magazine slapped the floor. "You've got to make friends where you can."

Bending down, Mitchell reached through the bars to pick up the magazine. Across the aisle, the little man hopped back up on his bunk, and sliding on his headphones, he began to adjust the knobs on his mini media system. Noticing Mitchell watching him, he pulled down the headphones. "You have to do two things in order to survive in here," he said pedantically. "First, you have to learn to live in your head. This place is like living in a ghetto. You know, you look around and it's all shit. So you live vicariously. You listen to the radio, you listen to tapes, you watch TV, read, daydream, whatever. You know, like what people do in big cities. But you have to make your own reality! Anything's better than what you got here!"

Mitchell smiled halfheartedly. "What's the other thing?" he asked, and seeming to wonder if Mitchell was mocking him, the little man puckered up his face. Then, apparently confident of Mitchell's sincerity, or unable to restrain himself, he went on. "You've got to do something to validate yourself," he said proudly. "Something that shows you that you're here, that you make a difference, recognition. Know what I mean?"

Standing up, Mitchell rolled the magazine up in his hand. "Like what?" he said.

"That's up to you," said the little man as he put his earphones back on. "Do anything, whittle, paint, write letters, talk to yourself, talk to God, talk to the walls. If you don't do something, they'll turn you into an animal."

Chapter Sixty Three

#

It was noontime when Noah came by the next day, and as he entered the cell, his arms were laden with books and a sack of clothing. Letting them all fall in a heap on the bunk, he let go of a big volume of Shakespeare, and some of Mitchell's mail spilled out across the blanket. As he surveyed the pile of books and toiletries, Mitchell ran his hand across the large volume of Shakespeare. "Well, what's happened?" he said when he turned to face Noah. "How's Fiver?"

Putting his hands on his hips, Noah straightened his back. "Fiver's fine," he replied with a slight moan, "and one of the girls at the pound is going to take him for his walks every day."

"And did you take in his meds? He needs those in case he has a seizure. He still has those once in a while."

"Sure did. Didn't take 'em all, though, just a few in a baggy. You had quite a supply there."

"I know. How 'bout Jesse? How's he doin'?"

Noah's forehead wrinkled as he caught sight of the little man in the opposite cell. "Jesse's fine," he said, still staring at the little man.

"And any news for me?" asked Mitchell. "How bad is it?" Then, pulling his gaze from the man in the opposite cell, Noah looked Mitchell straight in the eye. "From what I gather, they're gonna do what I said, try to charge you under the Good Samaritan law, and get as much as they can. It's technical, and they have to know that it's weak and won't fly, but we'll see how far they go. I still think we'll get it dismissed."

Mitchell stared blankly at Noah. "I see. Anything else I should know? What's the prosecutor like?"

Noah rubbed his chin. "Well, he's a young hotshot, and they say he's aggressive, trying to make a name for himself, and Snyder's people, investigators and all that, are doing a lot of research."

Starting to turn away, Mitchell stopped, and turning back around, he gave Noah a hard, questioning look. "So you think it could go to trial?"

"It's always a possibility," replied Noah as he continued to rub his chin, "but I doubt it. It's not in the cards, try to relax. I think we'll get the right judge. The arraignment will be tomorrow, and the hearing could be anytime, probably in a few days, or maybe a week at the longest."

Closing his eyes, Mitchell rubbed the back of his neck. "My God," he said flatly. "I really didn't think it could get this bad. It seems so absurd to me. What the hell can they be thinking? I didn't force him over the damned cliff."

"Now listen," said Noah firmly. "You've got to remember that they don't know exactly what happened, and they're trying to put it together. That takes some time. Let me go get the rest of your stuff, and then we'll talk. We'll beat this thing. Don't worry."

After Noah left, Mitchell sat on the edge of his bunk and sorted through the scattered letters. The second letter he picked up was from Nancy, and he pondered it a long time before abruptly tearing it open.

Dear Mitchell,

My showing was a success. I've never been so thrilled. We sold all but two or three of my paintings, and I have orders for more, and we're talking about making a run of prints. You know, signed and numbered. It's been a lot of fun. I wish you could have been here.

Funny, you know how I've talked about how cliquish it is here. I thought my success would break the ice and open some doors, but it seems it hasn't worked out that way. I think some people resent my success. Oh, well, they say it's lonely at the top, but I do have a couple of friends, and now and then we go out to a neighborhood bar for dinner and drinks. Lots of crazy artistic types there. I miss you. Please write.

Love always,
Nancy

"Sure," thought Mitchell, "and who were you out with all night, Picasso?" Then, dropping the letter, he lay back on the bed and closed his eyes. When he woke up a while later, he saw the little man lying on his stomach on the edge of bed. With his feet in the air, and his head and hands hanging over the side of the bed, he seemed to be poised for something. Then, suddenly pounding his fist on the floor, he grabbed wildly under the bed. "I almost got you that time," he said as he pushed himself back onto the bed.

"You trying to catch the mouse?" said Mitchell. "I thought he was your friend."

"He is," said the little man, almost beaming. "I wasn't trying to catch him. I just scare the hell out of him sometimes. Makes it more interesting for both of us."

After some thoughtful hesitation, Mitchell laughed, and for a moment his mood lightened. "You play God, huh?"

The little man threw up his shoulders nonchalantly. "Sort of. But there's a method to it. You see, if I don't do this, when I leave, the next guy in this cell will probably kill him when he comes out and he's not cautious. It doesn't pay to get too friendly around here."

"What's your name?" said Mitchell as he watched him lean over the edge of the bed and look under it.

"My name's Daryl," said the little man without looking up, "and I know yours. You're Mitchell Black. You're the one they say let that guy go over the cliff and all that."

"How'd you know that?"

Pushing himself up from the floor, Daryl rolled over on his back and casually clasped his hands behind his head. Then he nodded toward the radio and tape player. "Oh, I'm kind of in charge of information around here. It's kind of a sideline of mine. You know, everything you do has to pay."

Amused and somewhat puzzled, Mitchell smiled. "What are you in here for?" he asked, and looking back at him, Daryl struck a thoughtful pose.

"Oh, you could say I was in sales, just sellin' the wrong stuff, that's all. You know Ford can sell cars that blow up, and Reynolds Tobacco can sell cigarettes that kill you, and the government sells arms to anybody that wants them. But me, I just wanna sell some grass. You know, an elixir for the downtrodden masses, something to kill the pain, and I get busted."

"You were selling grass?" Mitchell said quizzically. "What happened? I didn't think that was too serious these days."

Still lying on his back, Daryl looked at the ceiling while he spoke. "Well, problem is, I had a truckload of the stuff in the back of my truck, and I was doin' uppers and downers, and I got weird and crashed just this side of the Utah border. Flipped the truck, rolled it a couple of times. I shoulda been dead, and you know most of the damn weed spilled out and blew all over the place. I've probably seeded the entire Rocky Mountains. Should be a nice crop there next year."

Mitchell snorted as he began to laugh, and Daryl shook his head as he continued. "They took me to the hospital and then here. They'll probably get around to trying me in a few weeks. Best-laid plans of mice and men, huh?"

Chapter Sixty Four

The next day Mitchell met again with Noah, and he was still optimistic about getting the charges dropped. That possibility, along with visits from a few friends like Tom and Glen, and Daryl's tales of woe and misbegotten adventures, made the confinement a little less unbearable. It was only the recurring images and dreams about the scene on the cliff and the constant longing for Fiver and Nancy that made the time go so tortuously slow.

When Noah left, Daryl saw Mitchell dejectedly staring down at the floor, and asked him if he wanted to listen to any of his tapes. "I've got some good stuff from the sixties. That's your era, isn't it?"

Mitchell smiled. "Do you have any classical things in there?"

Daryl lit up. "Ah, I've got a whole set of classical pieces. It's one of those *Life* magazine music library things for people who really don't like classical, but feel insecure about it. How about something by Schubert, or maybe Dvorak?"

Flipping through the tapes, Daryl stopped and held one up. "Ah, here we go," he said as he snapped it into the player. Then, bending down, he took the headphones and, reaching through the bars, slid them across the floor. "The cord won't reach to the bed. You'll have to sit by the bars."

Kneeling down, Mitchell picked up the headphones, and sitting on the floor with his back to the bars, he put them on. When the music started, he closed his eyes, and for an hour he rejected his surroundings completely. Then, through the bars at his back, he felt the guard open the door to his cell, and looking up, he saw Noah gazing down at him, and his demeanor was pained. As he rocked forward, Mitchell took off the headphones. "What's up?" he said, and still staring down at him, Noah remained silent. "What is it? It can't be that bad," said Mitchell as he got to his feet.

"Fiver escaped from the pound. They're out looking for him now."

In utter disbelief, Mitchell fell silent, and with his arms dangling hopelessly at his sides, he searched Noah's face. "What do you mean? Where is he? How could he escape?"

Tilting his head, Noah recounted what happened. "They were walking him, or the gal at the desk was. They were outside in the compound, and it seems he just pulled out of his collar. She said that before she knew it, he ran and jumped a six-foot fence and was gone, just like that. They went after him, but they say he just vanished. I guess he just bolted. Took them all by surprise. It's almost like he planned it."

Turning away, Mitchell grabbed the bars of his cell, and holding onto them, he dropped his head.

"It's a small town," said Noah. "They'll find him. They're going to send a truck out to your house. He might show up there."

#

Chapter Sixty Five

#

It was late that afternoon when the truck from the pound pulled up in front of Mitchell's house. "Well, let's go check it out," said the driver. "It's four thirty. I wanna get home."

"OK," said the man sitting on the passenger side. "You check out the front, and I'll go around the back. Then let's get out of here."

Slamming the doors of the truck behind them, the two men in blue uniforms made their way through the front gate. As they scoured the yard, Fiver watched from inside the garage. Peering out from the darkness just behind a broken slat in the wall of the old garage, he carefully monitored their every move. When he heard one of them call his name, he lowered his head, and, scooting backward along the ground, he pulled back further into the darkness. Still able to see out, he watched as one of them stopped and, looking in his direction, rubbed his chin. Then, walking toward the garage, the man called out again. "Fiver. Here boy."

Tensing as the man drew closer and closer, Fiver rose up, and in a low crouch, he was about to leap out when, already back at the truck, the other man yelled, "Come on, Ed. Let's go. He's not here. It's quittin' time."

At the entrance to the garage, the man who was now only a few feet from Fiver yelled back, "I'll be there in a minute," and shielding his eyes with his hand, he leaned forward and looked into the garage. But before his eyes could adjust to the darkness, he turned away. "Ah, to hell with it," he said. "Let's go."

The truck from the pound was well down the road when Fiver peeked out from the garage, and as he stepped out into the afternoon sunlight, he carefully looked around. Then, glancing back and forth, he trotted across the yard. For a second, he stopped and stared at the place by the front gate where Mitchell used to park the car. Then, turning away, he headed around to the back of the house. Running up the back steps, he pushed on the screen door with his paw, and when it moved freely, he scratched at it until he was able to catch it with his nose and nudge it open.

With the door stuck open, he trotted past Nancy's painting, and with hopeful eyes, he went directly to the door that led into the kitchen. But when he nudged it, he found that it was closed tight. Sitting back on his haunches, he scratched at it. Then he barked. But no one answered, and with his head cocked to one side, he scratched again and waited, and still no one answered. Lowering his head, he looked over at Nancy's painting, and for a moment he seemed to study it. Then, walking toward it, he lay down by the chair that Nancy used to sit in when she painted. As his eyelids got heavy, he stared at the big bag of granola that sat next to the screen door, and soon, with his head resting on his paws, he was asleep.

At the cry of a meadowlark, Fiver woke up early the next morning, and as he rose up and stretched, the warm glow of the morning sun sparkled on the gold highlights of his coat. As he looked around at his surroundings, he seemed to ponder what he was going to do. Then, trotting across the floor, he scratched at the kitchen door. When no one answered, he turned away, and perplexed, he looked again at Nancy's painting. Then, directly behind it, he saw the big bag of granola, and with his eyes suddenly brimming with possibilities, he padded over to it. A moment later, like a bear getting into a honeycomb, he rose up, and using his front paws, he pulled the bag over, spilling granola bountifully about his feet. Then, lowering his head, he sniffed the sweet grain and began eating.

After he had eaten his fill, he scratched on the back door one more time. When no one answered, he stepped through the spilled granola and went outside. At the bottom of the steps, he stopped and sniffed the air and cautiously gazed around at the yard. Then, trotting leisurely across the back lawn, he ducked under the fence and headed across the field toward the small irrigation stream bordering the property. At the stream, he drank for a long time, and when he finished, he began to meander around the field, stopping here and there to appraise a different scent. A while later, he was pawing at a gopher hole when out of the corner of his eye he saw the truck from the pound pull up. Instinctively, he lay down in the tall grass, and like a crouching lion, he watched the men wander about the yard. Had they had better vision and a better sense of smell, they might have discovered him, but after a few minutes they abandoned the search and drove off.

That afternoon Fiver maintained at the house, and except for a constant longing for Mitchell and a growing sense of sad confusion as to what had happened, he got along. However, the next morning, when he was still asleep on the porch, something woke him up, and opening his eyes, he saw the curious face of another dog peering in through the screen door. As he rose up, he saw a very pretty but gaunt, half-starved black Labrador. Shrinking back, with her brown eyes darting nervously back and forth between Fiver and the spilled bag of granola, the Labrador vacillated between her apprehension and her hunger. Standing erect, Fiver stared back at her with his tail slightly elevated and wagging ever so slowly. Then, cautiously, a step at a time, he edged forward and sniffed her nose. Gently, he carefully stepped closer, and the Labrador tensed when, moving his nose along her back and side, Fiver began to sniff her hindquarters. But sensing that he was not a threat, she edged forward, and after giving him one last look, she briefly sniffed his underside. Then, with a quick step, she trotted past him through the open screen door, and after a couple of furtive glances about the room, she began to frantically gorge on the granola. Following her in, Fiver watched her eat, and when she glanced up at him with eyes that were still wild and distrustful, if not fierce, he returned her gaze with his own Buddha-like countenance.

After she had eaten all she could, the Lab turned from the granola and seemed to take Fiver's measure one more time. Then with a still-cautious eye on him, she lay down next to Nancy's easel, and after raising an eyelid to check on him, she was soon overcome by sleep. When she awoke hours later, she found Fiver watching her from his repose across the porch, and for a long time, like two shipwrecked strangers, they just stared at one another, wondering. Then, finally, the Labrador rose up, and after sniffing the easel and a pair of Mitchell's old work shoes, she gazed at Fiver with eyes that were now more trusting. As she moved cautiously toward him, Fiver rose up, and they were both gentle in their investigation of one another. Then, with a wag of her tail, the Lab shyly licked Fiver on the nose. A few moments later, he went down the steps, and then the two of them bounded across the lawn, ducked under the fence, and loped off into the fields. When the sun set, Fiver and the Labrador were lying down side by side underneath the big cottonwood at the side of the house. Later, when it was dark, they moved to the porch, and curled up on the floor, they slept back to back, and only the crickets that sang in the backyard seemed to know of their presence.

For the next two days, while Mitchell was slipping into a dark depression, the two dogs became inseparable, and when they weren't lying around in the yard, they went out exploring in the fields. In the foothills they chased rabbits, and the Labrador almost caught one. Later on, when they came upon a snake, the Lab was quick to back away and signal the danger with a bark. But whatever they did, they always came back in the afternoon, and at sunset it was their habit to sit beneath the cottonwood tree. Like an old couple that over the years had outgrown the need for words, they sat silently and watched.

It was on Wednesday in the late afternoon when Fiver looked out from beneath the cottonwood tree and saw a different truck pull up in front of the house. He and the Labrador were poised to escape when, to his surprise, Fiver heard a familiar voice call his name.

It was Grandpa from the farm, and he had run into Glen and Tom at Lucille's. When Tom told him about Mitchell, and Fiver escaping and now being lost, he was surprised and worried. As he was driving home, something about the story bothered him, and playing a hunch, he turned abruptly onto the street where Mitchell lived. "I'll bet he's here," he thought as he came through the gate. "He's like old Ben, he's a smart one. I'll bet he's hiding."

"Fiver," he called out again, "where are you, boy?" and this time Fiver's ears stood up while he tried to identify the voice. But still, his instincts urged him to flee, and he was just about to give in to them when, in his mind, he saw images of Grandpa and Isabelle, and then Mitchell and Nancy on the horses. Moments later, Grandpa came around the side of the house, and coming toward them, he was whistling and calling out his name.

"Fiver." Glancing at the Lab, Fiver saw that she was already in a low crouch, and with fearful eyes, she was waiting for a cue to run. Looking back to Grandpa, Fiver hesitated and then stood up tall, and with his tail wagging from side to side, he trotted slowly toward him. "Fiver!" cried Grandpa, and dropping to one knee, he began to rub him behind the ears with both hands. "Boy, am I glad to see you!" he exclaimed. "You son of a gun. You broke jail, huh! I knew you were here."

As she watched them from beneath the cottonwood tree, the Labrador glanced nervously at the field behind her, and when Grandpa stood up, she shied and stepped back, as if about to flee. "How would you like to stay out at the farm for a while?" said Grandpa as he looked down at Fiver, oblivious to the Lab. "Why don't we take you out there. You know the place, and then tomorrow I'll run into town and tell Mitchell."

Hearing Mitchell's name, Fiver swished his tail across the grass. "C'mon," said Grandpa. "We'd better get goin'." But as he turned to head back to the truck, he heard Fiver bark. When he turned around, he saw him step backward and glance at the Labrador who was still standing anxiously beneath the tree. "Well, I'll be," said Grandpa. "It looks like you've got a friend," he said, and rubbing his forehead, he studied the skinny Labrador. "She's been on the road a while," he thought. Then with a knowing nod of his head, it became clear to him. "She must be the one that was getting into the trash," he thought. "Mitchell mentioned that."

"Well, we'd better take you both," he said, smiling. "You'll make a handsome team." Then, kneeling down, with Fiver at his side, he whistled at the

Lab, and her first response was to step back. But then, looking at Fiver, she stopped, and after a lot of gentle coaxing, she timidly came over and stood next to Fiver. "So you two are a couple, are ya?" said Grandpa. Then he put his hand out to the Lab, and in time he was able to touch her and softly stroke her.

After petting the Lab for a long time, Grandpa managed to gain her confidence, and soon he had both dogs next to him on the seat of his pick-up. It was sunset when he drove off, and he didn't pay much attention to the nondescript county truck that zoomed past him down the lane. It was only when in his rearview mirror he saw it come to a sudden halt in front of Mitchell's that he realized it was from the pound. "We got out of there just in time," he said as the two men jumped out of the truck, and as he turned onto the highway, he didn't see the woman coming out of Snyder's house, motioning to the men.

Chapter Sixty Six

The next morning, while Grandpa headed into town with the news of Fiver and his new friend, Noah had gone with Mitchell to the arraignment, and just as Noah expected, under the Good Samaritan law, the prosecution proposed charges, both civil and criminal, against Mitchell. "They're really pushing it," said Noah as he paced slowly back and forth. "They're claiming that you were willfully negligent and wanton in not helping Snyder. That's the bottom line. It's bizarre, and the statute only pertains to people in professional organizations, you know, like paramedics and doctors, who stop to help someone. But they're saying in your tow truck you were acting in a professional capacity, and because of the bad blood between you and Snyder, you maliciously avoided helping him."

Sitting on the edge of the bed, Mitchell looked up at Noah. "They're really going after it, aren't they," he said quietly.

"It's not as bad as it looks," replied Noah, "but we've got to be careful. They're hinting at some stronger charge, maybe manslaughter, which is malarkey, but we've got to be careful. They might play that up just to scare us, then try to get you to cop a plea and accept the lesser charge under the Good Samaritan law, and then go for damages."

"I get it," said Mitchell dejectedly.

"Yeah, but we can handle it," rejoined Noah. "They're on thin ice, it's a bluff, just a bluff. So the hearing is set for later in the week, and I want you to be in decent shape, so don't get sideways on me. You can handle this, and today they'll want you to meet with the court counselor, a psychologist. It's just routine, some new program they have here, but it's important that you have a good attitude. You do realize what's at stake? You've got to play the game here, and make a good impression."

Looking down, Mitchell sighed, and in his mind he saw Fiver fleeing and hiding. "I see," he said. "But you know I can't lie. It's the only freedom I have left. They'll have to deal with it."

"I don't want you to lie," retorted Noah as he slipped off his glasses and pinched the bridge of his nose. "Of course not, that would unhinge everything and we'd have nothing to stand on. But know that there is some politics here, whether you like it or not. Just don't give anything away, and don't give them any ammunition to use against you. Got it?"

"I got it," replied Mitchell with forced enthusiasm.

"Good," said Noah. "Things will work out. It'll just take some time."

When Noah left, Mitchell reflected on the whole thing, on the accident, the court, and the coming hearing. "I know the game," he thought. Then his mind flashed back to his days at the brokerage house, and the many times he had held his tongue and agreed with things he thought were clearly wrong and how he smiled and shook hands with people he didn't respect and sometimes despised. "It's all the same," he thought bitterly, and as he thought back on it, his self-contempt grew. "I was part of it," he thought.

Then he heard the guard coming down the aisle, and moments later they took him to a small room away from the cells. He was sitting at a table when a woman entered the room and demurely closed the door behind her. With long auburn hair that turned under at the shoulders, she was rather handsome. Wearing a dark suit and a pale-yellow silk blouse, she seemed overly composed as she sat down, and her meticulousness reminded him of Susan.

"I'm Dr. Oveson," she said confidently.

Mitchell nodded. "Hello."

"This won't take long," she said cheerfully as she jotted on her note pad. "We just need some background information, and then maybe we'll give you a couple of short questionnaires to fill out. According to our records you did well in college, and looking at your transcripts, it seems you studied philosophy, math, sociology, and then psychology, and lots of liberal arts. Interesting, and you either got As or Fs. It appears that you spent six years getting a bachelor's degree and then you went to work for a large company and then a brokerage house. Very unusual life trajectory. Have you ever taken an IQ test?"

"Don't think so," said Mitchell dryly. "They're just measures of efficiency. Governments and corporations use them to see how much work they can get out of people, you know, like foot pounds in physics or horse power."

"Measures of efficiency?" said the psychologist, doubtfully. "That's a rather unconventional way to look at it, don't you think? They are important diagnostic tools. We use them to help people."

"The tests are for your sake, not mine," retorted Mitchell, and as he spoke, he started to feel irritated like he did when Susan kept trying to straighten him out. "It's a management tool," he went on, "and you give the tests because it's part of your job as manager. You and the jailer out there, you're doing the same thing, in a way. He's just more honest about it. I've been in management. We used attitude tests all the time, and it sure wasn't for the benefit of the workers."

Clearly surprised by Mitchell's less-than-subtle criticism, the psychologist coolly set her pen down on the note pad. "I see," she said. "It seems you have a rather jaundiced view of psychology, Mr. Black. Do you think we're really that hypocritical and self-serving?"

As he tried to manage his emotions, Mitchell stared at the poised figure in front of him. Then in a slow, methodical voice, he said, "I think you have a new Volvo out in the parking lot, and I bet your husband's a professional type, isn't he, maybe a professor or a lawyer?" Lifting her chin, the woman stiffened as Mitchell went on. "And you both went to the better schools. With your upper-middle class background, you could do that." Mitchell paused. "And in a couple of years you'll have enough money to decorate the house the way you want, and take those vacations in the Bahamas."

Sitting up in her chair, the psychologist studied Mitchell. "That's a normative description," she said. "It's shrewd, but it could fit hundreds of professional people. I fail to see what that has to do with psychology."

Mitchell looked down at the table. "That's the point and the problem," he said. "As a psychologist, you should see the big picture, the context, the system, and you don't, and in ignoring it, you blame the victim and capitalize on the whole damn thing. Sweet deal for you."

"I see," the woman said curtly. Then, picking up her pen she began to jot things down on her note pad.

"And I'd appreciate it if you wouldn't do that," said Mitchell, noticeably irritated. "Don't you think it's condescending to sit there and take notes on someone, like they're some kind of oddity. It's a put-down."

"Well," said the psychologist indignantly, and then, like a soldier surrendering his weapon, she slowly set her pen down. "OK, Mr. Black. So, you think we're part of the problem. I see your point."

Looking back at her, Mitchell watched as her professional demeanor gave way to a mixture of indignation and curiosity. "Well, let's just say you're working both sides of the street," he said as his own indignation rose, "and I think you help people cope, but you don't empower them by helping them to understand the world they live in, and how the problem may not be them, but the way things are set up to take advantage of them, and that keeps them down. It's pretty safe and conservative, what you do, but you perpetuate the problem and you profit from it." As he paused, Mitchell's eyes were now shining with a defiance that bespoke years of holding back, and years of trying to figure things out. "To do all that you have to lie, and worst of all, you lie to yourself about what you do and what you are. That's the hell of it, isn't it, for all of us. I know; I've done it. Done it for a living, literally."

As if the slightest movement would unleash an avalanche of unprofessional anger, the psychologist sat absolutely still. Then, raising her chin high in the air, she said, "We can't change the world overnight. We're just trying to minimize the suffering as much as we can. You have a unique perspective, and I wish we could talk more about it. It's been interesting. However, we need to have you complete these questionnaires."

"I'm sorry if I offended you," said Mitchell as his anger was slowly quelled by a rising sense of guilt that gradually gave way to compassion.

"You didn't offend me," replied the woman in an overly formal voice. "In spite of what you think, my work is not always easy. Actually, in comparison to some of the more recalcitrant cases I have, you're quite manageable...or I should say, considerate."

Smiling at her obvious slip, Mitchell opened his booklet. "Is there a time limit on this?" he said dryly.

"This is not an IQ test," retorted the psychologist as she stood up. "There is no time limit." Then, as if to stop what was now clearly becoming banter, the psychologist smiled. "You're an interesting man," she said almost warmly. "How much psychology have you read?"

"Not that much," replied Mitchell, staring off. "But I did read some Pavlov once. He said that the two strongest drives in animals are for security and freedom. I never forgot that."

As she left, the psychologist was smiling to herself when she ran into Noah in the hallway.

"Hi, Nora," said Noah. "I assume things went OK. He's a good kid."

"Well, I'll be filing my report today," said the psychologist. "You'll get it tomorrow. He's an interesting case, though, and I think he does have a guilt complex, but he's quite sane." Then, looking up, she laughed awkwardly. "He thinks we're insane," she went on, "or rather, that we really don't know what we're doing."

Before Noah could reply, the psychologist turned and walked away. Wondering just what Mitchell had said, Noah rubbed his chin as he watched her leave. "I hope he didn't go off on one his tangents," he thought.

After Mitchell finished the questionnaires, a guard took him back to his cell. Moments later Grandpa appeared at the cell with a guard. "I've got some good news for you," said Grandpa as the guard opened the cell door, and the comment brought a flicker of hope to Mitchell's face. "I ran into a friend of yours, and he's about the handsomest devil I've ever seen."

Standing up, Mitchell almost leaped forward. "Fiver?"

With a broad smile, Grandpa nodded in the affirmative. "He's got a friend, too, a black Labrador. She's awful skinny, but she's a pretty thing. I found them camped out over at your place. But since I didn't think it was too safe there, I threw 'em in the truck and took 'em out to the farm." Tears started to come to Mitchell's eyes, and turning away, he wiped them with his fist. "I could take him back to the pound?" said Grandpa, and abruptly Mitchell turned back around.

"No, don't do that! Keep him out there as long as you can."

"That's what I thought you'd say. It's a good thing, too, 'cause I'm gettin' kind of attached to him. Can't help but like him, and the Lab too, but I've got to get back."

Smiling, Grandpa turned away, and he was waving to the jailer to let him out when Mitchell took him by the shoulder.

"He might need his meds," said Mitchell. "They're at the house in the bathroom. Once in a while he has a seizure, from when he had distemper. If he seizes, just give him one. That'll do the job."

"Sure," said Grandpa, "I'll pick 'em up."

"I can't tell you how much I appreciate it," replied Mitchell with deep appreciation in his eyes. "And have you? I mean, have you heard anything from...from Nancy?"

Shaking his head, Grandpa closed his eyes. "No, we haven't heard from her. Just the one letter. Are you sure you don't want us to contact her? I think someone should."

Mitchell shook his head. "No, no, I think...well, it looks like she's moved on." Cocking his head, Grandpa raised his eyebrows. "I doubt that. It's none of my business, but I really doubt that."

Chapter Sixty Seven

Back in his cell, Mitchell was visibly less depressed, and if not optimistic, at least less worried, particularly about Fiver. As he sat on his bunk, he looked out the small window in his cell and saw blue sky with willowy white clouds rolling like a river in slow motion. Then, from across the aisle, he heard Daryl. "Well, how'd it go?" he said cheerfully. "Better," said Mitchell, "they found Fiver."

"Oh, your dog, huh. That's great," replied Daryl.

"How's your mouse?" said Mitchell as he looked over at him. "Does he have a name?"

"Sure does. I call him Flash 'cause he's so fast when he comes out for his food. You know, he's a crafty little bugger. Comes out at different times for the food, and sometimes he'll just come and look out and not touch it and then run back, like he's casing the joint. Sometimes I think he's actually thinking, you know, trying to figure out a strategy."

"Flash, huh," said Mitchell with a short chuckle. "That's a good name."

"Do you think he's really thinking?" said Daryl almost sarcastically. "I mean, can they do that?"

"Sure they can," replied Mitchell casually. "You ever watch a bird take a bath in the sprinkler? They're very methodical, they lift their wings and spread their tails. They know what they're doing."

"I know, but that could just be instinct, couldn't it? It's not really think-ing like people do."

Before he responded Mitchell paused, wondering if he should get into it. "No, they think," he said after a moment, and in his mind he saw a some-thing from a nature program on TV that he had watched. In the scene, a young zebra colt was separated from her mother and was being stalked by a lioness. Seeing the approaching lion about to kill her foal, the mare zebra left the safety of the herd, and just as the lion pounced, she placed herself in front of the colt. With the lion attacking in midair, the zebra kicked the lion square in the jaw and sent her tumbling. Then, after nudging the foal back to the herd, with ears back, the mare scolded he colt with a variety of ges-tures and looks, and generally gave him a good talking to. "No doubt they think," said Mitchell forcefully, "They do all the things we do—they bond, and they love and raise their young. They play, and they fight to survive. They live in families, they communicate, and they feel things and they ex-perience loss and joy, and they dream!"

"Hey, you're overdoing it a bit," declared Daryl as he sat up straight on the edge of his bunk. "You're anthropomorphizing, aren't you?" he de-clared. "Giving them human traits. That's what they called it in college."

"Not at all," replied Mitchell, and for a moment, lost in his thoughts, he surveyed all he had read. "Elephants live complex social orders," he went on, "and they're matriarchal, the females run the show. And they commu-nicate with a wide variety of sounds, sometimes from miles away, that we can't even hear. The matriarchs lead the troop, and they make all kinds of decisions—where they're gonna go for food, and things like that. Some researchers say elephants have a sense of death, and they have rituals that they go through when they find one of their own dead. I always thought that might be the beginning of religion."

"Really?" said Daryl in amazement. "I didn't know that. I mean, it's not something you think about very often."

"That's true," said Mitchell, "but see these." Mitchell grinned, and pull-ing back his upper lip, he tapped his canine tooth with his finger. "These are fangs, and we have finger nails, right? They're really claws. Tooth and claw, we're animals! We spend a lot of time denying it, but we have a lot in common with the other creatures."

"Well," said Daryl, "but you know..."

Mitchell interrupted him. "Listen, once I read about an elephant in a zoo that paints, and there's a gorilla that paints, too. She actually names her paintings, and she communicates through sign language, and she loves kittens. And I've seen studies of dolphins. They have a rich language, and a powerful sense of self. They can recognize themselves in a mirror, and they can understand sentences and grammar. And whales sing long, complicated songs. Soon, they'll find out that most other species have a sense of self. It's pretty clear. And wolves, there's all kinds of research about wolves and how they live in family groups, and how they hunt and play and raise and nurture their young, and how they communicate and how musical and heartfelt their howling is. All the animals sing and make music. It just seems so damn obvious to me. We really have more in common with them than not. We're all related, and we're not that different. It's delusional to think otherwise, prejudiced. And we're certainly not more civilized than they are. Anybody knows we're infinitely more destructive and violent. Look at all the wars. Basically, we're just more powerful, not more civilized."

Put back by Mitchell's long discourse, Daryl was quiet, and for a moment there was long period of silence. "Just more powerful, huh," he said finally.

"Yeah," said Mitchell, still looking off, lost in his train of thought. "It's because we have a complex language, and we can write things down and store information, and we can use our hands and make tools, man the evolved tool-user. That's the short story, evolution, technology, driven by human creativity, fueled by hope, and fear, and some kind of deep, marvelous drive for life. But somewhere we lost our way, and now the machines are running roughshod over everything."

"Whew," said Daryl with both awe and considerable skepticism. "But, c'mon, let's get real. Animals can't even add. I mean, everyone knows they can't do any kind of math." Looking back at him, Mitchell smiled and cocked his head. "Sure they can," he said almost in a whisper. "Ever see a chipmunk carry nuts up to his nest? He's stocking up, right? And that's because he knows he got more than one. Ever see a bird find some seeds and take one and hide it somewhere? Ever give a dog a few bones and see him take one and bury it for a rainy day? To do that, he's got to know that he's got more than one, doesn't he? That's math, isn't it? And he's thinking about the future, what he's gonna do with the surplus, that's economics. He's thinking, maybe not in the same terms that we use, but he's thinking."

With doubting eyes, Daryl nodded sideways. "Yeah, OK, and did anyone ever tell you, you're a little nuts, yourself?"

Chapter Sixty Eight

The hearing began at ten in the morning, and there were a large number of people in the courtroom. Jesse sat in the back with Tom and Glenn. Up in front there was one older woman whose dark eyes and severe expression caught Mitchell's attention. Then Noah nudged him. "I thought Nancy's grandfather would be here," he whispered.

"He's looking after Fiver," replied Mitchell with a slight smile. "He's at the ranch." "What?" questioned Noah. "Well, you're just full of surprises, aren't you."

When the judge, a short, stout man with a full mustache, a man who seemed uncomfortable in his judicial robes, entered the room, Noah smiled confidently. "We won that that one," he whispered to Mitchell. "He's the one we needed."

After hearing three cases, two of which were dismissed, the clerk read the charges against Mitchell, under the Good Samaritan law. Then the prosecutor, a tall, thin, balding man, addressed the judge. "Your honor," he said in a confident but high voice. "I am Arthur Seegmiller, and the prosecution moves that Mitchell Black will be proven guilty on all criminal and civil charges and should be tried in a court of law and held accountable. To that end, we have a number of depositions and affidavits which when presented in court today will indicate that there is sufficient evidence that Mitchell Black committed a criminal act with criminal intent, mens rea and actus reus, and should be tried on these charges. We think that, ultimately, the court will find that, beyond a reasonable doubt, he committed this crime and should be punished for it."

When the prosecutor finished and sat down at his table in front the judge, Noah stood up with his hands at his side. "Your honor," he said. "My client is innocent of this charge, and we will prove decisively that there are no grounds whatsoever for these charges and that the charges should be dismissed immediately. Moreover, we will prove that the information presented by the prosecution is nothing more than hearsay, and that there is no probable cause and no indication at all of intent or criminal acts in terms of the laws cited. Had the court not acted so expeditiously, I would have filed a writ of habeas corpus. Thank you."

"Very good," said the judge. "Let's begin with the prosecution. What affidavits and depositions do you have?"

Standing up, with a pile of folders in front of him, the prosecutor replied, "I have affidavits from people at the scene, and I have others from local people familiar with Mitchell Black and some other people who have known him in the past."

The first deposition that the prosecutor presented was from Ann Delaney, the waitress at Lucille's. In the deposition, she noted that Mitchell brought his dog in one night, and how he really loved the dog. Then she described the altercation between Mitchell and Snyder that took place at the restaurant, and while she couldn't remember the exact words, she said, "He did say something to the effect that if Snyder hurt his dog, it would be the last thing he did," implying that he would attack him. This last statement brought rapt attention from the people in the gallery.

The second deposition was from a man at the scene of the accident who said he saw Mitchell go down to the truck and let out the rabbits and the dog. In his statement, he said Mitchell should have just got Snyder out, and that he should have hooked the cable to the truck and not "messed around with opening the back door and freeing the damn rabbits."

The third deposition was from Jesse, and in answering the questions about any animosity between Mitchell and Snyder, Jesse first attested to Mitchell's good character, but eventually he was forced to admit that Mitchell didn't like Snyder, and that he was particularly upset about what went on in the slaughterhouse and that he was shocked by all the animals in Snyder's trophy room. As he listened to the deposition, Mitchell's eyes fell. "That must have been tough for Jesse," he thought.

The fourth deposition came from the court psychologist who interviewed Mitchell. In her testimony she noted that while Mitchell was quite sane and very intelligent, he did display some signs of guilt, maladjustment, and depression, along with antisocial tendencies, and a deep distrust and dislike of authority. When the prosecutor finished summarizing her statements, Noah looked over his shoulder at Mitchell and rolled his eyes.

The next deposition was taken from court records in Denver. As it turned out, the postman in Mitchell's neighborhood had filed a routine report about the incident with Fiver and Mitchell, and how Mitchell had knocked him down. No battery charges were filed, but the record of the incident was still there, and the prosecutor went to great lengths to underscore how Mitchell was clearly capable of violence. Other depositions came from various people who knew Snyder and respected him and highlighted his contribution to the local economy, and there was one patronizing deposition from Mitchell's old boss in Denver that read, "Mitchell was smart, all right, but he was also eccentric and downright strange at times. Never knew what to expect from him. At times I worried about him."

The last deposition came from Jerry Engam, Mitchell's good friend and drinking buddy in Denver, and Mitchell guffawed when he heard his name. "Jerry?" he said. "My God."

"I know, they really did some digging," replied Noah. "That's their method, dig and twist."

In his statement, Jerry initially said favorable things about Mitchell, but when pressed with particulars regarding Mitchell being antisocial, he did say that Mitchell has "unusual views."

"I don't think he's a believer," he went on. "He seems to think that animals are as important as people, and he did say once that people aren't special." Amid a buzz of whispers, the statement hung in the courtroom like a dark cloud. "With friends like that, you don't need enemies," said Noah finally. "A real piece of work, that guy."

After he had finished the affidavits and depositions, the prosecutor addressed the judge. "With the court's permission, I would now like Mitchell Black to briefly take the stand and answer one or two routine questions."

"I knew that was coming," said Noah as he leaned over to Mitchell, "but it will be all right. Go ahead."

The crowd was quiet when Mitchell took the stand, and the prosecutor was quick to speak. "I just have a few questions; please just answer yes or no. Did you dislike Robert Snyder?"

Pausing, Mitchell groaned softly. "Yes, I didn't like him."

"As indicated by other testimony, did you say that people are not special, and are just animals?"

"Yes," said Mitchell, and as he shook his head in disbelief, the courtroom became absolutely quiet.

"And did you threaten Robert Snyder, saying something to the effect that if he hurt your dog, he would regret it, and it would be the last thing he did?"

"Yes, I did," said Mitchell, "but he had..."

Interrupting, the prosecutor said, "Please, just yes or no. And, on the day of Robert Snyder's death, was there something you could have done that might have saved him? Tied the cable to the truck, or pulled him out first, a different approach?"

"I don't know," said Mitchell as he his ran hand through his hair. "It all happened so fast. I was..."

Interrupting, the prosecutor said again, "Please, just yes or no. So, if I may summarize, you didn't like Snyder. You don't think people are special, and it's possible that you actually could have saved him. That will be all, your honor."

After Mitchell stepped down, the prosecutor made his closing remarks. "So you see, your honor," he began, "we have ample evidence to prove that Mitchell Black is an antisocial person with eccentric if not delusional views about things, and he did in fact have motive, and was engaged in a crime that followed directly from that motive, his deep hatred for Robert Snyder. And, this crime, however subtle and well executed, entailed deliberately and with malice, not giving obvious and proper aid to Robert Snyder and causing his unnecessary death. In that Mitchell Black was driving a tow truck, and acting in terms of a professional capacity, a profession that is regularly called to accident scenes, he was willfully negligent and malicious and thus should be tried under the Good Samaritan law of Colorado. The prosecution feels this is self-evident."

When the prosecutor returned to his seat, Noah patted Mitchell on the leg, and stood up. He began his final summation by going through some of his own affidavits and depositions, many of which were from friends of Mitchell's. These included strong character endorsements from Jesse, and Glenn and Tom, along with a statement from Grandpa. When lastly, Noah read a brief and very flattering statement from Nancy, Mitchell shot him a puzzled look, to which Noah only raised his eyebrows.

When he sat down, Noah told Mitchell that he had contacted Josh, Nancy's grandfather, who told him that Nancy had gone to New York to set up an art show, and that she was actually on her way here. "She tried to reach you, but couldn't," he said, "and evidently, the prosecution sees her as a hostile witness, so they didn't want any testimony from her. I just got the information this morning."

After he presented his own affidavits and depositions, Noah went over those submitted by the prosecutor, and he was very careful to highlight favorable things that the prosecutor had de-emphasized or omitted. In particular, he noted how the waitress at Lucille's had said Mitchell was a fine person, and how Mitchell's boss in Denver might be mad about Mitchell quitting because Mitchell made him a lot of money.

"The potential for bias is obvious," declared Noah. "Moreover, all of this is hearsay and doomed by the lack of clarity that follows from the passage of time, which also makes much of it irrelevant." Then as he addressed the affidavit by the court psychologist, he paused and looked thoughtfully around at the court. Turning to the judge, he said. "There's nothing concrete in this other than she said he's sane. That's it! As to her implying things about Mitchell's depression and hostility toward authority, in this world, who doesn't get depressed now and then, and who doesn't get tired of the government jumping into every little thing you do? All Mitchell did was be honest about it. As to the innuendos about Mitchell's antisocial tendencies, and his strong concern for animals, who doesn't look around at all the violence in the world and wonder about human nature and not get a little cynical? At my age, if you're not a little cynical, you haven't been taking notes. And, may I say, how many people, when asked, would freely admit that their pets are part of the family, and they love them as family, and how many people, like Mitchell, would defend them as family? Again, Mitchell Black's only crime is that he's honest, and people don't always like that, someone holding a mirror up to you. He's not a misanthrope, and that's what the prosecution is insinuating because that's all they can muster up, innuendos and vague recollections. If I may, I can demonstrate by asking Mr. Black some straightforward questions."

As Mitchell took the stand, Noah gave him an encouraging look. Then, after Mitchell was seated, Noah asked him, "Did you intend to do harm to Snyder on the day of the accident?" and Mitchell replied with a succinct, "No." Noah then asked him if he had followed Snyder that day, and if he planned to harm him, and again Mitchell responded with a plain and simple, "No." His last question to Mitchell was just as simple and direct. "Did you, in fact, intend to help him that day?" "Yes," replied Mitchell. "Thank you," said Noah. "You may step down.

As Mitchell returned to his seat, Noah continued. "Your honor, the prosecution has no case, and they know it. There is no intent, and there was no plan, no scheme. Mitchell didn't know Snyder was going over the cliff, and he had nothing to do with it. In fact, he risked his life to save him. So again, I say there is no motive, no intent, and no crime, and all this evidence is mere hearsay. In the last analysis, the charges are without merit, and what they really display is the power of money, and the subordination of law to the power of money, and how people and corporations can use money to pay lawyers to manipulate the law and punish people who get in their way, people like Mitchell Black, a man who was simply trying to do the right thing and be honest. Basically, this is a modern-day witch-hunt, and there's no way this should go to trial. The prosecution's case is hearsay, no motive, no crime, no probable cause, no habeas corpus. Your honor, there should be no trial, and most importantly, in regard to the Good Samaritan law, Mitchell was not acting in a professional capacity to help Robert Snyder. As noted in the record, he was not sent there to do that, to pull Snyder's truck out of the canyon, and he was not trained in search and rescue techniques. He had no foreknowledge of what had happened, and he only attempted to help him with the best of intentions, using whatever he had on hand. In short, the Good Samaritan law is irrelevant and not applicable. So, again, I say the charges should be dismissed."

As Noah sat down, the judge sat back in his chair and fingered his mustache while he thought. Then he gave each attorney a long penetrating look. "Thank you," he said finally. "I'll give you a decision on this at two o'clock tomorrow afternoon. Court dismissed."

As people began filing out of the room, Noah and Mitchell visually commiserated as they looked at one another. "What's that about?" asked Mitchell. "Is that a bad sign, him making the ruling tomorrow?"

"I don't know," replied Noah, looking down. "He's a cautious judge, and he's rarely overturned. Maybe he just wants some time to mull it over. I guess it's not a slam dunk, either way. I'd hoped for an early dismissal, though. We're not out of the woods."

As Mitchell and Noah stood up to leave the courtroom, Mitchell again saw the stern-faced older women, and now sitting alone with vacant seats around her, she glared at Mitchell. "Who is that?" he asked as he looked away from her.

"That's Snyder's mother," replied Noah. "She's been staying at his house."

# #

Chapter Sixty Nine

# #

When Noah left the courthouse it was midafternoon, and unbe-
knownst to him or Mitchell, that morning the pound had received a
call from a woman, Snyder's mother. She said she had seen an old man in an
old truck pick up two dogs from Mitchell's house. She had written down the
license plate number, and demanded they find out who it was. Two hours
later, officers from the pound and the sheriff's department were descending upon Grandpa's farm. When the truck pulled up to the house, Fiver and
the Lab were lying on the porch, and when Granny came to see who was
there, her face dropped when she saw the men in blue uniforms getting
out of the trucks. On the porch, Fiver stood up slowly with the hair on his
back standing up. Then after looking at Granny and back at the officers, he
sprang from the porch, and with the Labrador at his side, he headed out
across the fields toward Silver Mountain.

Out on the far edge of the farm, the back forty, they called it, Grandpa
was irrigating, and with a couple of irrigation gates half open, he was almost through watering the field when he saw the dogs running, and the
trucks coming across the field behind them. "Ah, hell," he cursed. "Why
don't they leave things be." Then, as he was about to close up the gate he
was working on, he stopped and looked at the approaching truck. "OK," he
said under his breath, and instead of closing the gate, he opened it wide,
and water a foot high came gushing out. Then, taking a few more quick

steps, he opened three more gates and watched as the field began to flood. "That'll slow 'em down. This is my land."

When the dogs were just fifty yards away, the truck was almost up to them. But then, with wheels spinning and throwing mud, the truck started to slip and slide sideways. When the dogs were almost within Grandpa's reach, the truck slid to a halt, and with a great deal of cussing, the men inside jumped out and started tromping through the mud toward Grandpa and the approaching dogs. Glancing behind him, Fiver saw them, and after giving Grandpa a quick kind of knowing look, he and the Lab kept running. After they ducked under the last fence, they started up the trail on Silver Mountain.

As the men trudged toward Noah with mud caked on their boots and pants, Grandpa was leaning on a shovel. "What the hell are you guys doing?" he said. "You've ruined my field. I might have to file a lawsuit."

"You know why we're here," said one of them. "To get the dogs. We got a call from the sheriff's department; the court says we have to. You know that."

"Well, this is private property," retorted Grandpa, "and you'll need a court order to search the place. So now, why don't you guys just go home."

"Oh, I get it," retorted one of the officers. "So you're gonna play that card. So, all right, what about the truck? How are we gonna get it out of there?"

"You can get that tomorrow, when the field's dried out," said Grandpa. "Damn fool thing to do, drive into a wet field. You should have known better than that. Granny'll give you a ride back in the old Studebaker. 'Cept you're all muddy; you'd better ride in the back."

As the men trudged back across the field, Grandpa closed the irrigation gates. Then after studying the truck, now moored in the mud with its door still flung open, he looked up at Silver Mountain. It was dusk and some dark clouds were moving in on the peaks. "It could rain," he thought, and for the next two hours he hiked up the trail whistling for the dogs and calling Fiver's name. He did find some tracks, but when he knew he had only an hour or so of light left, he stopped just short of the lake and turned back. "Aw, hell," he said, "I'll have to come back in the morning. I'll saddle up Sunny."

By this time, Fiver and the Lab were well up the mountain, and every so often Fiver would stop, and after sniffing here and there and looking around, he would take the lead up the trail. It was still light when they passed the lake and reached the crest of the mountain, and it was here that Fiver slowed up and sat down on his haunches, and with the Lab next to him, he looked all around at the forest. Then, just at dusk, the rain started to fall, and seeming to have made a clear decision, Fiver stood up and started following a smaller trail that would eventually dissect the highway over Silver Mountain. But just then the rain started falling more heavily, and suddenly a bolt of lightning struck the ground a few feet from them. Stopped dead in their tracks, the dogs crouched, and then ahead of them, on the mountain side of the trail, they saw a short path leading up to a big pine tree that stood next to a large overhang of rock. In an instant they ran up the path, and standing next to the tree, they looked under the huge overhanging rock. The space underneath it was deep and cavernous, like a cave.

After looking at one another like two doubtful pilgrims, with the Labrador taking the lead this time, the two of them moved under the large rock. But, suddenly the Labrador froze, and behind her, with the hair on his neck standing up, Fiver sniffed the air and began to growl. Then they heard it, the scream of a panther, and from deep under the rock in a cave obscured by the darkness, the mountain lion with a cub at her feet, stood up, and an in instant she leaped forward and grabbed the Labrador by the neck. Then, growling, Fiver lunged and with bared fangs, flew at the cougar, and biting with all his might, he tore at her throat. Dropping the Lab, the cougar whirled, and with one slap of her huge paw, she knocked Fiver back down the trail. Landing against the roots of a tree, he quickly got to his feet, but there was blood trickling from three large gashes on his shoulder, and his eyes were wild with fierce anticipation. Then, yelping, the Labrador ran past him as she fled down the trail in the darkness. Behind her, the cougar snarled and pawed at the air as she looked down at Fiver.

Taken by her menacing ferocity, Fiver growled and readied himself for the attack. But then the panther paused and just stared down at him incredulously, as if to give him time to come to his senses. Then, with his eyes fixed on the cougar, Fiver stepped back slowly, and turning away, he leapt down the trail after the Labrador. As they fled, the cougar stood on the ledge and watched, then turning slowly away, she returned to her cub.

When they were safely down the trail that led toward the highway, the Labrador stopped and lay down under a large pine tree. As Fiver approached, she whined and cried, and arching his neck, Fiver whined too, and crouching down, he howled out into the darkness. Then, moving close to her, he studied her eyes and then carefully started to lick the blood flowing out of the deep puncture wounds on her neck. Moments later he nudged her, and with blood running down to his paw, he was limping badly as they started down the other side of Silver Mountain.

#

Chapter Seventy

#

Back in Mitchell's cell, Noah and Mitchell were talking, and Noah could see the growing concern in Mitchell's eyes. "It's not that bad," he said. "This is the right judge, and he's a good man."

Nodding, Mitchell sat on his bunk. "You were good today," he said. "Nobody could have done a better job."

"Thanks," said Noah. "Now listen, I've got another case to attend to, just an accident, car and a bus, but I'll be back in a bit."

"Sure," said Mitchell. Then he stared off, and before him, in his mind, he caught a glimpse of a bus, a yellow bus, and bright blue sky all around, and clean, white sparkling snow, then a little dog running, then the bus, then the dog in front of the bus. Then, wincing, Mitchell closed his eyes.

"What's the matter?" asked Noah. "You look like you've seen a ghost."

"Huh," said Mitchell in a weak voice. "That's when it all started."

"What?" asked Noah.

Still taken by the vision and puzzled by his own words, Mitchell went on. "When I was a kid, I saw a dog get hit by a bus. It was on Christmas day, a beautiful winter day. I couldn't have been more than eight years old. I remember the dog was...was smashed flat, and his tongue was out, and eyes bulged out. The bus tried to stop, but it slid on the snow." Pausing, Mitchell shook his head doubtfully. "Huh, I'd forgotten that, or maybe I repressed it," he went on. "But, I was just a kid, but it made me think, and right then and there I started doubting everything, everything people told me in church, in school."

"That's too bad," said Noah.

But before Noah could say more, Mitchell, still mesmerized by his own reflections, went on. "Here was this dog, playful and happy, and then right before my eyes, he's gruesomely killed, and I couldn't deny it, and I wondered why. Why? The funny thing was that I used to ride that bus once a week, and I decided right then and there that when I was on that bus, I would think about things, anything, everything, figure it out. I remember one day I was at the bus stop, and I was looking up at the sky, wondering if heaven was really up there, and where it could be. It didn't seem possible, floating around on a cloud." Blinking, as if waking from a dream, Mitchell looked at Noah. "That's when all the trouble started," he said with an ironic chuckle. "When I started to think and doubt. That's when it started, that day, and here I am."

After comforting Mitchell as best he could, Noah left, and he was shaking his head as he walked down the hallway. Lying on his bunk, Mitchell was looking out the small window that, like a painting, framed an empty but brilliant blue sky. Then, from behind him, he heard two sets of footsteps. One was the familiar clunk of the guard's boots, but the other was crisp and new-sounding. When they stopped at his cell, Mitchell cast an eye over his shoulder, and next to the guard's boots, he saw a shiny pair of Italian leather shoes. As his eyes moved up the brown, pinstriped pant leg of an expensive suit, he saw Jerry looking down with his Cheshire Cat smile, exuding confidence.

"You've got a visitor," said the guard, and in disbelief, Mitchell looked up at Jerry.

"I came down to help," said Jerry as he beamed down at Mitchell. "When they contacted me about the deposition, I thought I'd come over and see what I can do to help."

Getting up and sitting on the edge of his bunk, Mitchell gave Jerry a skeptical look. "Yeah, you really helped all right," he said derisively. "Telling them I'm antisocial, and that I don't think people are special. That did me a lotta good."

"I said some good things," declared Jerry emphatically, "but, Mitchell, you know I couldn't lie, not now. You see, I've changed. I mean in a big way. And this whole thing is not as bad as it seems," he went on, "and I know you must think I'm a Judas, but I'm not. I'm here to help you, and I can if you'll let me. I know the truth, and I've changed. Believe me, I'm not the same man I used to be."

Waiting for Mitchell to respond, Jerry paused, but seeing Mitchell's silent but growing incredulity, he went on, "You have to let me help you. Don't let your pride get in the way. That's what I did. God has done this to you for a purpose. Sometimes he has to break you down just to get your attention. That's what he did to me. You see, after you left Denver, everything fell apart, and I ended up selling used cars for a while, then furniture. Eventually, I lost it all, everything. I was so desperate, and I was praying and praying, and then it happened! Just like that, and I got this position with the Prosperity Church, just doing some PR work at first, and then everything took off, and, well, I was saved, and everything is working just like I always said it would. But now it's God's work, and I'm just part of it. He had to break me down to get me to see it, and that's what's happening to you. Don't you see?"

With Jerry's Cheshire Cat grin bigger than ever, Mitchell stared back at him in complete amazement. Then, raising his arms in the air like a preacher, Jerry went on. "You have to lose everything before you get it," he declared. "Then you can have it all, in this world and the next. That's what God wants for all of us, ultimate, complete prosperity forever and ever."

From his bunk, Mitchell marveled at Jerry. Then slowly he rose from his bunk. "You're serious, aren't you," he retorted. "And that's why people go hungry, and babies starve, and people are killed in factories and in wars, and the holocaust, just so God can save them? Give me a damn break. I'll tell you what happened. When you lost your money, you lost your damn mind! That's all that happened, a classic conversion experience. Sober up!"

"Mitchell, this is the real deal," said Jerry, unshaken.

And to check his anger, Mitchell laughed bitterly. "Such a deal," he retorted. "So, what are you selling? What kind of package is it this time, land, or a pyramid scheme?"

"Nothing like that," replied Jerry. "Absolutely not. We do have some motivation courses, and some counseling services, but that's different. One of the courses is called 'Dare to Have and to Be.' It's a course on personal empowerment through faith.

"Oh, I get it," said Mitchell, raising an eyebrow, "like Scientology."

"Of course not," Jerry retorted quickly. "That's a cult. This is legit, and it's not about the money, it's about faith and peace and happiness, prosperity, you know, the city on the hill. It's all in the prophecy. Let me share it with you. Please."

As he rose from his bunk, Mitchell felt his frustration smoldering toward hot anger. "I may be beat," he said when he got to his feet. "In fact, it may be all over for me. But I'm not crazy, and I don't need your malarkey! If you had the truth, you wouldn't have to go around gathering up converts. You're still scared, and you just want the converts to allay your own fears. You don't want to help anybody but yourself."

Jerry's expression grew stern. "No, that isn't the case at all. I do have the truth, and I want you to have it. I want everyone to have it. It's so wonderful."

"What about helping the poor and living a Christ-like life?" Mitchell asked in a more calm voice.

"That's just what we're doing, helping them prosper," Jerry asserted proudly, "and it's taking off like wildfire all over Texas and the Midwest. Mitchell, I am the future, the future of America and the world, and I want you to be part of it. I want you to be saved. I've never been so sure about anything in my life."

"You're kidding," asserted Mitchell derisively as he shot Jerry a bewildered look. "You know, I could be wrong about everything," he said loudly as he stepped toward him. "I mean, I might have it all wrong. Everything!"

Raising his eyebrows, Jerry looked at him with condescending pity, but before he could respond, Mitchell went on. "How about you? Is there any chance that you're wrong? Any chance in hell?"

Jerry pulled his eyebrows down tight. "No, not on the important things. That's the miracle of it."

Mitchell groaned. "No, that's not the miracle of it. That's the danger in it. You know the story about Abraham?"

Jerry folded his arms in front of him. "Yes, of course."

"Well, if God told you to kill your child, to kill me, to destroy a city, you'd do it, wouldn't you! You crazy son of a bitch!"

Jerry unfolded his arms and threw his hands up. "That's ridiculous. That won't happen."

Mitchell moved closer. "Are you saying you wouldn't, that Abraham should have said no? That's what I would have done. You could burn me in hell, but I'd say no. I wouldn't do that, not for God or anybody."

Jerry dropped his hands and pushed his chest out. "Mitchell," he said loudly. "Abraham did the right thing. I know it's hard to understand, but God's omniscient, and sometimes we can't see his purpose." Then, pausing to reconstruct his composure, Jerry widened his Cheshire Cat smile. "I know I have the truth. I don't know why God chose me, but he did, and you can have it too, all of it, everything."

Turning away to curb his anger, Mitchell looked up at the small window. It was getting dark outside. "You'd better go," he said in a restrained voice as he turned back around. "This is not the right time, man. But let me say this. I've spent a lifetime trying to grasp things, inductively, bit by bit, and what I see doesn't always make sense, and sometimes it's terrible. All you've ever seen or wanted to see was what made you feel good. That's truth for you, a feel-good thing. That's all. You can't stand the uncertainty, never could. It's not about them, the downtrodden, it's about you, and you've made your God in your own image, and it's your own hide that you're interested in. You're too overwhelmed and scared to have anything but the absolute truth!"

Jerry stepped back and pulled on the cuffs of his suit coat. "Mitchell, you don't understand," he said with pious calmness. "If you could feel it…"

"Feel what?" said Mitchell, interrupting. "The security of being omnipotent, the relief that comes from handing all your responsibilities to your God? I'll bet that does feel good, doesn't it? If you were a true Christian, you'd be terrified by what you see on this planet. But you're not, are you?

No, you sleep soundly, don't you! Your religion's just an expedient, lets you feel good without really having to sacrifice anything."

Still backing up in disbelief, Jerry bumped against the bars. "Mitchell, you just don't understand. God..."

Mitchell cut him off, and stepping closer, he said loudly, "I'll tell you what your God is. It's power. And you don't save people with it, you sell them the illusion of it. And you sell it to the poor and the weak, and you keep 'em down with it. You sell it to lonely little housewives, and to men who have no idea of the world around them or how they fit into it, and yes, you do make them feel better, and more powerful, and pretty soon they're worshipping you, aren't they? And then you feel more powerful, and all of it's wonderful, isn't it! It must be true, if it feels that great!"

With his chest heaving with frustration, Mitchell paused. "You haven't changed," he said as he grimaced at Jerry. "You're the same petty crackpot despot you always were. You're the one who's a sociopath, not me. You just want followers, like any other fascist."

"Mitchell, I really care! I really do!"

"The hell you do! If you cared about people, you'd give 'em some real awareness, understanding of things, the nature of things. But, naw, you can't do that, no profit in that, and no glory."

Looking back at Mitchell with alarm in his eyes, Jerry was slow to respond. Then with priestly piety, he said softly, "My job is to spread the word of God. I don't have to defend it. It speaks for itself."

"That's right," retorted Mitchell, angrily. "You don't defend it. What you defend is power and the system. That's what you do, you and all the other despots. That's what you sell. Spiritually, you're a slum landlord. You tell people you're giving them shelter, when in fact you're taking. You're a taker, always were. Now get of here, and don't do me any favors, huh. I'm honest with God, and I'm honest with myself!"

Stunned by Mitchell's final outburst, Jerry tripped as he motioned the guard to open the door. After the door closed behind him, Jerry straightened his suit coat, and regaining his composure, he turned back to Mitchell and said, "I'm concerned about ultimate things, eternal life. That's what I was offering you. I'm sorry for you. Christ loves you. I'll pray for you. I will."

"You do that!" yelled Mitchell. "And put in a plug for your stocks and bonds, huh! You know, you're the one who doesn't get it. The ultimate power is creativity. Artists, scientists, craftsman, they create. That's where the real power is, creativity, and that's why we give God so much power. 'God the Creator,' isn't it?"

Baffled, Jerry fell silent, and then slowly, his Cheshire Cat grin faded to sad, condescending pity. "I will pray for you. God loves you," he said as he turned and walked away.

After Jerry left, Mitchell stood holding onto the bars with his face pressed between them. Like Lot's wife, frozen in bitterness and remorse, he was lost in his thoughts when he heard Daryl's plaintive voice. "You really know how to make friends and influence people, don't you," Daryl said cheekily from the edge of his bed, and the friendly sarcasm pulled Mitchell away from his grief.

"I guess I lost it," he said with a weak laugh.

"Hey, man, you'd better take it easy," replied Daryl. "You sound like you're going over the edge, man, really comin' undone."

"Not really," said Mitchell with a sudden calmness that bespoke a new insight. "I'm actually just starting to understand."

"Understand what?" inquired Daryl.

"I'm a heretic," Mitchell said in almost a whisper. "A heretic, and I think I'm gonna lose tomorrow." Then, in his mind, he saw the big cottonwood tree shed all its leaves and stand dark and naked against the sky.

Chapter Seventy One

#

That night, tossing and turning, lost in images of Snyder screaming and wide-eyed rabbits looking down at him from the hill, Mitchell hardly slept. The next morning, gaunt, with tired eyes, he looked older than his years. When Noah came by to walk with him on the way to the court, Noah was cheerful, but there was something, something about him that was different. To Mitchell it read like a Greek tragedy, and in spite of his best efforts, his heart sank as he entered the courtroom. But when he saw Nancy sitting next to Jesse and Grandpa, his spirits rose, and for a moment, like an old man trying to remember a fond memory, he stopped and gazed at her. Then a faint smile touched his lips. With her eyes welling up with tears, Nancy smiled back at him. "I love you," she whispered as he passed.

As the judge took his seat behind the podium, a large gallery of spectators poured in. In the back, Jesse and then Glen and Tom took their seats. As he looked over the papers in front him, the judge looked reluctant, and this bothered Mitchell, but expecting the worst, he didn't say anything to Noah, who was also studying the judge. "It's there," Noah said. "That's good."

"What's there?" inquired Mitchell weakly.

"You can't see it?" said Noah, holding back a smile. "The dog hair on his tie and his robe, some red and some yellow, a Lab and a Setter. He loves them more than life itself. That's our ace in the hole, kid."

Looking back at Noah, Mitchell was speechless. Then the judge began the proceedings. "We'll start with The State of Colorado versus Mitchell Black. I see that both attorneys are present, and I must say for a variety of reasons, this has been a difficult decision. However, the heart of the matter is that to be found guilty under the Good Samaritan law, a person must be acting negligently or wantonly in the performance of a professional duty, and in that Mitchell Black was not acting in a professional capacity, but rather as a private citizen who just happened on the scene, the court finds that there is not sufficient evidence to have a trial. Accordingly, all criminal and civil charges are dismissed and the defendant is free to go."

Stunned by the brevity and succinctness of the decision, Mitchell sat wondering if he had heard right. Then Noah reached over and hugged him. "Well, quite a process, isn't it. And it's amazing what a little dog hair will do. I knew we could beat this, but this saved a lot of time and expense."

"Thanks," said Mitchell, "I don't know what to say. Thanks so much."

"I kind of enjoyed it," said Noah, smiling, "fighting the good fight for once, and besides, my Olds needs a lot of work. I think we'll take it all out in trade, OK?"

As the courtroom slowly emptied, Mitchell and Noah stood up, and as they stepped into the aisle, they were immediately greeted by Jesse and Tom from the garage. Behind them, Nancy and Grandpa, both beaming with satisfaction, waited patiently. "I finished up the Healey," said Tom. "The right parts came, and putting the clutch in that thing is a bit of work, but it's all done. She's parked out in front, and here are the keys. I thought you might need her."

"Really," said Mitchell as he grasped the keys. "I'm blown away, man. That's a lot of work. Thank you. Thank you." Then he shook hands with Jesse, and the two men hugged unabashedly for a long time. "You gonna be all right?" asked Mitchell as they parted.

"I'm fine," replied Jesse. "In the end, they actually wanted me to stay on for a while. Can you believe that? But I told them to hell with it. It was way past time. Time to move on."

"Good for you," said Mitchell. "Good for you." Then, stepping past Jesse, Mitchell took Nancy in his arms and hugged her.

"I couldn't get here fast enough," she said with tears rolling down her checks. "I didn't know, and I tried to reach you."

"I know," said Mitchell, "I was dumb, so dumb."

As Mitchell stepped back from Nancy's embrace, he saw Grandpa extend his hand. "I'm glad for you," he said. "I knew that was all a load a manure." Then his faced hardened. "I don't know how to say this, particularly now, but I'd better. You see, Fiver and the Labrador took off. The guys from the pound came out yesterday to get 'em, and when Fiver saw 'em, the two of them took off up Silver Mountain."

Deflated, Mitchell's eyes tightened with worry. "You couldn't find them?" he said.

"Not yet," replied Grandpa. "I tracked them this morning on Sunny. Pretty good tracks in some fresh mud, but I lost 'em on this side of Silver Mountain. I think Fiver's staying close to the highway. I think he's heading back to your place. That's the way it looks to me."

"Well, let's go!" cried Mitchell. "We've got to find them."

"All right," said Grandpa. "I'll get Sunny and retrace the trail over the top and start headin' down this side. Why don't you start over by the old homestead, check by the river, and then work up, and we'll meet. We'll find them."

"OK," said Mitchell as he started toward the door.

"And Mitchell," said Grandpa, "there's one more thing. There's some blood on the trail. I think one of them is hurt."

"I've got to find him quick," replied Mitchell. "He could have a seizure, damn it!"

With fear in his eyes, Mitchell ran out of the courthouse and down the steps to where the Healey was parked. Jumping over the door, he slid down on the seat, and pulling on the starter button, he brought the engine to life. Checking the gauges, he saw that the oil pressure was good. Then he pumped the clutch and it was stiff and sound. Next to him on the passenger's seat, he saw his navy pea coat.

"It's cold in the evening. You'll need that!" yelled Nancy from the court steps.

"Thanks!" he yelled back. "And could you go over to my house and see if Fiver shows up there?"

"Tom is gonna take me over!" she yelled, still waving. Then, as he backed out, he spun the steering wheel and turned sharply. When he stopped, he put the Healey in first and drove off with a mellow roar in his wake.

As he drove, the Healey felt strong and powerful, and for a brief moment a surge of optimism ran through Mitchell, and he marveled at the mere ability to move, to be free. As he passed the quaint old buildings in the center of town, he had the unusual impression of moving through time. Had he not been engrossed in his worry over Fiver, he might have given the impression more thought, and in his new freedom, he would have been ecstatic. As it was, he drove almost unconsciously.

Chapter Seventy Two

Out on the highway, Mitchell was quick to bring the Healey up to cruising speed, and with the engine running smoothly, the deep hum of the exhaust added to his resolve. Although the skies were clear, the fall air was chilly. As it cut past his neck, he glanced down at the pea coat beside him. When he looked up, he saw the shiny metal roofs of Snyder's slaughterhouse, and for a second he saw Snyder's terrified face as he fell back in the truck. Then, with his eyes narrowing, he pushed down harder on the accelerator, and shooting past the slaughterhouse, he saw that the front gates were closed and the Dobermans were gone. In the rearview mirror, the place looked abandoned and archaic, and it shrank as it receded behind him.

Turning onto the road that led up to the gorge, he accelerated hard, and as he rounded the tight corners, he put the Healey through the gears. Around the next bend he saw Grandpa's truck and his horse trailer. "He'll be covering everything from here up," he thought as he slowed down. Then he scanned the forest and the rapidly rising foothills, and the mountain looked bigger and more formidable.

Moments later, coming up on his right, he saw the dirt road that led over to the old homestead, and shifting down, he slowed up, and pulling the Healey into second, he turned onto the rutted dirt road. "I'll start here," he thought. "One of us will find them." As he drove up the road, the

Healey squeaked and rattled as its wheels fell in and out of potholes and ruts, and on both sides of him, the passing trees seemed taller and denser than he had remembered. About halfway up the road, he pulled into a small clearing. As he shut off the engine, a cloud of dust rolled past him. Then, with the dust settling on the windshield, he saw a trail directly in front of the car that, leading off into the trees, seemed to head up the mountain toward the gorge. "I'll follow the trail to where the mountain gets steep," he thought as he got out of the car. "Then I'll come back by the river."

Standing next to the Healey, he threw his pea coat over his shoulder, and peering into the aspens that surrounded him, he whistled Fiver's special call. Then, leaving the car behind him, he started to follow the trail. As he walked into the dense forest, he called out for Fiver every so often. Beneath his feet, the path was hard and rocky, meandering this way and that.

Calling and then whistling, he had been walking for about a half an hour when he first heard the hum of the river in the distance. With the trail now starting to descend, he continued on, and as he wound his way down, the roar got louder and louder. Gradually, the sweet fragrance of the pines gave way to a cool mist that in its own way was even richer and more essential.

When he got to the river, he stood on a grassy outcropping that jutted out into the water and gave him a look upstream. With his pea coat still over his shoulder, he knelt down, and for a moment he gazed into the turbulent green water. Tumbling and swirling with a natural precision unmatched by any machine, the river bespoke a profound purpose that was beyond his grasp, and for a moment, staring deeply into this dancing vortex, he saw without words. Then, as if waking from a dream, he looked up, and following the stream upward with his eyes, he saw the canyon as it narrowed, and not far from where he stood, the rocky walls were steep and jagged. "Fiver wouldn't come through there," he thought, and looking back to the trail, he searched it for any tracks. "I'll follow the river back downstream. Maybe I'll catch a track. They might come to the river for a drink."

As he stood up Mitchell pulled on his pea coat, and for a second he thought he heard a tinkling metal sound, but looking around he saw nothing. After scouring the trail and the surrounding trees for any sign of the dogs, he headed downstream. As he walked, the pea coat kept him warm, but it failed to insulate him from a growing sense of dread and futility, and as he trudged on, his apprehension, like the constant hum of the water, seemed to surround him. Calling out every few yards, his voice began to get rough and hoarse, and he had to wet his lips in order to whistle.

After following the river for about an hour, he was coming around a bend when he was confronted by an immense tree that had fallen across the trail. With its huge trunk protruding down and into the river, its roots, like the viscera of a slain giant, lay exposed in front of him. Staring down at them, he felt the last of his forbearance begin to wane. "He's dead," he thought, and from someplace deep inside of him, the anguish of it pulled at him as if to drag him into the ground. "You don't know that," he said back to himself defiantly. "No, he's somewhere. I'll find him. If I have to die out here, I'll find him!" Then, as he walked, he felt like he could hear the forest, or sense it or understand it, in some new, unorthodox way. "I'll cut up here," he thought. "I'll keep searching!"

Grabbing onto the rocks that jutted out from the steep embankment, he climbed up from the river. When he got to level ground, he was in a thick undergrowth of vines and bushes, and with a new sense of urgency, he waded through them like a gorilla in the jungle. Stopping to catch his breath, he pulled a vine from around his throat. Then, for a second he wondered if he should turn back and try to catch the trail, but the thought of conceding fueled his resolve, and he continued to march through the brush.

Moments later, as if he had just come out of the clouds, suddenly he came to the edge of a clearing. As he gathered his bearings, he realized that he was just a little ways below the old homestead, and through the trees on the other side of the clearing, he could see the side of the barn and the old house. Wetting his dry lips, he whistled for Fiver. Then, placing his hands in front of his mouth to make a cone, he took a deep breath, and thrashing his already raspy throat, he called out Fiver's name. The silence that returned was like water slowly oozing into a muddy footprint, and it seemed to mock his efforts. As he gazed across the clearing, hopelessness inched up on him from all sides. Then he dropped his head, and like an old tired horse, he began to trudge across the field. With his mind silenced by the grief that was settling within him, only the sound of the tall grass swishing past him vaguely penetrated his consciousness, and now his remaining hope was just the sound of his own movement through the grass.

With the afternoon sun about to set, Mitchell slipped under the lodgepole fence that bordered the property. Rising up, he took a long look at the old homestead. Underneath the trees and a sky that was just beginning to turn orange, it seemed to be resting as if after a long and tiresome journey it had finally found peace. Moreover, it was accepting, accepting of everything and anything. Then a big gray rabbit darted across the front porch, and with a curious but beguiling glance, it disappeared through the half-open front door, and without thinking, Mitchell began to follow him.

As Mitchell went up the front steps, the old boards creaked, but lost in his pursuit, he heard nothing. As he looked through the partially open door, he waited for his eyes to adjust to the darkness. Then carefully, he pushed the door aside and went in, and with the loud knock of his steps ringing up from the old hardwood floor, he unwittingly glanced around for the rabbit. As the shadows began to give up their secrets, he saw that the back door was wide open, and from the darkness within, it framed the old barn that sat out in back. Like someone standing before a painting, he tried to fathom what he saw. Then, out of the corner of his eye, he thought he saw something move, and turning his head, he searched the dim surroundings for a sign of life. But finding only stillness, in the quiet, his eyes surveyed the room, and among years of dust and debris, there was an old table with an empty metal pan on it, and a chair with a broken armrest. Then across from the dilapidated fireplace, surrounded by scattered bricks and old bottles, he saw the remains of an old upright piano. Covered with dust and cobwebs, with its top and front piece missing, and the front legs gone, it sat broken and violated, lost to time.

As he looked at the exposed strings and the broken and yellowed keys, he ran his hand across the dusty ridden keys. "I'm beat," he thought. "The damn mountains got them." Then, pushing down slowly on a mutilated key, he watched as one of the wooden hammers rose like something from the grave, and when it fell forward, it made a thunking, clinking kind of sound. Pushing it again, he tried to trace the movement back from the hammer through the maze of levers and joints that made it work. As he let the hammer settle slowly back to its resting place, his eyes ran along the cabinet. Then, unconsciously, he struck three solitary notes that in their metallic shrillness left a terrible, long, empty silence. Then, from somewhere in the distance, someplace far away, he thought he heard something, and with every tissue and cell in his body, he listened, and then, ever so softly, he heard it again. It sounded like a soft cry or a howl, and it wasn't so far away, it was just weak. In hopeful astonishment, he turned from the piano and saw the barn framed by the doorway. Then he heard the sound again. It was a faint cry, and in an instant, with his whole body tingling with hope, he stood up, and running from the house, he jumped from the back porch and started to sprint toward the barn.

With his arms and knees pumping high, he stepped across a ditch, and then jumping over a pile of old pine poles, he slid to a stop in front of the barn door. Seeing the door was slightly ajar, he grabbed it with both hands and pulled. But the door didn't move and as if it were guarding something, it seemed to resist. Then, gritting his teeth, he pulled with all his might, and with a creaking moan that seemed to echo all the way back to the beginning of time, the old wooden door suddenly gave. Flinging it aside, Mitchell peered in, and before him he saw the beam that, as a youth, he had pondered years before. With the wide-eyed amazement of a child, he followed it down from the break in the roof. Then he shuddered. On the floor, he saw Fiver lying on his side, motionless and covered in blood. When he saw Mitchell, Fiver raised his head and, with a thump of his tail, he feebly acknowledged him.

With his heart pounding, Mitchell raced to his side, and dropping to the floor in front of him, he tried to gauge the extent of his injuries. "You're gonna be all right," he said as he stroked him, and looking up at him, Fiver again lightly thumped his tail on the floor. Then, seeing the three gashes on his shoulder, he leaned forward, and parting the bloody and matted hair, he saw that the wounds were deep and long. Grimacing, he closed his eyes and looked away. When he opened them, in the shadows he saw the Labrador. A few feet behind Fiver, she was lying on her side, and with her head on her paws, she looked like a child that had lain down and gone to sleep.

Patting Fiver on the neck, Mitchell carefully stepped over him, and crouching, he knelt down by the Labrador. In front of her, he saw where a small pool of blood had soaked into the dirt floor, and then he saw a gash and the puncture wounds on her neck. Leaning over, he petted her head and rubbed her back, but she didn't respond. Then, hopefully, he put his ear down to her nostrils, but there was no breath. She was gone. As he stroked her head the last time, he was struck by her beauty and her dignity. Then, standing up, he quickly stepped back over to Fiver, and getting down on his knees, he scooped him up in his arms and rose up. As he turned to leave, Fiver gazed over his shoulder down at the Labrador. "She's gone, Fiver," said Mitchell. "I'll come back for her. I promise."

Chapter Seventy Three

S tanding outside the barn, Mitchell realized that the Healey was parked quite a ways up the dirt road. Tightening his grip on Fiver, he began to jog, and he kept running until, up ahead, he saw the rear fender of the Healey protruding out from the trees at the side of the road.

When he reached the car, he was breathing heavily. With the muscles in his lower back starting to burn, he leaned over the door and laid Fiver on the passenger seat. Taking off his now bloody pea coat, he draped it over him. Then, grabbing the windshield, he jumped over the passenger door, and flinging himself forward, he landed in the driver's seat. As he slid down behind the steering wheel, he reached into his pocket and groped for the car keys. Not finding them, he frantically checked his other pockets. Then it hit him. Somewhere he'd lost the keys. "Damn it!" he shouted, and looking down at Fiver, he was struck with fear. "How am I gonna get her started?" he thought frantically. "What can I do?" Then, almost instinctively, he pulled the hood latch and threw open the door.

Jumping out, he undid the leather straps on the hood and raised it. Then, after pulling down the brace that held it up and snapping it into place, he leaned over the engine and scanned the firewall for the fuse box. When he found it, he ran his finger over the clips that held the two main fuses. "That'll do it," he thought, and stepping around to the passenger door, he reached in and grabbed the pea coat that he had laid on Fiver.

Then, holding it firmly in one hand, he ripped off one of the metal buttons, and then he carefully laid the pea coat back over Fiver. "I'll just be a sec," he said as he ran back to the front of the car, "and we'll be out of here." A moment later, leaning over the fender, he wedged the brass button between the two fuses. Then he stepped around hurriedly and looked in at the dash. When he saw that the ignition was on, glowing red, he stepped back to the front of the car and quickly dropped the hood. "That should do it," he said as he sat behind the wheel and pulled the starter switch. "Yes!" he shouted as the Healey first whined and then starting, began to purr. "We're out of here!" he shouted as they backed up and then headed down the bumpy dirt road.

Out on the highway, Mitchell raced through the gears, and as he sped down the road, his mind went back to the barn and the dead Labrador. Then, slowly, his eyes filled with tears. "I'm sorry," he said as he looked over at Fiver. "I'm sorry." Then, with the corners of his mouth pulled down, he drove with both hands on the wheel, and catching the wind, his tears lifted from his cheeks. When ahead he saw the stop sign at the highway, he geared down, and without stopping, he slid across the intersection. Then, pressing hard on the accelerator, with the car fishtailing just a bit, he raced toward town.

It was after six when he shifted down and pulled into the parking lot in front of the veterinary clinic. Seeing that there was still one car in the lot, he honked the horn frantically as he brought the Healey to a stop. As he got out of the car, he saw someone peek through a blind, and with Fiver cradled in his arms, he headed up the front steps. Then a balding, blond-haired man held the door open. "Take him into that first room and put him on the table," he said. "I'll be right there. It's lucky you got here when you did. I was just walkin' out the door. Another minute and I'd have been gone."

While the doctor flipped on some lights, Mitchell carried Fiver into the examining room and laid him down on his side on the table. With Fiver looking up at him, Mitchell was stroking his head when the doctor came in and started to inspect the wound on his shoulder.

"He's lost a lot of blood," said Mitchell.

"I'll bet he has," said the doctor, "those are mean gashes."

"I think it could have been a bear or maybe a cougar," replied Mitchell, "up by the old homestead."

"I see," said the doctor as he felt Fiver's abdomen. "I've heard tell of a cougar around lately. They're coming down because we've killed off too many deer and there aren't as many rabbits and varmints as there used to be, no habitat left for them," said the doctor as he continued to probe Fiver's abdomen. "He's lucky he's alive. My concern is internal bleeding."

"And, I should tell you, he has seizures," said Mitchell. "He had distemper, and...and it's an aftereffect, I guess. I give him phenobarbital when it happens."

"Distemper's fatal," said the veterinarian. "Sure it wasn't something else?"

"It's a long story," said Mitchell.

"I'll bet," replied the doctor as he rose up. "I'll bet."

After leaving the room for a moment, the doctor returned with a syringe. "I'll have to call my assistant," he said as he gave Fiver an injection. Then the doctor stepped out into the hall, and Mitchell heard him rapidly punch some numbers on the phone. "Linda, I've got an emergency down here. I need you right this second." Not waiting for a reply, the doctor hung the phone up, came back into the examining room, and again started feeling Fiver's chest and stomach.

"Is he gonna make it?" asked Mitchell as he watched the doctor put his stethoscope on Fiver's side.

"I don't know," replied the doctor without looking up. "I'll have to open him a bit to be sure. We'll do everything we can." Letting his stethoscope fall to his chest, the doctor rose up, and turning to the sink, he started to wash his hands. "I haven't had a dog attacked by a big cat," he said. "Lately all we've had are dogs that have been hit by cars. More traffic now than there used to be."

Then a young woman came through the front door and tossed her coat on the counter. Looking up at her, the doctor nodded and then gave Fiver another injection. "It'll be a while before we know anything for sure," he said, looking over at Mitchell. "You can wait out in front there."

"Can I wait until he's out before I go?" pleaded Mitchell, and leaning over, he kissed Fiver on the head. "You'll be all right," he said. "I love the Fiver," and with a thump of his tail, Fiver gazed up at him lovingly. Then, as the anesthesia began to work, Fiver blinked, and after looking at Mitchell one more time, his beautiful almond-shaped eyes slowly closed. Looking down at him, with a tear running down his cheek, Mitchell said, "I love the Fiver."

The surgery went on for two hours, and it was dark outside when the doctor finally appeared in the doorway. Looking up from his chair, Mitchell felt his soul quake when he saw the tired, blank expression on the doctor's face, but before he could speak, the doctor smiled. "Well, I think your dog's gonna' make it," he said. "Wasn't quite as bad as it could have been, no internal injuries or bleeding. He's got a lot of heart."

Standing up, and with tears pushing out from the corners of his eyes, Mitchell smiled like a forlorn clown. "Thank you," he said in a whisper. "Thank you."

The doctor nodded. "He'll be out for the rest of the night. Why don't you go home and get some rest. Give us a call in an hour or so. We'll be here all night."

Mitchell took a deep breath. "Thanks again. You'll never know how grateful I am."

"Don't thank me," said the doctor. "It's modern technology and science that saved him. We can do things now that we couldn't just a few years ago."

Chapter Seventy Four

As he stood on the front steps of the clinic wondering if he would go home or just stay at the clinic, Mitchell saw the headlights of a truck as it turned off the highway into the parking lot. It was Grandpa's truck, and when it stopped next to the Healey, he saw the passenger door fly open. "What happened?" cried Nancy as she rushed toward him. "Is it Fiver?" she asked. Then behind her Grandpa got out and slammed the door of the truck. As he came down the steps, Mitchell waved at Grandpa and then threw his arms around Nancy. "Yeah, I found him," he said as he held her tightly. He's cut up pretty bad, but he's gonna make it."

"Oh, I'm so glad," said Nancy, crying. "So glad. When it got dark, I was getting scared. Then Grandpa came by to get me and he was worried about the cougar up there."

"You were right," said Mitchell. "It looks like it was the cougar, and the Labrador didn't make it. She's back at the homestead. That's where I found them."

"That's too bad," said Grandpa with his hands in his back pockets. "I saw the tracks, and she had a cub, they're very protective. Well, at least you found him. I was worried."

"No, I didn't find him," said Mitchell shaking his head. "It's more like he found me, and it would've never happened if you hadn't trailed him over the mountain. If you hadn't done what you did, he'd be dead." Letting go of Nancy, Mitchell reached out and shook Grandpa's hand.

"Well, I'm glad he made it," said Grandpa with a broad smile. "There's something about him, something about his eyes. They've got an eternal quality to them." Smiling, Mitchell pulled Nancy close.

"Too bad about the Labrador," said Grandpa, "She was beautiful, and you could see that Fiver was fond of her, more than that, really. And I was too. They were a pair, romping out in the fields. Well, I'd better be going. Isabelle will be wondering where the hell I am. I'll see you kids later."

Standing next to the Healey, Mitchell and Nancy watched Grandpa climb back into his truck. He waved as he pulled away. Then, leaning back against the front fender of the Healey, Mitchell looked down.

"What's the matter?" said Nancy.

Scuffing his foot against the ground, Mitchell struggled for words. "I was losing it at the end," he said finally, "when I thought Fiver was gone. I mean, when I thought he was dead, I was comin' undone. You know, the mountain's gonna take him someday, and I don't know if I can handle that. I really don't."

At his side, Nancy nuzzled in closer. "You'll have to handle it as well as Fiver did," she said. "For his sake, you owe him that."

Chapter Seventy Five

That night, Nancy stayed at Mitchell's house, and in the morning Mitchell went straight over to the clinic to check on Fiver. When he got back, Noah was at the house, and over coffee, Nancy and Mitchell told him all about finding Fiver and the Labrador at the homestead and the cougar. As he was leaving, Noah stopped at the front door, and turning to Mitchell, he said, "By the way, a guy named Daryl wants me to defend him. He said you'd give him a character reference, asked me to tell you that Flash made a break for it, and he's free. What the hell is that all about?"

"It's a funny story," said Mitchell with a laugh. "He's a character all right, but he's OK. He deserves a break."

After Noah left, Mitchell found his spare keys, and with the still-bloody pea coat on the passenger seat, he drove back up to the homestead. In the barn, he knelt down and carefully wrapped the Labrador in the pea coat. As he stood up with the Labrador in his arms, he looked around at the interior of the barn. In the back he saw a broken wagon wheel, and the remains of some sort of wagon or carriage, and there was an old shovel with a broken handle leaning against the wall. For a long time, he stared at the broken shovel, and then firming up his grip on the Labrador, he carried her out to the car.

When he got back to the house, with Nancy at his side, Mitchell laid the Labrador down on the grass in the back yard by the old cottonwood tree. As they looked down at her, Nancy wept openly. "I'll bury her here," said Mitchell, rubbing a tear from his eye. Then, bending down, he pulled the bloody coat over her shoulder, leaving her beautiful head exposed. "I'll get some tools," said Mitchell as he turned toward the garage, and when he returned a moment later, he was carrying a pick and shovel.

Still crying, Nancy watched as Mitchell aimed and then swung the pick, and with every stroke, it bit and carved up chunks of earth. After a bit, he groaned, and then throwing down the pick, he picked up the shovel. When, a few minutes later, he finished digging the hole, he looked over at Nancy and sighed. Then he carefully knelt down and picked up the Labrador, still wrapped in the pea coat, and gently set her in the ground. When he stood up, Nancy came to his side and took his hand. "I need a pair of scissors," he said. "Could you get them for me? They're in the desk." Nodding sadly, as if she understood, she let go of his hand, and moments later she returned with a shiny pair of silver scissors. "Here you go," she said as she looked down at the Labrador, and taking the scissors, Mitchell knelt down and clipped off a lock of hair from the Labrador. "She is beautiful," he said as he stood up and put the lock of hair in his pocket. "I know Fiver must have loved her, and he'll miss her, and he'll dream about her."

"I'll sculpt a marker for her," Nancy said softly. "But it won't be as beautiful as she was."

After standing at the grave for some time, Mitchell took Nancy by the hand, and together they walked slowly back to the house. Inside, Mitchell went to his father's desk, and picking up one of his father's round tobacco tins, he held it up and admired it. Then he opened it and poured out the few remaining strands of tobacco, and reaching into his shirt pocket, he pulled out the lock of hair from the Labrador and put it in the tin. Then, pausing, he thought for a moment, and with a sigh, he reached into his pant pocket and pulled out the brass button that he had used to start the Healey. Holding it up, he admired it. Then, carefully, he put it next to the lock of hair in the tobacco tin. As Nancy watched from the doorway, he closed the tin and placed it on the mantel over the fireplace. Then he felt Nancy's hand on his shoulder. "It's hard," she said softly. "Death's hard. Van Gogh says it's just a traveling to another star, but it is so hard."

"A changing of worlds," said Mitchell with tears in his eyes. "That's what Chief Seattle said. But eventually we all run out of time. I don't know. I don't know."

Pulling herself closer to him, Nancy embraced Mitchell. "It's part of the changes," she whispered. "Maybe it's necessary, like the changes you talk about in music, and the contrasts in my paintings."

"The last change," said Mitchell forlornly. "You know, I've never told anybody this, but I've always thought when you die, there is no time. Time is just an abstraction, a measurement. Apart from that, it doesn't exist, and it doesn't do anything. It's like when you have surgery. You take the anesthesia and you wake up and it seems like no time has passed at all." Pausing, Mitchell took a deep breath, and then continued. "So, after you die, billions of years can pass, and you'll wake up somewhere with some kind of consciousness in some world. You might be somebody else or something else, but alive. With no time, life is inevitable, just look around you. It's everywhere. It's as inevitable as death...Inevitable, but you know, I really don't know, not down deep, and I'll have to live with that. That's all there is to it. To say more is just arrogance born out of uncertainly and fear."

"I guess Shakespeare's right," whispered Nancy. "Time makes fools of us all. So who's to say what it's all about? We are, as he says, mere mortals."

Beginning to tear-up again, Mitchell laughed. "Boy, you can say that again." Then, pausing, he tilted his head and pondered. "I know one thing," he said firmly. "I know Fiver's eyes are beautiful, and he is beautiful. It makes it all worth it, all of it, as fleeting as it may be. Life's a miracle, the whole wonderful, terrible, all of it."

Chapter Seventy Six

It was late in the afternoon when the vet called and said that they could pick up Fiver that evening around nine. The doctor wouldn't be there, but his assistant would, and she could do up the paper work. When Mitchell left the house, Nancy was on the porch by the painting. "I won't be long," he said as he went out the back door and headed toward the Healey.

"I'll be working on the painting," replied Nancy in jest. "This one could take a lifetime, don't you think?"

Smiling, Mitchell cocked his head and nodded. "As far as I'm concerned, it could take forever."

When Mitchell got to the vet's it was dark, and as he went up the front steps, he gazed up at a canopy of orange and gold stars set in a dark-blue sky. When he went inside, he shielded his eyes from the bright, colorless florescent light, and while he was waiting for someone to come to the desk, he marveled at the array of medicines on the shelf and racks of tools and appliances that included a variety of gadgets and tubes and clamps. He was looking at a mobile monitor of some sort when the vet's assistant appeared in a doorway and motioned for him to come in. In the room, he saw Fiver lying on a padded mat with a large bandage on his shoulder and leg, and a smaller bandage over an incision in his abdomen. When he saw Mitchell, he thumped his tail, and his beautiful almond eyes were filled with love and deep gratification. As he knelt down and hugged him, Mitchell couldn't help but cry, and hearing him cry, Fiver whimpered. Then, as if to say, "That's enough," Fiver pulled away and slowly rose to his feet. A bit shaky, he limped to the door, where he looked back at Mitchell with his knowing eyes. "I'm coming," said Mitchell. "I'm coming."

Moments later, with Fiver seated beside him in the Healey, Mitchell pulled the starter button, and as his machine came to life, he felt its power surge through him. As it idled, it seemed to pant like a restless dog or a horse just after a hard race. After giving Fiver a hug, Mitchell snapped on the headlights and took hold of the steering wheel. In front of them, the beams of the light cut a long, narrow path through the surrounding darkness. After he checked the gauges, he reached over and patted Fiver. "I love the Fiver," he said. "I love the Fiver." Then putting the Healey in gear, he revved the engine, and the two of them edged forward into the night.

CPSIA information can be obtained at www.ICGtesting.com
Printed in the USA
LVOW11s0109100115

422261LV00002B/581/P